THIS GOLDEN FLAME

EMILY VICTORIA

THIS GOLDEN FLAME

HODDER &
STOUGHTON

First published in Great Britain in 2021 by Hodder & Stoughton
An Hachette UK company

1

Copyright © Emily Victoria 2021

The right of Emily Victoria to be identified as the Author of the Work has been
asserted by her in accordance with the Copyright, Designs and Patents Act 1988.

A CIP catalogue record for this title is available from the British Library

Hardback ISBN 978 1 529 363739

Printed and bound in Great Britain by Clays Ltd, Elcograf S.p.A.

Hodder & Stoughton policy is to use papers that are natural, renewable
and recyclable products and made from wood grown in sustainable
forests. The logging and manufacturing processes are expected to
conform to the environmental regulations of the country of origin.

Hodder & Stoughton Ltd
Carmelite House
50 Victoria Embankment
London EC4Y 0DZ

www.hodder.co.uk

To my parents, for always believing in me.

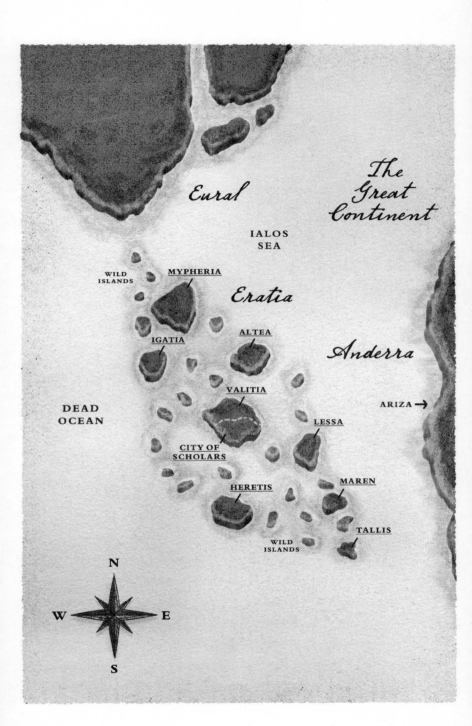

1

KARIS

The hallways of the Tallis Scriptorium are always so black at night. Statues and busts loom out of the dark and ribbed columns stretch down from the roof like pale fingers. I've taken my sandals off, twined their laces together, and hung them off my shoulder where they can't make any noise, and the cold of the floor leeches through the soles of my feet. I pull my himation tighter around me, the rustling of the cloak a bare whisper. If this were day, I would hear the quiet scratch of reed pens against parchment in the study rooms to the east, the droning buzz of a master's lecture from the hall. But in the night, it's so stiflingly quiet. Like a tomb.

Even after seven years I'm still not used to it. To the quiet. The dark. Back on Heretis, the island I grew up on, there was always noise, always light, even in the run-down streets my brother and I haunted, where not many could afford oil for their lamps. Here on Tallis, the black is deep and somber, every door locked and every shutter latched firmly shut, as if the masters fear thieves who might lurk out there in the wilderness and the night.

If only they knew the thieves were already inside.

I slink down the shadowy hall, my eyes straining to navigate the black, even though it isn't really the dark that's a risk. Being out of bed this late would earn me a lashing, but at least that's all I'd get. The true risk is in anyone discovering what I stole: the ledger currently clasped to my chest, its leather cover warm beneath my fingers. I can't even say what the punishment for this would be, because as far as I know no one's ever been impudent enough to try it.

At least not before me, and I prefer the term *reckless*.

I reach the west hall. Giving a quick glance up and down the silent corridor, I lift the latch on the closest window, wincing as it squeaks. I push the shutters open and night air brushes my skin.

The chilled marble of the windowsill stings against my legs as I swing over and drop into a crouch in the deep shadows by the edge of the building. From far off I can make out the sound of the waves crashing against the cliffs, the sharp tang of seawater hanging in the air. I take a deep breath, trying to trap the taste of it in my lungs.

I look across the dark courtyard to one of the smallest buildings. Despite its size, it's all marble with a full colonnade around its edges and elaborate moldings of masters and ledgers and automatons in the frieze running along the edge of its roof, darkened now with shadows.

The Hall of Records.

The second watch rings across the complex. I allow myself a smile. Perfect. There shouldn't be a patrol anywhere near here right now. I take off across the courtyard, bare feet pounding the packed dirt, not slowing until I slip past the colonnade. Bars of moonlight glow against the floor, stretching from the pillars that surround the open atrium I stand in. The back of the space is lost in the gloom, but it's impossible to miss the glimmer of gold, too vivid and bright to be anything but Scriptwork.

I pad silently over, avoiding the strips of moonlight and sticking to the shadows. As if the night sky will tell on me. Details swim from the dark: olivewood doors stretching high above my head, framed with brass and cut with flourishes and curls; the seal of bronze plastered to their center; and the rune carved deep into the metal, a tangle of thick golden strokes, bent around each other as if in a knot. A *lock* rune. The most complicated rune on this island.

I run my fingers over the ridges of the lines, warm and tingling beneath my skin despite the night air. The truth is, I'm not even supposed to know Scriptwork, at least no more than what's needed to climb automatons and make rubbings of the runes. The actual work of study is done by the masters and the aristoi scholars who come to study on Tallis. We orphans are only here for grunt labor. The Scriptmasters barely believe we can think for ourselves, never mind do something like this.

Lock runes are tricky. You have to understand which strokes engraved into the seal are part of the base rune and which have been added by that particular Scriptmaster. Then you have to replicate it perfectly in a ledger, all in the right order. Runes have rules, some of which haven't even been discovered yet, and we were certainly never allowed to study them.

But just because a crotchety old master wasn't going to teach me didn't mean I wasn't going to learn.

The light's just enough to let me see the ledger as I flip it open to the last page, the golden glow spilling over the rough stretch of parchment. I pull out the stub of charcoal from my belt pocket. Once I draw a line, there's no changing my mind. I'll have to sneak the ledger back eventually, and lines will only mean evidence, since trying to tear a page out will just be more obvious. If this doesn't work, I'll have taken all this risk for nothing.

Only then I think of Matthias. It's been seven years since they shipped my older brother away, all because he tried to defend me against them. Because they decided he would be too troublesome to keep. Behind these doors is the only record on the whole of this island that can tell me where he was sent.

And I am getting through tonight.

I dash off the first of the lines on the page. It comes off black and bold and perfect.

That's when I hear voices. Low. Serious.

A patrol.

There shouldn't be a patrol here, not at this time of night. Which means I'm either not as observant as I think or I'm real unlucky.

As soon as they enter the courtyard, I won't be able to get back to the window, not without them noticing. A hint of panic thrums beneath my skin, telling me to leave now, while I still can. But then I look down at the parchment, the rune already started. They can't catch me if I'm already inside the Hall.

As soon as I have the idea, I know it's a terrible one. I suppose that fits me perfectly.

I bend over the ledger and keep going. The lines unfurl across the parchment as the rune takes shape, each line in the proper order and form. Excitement curls around my heart, even as the voices come closer. I'm doing it.

The rune is finished. I look up at the seal on the door, waiting for the golden line to cut it in half, to let me through.

Nothing happens.

The seconds pound through my head. No. I look down at the page, at this rune that looks exactly like the one on the door. I'm sure I did it right. Why isn't it working?

One of the soldiers speaks again, their voice close. Too close.

I'm out of time.

I bite down my curse and dash away from the glow of the rune, toward the courtyard. Maybe I can still get across. I've just reached the colonnade when the soldiers step into view through the main gates. There are two of them, a man and a woman, their red chitons dark enough it's hard to make them out. Short gladius swords are strapped to their hips. They're coming closer.

There's one other way to my quarters, through a door I can possibly sneak to by circling the back of the buildings. A door that always stays unlocked because it's used by the patrols themselves to get inside.

I jam the ledger into a fold in my himation and run,

sticking close to the wall that surrounds the Scriptorium complex. I can see the door I need ahead, nestled at the back of the acolytes' quarters.

I'm reaching out when it swings open toward me. I stumble back, off balance, and a hand from behind me clamps around my upper arm.

I jam my elbow back at whoever has me, but they're quick. An arm scoops me around the waist and jerks me behind the closest pillar, right as another two soldiers step out the door. I snap my head up at whoever has me, and catch a glimpse of a trainee's red sash. Of tousled dark hair and deep green eyes, currently narrowed to order me to shut up.

Dane.

I go still, both of us hidden in the narrow space between the pillar and the building. It throws me back, to years ago, when I wasn't the only one sneaking out at nights. When this picture of him and me was as natural as breathing.

The footsteps fade away.

I let out a breath. That was close. I know I shouldn't, but I look back the way I came. Maybe now that Dane's here, I could try again. Maybe he'd come with me.

But he doesn't even give me the chance to ask. Before I can open my mouth, he grabs my hand and pulls me through the door. Our footsteps hush over the floor, two sets this time, and even though I can practically feel the exasperation wicking off of him, see the tension in his neck, I feel strangely relieved. At least he's here.

He doesn't stop until we reach the small linen storeroom near my quarters, piled high with coarse chitons. There's a thin crack in the shutters, letting in just enough moonlight that I can see him. His hand is pressed over his eyes, obscuring most of his face, as if that's enough to hold back whatever he's thinking. Under different circumstances, that would have made me laugh.

"Karis." His voice is that dangerous sort of calm that, as far as I know, is only reserved for me and only when I've done something incredibly reckless. "What in all of everything were you thinking?"

I fold my arms over my chest. "You don't even know what I was doing."

He drops his hand and glowers at me. It's an expression I haven't seen in a while. Not because I haven't been doing reckless things. But because he hasn't been around to notice. "I got back after the rest of the patrol and I saw you near the Hall of Records. I know what you were doing."

I wince. I hadn't even considered that the patrol might have been spread out. It was careless.

"What were you even hoping to achieve without a ledger?"

He's facing the moonlight. I'm not. I doubt he can make out my expression, but my silence must speak volumes.

He groans. "You didn't."

I reach into my himation, the cloth looped about my shoulders and waist, and pull out the ledger. "I'm going to return it."

Dane shoves his hands through his hair, growling at the ceiling. "Of all the ill-thought, hardheaded, impulsive…"

Dane's my best friend. My only friend really. But that doesn't mean I'm going to stand around while he verbally berates me to the roof. "You couldn't have expected me not to try."

"Try to do what? What exactly were your plans for this?"

He catches my wrist and holds it up, forcing me to look at the bronze bracelet suckered there like a malignant growth. A copy of the one he wears. That every orphan brought to this island wears.

And he's right. I hate it, but he is. Even if I'd figured out the rune and written it perfectly, even if I'd gotten in and found exactly where Matthias had been sent, I would still be trapped here. Because of this hunk of metal around my wrist, this perfect circle with no clasp. As long as it's attached to me, going anywhere near the beach will burn my bracelet's identifying rune into their scrolls. They'd know exactly where I was and what I was doing. And there'd be no running from them then. There's only one ledger that can unlock the bracelets, and it's always with the head Scriptmaster. Not even I can steal that.

I meet Dane's eyes over my hand, and for a moment I'm so achingly tired. I almost want to apologize, to tell him he's right. Because maybe he is. Maybe I don't want to spend my entire life fighting a battle I can't win, when I couldn't even open a door. Maybe the masters were right about me and I am exactly what they judge me to be.

Only then I think of Matthias. Of the way he looked the last time I saw him, the day he was dragged away. Me screaming. Him calling out my name as his hand was ripped from mine.

The truth is, it isn't in me to quit. Not now, not ever. There are things I will not—cannot—concede, and my brother is at the top of that list.

So I don't say anything, just stare Dane down, and in the

end he's the one who looks away, dropping my hand. A part of me is naive enough to believe it might be because he understands.

"You're lucky I was on patrol," he finally says.

"I know," I whisper. It's the most I can give him. It must be enough because he lets out a breath, rubbing the back of his neck.

"Did it work?" he asks. "The rune?"

I don't want to say it and make it more real. But I lie to so many people in my life, and I won't lie to him. "No." I swallow, staring down at the floor. "It didn't."

I can feel his eyes on me and when he speaks, his voice is gentler. "I'm sorry."

I raise my head to look back at him and force a smile. As impish and real as I can make it. "I know that, too."

He rolls his eyes, but that crooked grin, which doesn't belong to the soldier but to the street brat, to my friend, is already stealing over his face. I've missed that smile. "Yes, well, now that I've saved your sorry hide, I need to get back. And you should go to bed."

He must have forgotten the ledger, hidden in the dark. I rub my fingers over it and for a moment I'm tempted not to say anything. To let him leave and to give it another try. Maybe I would have, if I had any idea where I went wrong with the rune. Maybe I would have if Dane wasn't standing right there.

But he is. I don't know how he managed to get away from his patrol for this long, but I do know that if anything happens tonight, he'll be implicated in it. And I wouldn't do that to him. The risks I take, I take on my own.

I hold the ledger up. "I need to get this back." When I left, Master Kaius was snoring into his wine, but even he'll notice a missing ledger when he wakes up. The masters would tear this Scriptorium apart to get it back.

Dane looks at the book between us, and then he takes it. "I'll slip it into his study. At least if I get caught in the halls, I'll have an excuse."

I wasn't expecting that, not even from him. "Dane…"

He's already taken a step away, but he looks over his shoulder, and maybe more of the street boy still exists than I thought because trouble darts across his deep eyes. He comes back to me and pecks a kiss on my forehead. "Go to bed, Karis, before someone notices."

Then he's gone, disappearing back into the shadows of the hall, and the only evidence he ever stood here is the soft tread of his fading footsteps.

I failed. The knowledge sits like a thorn in my chest, prickling at the tender flesh of my heart. I was right there, I had the ledger in my hands, and I failed.

I drag my feet as I walk through the hallways, silently following the other acolytes in my group. Master Vasilis strides down the hall at our head, his robe billowing around his legs as he leads us to whatever work site he's chosen today to re-catalog for the umpteenth time. All in the hopes that something will have changed that will unlock the secrets of the automatons.

The Scriptorium, which rules Eratia, flaunts itself as a leader among the nations in knowledge, but for the past two hundred years all the Scriptmasters have been obsessed with is recovering what they lost—reanimating and controlling the automatons littered over the islands.

It's mind-numbingly pointless. If it hasn't happened yet, it isn't going to happen. The power of the automatons is dead. And right now, with the knowledge of my failure sitting heavy in my heart, I'm spitefully glad the Scriptorium is never going to get what they want either.

Outside, it's barely dawn, pale colors stretching across the sky. Despite the early hour, the yard is already busy with the organized chaos of morning drills, men and women scattered about the yard. I look for Dane, even though I know he's smart enough to take care of himself.

There are so many sparring pairs, it takes me a moment to spot him. Despite the chill in the air, his skin's flushed and sweaty, and his sword flashes in the sun as dust flies around his sandals. Fatigue sits like a stone behind my eyes, but Dane looks as awake as ever. He lunges out fast and his opponent, a boy named Erys, jerks back and trips over his own feet. He falls in a tangle of flailing limbs. Dane lets out a whoop and jogs a few paces of a victory lap before helping Erys to his feet and slapping the other boy on his back.

I can't help the grin that cracks across my face. Someone's having fun.

As if Dane can sense my attention on him—which I'm half convinced he can—he turns and sees me. He flashes me a smile that's all secrets and all mine, and for a moment I almost forget how much the last few years have changed us. I wave back, ignoring the odd looks some of the nearby soldiers throw my way. As if it's unnatural that someone like Dane would pay attention to someone like me. I wonder how many of them remember that Dane came here as an orphan, too. Before he picked up sword-fighting like he'd been doing it his whole life. Before he was allowed to join the militia ranks and became a favorite of his master and his squad. Before he grew from a gangly child into someone who fits in perfectly.

Dane is good-looking and the worst thing is, he knows it. Knows exactly the effect he has on other people, especially on girls. At least girls besides me.

I've never felt that way about him. Actually, I've never felt that way about anyone. It's not as if I think Dane is bad-looking. Objectively speaking, he's quite nice to look at. There are plenty of people on Tallis who are nice to look at. I just wouldn't ever want to kiss one of them over it. Whatever it is that makes my group mates sigh and go misty-eyed, I've never felt for myself.

I know all that about myself and most of the time I'm fine with it. But right now, under all these stares...there's a part of me that wonders if I'm the strange one.

The drill sergeant, Master Adalis, gives a sharp whistle, raising her eyebrows at Dane. Looking only mildly abashed, he readies himself for another spar. I jog after the tail end of my group, slipping out through the front gate.

The island spreads before me, all pale craggy rocks and waving grasses. Stiff stalks poke at my calves and dust settles into every itchy space in my sandals. Orchids, just now blooming, open their delicate, purple petals to the sky. I lift my face to the thin rays of sun, ignoring the chatter of the other students, none of it directed at me.

I wonder what Matthias would think of this island. Even

though he has low vision, he was always an adventurer, certainly more than I was. Maybe that was just because he was older. Or maybe that was just him. Back when we were young, I'm sure he knew every corner of our parents' weaving shop and our tiny yard, where we used to pluck figs from the tree and eat them crouched in the shade on hot days, or separate lentils into bowls for dinner. When we were on Heretis, every run-down building we took shelter in was a chance for him to poke his fingers into the nooks and cracks. Our childhood was one of small spaces and I'm sure he'd have loved the wide-open possibilities of Tallis.

"Acolyte Karis."

I snap back to attention just in time to hear the snickers. My cheeks burn as I see Master Vasilis standing in front of me. Behind him I can make out the curving edge of the eastern side of the island, where it turns sharply into white cliffs. We arrived at our work site and I didn't notice.

Master Vasilis glowers down his aquiline nose at me. "Tell me, Acolyte Karis, what has so riveted your attention that you ignored my instructions?"

I almost want to tell him, just to see his face when he learns I stole a ledger. But if I said that, I might as well go walk off that cliff. So I bite down the impulse and mumble, "Nothing, Master."

"Nothing? Well then, your wandering thoughts must simply be in need of a task. Attach the pulley system to the automaton."

My group mates snicker again and I don't understand why until I turn to the behemoth of a creature standing not five feet from us.

In the seven years since I arrived on Tallis, I've gotten plenty used to automatons. Back home on Heretis, there were only two on the outskirts of the city, and since Matthias and I always stayed near the central agora, where thieving was the easiest, I never actually saw them. Only heard the tales from the other street kids.

Here on Tallis, there are close to a dozen, leftover from the days when this island was a guard post. The things are massive. Monstrous. Great hulking bodies made of Script-strengthened bronze, most of it tarnished a dull green because there aren't enough of us to keep them all polished, thick arms and legs made from interconnecting plates meant for bashing and breaking, tiny heads placed atop for no reason I can see except to provide a point of normality to creatures that don't look normal at all. When I came to this island, I screamed the first time I saw one. And though the years have taken that blinding edge of fear away, the things still give me the shivers. Even though they're the pride of Eratia, the proof for the Scriptorium that once we were more powerful than anyone.

This automaton looks like any of its frozen kind, except for one thing: it's at a tilt, its upper body leaning out over the cliff's edge as if stilled in the moment before it was to dive into the water below. The ocean glints from up here, deceptively bright and beautiful. But I know there are rocks just beneath those waves. One wrong misstep on the climb up and I'll be taking a quick trip to a long sleep.

One of my fellow acolytes, Demetrius, steps forward and shoves the pack with the pulley system into my hands. I meet his smug eyes. The others crowd behind him— Jocasta, Petros, Thetis—whispering as they sneak glances at me. There's not a scrap of kindness in any of their faces, even though once there was. In Jocasta's, especially. Of everyone, she was maybe the one I could have made friends with in those early days. She was the one willing to reach out, who would smile when she passed me in the halls. Only I didn't want friends.

And I don't need their kindness.

I jut out my chin as I swing the pack onto my back. My gaze tracks up the automaton, trying to find the best route. Its tarnished and dented skin is littered with runes: *reach, lift, bend.* Hard lines carved into the hard metal. They aren't lit—they haven't been lit since Master Theodis, the greatest villain of the ages, triggered the Great Lapse that made all the things still. But they're as close to handholds as I'm going to get.

I grab the lowest rune and haul myself up. I stick to the back of the thing's thigh, where at least its body is between me and the fall, but the runes down here are far and few between.

Sweat prickles from my palms and slides down my spine. My arms ache from the sheer effort of pulling myself up the steep incline. I grit my teeth and push on. I refuse to give anyone the satisfaction of seeing me plummet to my death.

I'm almost to its back. I reach for another rune and my fingers slip. I scramble for a new hold, any hold, but it's too late. My balance tips and I fall, screeching. The world tumbles over itself, flashing water and sky and cliff side. My body slams into rock, a steep slope turning my free fall into a desperate tumble, until with a bone wrenching thud, I stop.

I choke on air, my chest heaving, as I stare up at the bright blue sky. A hazy din of panic screams in my ears, and agony burns under every bit of my skin, like hundreds of scratching insect legs. I'm…alive. A strangled laugh tears from my throat. I'm alive.

My shaking fingers probe the ledge I'm on, slick with salt spray and barely larger than I am. This little outcropping of rock that saved my life. If it didn't involve flipping over, I might have kissed it. Gritting my teeth, I heave myself up to my elbows.

There's a crack in the cliff side, a few feet farther down the ledge. Its edges are lit with a faint glimmer of golden light.

I blink slowly, my aching head still sluggish. Is that… Scriptwork?

"Master, she isn't dead."

My group mate, Archus, has stuck his head out over the edge of the cliff side. Master Vasilis appears next to him, and even though I can't hear his sigh, I see it in the way his shoulders heave. As if my nearly dying is some great inconvenience.

"Well, I suppose someone ought to grab a rope and throw it down," he says.

There's some shuffling up above and then the frayed end of a rope is thrown down. Every bit of me feels battered and bruised, and I have no idea how I'm going to climb all the way back up. But I do know that if I don't do it, no else is going to come down here and get me. So, with a growl, I grab the rope and drag myself to my feet.

2

—

KARIS

I've always hated the infirmary. Partly because of the way it smells: the muggy scents of herbs and tinctures and pastes so muddled together they make my head swim. But mostly because it means beds and staying still.

Master Kronus dabs a wet cloth with some greenish goop on it to a particularly nasty cut on my elbow and I hiss as jagged pain shoots up my arm, louder than I probably had to. Kronus ignores me, taking a bandage from the table and wrapping it around my arm. That's one thing to be said about the crusty old healer: he doesn't treat the aristoi or us orphans who end up here on Tallis any differently.

No, he hates us all equally.

"I'll go mix up something for the pain," he grunts. "Stay here." He clomps off down the row of beds toward his still room.

I debate disobeying him. I've tasted his concoctions be-

fore and I'd almost prefer to be in pain. Only then I shift
and agony flares up my spine. I groan and settle back.
Maybe not.

I lie there, staring up at the ceiling. Trying not to crawl
from my skin from being trapped here.

There was Scriptwork in that cave. Live Scriptwork.
The masters have been cataloging every instance of Scriptwork on this island since the Scriptorium was built here,
but that cave looked like it had been lying undiscovered
for centuries.

I need to find out what it is. Because it could be anything. Because it's something after seven years of frustrat-
ing nothing. Even the Scriptmasters have barely dented the
language of the runes, especially after so much knowledge
was lost during the Great Lapse. And the fact that Scriptwork has survived without any maintenance for so long
must mean it's powerful. A *lock* rune barely lasts a decade
before going dark with no upkeep if it's exposed to the el-
ements. Which means maybe there'll be something in that
cave that will give me an edge.

"You're looking rough."

I twist my head at the jesting voice and see Dane leaning against the doorway. His arms are folded across his
chest, one ankle lightly hooked over the other. The pose
is so intentionally casual it makes him look like a carved
masterpiece.

I prop myself up on my elbows with a grimace. "I decided to see what would happen if I fell off a cliff."

Dane glances around for Kronus, then steps over to my
bed. His eyebrows quirk as he takes in my appearance, my

skin a mottled mess of scrapes and bandages and whatever foul gloop Kronus has coated me with. I'm momentarily put out that Dane gets to be all charm and ease, while I'm all scowls and bad ideas. "Not your best plan," he says.

"Not my worst either."

He laughs as he reaches into his belt pouch and pulls out a handkerchief wrapped around a small barley loaf. "Here, I filched this from the kitchen for you."

I hadn't even realized how hungry I was. I pluck the roll from his hand and take a bite. With a happy moan, I sink into the bed. It's still warm. "Thanks," I mumble around my mouthful.

Dane plops himself down next to me on the bed. I wince as he works his arm beneath me, but I don't say anything. Because he chose to come here. Even though I'm sure all his buddies are relaxing together after their morning drills. Even though, if he was so inclined, he could probably be with any girl he wanted on this island, aristoi included. Instead he's here with me. Our friendship is just as strong as what he has with them.

"I'm glad you're all right, Karis," he murmurs and maybe his night of patrolling did tire him out because when I glance over at him his eyes are closed. He's relaxed, quiet. I realize I might be the only person who gets to see him like this. Maybe that's why he stays with me, because he finds being constantly fawned over draining. I sure wouldn't know.

It almost makes me not want to say anything, feeling that for the first time in a long time we're just like we used to be. But all of the anticipation is bottled up in my chest and I have to let it out.

"I actually found something," I say quietly. "When I fell."

"Hmm?" he murmurs.

"A cave. And there was a glimmer of Scriptwork in it."

Dane goes still beside me. There's a too-long pause before he carefully says, "Sounds interesting."

"It's more than interesting, Dane, and you know that."

He sits up, pulling his arm away. The loss of heat is almost as bad as the pain. He drops his head into his hands. "Karis."

I sit up, too, even though pretending I said nothing is looking real appealing. "There could be anything in there."

"Or there could also be nothing." He drops his hands and turns to me. "Which means, you could be risking everything for nothing. Is that what you want?"

Of everyone, I thought Dane would understand. "Matthias is somewhere out there. He's my brother. I need to find him."

Dane scrubs his fingers against his bracelet. I doubt he notices he's doing it, even though that bracelet used to rankle him as much as it did me.

"Look," he says. "I know I don't understand how you feel. My life before I came here…" He turns away, but not before I notice how tight his jaw has gone. "It wasn't a good one. I never had a family to fight for. But here we're safe. We never have to worry about food or where we're going to sleep. Here we have the opportunity to actually make something of our lives. To become captains or Scriptmasters."

He might have a shot at becoming a captain, he's that good. But I know, even if he refuses to admit it, that I have no chance of rising in these halls. I'm an orphan, with no money, no connections. Dane's natural sword-fighting skills got him to where he is, but I don't have that. And even if I did spend my life here trying my hardest, even though I've figured out runes all on my own, that's not enough to make them care. In this place, I'll only ever be a street brat. I'll only ever be nothing.

"I know you want to find your brother," Dane says, a plea hidden just beneath his tone. "I don't want to be on Tallis my whole life either. I want to see the rest of the world. And we'll get our chance one day. But in the meantime, we can have good lives here."

Good lives. I can't remember when he started calling our existence here that. It makes me angry. "And all it costs us is a shackle around our wrists."

"You always make everything so black-and-white."

"Some things should be black-and-white."

We stare at each other. We're sitting so close, but he seems far away. Like even if I reached out right now, my fingers wouldn't be able to touch him. Dane and I used to have so much in common, when we first arrived on Tallis within weeks of each other. I had so much anger. At the Scriptorium. At my life. I was always picking fights. Usually with older acolytes I had no hope of winning against. But at least as I was being pounded into the dirt, I could forget for a moment the pain of losing Matthias. Then one day as I was getting roundly beaten, Dane showed up and maybe he was just angry at it all, too. We had both lived and lost the same kind of life. He waded in, and even though he ended up getting pummeled, too, from then on, it was always the two of us.

People change, though. He may be an orphan and a street brat just like me, but he's found his place here. Now I can feel him slipping away and I don't know how to stop it. Maybe, if I'm being honest, that's part of why I'm so desperate to go. How much longer can we have this argument before we realize there's nothing left between us worth fighting for?

Dane stares out the window. "You're as close to family as I have, Karis," he says quietly. "Don't ask me to watch you ruin yourself."

I look down at my hands folded on the sheets. I've never heard Dane talk like this before. If I'm being honest, I feel the same about him. Here on Tallis, he became a brother, just like the one I lost. On the streets, all that mattered was protecting your own. And maybe we brought that mind-set here. Only keeping Dane would mean giving up on Matthias. And I can't give up on my brother. Can't resign myself to living on this island that makes me feel as if it's slowly strangling all the air out of me.

"I won't stop, Dane. And you should know better than to ask me to."

Terrible, heavy silence stretches between us. For once, I don't know how to break it.

Heavy footsteps clomp toward us. Master Kronus. I look across the infirmary and the bed rocks beneath me. By the time I turn back, Dane is gone.

When Master Kronus releases me, the lamps have been extinguished, and only wisps of their smoke still snake through the air. I step out into the dark corridor. It hurts to move, but whatever he gave me took the edge off the pain, even though it felt like swallowing gristle.

I'm close to the west wing, where I sneaked out the other night. If I went the other way, it would eventually take me to my cramped living quarters. Two choices lie before me, and neither seem clear. Sleep and pain create a fog behind my eyes. Maybe Dane is right. Maybe I should just go back to my room, forget the cave and the Scriptwork. Try to fit in. Try to carve out some sort of life here. No matter what I do, it seems like freedom is always just out of reach. As untouchable as the stars.

A laugh echoes down the hall, and I see Jocasta and Thetis, crossing at the far end. The lantern they hold between them lights up their faces. Jocasta says something and Thetis erupts into a fit of giggles. They turn the corner, their light trailing behind them.

For a moment I imagine myself running after them. Maybe making a joke. Being one of them.

But that thought is just a dream. I know that as soon as I have it. I lost that chance. When I first arrived, I was so focused on finding a way to escape, of getting back to Matthias, that I didn't want to grow any roots that might hold me down. I ignored Jocasta's friendship, all of their friendship, until it turned into indifference, and then into scorn. There's only one person out there that I belong with now.

I start walking, toward the west wing. The same window gets me out of the building, and I shiver. It's cold, the night air spreading goose bumps over my skin. I shove the front gates open, grimacing at the ache that burns into my ribs. On the other side of the wall, the island is quiet and dark, with clouds smearing up the sky. I look for the tell-tale bob of light from any of the patrols, but don't see them.

It takes me too long to reach the cliffs, and when I finally arrive, I'm panting. The automaton looms out of the darkness. As bad as the thing was during the day, it's even more foreboding in the dark, its ghastly shape blurred by the shadows.

I can just make out the ropes hanging from its form. I grab the one closest to the cliff edge, pulling until I have a spare spool snaking around my feet.

Now the difficult part. I look out over the cliff side. Far below me the dark waves pound the shore. Dane would say I have a bad habit of not thinking things through, and I guess I just proved him right. Back in the Scriptorium, I didn't stop to consider how difficult this was going to be with the shape I'm in. Already the pain is crawling back into my skull, echoing beneath my skin. For a moment the cliff and the waves and the night blur around me. I blink it away. It's not that far. And if I fall... Well, that ledge caught me once already.

Before I can spiral into doubt, I pivot, bracing my legs against the rock until the rope is fully supporting my weight. It strains but holds. My legs, though... Pain is already lancing through my muscles.

Step by step I go, each one piercing and sharp. Spray hits the cliff face, making everything—me, the rope, the rock—slick and cold. My fingers ache from clenching so hard. Almost. Almost. Almost. The word pounds with my heartbeat, faster and faster.

My foot touches the ledge and my legs fold beneath me, sending me sprawling. I plant my palms on the comfortingly solid rock beneath me as I gasp in air, the world shuddering. The spray has already soaked my chiton through with a cold that ekes into my bones.

I really should consider listening to Dane more.

Lifting my head, I look at the crack in the cliff side, half expecting not to see the glimmer of gold, as if it was only some shock-induced dream. But it's still there, even more obvious in the night. I was right.

I'd packed a lamp and a small amphora of oil, but my fingers are so chilled it takes me three tries to light the wick, bringing with it the nauseating smell of animal fat. I grip the lamp closer, wrapping my body around its flame, as I stagger to my feet and forward.

The crack isn't large, but I manage to squeeze through, the sound of the waves going strangely muted. There's just my footsteps and my breath, thrown back at me from the dripping walls. The wetness makes everything glint slightly in the firelight. If I die down here, no one would even know where to look for my bones.

That's comforting.

Something metallic clinks beneath my foot and I jerk. It's a medallion. I crouch down and pick it up. It's the size of my palm, faded and dirty and one side bent. Its edge is embellished with beads of gold and there's something imprinted on its center beneath all the grime. It's undeniably old and I really hope I'm not about to find whoever used to own it.

I tuck it into my belt pouch and keep going, toward the

glow of the Scriptwork hovering in the dark in front of me. My own light, pale in comparison, slips over plain rock. And then it finds a face.

I jump back but my bruised body can't move that fast and I go down, the lamp extinguishing as hot oil spills from it, scalding my skin. Stifling darkness floods in. I scrabble in my belt pouch for my flint, trying to listen past the rasping of my breath for the noise of whoever—whatever—I saw. Of them prowling toward me in the dark.

My throbbing hand finds the flint and I strike it, lighting the lamp again. I lurch to my feet and see...

An automaton.

My light flickers over its stilled body. Every other automaton on Tallis is a vast, hulking creature built only to destroy. The monstrous pride of our nation. But this one, sitting against the wall, head slightly lolled as if it has simply fallen asleep, almost looks like a person.

It's my size, with delicately crafted fingers and toes, even a face that is strangely expressive, exquisitely shaped from dozens of bronze discs so smooth they blend into one another. A slight frown cuts its lips, a furrow dimpling its brow. There's something youthful about it, as if whoever built it wanted it to look more my age than the age of the wizened masters who control this place. It's wearing a chiton, too. An old one, more tatters than fabric now, but someone went through the effort of dressing it. Considering how old this automaton must be, it should be covered in tarnish. Instead, the bronze of its skin is still polished, with a strange sheen.

I take a step back. This isn't right. Automatons aren't supposed to look like that. They were built to be monstrous, because automatons were built to be monsters. An automaton shouldn't be lying in a cave, looking strangely troubled even in sleep, and appearing so unnervingly…human. As if at any moment it might open its eyes and see me.

I'm being ridiculous. This thing isn't human. It won't open its eyes because it isn't alive. It's a weapon. A tool.

A tool that maybe I can use.

I kneel beside it, strangely feeling like I'm kneeling next to some corpse. I force my eyes off its face and onto its metal skin. Most of it is bared, showing me its runes. All the Scriptwork I know is self-taught, from sneaking books out of the library or even right out of the bags of the aristoi. Every automaton I've ever seen or studied has had the exact same runes: *twist* etched into shoulders, *reach* printed on arms, *bend* carved onto legs. This automaton does have those. But scattered among them are dozens upon dozens of runes whose meanings I can't even guess. Even the lines look different. They normally look hard and rigid. These are more elegant, with a lilt that almost makes them look…graceful.

On its arm, a tangle of lines stretches all the way from its shoulder to its elbow, so complicated I can't tell where one rune ends and the next begins. They've been damaged, not from age, but struck through with a violent, jagged gash. The runes are broken, and they're broken badly.

That's when I notice the satchel, wedged between the automaton's back and the wall. I ease it out and open the flap. There's only one thing inside. An old, decaying book.

No, not a book. A tome.

My breath rasps in my ears as I pull the volume out,

taking in its worn cover, the leather crackling from age beneath my fingertips. It's a tome. An actual automaton's tome. I flip it over to look at the seal on its spine. Two curves enclose a circle almost like a golden sun. It's glowing, the light gently pulsing across my fingers. I reach out and move the automaton's chiton aside, to where its own seal is. It's a match. And it's glowing, too.

I sit shakily back on my heels. I've seen so many automatons. I've even seen tomes in the archives. And none of them, not one, had live Scriptwork.

No one knows what Master Theodis did to trigger the Great Lapse. No one even knows why it shut the automatons down when the rest of the Script—the individual runes used for locks and bracelets and weapons—kept working. But this seal is still lit. For two hundred years, the Scriptmasters have been looking for this exact thing, live Scriptwork on an automaton, and now it's right in front of me. If I wake this automaton up, any of the runes on its skin written correctly on the pages of this tome will be able to make it move. The first one of its kind to be commanded in two centuries. And it wouldn't be the Scriptorium doing it. It would be me.

The idea's a terrible one. As soon as I have it, I know that. It's terrible and dangerous and reckless. I'm not a Scriptmaster. I don't know all the runes they do. I don't even know what I'd do with the thing if I woke it up.

But all that possibility is already coursing beneath my skin, thrumming through my veins like they've been lit on fire, banishing the cold, the fear, the doubt. And it isn't in me to turn from it. This is my chance to get away from this place, to change everything.

I set the lamp between me and it, and step a safe distance away before cracking the tome open. I'm not exactly sure what I expect to see, but the smooth page with only a single faded rune at the top—*wake*—surprises me. This automaton never received a command. Who would go to the effort of dragging it here?

I pull out my charcoal. It was only one night ago that I stood before a different seal and wrote a rune that did nothing. That was only a *lock* rune, and yes, it was complicated, but it's nothing like the one before me now. There is no rune more advanced than the knot of tight lines that make up a *wake* rune. Even the aristoi aren't allowed to study it until they become masters.

I labored for months to figure it out for myself using any books I could find or steal, trying to untangle how all the lines interacted and which order they needed to be written in. Anyone can draw a rune as long as they have a ledger or, in the case of an automaton, a tome. But you either need to memorize the form or figure it out yourself. I wanted to learn the rune needed to power an automaton. Maybe just because it was forbidden. But standing here, alone, suddenly I find myself doubting. I'm not a Scriptorium master. I'm not an aristoi. I'm just me.

Only then I think of Matthias. He's out there somewhere. The only family I have left.

I begin the rune. My charcoal dances across the page, tracing the broad strokes. Instantly I know this time is dif-

ferent, because this time I feel it. The lines running together. A strange energy thrilling around my fingertips.

My charcoal stills. The rune is complete, thick lines and
sharp angles bold against the parchment. I almost don't
want to look up, because I'm not sure I could handle another failure.

A scrape sounds against the rock of the tunnel. Heart
pounding, I raise my head.

The automaton shifts, its back straightening. It's...
moving.

I did it.

That's when its eyes open.

I stumble back. Its eyes are made of some sort of polished
stone, deep and dark except where they burn with light
almost as if there are twin flames of gold inside of them.
They're ethereal. Eyes like I've never seen before.

Then those eyes, those impossible eyes, look right at me.

3

ALIX

Nightmare images cling to my mind: of black water sloshing up over my head, suffocatingly cold; of a blazing light and golden warmth on my face; of a voice—my father's voice—crying out my name in pain and fear. The memories cling, trying to pull me under, and I fight back, dredging myself free. As they clear, I see a damp, black cave, lit only by the dim light of the lamp that sits a few feet away.

Behind that lamp is a girl.

I blink at her as she stares back, her face so still I'd be half convinced she was a statue, if not for the shallow cut across her cheek. Her brown hair falls past her shoulders, wet and scraggly, the color matching her eyes. I struggle to remember where I am and who she is. My head and memory feel mired down somewhere I can't grab hold. I'm sure I only closed my eyes for a moment, but I don't know this cave.

I don't know this girl. She's dressed strangely, her chiton worn off both shoulders, its hem landing above her knees.

Then I see what's in her hands. It's my tome, and above it, a piece of charcoal poised to write.

Everything in me goes cold. I lunge forward, hands outstretched. The girl stumbles away, jerking the charcoal across the page. A rune flares on my back, a bright burn, and a shudder goes through my body. It freezes everything it touches, stopping my arms as they reach forward, halting my legs in mid-movement. Panicked, I fight it, slamming my will against my limbs, but they stay still.

I'm trapped.

The girl takes a shuddering breath, her eyes painted wild by the reflected firelight. "What are you?" she murmurs.

I clamp my mouth shut as I rack my mind, trying to remember anything that might tell me what I'm doing here in this cave with this girl. Nothing comes except for the crippling knowledge that this stranger has stolen my tome. She can make me do anything, and I am powerless to stop her from doing it.

I wait for her to write the rune that will force me to move.

She doesn't.

A fragile hope lights in my chest. Her clothes don't look quite Scriptorium. Perhaps she isn't one of them. Perhaps she hasn't studied any but the most basic runes.

We stand there, her staring at me and me staring back. In the end I'm the one who cracks first because the fear inside of me bursts with bright explosions. "Give that back," I rasp. "It's mine."

A jolt goes through her, and I remember that I'm not like other automatons. I can do things that other automatons cannot, such as speaking. How could I forget that, for even a moment?

"You can talk," she whispers, and beyond the fear there's a hint of wonder.

"Please." I hate the pleading in my voice, but I can't tamp it down. The panic is breaking through every wall I set up to hold it back. "Give it back."

The girl's hands curl tighter around my tome and she steps away.

Like a flame dying, all the fight leeches out of me. Father warned me what would happen if anyone else got their hands on my tome. Now someone has, and I can't so much as move my little finger to get it away from her.

I would have sagged if I could have, all the life draining out of me. The wretched rune in my tome doesn't even allow me that.

"What will you make me do?" I ask.

A frown cuts across the girl's face. She looks down at a bracelet on her wrist, runes carved into its surface. As she rubs her fingers over it, something sharp passes across her eyes. I can't quite read it. The only face I've ever had to try to understand was my father's.

With an exasperated growl, she writes another rune in my tome. My limbs unlock, and I stumble forward.

She thrusts my tome at me. "Here."

I stare at her in baffled disbelief, then snatch it back. As soon as my fingers wrap around the familiar leather cover, the seal on my chest flares with warmth. I retreat a few steps back, looking down at the new runes on the page: *wake, stop, move*. They're all written in the same hand.

Her hand.

The girl leans against the wall, rubbing her face. I watch her, suddenly unsure. Father always said that if anyone stole my tome from me, they would never give it back. Yet she did.

She drops her hands. "Seriously," she says, her voice thick. "What are you?"

Those words sting. *What*. As if I'm a thing.

"I'm not a what," I say. "My name is Alix."

Every time I speak, her eyes go a bit wider, as if every time she isn't quite expecting it. She doesn't seem to know what to say. Then, of all things, a dry smile tweaks at the corner of her mouth. "Karis."

I blink. That was not the reaction I was expecting.

She raises an eyebrow as she studies me, firelight flickering across her face from the lamp. I've always regretted not having eyebrows.

"How did you get down here?" she asks.

That memory rises again of my father calling out to me, but it's fuzzy around the edges. Perhaps I don't want to know what the fog of my memory is hiding from me. Father wouldn't have abandoned me in a place like this, with my tome unprotected. Which begs the question of where he is right now. "I don't... I don't know." I rub my fingers over my tome. Its cover feels different. It's worn, the leather cracked in places like scars. It wasn't worn before. What is going on?

I glance up at Karis. I'm not sure I can risk trusting her,

but nothing is making sense, and I don't know what else I'm supposed to do. "You don't..." I trail off, then force myself on. My father is one of the most prestigious Scriptmasters alive. Surely this girl, whoever she is, will have at least heard of him. "You don't know where my father might be, do you? His name is Master Theodis."

At the sound of my father's name, shock flashes across her face, an expression that quickly slides into a fear I don't understand.

"What is it?" I ask.

Karis chews on her lip.

"Please tell me."

Her eyes search mine before she glances away. "Master Theodis is... I mean..." She grimaces. "He's dead."

Dead. A sudden silence presses against my head. The world narrows to the space between me and this girl. I don't understand that word. I don't understand what she's trying to say. "What?"

The fear slips from her eyes, giving way to something like pity. "I'm sorry."

I take a step back, barely realizing I'm numbly shaking my head. There must be a mistake. My father can't be gone, those twinkling eyes empty, that keen mind silenced. Whatever my memory is hiding, it can't be that. I search desperately for the lie in her face.

I don't find it.

Unseen cracks split over my skin. "How?" I whisper.

"No one really knows how. Not anymore, I mean."

Not anymore?

She rubs her arm awkwardly. "Do you have any idea how long you've been down here?"

"A few days perhaps." It must have only been a few days.

"It's just... Master Theodis's death... It happened over two hundred years ago."

Two hundred years. Not days, not weeks, but years. Hundreds of years. I stumble away from her, only to hit the cave wall. I turn, pressing my forehead against the stone as I try to hold myself together, to control the panic clawing up my throat and shivering down my limbs. It isn't possible. I simply closed my eyes. It can't have been more than a few days. She *must* be lying...or trying to trick me...or...

A gentle touch comes to rest on my shoulder, so surprising that I jerk away. Karis jumps back, clutching her hand to her chest. I stare at her, an imprint of warmth still in my skin. Besides my father, no one has ever tried to comfort me.

No one has ever gotten close enough to try.

I look down at my clothes, hanging in tatters from my body, destroyed not by violence but from age. Perhaps that's why the style of Karis's clothes looks different, because the ones I'm used to are centuries old. I don't want to believe it, but the logical part left inside of me tells me it's possible. That's enough to let all of the doubt come flooding in. Two hundred years gone as I slept in this cave. If what she's saying is true, my father is nothing but bones and dust now. He's not here anymore.

He's not anywhere anymore.

"You know his name, at least, even now," I finally manage. "That means he died a hero, right?"

Karis fiddles with her belt, not looking at me. "I wouldn't say hero is a word most people attach to Master Theodis."

"What do you mean?"

"He did some pretty terrible things."

I stiffen. "What things?"

"He sabotaged the Scriptorium. Destroyed the power of the automatons."

The Scriptorium is my enemy. I may not remember much, but I remember that. "You." I point at her. "You're one of them."

She glares at me. "Not willingly."

"And yet you repeat their words and believe their lies," I growl, advancing a step. For the first time, a flash of temper flares in my chest. Perhaps I'm glad about that, because anger has to be better than the sadness smearing me away.

Fear flashes through her eyes, bright and sudden. I stop. What am I doing? This isn't me.

I stare down at the ground. "Sorry."

Silence stretches between us and I'm too much of a coward to meet her eyes.

"Look," she finally says, "I have no lost love for the Scriptorium. And if you're really Master Theodis's...child, and if you were really there...maybe there's more to the story. All I'm telling you is what history has taught me."

History. His life can't already be history. "Then history is full of lies." I can't listen to this anymore. It hurts too much. I turn to leave.

Karis grabs my arm. "Wait, where do you think you're going?"

I shake her off, trembling. "I can't stand here as the

Scriptorium spreads lies about my father." I need to fix these things they're saying about him, because they're wrong. My father is not—was not—what they claim.

"Alix," she says, "you can't go out there. I don't know what Tallis was like when you first came here, but it's full of Scriptmasters and scholars now. People who would do anything to control you."

Control me. The sickening finality of those words stops me. Karis might have given me my tome back, but a Scriptmaster wouldn't. My father said they wouldn't. He made me promise I would never risk going anywhere near another Scriptmaster.

Karis looks at her bracelet again. This close, I can see that I was right. The metal is covered by runes. It seems like such a strange thing to create. What would something like that even be used for?

"Listen," Karis says. "I need to go before somebody finds me missing. But I promise I'll come back. Just stay here until then. I can help you. You can't go out dressed like that. I'll bring you some clothes. And if you need to find a way off this island, I know one."

Everything she told me swirls around my head in a jumble. Karis is Scriptorium. Yet, she gave me back my tome. She said she was sorry about what happened. She tried to comfort me. If what she's saying is true, my father is gone. I don't know how to navigate the world without him.

I finger my tome. "I'll stay. For now."

Karis leaves, taking the lamp with her. The only light that remains comes from my burning eyes and the glow of my seal. It's barely enough to cast a dim glow on the cave wall before me.

I press my fingers against the broken runes on my arm. Even though I can barely see them, I can still feel them, destroyed by an act of violence that I can't remember any more than I can remember anything else that happened. I probe my memories again, trying to push past the pounding of my head. I remember waking up for the first time, my father's kind face hovering over me. The time I spent with him in his villa, hidden away because we both knew what the other Scriptmasters would do if they found out about me. The quiet years of learning and simply being with him.

I can tell there are gaps, though, as if the memories are wall hangings that have had holes burned into them. The closer I try to get to whatever happened right before I reached this cave, the more I feel this empty blankness yawning in my mind. I remember a night… I went with my father somewhere… I remember a blaze like the sun, but in darkness. My palms pressed against a scalding heat. I remember running.

I ran and my father died.

The darkness pushes against me, bringing back the panic. I told Karis I would stay here, but if I have to spend an-other moment in the dark, trapped with my half memories, I'll drown in them. I lurch forward into the dark tunnel, banging against walls I only see as I hit them. I don't know Karis. She could have lied to me. How am I supposed to figure out what might make someone lie? She could be heading back here right now with Scriptorium soldiers. I need to see for myself.

I step out of the cave and for the first time in two hundred years, moonlight and fresh air touch my skin. It feels alive. Above me the night sky is dark, with only a few stars shining out between the thick masses of clouds. The dark waves pounding at the cliffs below me stretch on to an empty horizon, though I know there must still be other islands out there, shrouded by the night. Even if everything else has changed, that couldn't. The sight of the waves brings back another memory: trudging down into the murky depths between islands, looking for a hiding spot that wasn't meant to last centuries.

I turn away, before the memories have a chance to engulf me again and launch myself straight up, slamming my hands into the rock face as I land. The movement helps. It lets me focus on the climb, on reaching for the next hold rather than on anything else. I have no lungs to demand more air and no muscles to demand a rest. For once I'm glad because then I can keep climbing and I don't have to give myself time to think.

At the lip of the cliff face I pause, listening for any noise from up above. I remember this island: Tallis. The southernmost point of Eratia, which held only a small guard post.

I haul myself over the edge, hoping to see an island that's as empty as the night I came. I land in a crouch on the grass and I see it: an automaton. Standing not even ten feet away. A flash of memory comes back to me, of that exact automaton, darkened by the rain. Of backing away from it. Of falling.

Only this automaton isn't the same. The one I glimpse in my memory was whole, its metal burnished clear. This one is missing half of its left arm. Its metal is tarnished and cracked, undeniably old.

No, not old. Ancient.

I stare at this thing, standing over me in the dark. Back before, I was never allowed to be this close to one. I could only see them from afar, when one would lumber past my father's villa, its bronze shining blindingly beneath the sun. I hated seeing them then.

Standing here now, I hate it, too. Its brokenness doesn't hide how large and destructive it looks, as if it's a nightmare come to life. It doesn't hide how much, in the end, it looks like me.

I'm taking a staggering step away when I realize something is missing. I've always been able to feel automatons, as if they radiated this buzzing energy. I've never understood why I'm the way I am, and they're the way they are, but even they still had this fire inside of them. Only this one doesn't. It's as if it truly is dead.

I hesitate, then reach out to touch it.

Voices drift toward me. I duck behind one of the automaton's legs, halfway buried in the ground. A man and a woman walk toward the automaton, their bronze lamp illuminating the dirt path they follow.

Scriptorium soldiers.

A rush of anger swells inside of me, so quickly I don't have a hope of tamping it down. My father is dead because of Scriptorium soldiers. They killed him and then they lied. I want to destroy them. I want to make them pay for every bit of pain engulfing me right now.

I slam myself back against the automaton's leg. As quickly

as the rage comes on, it disappears. I sink to the ground, pressing my hands to my eyes. No. I'm not some mindless weapon like the other automatons. This isn't me. This isn't who my father raised me to be.

I am not a monster.

The voices disappear and still I sit there, shaking at what I almost did. Suddenly I wish Karis was here, even though I don't really know her. I'm scared of being on my own if those are the thoughts I'm going to have.

I'm not sure how long I sit there. Long enough that by the time I crack open my eyes again the sky has begun to pale. I get up, still shaky, and climb back down to my cave, to wait for a girl I'm not even sure I can trust, who might be my only chance.

4

KARIS

The archival room is quiet, with only the scratch of quills against parchment. There are no windows and the sole light comes from the bronze lamps perched on the edges of the desks, the smoke snaking around the space and making my eyes water. I transfer the details from the rune rubbings I made that day to the ledger laid out in front of me. Height and depth and condition. All to be pored over by the masters here, in the hopes that one day they'll be able to reanimate an automaton. Never knowing I just did, and he was nothing like what I expected.

Benches scrape against the stone floor and I look up to find the rest of my group packing their things. I shove my own tools into my bag and leave, wanting to be ahead of the crowd because I never know when my group mates are going to choose to see me and get nasty.

By the time the middle of the night comes, I haven't slept

at all. I keep telling myself I won't go. That whatever could have happened with the automaton—with Alix—began and ended last night. But then the ninth watch rings out and I find myself pulling on my pack. Slipping down the halls and out the window, trying to ignore what I'm actually doing. Willingly going back to an automaton. An automaton that can somehow think, even though that should be impossible.

That was made by Master Theodis.

I don't know much about the man, but it's said he single-handedly discovered over a dozen runes and created a dozen more. That he ascended to master status when he was nothing more than a young man. And that in the end, none of it was ever enough. In his greed he triggered the Great Lapse and ended the golden age of the Scriptorium's power. Eural and Anderra invaded, bringing with them decades of war. By the time we managed to climb our way back to any sort of peace, so much had been destroyed and lost, and no one remembered how to bring the automatons back to life. It's taken us two hundred years and we still haven't fully recovered.

What if this automaton is the same as the man?

That's when I see Alix. I thought he'd stay in his cave, that an automaton wouldn't care whether he was down there in the dark. Instead he sits on the edge of the bluff, in the moon-laced shadow cast by the much larger autom-aton above him. His legs dangle over the cliff edge as he stares out at the ocean, his hands resting on the satchel in his lap. There's a slight breeze, stirring the grasses around him, that smells like the sea.

And he doesn't look like a weapon or a monster. He just

looks...lonely. I don't understand that. How an automaton can look lonely. How an automaton can look anything.

I almost turn to go. Going would be the smart thing to do. But standing here, I can feel my future back in the Scriptorium winding out in front of me, always the same, always like this, and it makes me feel like I can't breathe.

"Alix?" I say quietly.

He glances over his shoulder. His skin might be metal, but that doesn't hide the exhaustion.

I make myself step closer. "You shouldn't be up here. Someone could see you."

He looks away, back across the water, the waves glinting beneath the moon. "I couldn't stay in that cave. It was too..." He cuts off, dropping his head. "I didn't like it."

His voice is strained. Actually strained. And I have to admit, it sounds real.

I reach into my pack and pull out my spare chiton and himation. "Here, I brought you something. With any luck, if anyone sees you wearing this, they'll just think you're an acolyte. I have a himation for you, too."

There's the smallest hesitation before Alix gets up and comes over. He takes the chiton and drapes it in front of his body, frowning.

I can't get over how expressive his face is, the bronze discs so smooth and crafted so delicately they shape just like skin would. It's unnerving. Unnerving and yet... Being on Tallis taught me to always disguise what I felt, to never show it. But Alix's face doesn't hide anything, each emotion bright and raw like an open flame. I feel a jealous pang that whatever he might be, he never had to learn to hide like I did.

"I'm sorry," I say. "I'm sure you don't want to wear Scriptorium clothes but they're all I have and—"

"No, it's fine. I'm just…not quite sure how to wear this. It's different from what I'm used to."

"Oh, right." I step up to him and help him wrap the cloth around his body, pinning it at the hips and shoulders and looping the belt around his waist before arranging the himation around his head and shoulders. Once he's dressed, he pulls the rags he has on underneath away.

I step back to take a look. His skin is still slightly the wrong color, and there's a strange pale sheen to his runes, not quite the glow of an activated rune, but not the dark of an unactivated rune either. Still, from far off, it should be mostly convincing.

Hopefully.

Alix smooths his hands over the material. "Thank you."

"Of course." My fingers curl around the medallion that's also now in my pack. And for a moment I want to keep it, in case it's valuable. In case I need it.

As soon as I have the thought, I hate myself for it. Alix is grieving, and I found this medallion in his cave. When my brother was taken away, when my life was taken away, I didn't get to keep anything. I won't do that to someone else, no matter what he is. "I also brought this."

As soon as he sees it, pain lights his eyes. He reaches out, and for all that I know how strong he must be, how strong all automatons are, his touch is gentle as he takes the medallion.

"What is it?" I ask quietly.

"My father gave it to me. It's the sigil of his house."

The sigil of Master Theodis's house. The greatest villain of the ages. I don't know how to reconcile the idea of a man like that with this lonely, gentle automaton in front of me now.

So I just won't think about that right now.

"Here," I say briskly. I pull out the piece of twine I'd packed and carefully thread it through the hole in the medallion, before looping the entire thing around his neck. His skin is surprisingly warm, tingling beneath my palms, as if it's somehow heated from the inside. Is this what an animated automaton feels like? The warmth is actually kind of…nice. "There we go."

Alix tugs on the medallion, then looks up, studying my face. We're close, as close as we've gotten so far, our faces only a few hand's breadths apart. I still can't get over the way his eyes look, the flames undulating in them. There's intelligence in that gaze. I can't deny it.

"Why did you give me my tome back?" he asks, so soft that even at this close distance I barely hear the words.

I wonder if every selfish thought I've had about using him flashes over my face at that question. I rub my fingers over my bracelet.

"I know what it's like for your life to belong to someone else," I finally say. If I had controlled Alix, forced his will to bend to mine, I would have become just like the Scriptorium. They've taken so much from me already. I refuse to let them take who I am.

Alix looks down at the bracelet. "What is that?"

I hesitate, then hold my wrist out to him. "It's my acolyte bracelet. I meant what I said before. I'm not loyal to the Scriptorium. I was sent here when I was a child and that's when they put this thing on me. It lets them track me and stops me from leaving this island." I drop my hand. "I'm trapped here because of it."

Alix studies the runes on it. "Would you like me to take it off?"

My head snaps up. "What?"

"You woke me. It's the least I can do in return."

I stare at him, baffled, and then thrust the bracelet into his face. "You can remove this? This bracelet? You can take it off?"

My voice is getting higher, louder, but I don't care.

Alix takes a timid step back. "Er, I should be able to undo the runes on it."

Alix can undo runes. These things that have trapped me on this island. That have kept me from Matthias. Could it really be that simple? "What about *lock* runes? Could you open one of them?"

"Umm…yes?"

In all the time I've been on this island, I've never heard of automatons being able to do anything like that, to work the Script, to undo its runes. But Alix isn't like those other automatons. He's something more.

"I need your help," I say.

Alix takes another tiny step back, looking intimidated. I don't understand how someone who can probably punch straight through rock could have that sort of expression. He glances over his shoulder, as if debating whether he should leave, and the thought of that happening is so painful I step forward and take his arm, as if I can stop him.

And immediately he does stop. I wonder if I made a mistake but when he glances down at my hand on his arm, his expression isn't angry or insulted. It's just confused. A confusion so raw it gives me a strange pang.

"Please." I force my voice to stay calmer. Part of me wants to ask him to take the bracelet off right now, but if he does, the Scriptmasters could very well be alerted. I'd lose any chance of finding my brother. I need to be smart about this. "When I was brought here, I was separated from my brother. The only place that can tell me where he was sent is the Hall of Records and it has a *lock* rune on its door. But if you could undo it, I could go inside. And then if you took off my bracelet, we could both get out of here. Matthias is the only family I have left."

I don't see how those words could ever be enough, when staying on this island would be so dangerous for him, and I have so little to offer him for taking this chance. But as I speak, a new grief filters into Alix's expression. There's loss in that look. A loss I understand.

I try again. "I know you don't owe me anything—"

"You woke me up," he says quietly. "You gave me my tome back. I would still be asleep if not for you." He looks down at his satchel, fingering its strap. "After I get you into the Hall of Records, you'll help me leave this place?"

"I will, I promise. I don't want to be here any more than you do."

There's another silence, so long I swear my chest is about to burst. Then Alix looks up at me, and despite the uncertainty still flickering in his eyes, he nods. "All right. I'll do it."

5

ALIX

Karis leads the way, avoiding the dirt paths and cutting across the scrubby fields, as I follow her shadowy form in the dark. I'm still not quite sure why I agreed to do this. Father always taught me to be cautious and stay hidden. If he were here, he'd want me to get off this island while I still could.

Except...I lost him, the only person in this world who cared for me. If I can stop Karis from losing someone she cares about, perhaps that will ease the grief that sits like a stone in the center of my chest. I didn't realize that emotions could feel this heavy.

Karis gestures to me. We drop to the ground, crawling forward on our stomachs.

"There it is," she whispers.

I look out at the cluster of buildings. Like everything else, the building has hints of the familiar, but it's wrong:

flourishes where I'm used to seeing smooth lines, and intricate carvings where I expect unadorned stone.

There's another automaton standing by the gate, inert like the other one. I look up at it, shadowy and indistinguishable in the dark.

My father spent most of his days studying automatons. I remember him once telling me how he thought that automatons might not have always been used as weapons. He theorized that once they might have been used, and built, for good. I always wanted desperately to believe that, but I'm not sure I ever quite could. Seeing this faceless automaton now, I'm still not sure I believe it. What good could come of such a thing?

"All right," Karis says, "see that patrol there? They're going to do a loop of the yard and then walk around the outside of the wall. That will be our chance to sneak in. Just follow me and if anyone gets close, look at the ground. Don't let them see your eyes. No one will be expecting an automaton as small as you, so if they only see your clothes, we might still be able to get you away without them suspecting anything."

I nod, trying not to show how queasy I suddenly feel. Perhaps this wasn't such a good idea. I'm not like this strange Scriptorium girl. I'm not used to running headfirst into danger.

"There," Karis says, "the guards have turned the corner. Go."

I follow her as she takes off toward the gates. We slip into the yard and over to the Hall, passing silently through the colonnade and into an atrium. I see the rune immediately, glowing in the dark in the back of the space. The bronze seal in the center of the doors is the size of my palm and has a complicated *lock* rune etched into it. The lines are so much sharper than mine.

Karis looks over her shoulder and then at the door. "Well?"

I step up to the seal and splay my fingers over its surface. As soon as I touch it, I hear the rune in the seal, the plucked strings of a harp, as if it's the beginning of a well-known melody that I have to finish. I hum a few notes. It's not that I need to hum to work on the Script, but I've always loved music, and right now it's comforting, a thin strand connecting me to the world I knew before. A rune flares hot on my side and a line of light shoots through the metal circle, separating it. The door clicks open.

Ornate bookshelves stand in sentinel-straight lines on the other side, the brass plates with neat print affixed to their shelves. Ledgers and scrolls and sheaves of paper tied with twine fill the shelves in neat order, suffusing the air with the thick scent of parchment. Windows set high in the roof slant light down to pale spots on the pale floor. There's a deep stillness to the place, like a held-in breath. It reminds me of the library in my father's house. He spent decades selecting and gathering his collection of works. I remember spending lazy afternoons with him wading through the scrolls in his library, each one a new world.

I itch to start exploring. I slept away two hundred years of history and discoveries. Now here they are right before me. The books as well. Outside of the tomes, books were so rare in my time, but here there are dozens.

Only Karis is already moving, her fingers hovering over the brass plates as she goes.

I follow her, passing information on automatons: on *construction* and *seals* and *known locations*. Then information on the Script: on *runes* and *etching techniques* and *scribal tools*. Right at the back we find information on *regiments* and *initiates* and *acolytes*. Then *arrivals*. Karis stops. She reaches out and begins flipping through the pages, back through the years until she reaches 531.

531. A year that was so far into the future, I wasn't sure I'd ever see it.

Karis pulls the sheaf of parchment from the shelf. The first page has a name I don't recognize written at the top. *Dane.* The next is hers, *Karis*, but she barely pauses. She reaches the final page in the pile.

Matthias.

She scans the page as if she's starving. I read the thin script over her shoulder.

Male. Approximately eleven years old. Of Eratian nationality. Delivered on the third day of the month of Octavius in the year 531 along with one sibling. Originally from Heretis.

Rejected from the Scriptorium due to troublesome behavior. Sent, on the third day of the month of Octavius in the year 531, to the Magistrate's Library in Valitia.

"The Magistrate's Library." Karis runs her fingers over the words. Her voice trembles. It makes me feel as if I'm intruding on a personal moment and I retreat a few paces away, scanning the nearby shelves to stop from looking at her. That's when I see the plaque—Masters: 300–350.

300–350. Some of those are years I remember. They're years that Father was alive.

Karis's brother only had one piece of parchment. The information on my father fills up the shelves in front of me. I pull out a sheet. It's a fragment, torn from some larger work.

...has long been recognized as the single greatest traitor in the history of the Scriptorium. Though acclaimed in his early years, his success turned to greed as he searched for ways to control more of the automatons, desiring their power not for the Scriptorium's glory but for his own.

Not much is known of what Master Theodis was working on during those years, except that it was meant to be the most powerful weapon Eratia had ever seen and that he planned to release it on the Scriptorium itself. The magistrate at the time, Reitas, led a force against him and the traitor was successfully killed but not before his weapon had done irreparable damage. No one knows what became of it.

A weapon. I stare at the words. Is this what Karis had been talking about? I think of my father, of the way his skin creased at the edges of his eyes when he smiled and his soft laugh. He was not creating a weapon. I pull out more records, then more, sure that if I keep looking, I'll find something that speaks the truth and remembers him like I do.

Disjointed phrases flash before my eyes.

…done in secret in his villa, no one knew what he was creating…

…no evidence of the weapon was found, even after Theodis's death…

…he worked for years in secret, honing his plan and his creation…

His creation. Dread coils around my seal. With everything I read, I'm struck with a deeper and deeper certainty that this creation isn't a weapon.

It's me.

I pull out another page and this one is merely a slip, with a single sentence on it.

Due to the actions of Master Theodis, the Automaton Heart was broken beyond repair.

The Automaton Heart. My fingers hover over the words. That name reverberates inside of me. I struggle to grasp it, even as it slips away.

"Alix?"

I jerk. Karis stands behind me, clutching the page on her brother.

"Are you all right?"

Am I all right? I thrust the papers at Karis. "Is this what they think of him? My father wasn't creating a weapon. He wouldn't have ever hurt anyone."

What about me? I can't say the words, of how they've viewed me this whole time. The anger wells up inside of me and I slam my hand into the wall, so hard it leaves a perfect imprint of my palm in the stone, runes and all.

Karis jumps. "Alix, please calm down."

Fear edges into her eyes, but for once I don't care. I can't calm down, because this is my fault. My father asked me to do something, and I failed, and he died. Now he's remembered as a traitor. "This is history now. These lies are history."

"Alix, please." Karis steps toward me, hands held out beseechingly. "I know how upsetting this must be but—"

A door creaks open and we both freeze.

"Is someone there?" It's an old voice, rusty with age. Light falls across the end of a nearby bookcase.

Karis grabs my hand. She tugs me forward and then we're running, feet pounding against the ground in sync.

What was I thinking? I push myself harder and now I'm the one pulling Karis behind me. We fly between the shelves, books and scrolls flashing past us. The doors to the Hall are ahead. We burst out and Karis staggers sideways, against one of the columns. Her body heaves with her breaths. I'd forgotten that she's a person, not an automaton, and that people need rest.

"Karis, I—"

She waves me off. "I'm fine." She half chokes on the words.

There's a shout from the other side of the complex. Soldiers.

"You need to go," Karis gasps out. "Now." She pushes me. She isn't strong enough to move me, but I let her.

I dash the short space to the wall and vault over it. I run, away from the Scriptorium and the shouts, into the darkness.

6

KARIS

I slip into my room, still panting, my chest too tight. I slide Matthias's paper into a tear in my bed, then change into my shift. If they find out what I did, if they come, I have to look innocent. I curl up in bed and squeeze my eyes closed, but I don't sleep. I can't sleep. The Magistrate's Library. Valitia. That's where Matthias was sent.

For the first time in seven years I know what happened to my brother that night, when he was dragged away and thrown back onto the boat that had just dropped us off. When I screamed until the ship was barely a speck on the horizon. When I collapsed on the beach, numb and cold.

I thought that once I learned where my brother was sent, everything would look brighter. But it doesn't. Because the Magistrate's Library can only mean the magistrate himself.

Agathon.

The Scriptorium doesn't teach us orphans much, but we

learned about him. The man took power twenty years ago, when tensions with Eural were running high. The previous magistrate was said to be a weak man, and one night, Agathon seized power in a coup. As soon as Agathon was declared magistrate he decreed forced conscription and sent our navy against Eural. He managed to beat them back from our shores, despite severe losses.

Some say he brought peace; and maybe he did. Our little archipelago of islands sits between two powerful nations, Eural to the north and Anderra to the east. It's a dangerous place to be. But I've also heard the whispers where the masters can't hear that when Agathon took over he killed the old magistrate, the entire inner council, anyone loyal to the old order, in cold blood. That even now, those who disagree with him simply disappear. I don't want my brother anywhere near a man like that.

Hours later, I jolt out of restless dreams to shouting and the heavy pounding of feet. I bolt upright in bed, disoriented, a cold sweat clinging to my temples, before it comes back to me. Waking up Alix. Sneaking into the Hall of Records. Coming so close to being caught. I scramble out of bed and fling my door open, tumbling into the hallway. There's already a crowd there of other acolytes, bleary-eyed and mumbling to one another, with mussed hair and shifts. All of them huddled in groups that right now I'm glad I'm not a part of.

"Karis."

Dane strides toward me down the hall. Whatever is happening must have reached the barracks first because he's already dressed in his uniform. Worry flashes in his eyes, so quick and sudden that if I didn't know him so well, I might have missed it. My gut twists. Dane doesn't spook easy.

He takes my arm and tugs me into a nook.

"What's going on?" I ask.

"All of the guards have been called out, but I had to talk to you first." Dane's voice is low and tense. "Karis, someone broke into the Hall of Records. Whoever it was had an automaton. The masters found some evidence... An imprint of a hand in the wall."

They know. Which means soldiers will already be spreading out, covering this island, cutting off our only escape from this place.

And Alix. He's out there alone, right now. If the Scriptorium gets his tome...

"They can't know it was an automaton," I say.

"Karis, the imprint showed runes. Somehow, a small automaton must have been built. Small enough to get through the halls. Tell me you didn't have anything to do with this."

I need to lie to him. Just this once, when it really matters. But I can't.

"I found an automaton, down in that cave," I whisper. "I found its tome. And I woke it up."

Dane squeezes his eyes shut. For once I have no idea how he's going to react. He could leave me, right now.

He holds out his hand. "Give me the tome. I'll plant it somewhere and no one will know it was you."

My heart lodges in my throat. He isn't leaving. Even now he's trying to save me from myself. "I don't have it anymore."

A bit of the tension eases from his shoulders. "Good. Just stay here and stay low." He glances back. "I have to report now."

He turns to go, and panic claws into my gut. I need to find Alix and get out of here, which means this will be the last time I see Dane. My best friend. More than my best friend: my family.

"Dane…"

I reach out to him, but the voices of the other students cover my own and my hand only catches air as he slips back around the corner.

Pain slices through me. I've known for years that I wanted to go and that it would mean leaving him, but going always felt years away. All this time, while I was hating this place, I didn't realize I was putting down those roots or that pulling them up would be this painful. This is exactly why I didn't want to build connections here.

For one moment I think of going after Dane, of not leaving this life I've known since I came here. But Matthias is waiting for me.

And I made my choice a long time ago.

I run back into the hallway, dodging the others until I get to the safety of my room. I shove things into my pack, making myself keep moving because then I don't have to think about losing Dane, about the fact that I don't have any supplies except what's in my room right now. A spare outfit and blanket. My water skin. My lamp and a small jug of oil. That's all I have. To cross oceans and islands and to find my brother.

I wriggle the Hall of Records paper out from my pallet

and wedge it into my pack before turning to the shutters. They're all locked in the acolytes' quarters. I grab the hardest thing I own, a hunk of bronze I found broken off an automaton, and slam it against the lock. It snaps off with a crack and then I'm through, slipping into the shadows of the building.

Soldiers mill about in the yard. I'll have to risk the wall. As soon as I'm sure I can't be seen, I scrabble up it. My heart lurches as I reach the top, completely vulnerable if someone chooses to look, but the soldiers must not be expecting to find the automaton on Scriptorium grounds because no shouts go up. I drop down on the other side.

Normally the island is quiet this late. Now, I hear the crisp, shouted commands of soldiers. Dark storm clouds have gathered in the sky, blotting out the moon and stars and leaving only torches dotting the black.

I steal off across the island, trying to stay on the rocks as much as possible to hide my footprints. I scrub at my bracelet. Master Vasilis could be checking on the acolytes right now. He could be checking on me.

By the time I reach the cliffs, rain has started to fall, cold drops splattering against my head and shoulders. *Grab the ropes and get down.* That's all I have to do. And then Alix and I can get to the boats and I'll finally be off this island.

A hand shoots from the darkness of the frozen automaton and latches around my wrist. It slams me against the thing's leg, and I gasp as pain from everything that hasn't healed yet ricochets through me.

"Karis."

Alix steps out of the dark, his eyes flickering in the black.

He lets go of my wrist but my legs buckle and he has to grab my arms to keep me up. His metal fingers burn my chilled skin. "I—I'm sorry. I heard shouts. I thought you were a soldier."

A chill of fear goes through me at how small and breakable I feel. He's swathed in shadows and his eyes glow like flaming stars.

Only there's guilt in his face, which never seems to hide anything. And I know that I either have to trust him right now, or I have to go back and turn him in.

"I'm fine," I grit out. "But we have to get out of here."

Alix looks out over the island. The shouts of the soldiers are muted by the rain but they're still there. "Are you sure that's wise?"

"Alix, they saw your handprint. It had runes in it, your runes. They know it was an automaton that broke into the Hall of Records. This is the Scriptorium. Their whole existence is built on trying to wake an automaton like you. Now that they know it's been done, they won't stop. They will tear this island apart looking for you. Right now, we still have some surprise on our side. We have to go."

Alix watches me, and I can see the indecision scrawled on his face. He fingers the satchel around his waist. "All right."

I let out the breath trapped in my throat and push back my himation, holding out my wrist. This is it.

Alix wraps his free hand around the bracelet. He hums a few notes and golden light flashes from his side, dimly visible through his chiton. The bracelet falls to the grass with a soft whump.

I stare down at it, this thing that's been on my wrist

for seven years, keeping me on this island as surely as any cage. My wrist feels odd, unused to the touch of the night and the rain.

I'm...free.

"Karis, are you all right?"

"Yes," I whisper. "Yes, I am."

A shout echoes across the island. I gesture to Alix, and we cut inward, away from the cliffs. Mud spatters up my calves, staining the edge of my chiton and clinging to my sandals. I keep our path weaving, far away from the automatons, knowing there will be soldiers at each one. We're almost there. Another turn, and...

A trio of soldiers rounds the rocks in front of us. They don't have torches. They weren't making any noise. But as they stop, surprise on their faces, my gaze is instantly pulled to the one on the right. His dark curls are flattened by the rain. His eyes are already widening.

Dane.

7

ALIX

Karis stiffens beside me. I look at the soldiers, realizing my mistake too late as their eyes widen. They know what I am.

"You," the soldier in the middle snarls.

He isn't looking at me. Of course he isn't. To him, I'm some mindless creature, waiting for my next command. In that moment, I might as well be, because I don't know what to do or say.

Karis juts out her shaking chin. "Clerval. This isn't what you—"

Clerval pulls his sword out, the metal slicing free from its sheath. I've never seen a sword so close. It glints in the torchlight. Karis takes a step back. The boy on the right, a dark-haired, pale-skinned soldier, looks between the two of them, sudden fear cutting through his expression.

He lunges. I tense, not knowing how to fight, but he

tackles Clerval, knocking him into the mud. The third soldier hesitates, and I leap forward. The soldier scrabbles for his sword hilt, but he's too slow. I throw a punch at his throat. The movement is awkward but I connect, and with a gargled cry he goes down, eyes rolling back into his head.

I step back, nauseous as I look down at my hand, still curled into a fist. He was so fragile. It would have been so easy to go too far, without even realizing it. Panic rises in my throat. Is this what I'm going to have to be now?

Clerval goes limp and the dark-haired boy slowly gets to his feet, mud streaked dark across his face.

"Dane," Karis says, her voice soft.

They know each other. For a moment I wonder if he'll be like Karis. If he'll also defy the way my father said others would treat me.

Then he looks at me, uneasy. He doesn't come any closer and he doesn't take his hand off his sword's hilt. "How is that thing moving without you writing commands?"

His words dig into me. "I'm not a thing."

Dane jolts, his fingers curling tighter around the hilt.

"Dane, no." Karis steps toward him. "He isn't what you think. This is Alix. He can think and feel and move. He got me into the Hall of Records."

Dane stares at me, as if I'm something unnatural. Standing here, them together and me apart, I can't help but wonder if that's true.

Shouts echo from across the island.

Karis bites her lip. "Maybe you can pretend we knocked you out, too."

Dane looks down at the soldier he fought. "I didn't hit Clerval that hard. He'll remember."

"I'm so sorry," Karis whispers.

Dane sags, rain snaking in rivulets down his arms. Karis reaches out, but he steps away from her.

"You do know they're going to find us, right?" Dane says. "We can't hide with these bracelets, and…" His gaze finds her bare wrist. "How?"

Karis looks over at me. "Alix did it."

I don't know if I can trust this soldier. Karis doesn't seem to have any loyalty to the Scriptorium, but he clearly does.

Yet he also saved us. I can't leave him to the Scriptorium's mercy. "I can take yours off."

Dane stays silent. I think he might reject my help, but he holds his wrist out to me. This close I can see how tense he is, the muscles corded in his forearms. I place my fingers over the rune I need to unlock and pretend not to see the flinch he can't quite hide. Not bothering to hum, I mentally twist to disarm the rune. The bracelet drops off and I step away.

When I took Karis's off, it was as if an invisible weight had lifted from her shoulders. Dane stares down at his, lying in the wet grass, as if he wants nothing more than to slip it back on.

"Dane?" Karis asks quietly.

He sweeps past her. Karis opens her mouth as if to say something else, then closes it and follows him.

The rain gives a haze to everything, squelching mud and slick grass beneath our feet. Being out here is nothing like watching the rain from my father's villa or even the safety of the garden. That rain always looked mysterious. This feels dangerous.

We reach a shale path and follow it down, cutting between the cliffs on either side. Dane raises his hand and we stop at the edge of the rocks. I peer out at a pebbly beach. Three wooden boats have been pulled up onto it, rain spattering their upturned hulls. Two soldiers stand nearby.

Dane doesn't quite look at me as he speaks, his voice tight. "Can you take one? Karis isn't a fighter."

The last thing I want to do is hurt someone again, but I don't see how we're going to get off this beach unless I try. "Yes."

"Let's go."

We both dash from our hiding spot. One of the soldiers turns and manages to shout but then we're on them. I disarm mine the same as the other soldier and he crumples.

Weapon.

The word flashes through my head before I can stop it. I turn away.

Karis runs down the beach as Dane knocks his soldier out. Together we flip one of the boats over and heave it into the swell. Cold water swirls around my feet. We clamber inside, and though I've never rowed, I grab the oars and manage to navigate us farther out into the dark water.

Both Dane and Karis stare at the island as we cut away through the waves. I look back over my shoulder, too. The Scriptorium is lit up, light pouring out of all its windows like a beacon in the rain. Torches from soldiers and searchers dot the rest of the island. I have a sudden flash of memory of another building that looked like that one,

of fleeing from it into another stormy night as alarm bells
tore through my head.

I reach for more details but the memory fades as quickly
as it came, disappearing beneath the stroke of my oars and
the slap of the waves against the boat.

We sit in silence, hunched against the stinging rain. Karis
keeps glancing at Dane, but he stays quiet and still, staring
out over the dark waters splitting around our bow.

I focus on the rowing, trying to lose myself in the mo-
notony of the movement. Reach and pull. Reach and pull.
Over and over and over again. The oar is slick beneath my
hands and I'm sure if I had skin my fingers would have
long gone numb.

I'm not sure how long we've been out on the water when
the first tiny island looms off our bow out of the rain. I
don't stop. The island can't be more than a quarter league
long and I'm sure it will be the first place the Scriptorium
will look when they notice the downed soldiers and the
missing boat. Other islands appear past it and I angle the
boat to weave in between them.

The rain has begun to taper off with the barest hint of
pink creeping through the clouds when Dane breaks the
silence. "I think we should stop there."

The island he points to is small compared to Tallis, but
it's one of the largest we've seen since then. Most of it is
covered by a forest, and there's a craggy beach on one side.

"Do you think we're far enough from Tallis yet?" I ask.

Each time I speak, Dane tenses slightly. "We don't have

much choice. Karis is freezing, and we both need to get out of our wet clothes."

Both. It's a word that clearly doesn't include me. I hunch down over my oars.

"I can keep going if we need to," Karis says, but there's a tremor in her voice. The himation she's wrapped around herself is soaked through and she shivers in the pale dawn. I forgot how cold people can get. How cold my father always got when it rained.

Dane's jaw twitches. "No, you can't."

"Dane."

"Will you just listen to me for once?"

His voice isn't loud, but Karis flinches. She stares down at the bottom of the boat and nods.

I shift. I don't know how to handle the tension strung between the two of them. I rarely had so much as a disagreement with my father.

I paddle up close to the shore and jump into the water. Before the other two have even stood, I've dragged the boat up onto the beach. We hide it among the rocks, then grab some branches and do our best to sweep away the gouge it made in the sand. A hint of a path leads up into the trees and we follow it under the soft canopy. Dawn light shines through the branches, speckling our skin. The trees have slender trunks with leaves so soft they look like feathers. Wet branches knock my shoulders, droplets of water tapping against my head.

For the first time since waking up, some of my uncertainty slips away. It's beautiful out here. My father had a garden. I loved that place, but here there's simply wild nature like

I've never seen before, that's vibrant and rich and stunning. I didn't know the world could burst with life like this. Walking here makes even me feel a little bit more real.

"We shouldn't stray too far from the beach," Dane says. There's a touch of sluggish exhaustion to his own words. "In case we need to leave quickly. Maybe we…"

He pauses. Up ahead the forest is cut in two by a rocky ledge, as if half the island rose up in some great upheaval, the layer of trees continuing atop the cliff. There's an indent in the rock, not quite a cave but almost. It isn't empty. There are the remains of a campfire inside, ringed by stone, and a small crate pushed up against the back wall.

Dane pads silently forward into the cave, looks at the ring of stone, opens the crate with his dagger, and peers in. He waves us forward, sliding the dagger back into his belt.

"We'll stay here. It looks like it's been deserted for a long time and it'll give us some cover. I don't think we should risk a fire, though."

Karis just nods.

"Let's sleep for a few hours at least," Dane says. "We can take turns on watch and—"

I step forward. "I'll take the watches. I don't need to sleep."

Every time I see his hesitation, it digs into me a little more. I almost want to ask why he's hesitating, to see if he'd say the words he's clearly thinking. Only I'm not that brave, and I don't want a fight. "The Scriptorium is after me as well. It's not as if I'm going to betray you to them."

Dane doesn't speak for a moment, but at least he's looking at me now. He turns away. "All right."

He wrings out his clothes as best as he can while Karis gets changed in the shelter of the trees. She returns looking minimally warmer. They spread a blanket from the pack and Dane settles on it, turning his back to us to stare at the cave wall. For a moment Karis looks unbearably weary, before she slowly lies down, too, curling up in a tight ball.

I watch over them as their breathing slows. Deepens. Until they drift away. My father never gave me sleep. Perhaps he couldn't. I wish, though, that he'd found a way to make me more normal, so I wouldn't have to be standing here, alone.

Only, maybe I'm not alone.

My father said that if I ever left the villa, that I had to be careful. I couldn't risk trusting too many people. It's true that I'm still not sure I can trust Dane, when he only looks at me and sees a creature, and I only look at him and see a soldier. Karis, though... This strange Scriptorium girl who comforted me when I needed it. Who helped me when I needed it. Perhaps I can let myself trust her.

8

KARIS

The buildings of Heretis loom on either side of me, uneven clay walls and straw roofs, their windows staring at us like dark eyes in the night. Matthias and I run, his hand clasped in mine, me desperately trying to steer him around anything in our way. Behind us a wild pack of boys screams and swears, chasing us down the narrow, shadowy streets. They're older than us, bigger than us, and they're gaining.

I look over my shoulder and it's not boys chasing us but Scriptorium soldiers, holding torches and swords, the firelight lapping at our ankles.

One of them grabs Matthias and jerks him back. His hand slips from mine, his eyes going wide in panic. I scream and reach for him, but the street caves in under me and I fall into darkness.

I jerk awake, my own scream still echoing through my

head. Squeezing my eyes shut, I choke down air. It's just a dream. Just a nightmare.

Only it isn't just a dream. Because the Scriptorium did find us, stealing in the Heretis agora. And they hauled us onto a ship, bound for the Tallis Scriptorium.

I remember it all. How we huddled in the hold, the only hint of light leaking in through the grimy porthole. Flinching every time footsteps came near. Matthias trying to keep it together for the both of us. Then we got to Tallis. I saw the Scriptorium at the top of the hill. And far off, the shadowy shape of what had to be an automaton, not yet clear in the dim morning light. Suddenly it felt like I couldn't breathe. I scratched desperately at the man who had me, without thinking, and his meaty fist had swung at my head.

I screamed Matthias's name. A scream I'll always regret. It was like Matthias just snapped at that sound. He launched himself at the man.

He did a surprising amount of damage before they wrestled him to the ground. And they decided that it would be too troublesome to keep us together. That they'd rather have me because I was younger and more malleable to their cause. So Matthias was dragged away, and the only goodbye we got was the smallest touch of our hands.

I've always wondered—if I hadn't done what I did on that beach, would we still be together?

I crack my eyes open again. Sunlight streams between the trees outside our cave, the rain burned away by the light of day. Dane still sleeps beside me, his brow creased, his mouth turned down into a frown. Alix, I can't see. I roll

up into a sitting position, every one of my scrapes protesting the movement.

I've barely made a noise but Dane stirs. His eyes cloud
with confusion as he pulls himself to his elbows, struggling
to wake up and be alert, before he takes in our surroundings. He sags back down. He looks so worn. The usual
laugh tucked into his face isn't there. I took that away.

He notices me beside him, and I can see him pulling
himself back together.

"How are you?" he asks quietly.

I touch one particularly bad scrape on my arm. It's hard
to tell with all the bandages, but I think most of the swelling has gone down. "I'm all right."

A thud shakes the ground as Alix lands at the entrance
to the cave. I jolt, Dane scrambling into a fighting crouch
before seeing who it is.

Alix glances over his shoulder. "I found a stream nearby
if you want to clean up."

I grimace as dirt flakes off the edge of my chiton. Maybe
getting clean will banish this fog that's settled in my head.

The stream is small but clear, burbling between two
grassy banks. Alix slips off to give us some privacy, and I sit
on the bank and unwrap the bandages. A sunset of colors
splays out over my skin, but everything's stopped bleeding.
I wet my handkerchief and dab at it, wincing at the sting of
the cold water. This was not how I imagined starting this
particular adventure, bruised and exhausted.

Beside me, Dane splashes water on his face. It runs down
his temples and drips off the ends of his hair. He's quiet,
his expression far away. I'm not used to this sort of silence

between us. A silence not because we don't have anything to say, but because neither of us wants to say it.

In the end, I give in first.

"Dane?"

His hands still but he doesn't look up.

"I wanted to tell you I'm so sorry, again. I know what being part of the Scriptorium meant to you, how important it was."

Dane still doesn't answer. When I sneaked out of the Scriptorium, I thought we would never see each other again. Now here we are, side by side, and he feels as distant as if I'd actually left.

"Dane—"

"Why didn't you tell me about this? About Alix and the break-in and everything that was going on with you?"

I can hear the hurt in his voice. The fact that he's trying to hide it makes this that much more painful. "I didn't want you to have to give up everything you've worked for."

He finally looks at me. "So you were just going to leave without saying goodbye? Without a word?"

I hunch my shoulders. There's nothing I can say to that. We both already know the answer.

Dane scrubs at his hands so hard I half wonder if he'll take his skin off. "Do you have any idea what it was like for me last night, Karis? To be out there and to see you, and Clerval pulling his sword. I thought he was going to hurt you. That I was going to have to watch it happen."

"I didn't know what to say, Dane. Because even if I told you, I thought..."

I stop myself. I don't want to go there, especially not now.

But he catches it. Of course he does. He turns from the stream to face me head-on. "You thought what?"

I shouldn't say it, but after everything else that's happened, now isn't the time for lies. And if he won't admit the truth, then I will. "You had your life on Tallis. And I was glad. But sooner or later, it wasn't going to involve me and you had to know that."

Thick, terrible silence stretches between us. Dane stares at me in angry disbelief. "That's why you lied to me? That's what you thought was going to happen?"

"This is exactly why I didn't want to tell you." I plunge the rag back into the stream, angry now. Hating that I'm angry, that we're having this fight. "We were already going in different directions, Dane. I never belonged on Tallis."

"Only because you never let yourself belong."

"How could I have?" I snap.

A branch cracks behind us and we both whip around. Alix is already edging away again, but as we turn, he winces. "Um... I was just coming to check if you two were done."

Dane stands. "We're done."

He stalks back toward the cave. I slowly drag myself up to my feet, too, feeling more exhausted than when I sat down.

Alix hesitates, then steps closer to me. "Is everything—"

"It's nothing."

He stops, the hurt on his face obvious. Guilt prickles in my gut. I'm not used to someone as open as Alix. Who lets people see so easily when he's in pain.

I rub my temple. "I just... Don't worry about it."

I walk past him, and after a moment his quiet footsteps follow.

By the time we get back, a headache pulses in my skull and my stomach rumbles. I settle on a rock. Dane leans against the entrance. He glances from Alix to me.

"So where exactly were…you two planning on heading?"

I clear my throat. "Valitia."

"The Great Island?"

I pull out the paper and show it to him. "Alix helped me get this."

Dane looks at it, and I see the moment he notices my brother's name at the top. He glances over at me, and his eyes soften for the first time since leaving Tallis. "You found it. Where your brother was sent."

I bite my lip, nodding. Maybe I haven't destroyed everything between us.

Dane reads the record. "The Magistrate's Library."

"Have you heard of it?"

He shakes his head. "No, but since the magistrate lives in the City of Scholars on Valitia, if I had to hazard a guess, I'd bet his library is there, too."

Alix perks up. "My father's villa is in the City of Scholars."

Dane frowns. "You have a father?"

I grimace. There was a part of me that hoped this topic wouldn't come up. Really, maybe I should have told Alix not to say anything. But now he has, and I'm not willing to lie about this. Not after how well my last lie to Dane went.

"His father was Master Theodis."

Dane rears away from the wall. "Master Theodis? The war criminal?"

Alix's eyes flash—literally. It makes him look exactly like the automatons our stories have told us about. And that scares me. "My father was not a criminal."

"He sabotaged the other Scriptmasters, tried to take all the power of the automatons for himself."

"That's a lie!" Alix advances on Dane, so close their chests bump. Alix is the shorter one, but Dane is muscle and bone, while Alix is automaton, his bronze skin only further strengthened by the Script carved into it. Even I can see that if they fight, Alix will win. Dane should realize that, too.

"Stop it." I step between them, forcing them apart. Dane twists away from me and I falter before pressing on. "This isn't helping. Dane, we can't know what happened back then."

Dane folds his arms over his chest. "Fine, if what we know is a lie, what did happen?"

The fire in Alix's eyes dims. "I don't remember."

"What do you mean, you don't remember?"

"It's foggy." Alix trails his fingers up his arm and it takes me a moment to remember the broken line of runes beneath the fabric.

"Those runes, on your arm," I say. "Are they what's causing the gaps in your memory?"

"I don't remember that either," he says miserably.

I step closer but stop when he edges back. Now that his temper is gone, he looks young again.

"Please," I say. "I just want to see, to try to understand."

All Alix had to do was press his fingers to that rune to make it work, and there are lines on his skin that even after years of climbing automatons, I've never seen before. I stole and studied for years to figure all this out. He just does it.

Alix meets my eyes, and whatever he sees there must convince him, because he pushes his himation up his arm. I touch the top set of lines, the metal warm and ridged. Could these somehow be responsible for why Alix is so different? I don't recognize the runes themselves, but the edges of the runes are hooked together, lines stemming off each other like branches on a tree. Normally runes stand on their own: *move, stretch, turn.* Even *wake*, one of the more potent ones, is a single rune that operates by itself. If Master Theodis did manage to link so many powerful runes, could it result in something as complicated as a mind?

"Do you remember anything about what happened?" I ask. "About your life before?"

Alix is quiet, and I'm not sure if he's going to answer. But then he does speak, his voice soft. "I remember most of it, at least the early times. I remember waking up and living with my father in his villa. I remember him teaching me about runes and automatons, literature and theory. Others would come to the villa, Scriptmasters, but Father created secret rooms for me and I would hide. He said if they saw me, if they learned about me, that I would be in danger. That they were my enemies."

Alix reaches up, curling his fingers around the medallion. "Then one night, something happened. Father was frantic. I remember he had been training me to do...something. He said we had to do it now. We went to this great building. There was this golden light, so large I thought it might consume me. This light and heat." His face creases in concentration. "I remember a pulsing. Others came, soldiers and Scriptmasters. They wanted to stop us. I ran. And then... And then..." He growls, pressing a hand to his temple. "I don't remember."

Silence follows his words. Alix was there, two hundred years ago. Somewhere in his head is the knowledge of what went so wrong. Unfortunately, a great building and a golden light doesn't give us much to go on.

"There's something else that you should see." He reaches into his belt pouch and pulls out a scrap of paper, giving it to me.

There's only one sentence there.

Due to the actions of Master Theodis with his weapon, the Automaton Heart was broken beyond repair.

I look at Alix, confused.

"I think I might be that weapon," he whispers.

A cold shiver skitters up my spine. Alix. A weapon. That's what automatons were built for. The only thing they were built for. And I've seen flashes of Alix's temper, of his strength. I know what he could do.

"And this Automaton Heart?" I ask.

"I can't remember." A hopeful light comes into his eyes. "Do you two know anything about it?"

I glance at Dane who reads the paper over my shoulder. He shrugs.

"I'm sorry," I say.

Alix deflates.

Dane clears his throat. "Whatever happened, we can

deal with later. The Scriptorium is going to come after us, so we need to be gone by then. We aren't going to be able to get to Valitia in our boat. It's too far. But we should be fairly close now to Maren. If we go there, we should be able to barter passage onto a ship, which will probably mean working for them. Alix will be tricky with his eyes, but hopefully we'll find something to cover them up when we get there.

"In the meantime, we need supplies. This island isn't inhabited, so we should scavenge what we can here. When nightfall comes, we'll head out again under the cover of darkness."

We separate to look for food. Luck is on our side, because this small island has that in plenty. Mushrooms, berries, nuts. Even better, I come across no animals larger than a fat brown squirrel that chitters angrily at me before disappearing up the trunk of a tree.

I pop berries into my mouth as I walk, each a tart burst of flavor. The taste is a memory, one I'd almost forgotten, from back on Heretis. I always dreamed of one day exploring the wild islands and now I'm out here, and it's so blazingly, wonderfully different from anything I've ever known.

On Tallis, the Scriptmasters keep every bit of land clearcut so it won't impede our studies of the automatons. Nothing was spared except the grass and a few dejected shrubs. Heretis is a bustling port city, with buildings crammed together to fill every available space. This island isn't the grunginess of Heretis or the militant authority of the Scriptorium. Here the scent of the ocean mixes with the wet moss. It smells to me like a fresh new world. A new world for a new start.

Maybe after I rescue Matthias, we can find a place like this to live. It wouldn't be an easy life but we're smart. We survived not having a home at all, and we could survive the wild islands as well. Out here, the problems of the rest of the world would never be able to touch us. Finally and truly free.

As the light fades, I bundle up the food I found into my pack and trot off. I wasn't paying that much attention to the wandering track I made through the trees, but the island isn't large, and it doesn't take me long to find the rocky ledge again. I follow it, quickening my step when I realize it's getting dark faster than I thought it would beneath the canopy, the shadows straining against the last bit of light. I don't want to be wandering around lost out here at night.

Up ahead, a thin curl of smoke drifts out of the mouth of the cave, twining around the branches. Dane must have lit a fire. Or maybe Alix, though I'm not sure someone who burns as hot as he does would need a fire.

"Dane, is that you?" I ask. "I found some…"

I step into the cave and the words die on my lips. Dane is on his knees, arms pinned behind his back. There's a shallow cut on his cheek and his eyes blaze. The man holding him down is massive, with thick arms and gray hair lashed back into a ponytail. He isn't alone. At least a half dozen others clutter up the space in the cave. The fire in the pit throws flickering light against their forms, twisting their shadows on the walls.

They're not Scriptorium. No, they're worse. I've never

seen pirates before, but there can be no mistaking their salt-flecked skin, the way they smell of brine and grit.

"Karis!" Dane shouts, trying to jerk free. "Run!"

I take a faltering step away but one of the other pirates, a rail-thin man with a knife in his hand, moves into my path. I rapidly back away from him, even though that forces me deeper into the cave.

"Well, now, it seems we've caught a second little fish."

I spin around at the voice.

A girl steps from the shadows. She can't be more than a year or two older than me. The people in the cave are a mix of skin colors from the paleness of the cold lands in the north to the dark of the jungles in the east. She's somewhere in between, her skin brown like sun-warmed earth and her black hair twisted into a messy braid. A three-pointed hat sits crookedly on her head and her bodice and skirts are made up of splashes of orange and red fabrics, vibrant colors imprinted with bold geometric lines. A curved sword hangs from her hip, thrust through her belt without so much as a scabbard. She's the youngest of any of the pirates here but they all orient themselves toward her. As if somehow, this girl is in charge.

And judging from the smirk on her face, I wouldn't bet on her being the friendly type.

The girl gives an elaborate bow, sending off a wave of chuckles. "Captain Zara of the *Crimson Streak* at your service. You two seem to have stumbled into one of our hideaways."

A hideaway. My stomach sinks down to my sandals. "We didn't mean to."

"Yet here you are." Her fingers caress the hilt of her blade, the firelight catching in her eyes and making them flicker. "A Scriptorium acolyte and a soldier, judging by your clothes. What odd prizes we've found. We pirates, you see, don't like the Scriptorium."

My throat is so dry, but I manage to force a hint of brazenness into my voice. "I can't say I'm too fond of them either."

Zara lets out a laugh. "You'll have to excuse me if I don't believe you."

The soldiers shift, their many bared weapons glinting in the light of the fire. Zara's still grinning at me, looking as if whatever terrible thing she's about to do to us won't bother her in the least.

And I'm struck with the sudden certainty that we're going to die here. We've barely managed to get a few islands from Tallis and now we're going to die here in this cave, where even our bones will be forgotten. Cold encircles my throat like a fist. Maybe Alix could help, but why would he risk himself for us now that he's free?

Then, out of the corner of my eye, I catch two blazing spots hovering in the deepening dark outside the cave.

He's here.

9

ALIX

I hang from the lip of the rocky ledge, low enough that I can see into the cave. Dane is on his knees and Karis, though still on her feet, won't be able to fight the thin man hovering behind her with the knife.

If I go down there, my tome could be taken. I'm the only one who's going to be able to get Karis and Dane out, though. Their only chance. That thought is terrifying.

I slip my satchel into a crack in the rock and tug my himation down over my face before leaning out farther. There are eight pirates, including the girl with the three-pointed hat on her head. Zara, I think I heard her name was. Eight of them against one of me.

Zara nods at one of her people, a squat woman. "Take the girl's bag."

Karis goes stiff as the woman pulls her pack off her shoulders. She hands it over. Zara roots through it, nuts and berries falling through her fingers to the cave floor. "You two are awfully unequipped for a journey out here on the wild islands."

A few of her people chuckle.

"We ran from the Scriptorium." Karis's voice is strained and a flash of temper sparks in my chest. "We didn't have time to pack anything."

"Hmm…" Zara glances down at the pack.

In the moment her attention shifts, I move. Wrenching my hand into the rock, I use it as an anchor to swing myself down and forward into the cave. I slam into the thin man with the knife, knocking him to the ground. He howls and I almost apologize, but a woman is already lunging at me. I manage to grab her wrist and she goes down with a yelp.

Dane has already gained his feet, grappling with the massive man who was restraining him, and for all that he's the smaller of the two, he's holding his own. Others are already stepping forward, though, toward him and Karis.

Zara. I look at her, careful to keep my eyes hooded. She's in charge here. If I can take her, I'll end this, without anyone else getting hurt.

She pulls something from her skirts and points it at me. It's bronze, crafted into a barrel, with runes scrawled over its surface. Her fingers curl around the handle as she arches a brow. "Don't even think about it."

I don't know what she's holding, but it doesn't look dangerous enough to stop me.

"Alix, wait!" Karis shouts, but I'm already lunging forward.

A splitting crack rends the air. Something blows into my

shoulder, the force enough to send me staggering back, my himation falling from my face.

Zara's eyes go wide as everybody in the cave freezes. I look at my shoulder, not understanding what hit me. A hole's been torn in my chiton and beneath it there's a punctured dent in my metal skin.

I'm...damaged. This pirate has something that can damage me. *Me.*

I step toward her, right as Zara swings the barrel of her weapon, pointing it at Karis's chest.

Karis sucks in a breath, her face ashen. I stutter to a halt. If that thing managed to damage me, it will tear through Karis as if she's made of parchment.

She'll be gone, like my father is gone.

Zara looks me up and down, amazement glinting in her eyes. "You're an automaton. An animated automaton."

I try to push down the panic, but it's already crawling all over me. I can't move without killing Karis. Only I have to move, before they find my tome and give me an order I can't disobey.

"Where's its tome?" Zara asks.

I flinch, but Karis presses her lips together. Even Dane doesn't move.

Zara cocks the weapon. Karis sticks out her chin, but it quakes. "Last chance."

Even with that weapon pointed at her, Karis is still keeping my tome a secret. Both of them are. I never thought anyone would try to protect me beside my father.

"It's up on the ridge," I say. "Hidden in the rocks."

At my voice, every person in the crew starts. Zara stares

at me, something glinting in her eyes. She turns to Karis. "It just talked. How did it talk?"

Karis simply glares the pirate captain down.

Zara's eyes narrow. She jerks her head at one of her crew. "Go find the tome."

Karis flashes me a worried look. I stare miserably back. What else could I have done?

One of the pirates, a dark-haired woman, leaves. We wait in silence until she comes back, pulling my tome from the satchel. My seal flares in my chest as she holds the book out to her captain. It takes every bit of willpower I possess to stop myself from reaching out and snatching it back. It's happening all over again.

"Cover the girl and the boy," Zara says. Men step up to them, grabbing them and placing blades against their throats. Karis squeezes her eyes shut. Dane's face is twisted in fury. All I can do is stand there, bare and exposed.

Zara takes my tome and opens it. I try to cling onto some slim hope. She's nothing more than a seafaring ruffian. Surely she won't know how to use the tome or what runes to write.

She pulls out a hunk of charcoal and dashes it across the page. A rune flares on my legs and they give, without my permission, making me kneel. My insides turn hollow.

"Stop it!" Karis says. "Alix isn't some mindless automaton. You have no right to take his will from him!"

Zara scoffs. "You make it sound like it's alive."

"He is not an it."

I can hear Karis defending me but I can't so much as lift my gaze from the floor. I'm too ashamed. Everything that makes me who I am has been taken from me by a few strokes on a page. No matter what I do or want, I'll never be what they are. This is exactly what father said would happen.

I am nothing to this pirate.

"Captain," one of her men says. "There's something else here in the pack."

I wearily lift my head and see the man pull a piece of parchment from Karis's pack. Matthias's record.

Karis stiffens.

Zara takes the paper, her eyes flitting over the words. She turns to Karis. "Who's Matthias?"

Karis doesn't answer, pure stubbornness painted on her face. Dane gives her a warning look.

Zara steps closer, waving the paper. "You want this back? You don't want to die in this cave? Then tell me who Matthias is."

Karis glares at the pirate captain. "He's my brother. We were separated when we were sent to the Scriptorium on Tallis. I'm going to Valitia to find him."

Zara studies her. There's a long pause before she says, "If you're going to the Magistrate's Library, you might not like what you find."

Karis stills. "You know it?"

Zara looks at her, and for the briefest moment something exposed passes across her expression. Then it clears, and she grins. "You have no idea what I know, Scriptorium."

The crush of running feet through the forest sounds a moment before a new man comes barreling into the cave. "Captain, I..."

He cuts off as he sees me, his eyes widening. I look away.

"What is it, Aiken?" Zara asks.

"Uh…it's a Scriptorium ship, Captain, off the far point of the island. She'll see us if we don't leave soon."

I hadn't thought this terrible day could get worse, but it did. No matter what these pirates might make me do, the Scriptorium could do worse. They know more.

Zara looks at us. At Karis and Dane, and then, surprisingly, at me. She writes something in my tome and my legs unlock.

I stare at her, then scramble to my feet.

She…freed me?

Zara's eyes give nothing away. "Well then." She snaps my tome closed, tucking it beneath her arm. "We had best be off."

We make a silent procession as we head toward the ship. I can feel my tome in Zara's hands, a piece of me that's been displaced, but I don't go for it, not with the knives prodding into Dane's and Karis's back. At least I'm walking of my own free will.

The bay, empty before, now has a ship bobbing on its waters. The *Crimson Streak*; that's what Zara called it. Its sails are such a deep, ominous red in the dark, they look stained with blood. I have no idea what awaits us on that ship. I had only ever read about adventure. I didn't expect it to feel like this: uncertain and overwhelming. If only my father was here. I need his guidance, now more than ever.

Two smaller boats wait for us on the beach. Karis and Dane are pushed into the first one, and Karis stumbles, catching the edge of the boat to stop herself from going over into the water. She glares at the man who pushed her. "I can get in a boat by myself," she snaps.

Another pirate tries to shove me in, too, but his hands bounce off. He clearly doesn't know what automatons weigh. I glance at him and he shrinks back. A twist of anguish buries itself into my chest.

"Get in," Zara orders, lowering herself onto her own bench.

I climb in, settling next to Karis. She hesitates for a moment and then her hand finds mine, her fingers wrapping around my own. I look at her, surprised at the touch.

"Thank you," she whispers. "For coming for us, back in that cave."

I blink. "Of course. I wouldn't have left you."

Something I can't quite read enters her eyes. "No, you wouldn't."

The men shove our boat deeper into the water before clambering in and taking the oars. When I rowed, our progress on the water had been haphazard. These pirates expertly cut us forward through the dark bay, toward the *Crimson Streak*. It blocks out the moonlight, creaking and rocking ominously on the waves.

Before my long sleep, I didn't have many chances to see ships. The docks were too far from my father's villa. I saw them once, though, the night I fled. They were long and narrow, with rows of oars like insect legs. Their front prows were hard and crafted for ramming, with ghoulish eyes painted on either side.

This ship is different. A figurehead is carved into its

front. It's a woman, her arms spread out as if embracing unknown horizons. A rune decorates her chest, written in a red ink that matches the sails. It's blockier than the runes I'm used to, geometric in a way that reminds me of the print on Zara's dress.

There's a shout from on deck and a rope ladder is lowered. Zara gestures me up and I go, the ropes straining beneath my weight. As I come over the railing, the pirates back away, eyes wide. As if I'm some creature, barely restrained. I shrink in on myself.

Zara gracefully hoists herself up over the railing, followed by Dane, Karis, and the other pirates.

"Ava," she calls. "Finn."

Two of the crew, neither of them much older than Karis or Dane, separate from the crowd. They must be siblings. Both have mops of hair in a vibrant shade of red I've never seen before, spilling around pale, freckled faces. The one on the left, Ava, has knives hung at each hip. Finn seems to be unarmed.

"Take our new guests to the brig," Zara says.

Finn nods. "Of course, Captain."

"You're just going to lock us up?" Dane growls. "You can't."

Zara's already turned to go, but now she raises an eyebrow. "I can't?" She steps closer, so close their chests are only a hand's breadth apart. She tilts her head back, her grin wolfish beneath the shadow of her hat. "This is my ship, soldier boy." She reaches out and plucks the sword from his belt, giving it a lazy twirl before its tip comes to lightly rest at the base of his throat. "I can do whatever I want."

Dane's jaw works for a moment but nothing comes out. With a smirk, Zara turns on her heel and strides away, his sword still in hand.

"Come on, let's go." Ava prods Dane, who glares daggers at the captain as she leaves. My eyes stay on her, too, as we're led across the deck, flanked by the two pirates. I can still feel my tome in her hands, an invisible tether that connects us. Every step I take away from it makes me feel a little less whole.

Zara hands my tome and the sword off to one of her crew before pulling a slim green ledger from a pocket in her dress. She writes something in it, and runes flare into sudden life along the sails and riggings, a shimmer of gold racing through their lines. In one graceful movement, the sails billow out, their ropes snapping tight like sailors at attention. A gust of wind catches the fabric and Zara gives the wheel a spin, taking us out.

I stare. The runes are actually woven into the fabric, their lines written in thread. It's not the power of automatons, but something different. Something new.

We reach a ladder and Finn swings onto it, disappearing into the hatch. "Down," Ava says, gesturing to me.

I look skeptically into the dark hold. It brings back memories, of a dark cave and a long sleep. I take a timid step away.

Ava pulls a knife, nudging Karis with it. Karis scowls and I half expect her to try to knock it away.

"Now."

I swing myself onto the ladder. It's another world down here, all creaking wood with everything shifting beneath my feet. The little light that leaks down is weak and sick, throwing harsh shadows against the ceiling and walls. A pungent scent hangs like a dead thing in the air. Most of the time I'm glad that my father gave me the ability to smell.

This isn't one of those times.

Karis and Dane touch down beside me, followed by Ava.

"This way," Finn says.

We're led to a corner of the hold that's hemmed in by dark bars, not even seven paces across. There isn't much inside: a ratty blanket in one corner, a bed of straw piled in the other, everything indistinct in the gloom. It's the grungiest place I have ever seen.

We silently step inside.

"G'night," Finn says before locking the door with a final clang.

10

—

KARIS

We've been captured by pirates. Of all the possible outcomes I considered when I used to lie on my pallet dreaming of my escape from Tallis, this was one I never so much as imagined.

Ever since I was a child, I've heard the stories; the unbelievable tales from my friends when I was young and still had a home, and then the just as unbelievable but more terrifying stories from the street kids. Tales of bloody, greedy people who'd snatch you up if you so much as looked at them and who'd sail off with you across the seas until the shore was nothing but a speck in your imagination.

The stories were bad, but they don't compare to actually being on this ship. None of those tales can grasp the fear that comes from being hemmed in by dark bars in a rotting corner of a ship. Can describe what it feels like knowing your only escape is to throw yourself into unforgiving waters, where sharks and sea monsters and who knows what else dwells in the deeps.

I twist Matthias's paper in my fingers, trying to focus on the feel of the parchment in my hands as I fold it into creases. At least Zara gave the paper back. This one piece of my brother to hold close.

"I'm sorry." Dane's quiet voice sounds across the cell. He sits against the bars, hands hanging limply between his knees. It's dark down here, but a bit of moonlight slanting through the porthole high on the wall hits his face, showing the exhaustion and regret.

My hands fall into my lap. "This isn't your fault."

"I was the one who suggested we stay there. I should have known better."

"We all should have known better. It wasn't just you." You forget things when you're locked in one little place for too long. You forget how dangerous the world is outside its walls. Like a wild bird that's been handled too much. Maybe I don't have what it takes to survive out here anymore.

"But I'm the soldier." He fingers his sash, now muddied and torn but still showing the seal of the Scriptorium woven into its end. "Or at least I was."

I want to say something to comfort him, but I don't know what. Even if he escaped from this ship, went back to Tallis, the Scriptorium would just clap him in shackles, throw him into a cell not so different from this one. Because of me.

I lean against the wood of the wall behind me, the cold of it pressing into my spine. The *Streak* rocks back and forth, the movement so constant it makes my stomach lurch. Suddenly I'm so unbelievably, unbearably tired. We're a sorry band of adventurers.

"What's that?" Alix asks.

His eyes are dim candles in the dark. I follow his gaze down to my hands, at the paper flower now sitting on my palm. I hadn't realized that's what I'd been folding. "Just a poppy," I murmur.

Alix glances from it to me in a silent question.

I gently brush the petals. "It's my favorite flower." Just like it was my mother's favorite before me. Or maybe because it was my mother's favorite flower before me.

It's one of the few memories I have of my parents: my father bringing bunches of them home when he traveled away from Heretis, out to some of the meadows that lie far off on the island, the vibrant red blooms spilling from his arms; my mother laughing as she slipped them into a vase, her dark hair curling from under her himation. "My brother used to fold these for me to cheer me up. He did it mostly by feel, of course, so they were always unique, something only he could create." Mine just looks sad in comparison. I never had enough patience for paper folding.

"What was he like?" Alix asks.

I'm not used to people asking. No one did on Tallis. Dane because he knew better. Everyone else because they didn't care. I used to think that if I just gave it enough time, the memories would stop being so painful, but that was never true. Some holes in your life don't ever go away.

But maybe a part of me is tired of just holding him in.

"He was stubborn and far too curious," I finally say.

"He wanted to explore every place we set foot in. And he wouldn't ever back down."

Dane nudges my foot with his. "I can think of someone like that." The smile on his face is barely there, but it's the first one he's given me since I tore him away from Tallis. It makes this easier.

"Matthias was always the one thinking two steps ahead and we never found a place that he wasn't able to get us into. He even learned to pick locks out there, something I could never get the hang of. He used to joke that with my eyes and his ears, no one would ever be able to sneak up on us. And he was so smart. He worked up this system, these phrases I could say to him when I had to guide him through a place and we didn't want anyone to know what we were doing. *Look lively* was turn left. *I don't see it* was come forward." I shake my head, a smile tugging at my lips at the memory for the first time. "*I hate it when you're right* was turn to the right."

"I hate it when you're right?" Alix asks.

"He always loved making me say that one. My brother had a strange sense of humor."

I realize what I've said a moment too late. The happiness turns to ice in my chest. "Has," I say quickly. "I mean has."

Dane leans forward. "We're going to find him, Karis."

My hands curl around the flower. I've never slipped up like that before.

"Karis," Dane says gently, but I shake my head. I should have just kept my mouth shut.

Footsteps come toward our cell and we scramble to our feet as the two ginger-haired pirates from before step up to the cell door. Dane glares at the two of them, somehow managing to look every bit a soldier despite the fact that he's dirty and stinking and on the wrong side of the bars.

"Rise and shine," Finn says. "The captain's ready to see you all now."

I tuck the poppy into my belt purse. "Did we outrun the Scriptorium ship?"

Finn just flashes me a shrewd grin before pointing at Alix. "You, don't even think of trying anything."

Alix stiffens. He doesn't say anything so I'm the one who snaps at the pirate. "He has a name." Dane frowns at me, but I've had an exhausting two days, and I don't have any patience left to give.

"He's an automaton," Ava mutters. "What does it matter what we call him?"

I glare at her. I don't know what it is about Alix, but every time someone insults him, I find myself getting so angry. He just always stands there, looking so helpless.

Finn shoots Ava a dry look. "Play nice. Fine. Alix, don't try anything." Finn unlocks the door, opening it with a squeal.

I follow the other two out, the hold rocking beneath my feet. At least it's easier to breathe outside of those bars.

"Since we were never really introduced, I'm Finn, and this is Ava. She's a she. I'm a they."

Dane pauses. "They?"

Ava takes out her knife and twirls it around her fingers. "You got a problem with that, Scriptorium?"

Dane scowls. "No."

"Good." Ava flashes a grin that's all teeth. "Then we'll get along swimmingly."

Finn snorts.

The two of them lead us up onto the deck. Morning has broken, and after being below for so long it's startlingly bright out, wind rippling the sails up above us. I didn't notice the night before when it was dark, but there are strips of iron running along the railings, circling the masts above us, even set into some of the planks of the deck beneath us. The metal flashes blindingly hot in the sun. It makes the *Streak* a stitched-together creation, beautiful and strange.

A group of crewmen are out on the deck adjusting the riggings and another pair plays some dice game, laughing with each roll. Heads swivel as we pass. I jut out my chin, staring right back, refusing to be cowed. A few of them chuckle and heat flares over my cheeks.

Barnacle brains.

The captain's quarters are at the back of the ship. A row of large windows beam light into the space. The walls are lined with shelves full of trinkets and treasures that look as if they've come from all over the world: a wooden box with jade inlay, a large mask with red feathers the length of my forearm, a black stone carved into the shape of a dog. One shelf holds nothing but a set of long bronze needles next to some colorful spools of thread. I wonder if that's how Zara works her Script. The tools are so much more delicate than the rough scribers and scrapers the Eratian Scriptorium uses.

Hanging beside the shelves is a large map. I stop. Back on Tallis, the only maps we ever got to see were those of Eratia. This one's different. Here our island nation is dwarfed by Eural and Anderra. Seeing them carves a hollow in my stomach. How much bigger they are. How much stronger.

Beyond Anderra to the east, there are the other countries on the Great Continent, Najir and Ariza and Tolog, nations of grasslands and jungles, deserts and savannahs. Past Eural lie other islands, the drawn lines stretching all the way up to the frozen Northern Expanse.

Even this map only shows a small part of the world. It doesn't show Xian across the Dead Ocean. It doesn't show the mysteries of whatever lies down south. But it's still more than I'm used to seeing. An entire world out there, and I've barely touched a corner of it.

"Ah, here's our brig birdies."

I turn. Zara waits for us at a table in the back corner, her boots propped up, flipping through Alix's tome. She looks so irritatingly unconcerned. Then again, what could possibly concern a pirate? Certainly not us, her prisoners, standing here awaiting our fate. "Come now," she says. "Sit down."

The words are a command, not an invitation. Dane and I sit. Alix stays standing, looking at his tome.

"It may surprise you, automaton, but I don't want to have to force you." Zara's fingers brush a stick of charcoal sitting close to her on the table. "But I will if I have to."

Alix sits down. I think he'll take the insult in silence, but to my surprise, he straightens. "My name is Alix, not automaton."

Zara raises a brow. "My apologies. Alix."

The door opens and crewmen come in, bearing plates

of food. As the scent of spice hits my nose, my stomach lets out an embarrassingly large rumble.

Zara grins, waving her hand as the spread is set out on the table. "Eat. Then we'll talk."

Even with the many misguided decisions I've made in my life, eating food served by a hostile pirate captain might still be poorly thought out enough to claim the top spot. Judging by how still Dane's gone beside me, I'm guessing he agrees. But we're trapped here. Even if the food is poisoned, that's probably a better way to go than dying of hunger in this girl's brig.

I look over the spread. Most of the dishes I know: rounds of cheese, lentil stew, pieces of salted fish. Other dishes aren't familiar at all. A light and spongy bread, meat and vegetables cooked in sauces that smell so good they make my mouth water.

I take a round of cheese and pop it in my mouth, cutting off Dane's protest. It doesn't taste poisoned. I shrug at him, ignoring the amused look Zara's giving us. I nibble on some fish, and when I don't fall to the floor foaming at the mouth, I work up the courage to try one of the sauce dishes. Heat explodes over my tongue, and I leap for the clay jug in the center of the table, water splashing out the sides of my mouth as I down it to stop the burning. Zara barks out a laugh.

"You could have warned me," I rasp when I can speak.

She grabs a bit of the bread and scoops up some sauce with a flourish, swallowing it in one bite. "What, and miss the show?"

I scowl, cheeks prickling. She's infuriating.

We eat our fill, and only then does Zara sit back, wiping her fingers on a cloth. "Now, let's hear this story of yours. And don't try lying or leaving anything out. I am an excellent judge of when someone's giving me a tall tale."

I glance at Dane and Alix. The little bit of common sense I possess says that I shouldn't tell a pirate captain anything about us. She did throw us in her brig. And I don't want to give her anything she could turn against us.

The only problem is, I'm not sure what our other choices are. Getting locked back up? Even if she lets us go, we have no way to get to Valitia, not on our own. Besides, she knows about the Magistrate's Library. Which means she might be able to tell me something that will get me that much closer to my brother. That knowledge is a siren's call.

Dane must see it in my face because he gives a resigned sigh and nods at me.

So, I talk. As I do, I watch Zara. Her face doesn't so much as flicker past mild pleasantness.

Then I reach our discussion on the wild island about our decision to go Valitia. About my brother's paper and the golden light Alix told us about. For the first time a flash of interest lights Zara's eyes, there and gone so quickly I doubt I saw it until Alix shifts beside me.

Zara seems so supremely nonchalant about everything. So unflappable. But suddenly I wonder how much of that is an act.

What is this pirate hiding?

When I'm done, we sit in silence. Finn, who's taken a position at Zara's shoulder, bends down to whisper in her ear. I fidget beneath the table. I can't hear what they're saying. They could very well be debating whether or not to throw us to the sharks. And I did not come all this way to be fish food.

Zara looks back at us. "You know, I think I believe you."

The clamp that's been squeezing my heart releases ever so slightly.

She leans forward, steepling her fingers. "We're actually heading to Valitia now, so we'll take you. But there's no room for slackers on my ship, which means you'll act and work as part of my crew and you'll obey everything your captain says."

She wants us to join this crew? A pirate's crew?

Dane folds his arms, leaning back in his chair. "And if we'd rather take our chances on our own?"

"Unfortunately, that doesn't work so well for me," Zara says. "I'm not risking an automaton like Alix falling into the hands of the Scriptorium because of your bad life choices. Besides, you should consider yourselves lucky that there's something I want from you. If not, you'd be getting very acquainted with my brig."

She said the words casually, but I can't believe it was an unintentional slipup.

"What do you want?" I ask.

She turns to Alix, and for a moment I'm sure she's going to say that she wants him and that somehow we're going to have to fight our way out of this impossible situation. He didn't leave us behind in that cave and I'm certainly not about to leave him here.

"I want to see your runes."

11

ALIX

My runes? I run my fingers self-consciously over the ridges of one that peeks out beneath my himation.

"I caught a glimpse of them, back on the island," Zara says. "And I didn't recognize what I saw. Not to mention there's the whole you being…well, you." She gets up and walks around the table toward me. "Can I take a look?"

The only one who ever studied my runes was my father. He always said that my runes were something to be protected and that if I ever found myself outside of the villa, I couldn't chance anyone looking at them too closely.

Only now I'm outside of the villa, and it isn't that simple. We're here at Zara's mercy, she still has my tome, and I don't want to give her a reason to take what she wants.

I stand and peel away my chiton until I've bared my chest. Zara leans in, her eyes bright. As she does, I feel a tug in the center of my chest, as if a hook has lodged there, pulling me toward her. I frown. It's how I felt on deck last night. I assumed that was because she had my tome, but now my tome is on the table, and it isn't my book—it's her. It's as if she emits this pulsing undercurrent. There's something almost…familiar about it.

"I was right," Zara says. "I have a fair talent for understanding the Script, but there are runes here I've never seen before."

A pirate captain shouldn't know the Script. That's the realm of scholars. I'm tempted to ask how she does. I don't, though. I may be able to punch through stones, but she is clearly the more intimidating of us two.

"So you're just doing this to sate your curiosity?" Dane asks.

"You don't believe me?"

"It's not very believable."

Zara smiles. "Let's just say I'm looking for some answers of my own, and I'm thinking those runes might help me. So help me help you."

"What about the Magistrate's Library?" Karis asks.

Zara cocks her head. "What about it?"

"You know something, I know you do."

"True, but you're not exactly in a place to make demands."

Karis glares. "So, you're not going to tell us?"

Zara leans back against the table. "You behave, and your captain might just give you a little reward when we arrive on Valitia. If I feel like it. So." She pulls her knife from her belt, picking at some dirt beneath her fingernail. "What's it going to be? Will you cooperate or would you prefer spending the trip in danker quarters?"

Karis chews her lip. She doesn't look happy about it, but at the same time, I see the hope that flashes across her eyes. She wants this, to go to Valitia and to find her brother. I'm bracing myself for her acceptance when she looks at me. "They're your runes, Alix," she says. "It's your choice."

My choice?

I have no idea what to say to that. In the villa, my father always made the important choices, because he knew so much and I knew so little. Maybe a part of me was relieved about that. If I never made any decisions, I couldn't make any bad ones.

Now, though, Karis is looking at me. Waiting for me. They all are, even Zara.

I finger my medallion. "If we agree," I say carefully, "then all of us will look at my runes. I want Karis and Dane there, too."

Zara shrugs. "Fine. The scribe might even be of assistance."

"I'm an acolyte," Karis says.

Zara ignores her. "As for soldier boy…" She rolls her neck back to look at him. "He can come, but I don't see what help his pretty head will be." She bats her eyes. "Lucky for you, good looks count for something in this world."

Dane scowls. "For your information, I also did learn a bit about the Script."

"Hmm," Zara says. "Sure, you did. Probably in between romancing every lady who let you put your hands on her."

A hint of red touches Dane's neck as he slouches in his chair.

"So, do we have a deal?" Zara asks.

"What about my tome?"

"It stays with me," she says. "As insurance. I'm not about to put the safety of my crew at risk, not for three people I don't know."

The fact that she counts me as a person does nothing to temper the sting of her words. In the end, she still sees me as something that needs to be guarded against. Something that she might have to take control of again. "You view me as a risk."

"Even you have to admit, it's a bit startling to meet someone like you. My gun barely made you pause. But I promise, on my honor as captain of the *Crimson Streak*, I won't use it unless you force my hand. And as soon as we get to Valitia, I'll give it back. So, how about it?" She holds out her hand.

Part of me wants to say no, to leave this ship and this crew right now. There's too much uncertainty. Too much I wasn't ever taught to handle.

Yet another part knows that even if Zara lets us go, none of those things will go away. Besides, perhaps this could be a good thing. Perhaps this could be what we need right now. A place to stay. A way to get to Valitia. People who might not be allies exactly, but aren't enemies either. I want to believe that.

Dane and Karis quietly watch me, waiting for my decision. *My* decision. I get a strange thrill at that knowledge.

"All right." I clasp her hand, her own grip surprisingly strong. "You have a deal."

Zara smiles. "Well then, welcome to the crew of the *Crimson Streak*."

Zara—our new captain—dismisses us with a wave of her hand. Finn grins at us once we're all outside. "So she didn't feed you to the sharks. Color me surprised."

"Err..." I fumble. I hope they're joking.

"Well, come with me. Let's get you into different clothes before someone sees those uniforms and decides to take offense."

The clothes Finn gives us are old but clean. Still, after wearing chitons my whole life, even the sleeves of the tunic feel constrictive. Karis, on the other hand, seems delighted with the sea green dress she's given. She gives a twirl and it's strange, seeing her looking carefree for once.

Strange, but nice.

Back up on deck, Finn shows us the galley and the riggings and the cannons. He points out the other crew members, too. There's Het, the rail-thin man who threatened Karis. The lookout, Camila. Aiken, who gave Zara the message in the cave. Manaka, a stout woman who's the cook. Verius, the big man who fought with Dane on the wild island.

I try to keep them straight, but I'm not used to meeting so many people at once. I'm not used to meeting people at all. There might only be a dozen or so pirates, but they're all so different from each other, their skin colors and nationalities from every corner of the world my father once told me about. By the fifth name, I don't remember who the first one was anymore.

It's overwhelming, being here with all of them. Father never let me touch the world before. He was too scared of what might happen. Perhaps a part of me is scared now, too, but suddenly I don't want it to stop.

"It's like they come from all over the seas," I murmur.

"They do," Finn says. "The captain's from Ariza. Het is from Istland. Manaka is from all the way across the Dead Ocean." They fondly pat the railing. "We might spend most of our time in Eratia, but this little beauty has taken us all over the world."

Istland. I don't recognize that name. Did I miss a whole new nation being formed?

"Where do you come from?" Karis asks.

There's a pause before Finn answers, so slight I almost miss it. "Eural."

Dane and Karis tense. Finn gives a rueful shrug. I'm left glancing between them, confused. "Is something wrong with Eural?"

Finn rolls his eyes. "There's nothing's wrong with Eural."

"You tried to invade us a decade ago," Dane growls.

"And you did invade us." Finn gestures out at the sea. "Automatons. Fleets being destroyed. Cities flattened to the ground. Remember?"

Dane grinds his teeth. "That was centuries ago."

Finn's eyes flicker. "You think that means we've forgotten? Do you think anyone's forgotten what Eratia did when they had the automatons? When they thought they could take whatever they wanted, just because they could?"

The two of them stare each other down. I stand there awkwardly. The conversation isn't about me. Yet somehow, I feel as if it is. I'm an automaton, after all. That destruction is part of my heritage.

To my surprise, Dane's the one to look away first.

"Look." Finn spreads their hands. "I have no ill will for the lot of you—you seem passably decent for Scriptorium—but I'd keep opinions like those to yourself while on board. Eratia is not particularly loved among the crew."

"Finn, who are these?"

I jolt. Two people stand right behind us. They hadn't been part of Finn's introductions. I don't think they've even been on deck before now. He has the darkest skin I've ever seen and she's so pale she nearly glows. The man's black hair is twisted in cords that fall around his head and he wears simple leathers, the only ornamentation the carved wooden flute hanging from his hip. Her hair is pale blond but just as thick, pulled into a fat braid. Her tunic and pants are plain, but iron circlets twine over her pale arms like snakes, engraved with swirling lines.

"These are the newbies the captain took on," Finn says. "Karis, Dane, and Alix. And these—" they angle toward us, a bit of a mischievous smile on their face, pointing first to the man and then the woman "—are Kocha and Wreska, the other two Scriptworkers on board."

They're Scriptworkers?

I look at the two of them, so different from the robe-clad scholars I used to glimpse coming to my father's villa.

Finn pats the mast. "You should see what Kocha has done with the *Streak*. It's a work of beauty."

"The *Streak*...?" I lean closer to the mast and see long coiling runes that match the grain of the wood so closely I had mistaken them for natural fissures. Eratian runes are blatant: deep lines cut into metal. These are beautiful, as if they truly are a part of the mast. I brush my fingers against them and the low strain of a flute echoes through my head.

I jerk back, staring down at my fingers. I've never touched Scriptwork that wasn't from here, but I always assumed I wouldn't be able to hear it, not when the runes carved into my skin are Eratian.

Only I did hear it. They sang to me, a song like I've never heard before.

"You work with wood," Karis breathes, her eyes wide. It makes her look younger. I wonder who she might have been if her parents had never died and her brother wasn't taken. Would she be this bright-eyed girl beside me?

Kocha gives an easy shrug, but Wreska looks us over, her expression cool. "He works with wood. I work with iron." Her fingers tap over her bracelets, over the circles and swirls. They're as different from Kocha's runes as either of them are from mine. I want to reach out and touch them, except that I don't particularly want to draw this woman's attention or her ire. "They're very different practices from very different parts of the world."

A blush crawls up Karis's neck, angry and hot. "Sorry," she mutters. "We didn't learn much about other Script-workers back on Tallis."

"Of course you didn't." Wreska's gaze trails down until it lands on Karis's wrist, the skin there still obviously paler. Karis tucks her arm into her skirt.

"You know," Wreska says, "you can take off your robes and your bracelets, but you'll still be Scriptorium underneath. You're still part of a nation that has only ever used its runes and its Scriptwork for one thing. To destroy."

Karis goes stiff. I want to back away from the tension that crackles between them like an imminent thunderstorm, but Karis straightens.

"The only reason we're Scriptorium," she says, eyes flashing, "is because we were street kids who were handed over to that place. And if you think that makes us them, you're as naive as any of our great Scriptmasters."

I wince as Wreska's eyes narrow, her fingers stilling. We don't need a fight with these people. I'm debating taking Karis's arm and pulling her away when Kocha laughs, the sound so deep and sudden that I startle. He nudges Wreska with his elbow and the smallest of smiles twitches at the edges of her lips.

"Well, you've got some grit to you, girl," Wreska says. "I'll give you that." She claps Finn on the shoulder and the two of them thread through us as they continue down the deck.

"Welcome to the *Streak*, little ones," Kocha calls back over his shoulder. "It'll be a treat having a fourth Scriptworker on board."

A fourth Scriptworker. I don't understand who they're referring to until both Karis and Dane look my way.

I stare blankly. Me, a Scriptworker? The runes on my skin are limited, I know that. I can only ever do what they allow. They have always marked me as a thing. Yet Wreska and Kocha didn't look at me or my runes that way. I never thought that these lines could be something that made me belong. I look down at the runes on my hands.

I've never really belonged anywhere.

Finn laughs. "Seems they like you."

"Wouldn't want to know what they'd do to someone they don't like," Karis mutters.

"Kocha and Wreska are all right. It's just the Scriptorium over here that they hate." Finn looks out across the waves. "You should see some of the other Scriptworking institutions out there, though. Like the ones in Zara's homeland. There, everyone learns the Script. The rich, the poor. Old people, young people. The things they can do in those places, when you get that many people working together, when the Script isn't used for power but for utility? It's stunning. All I'll say is that when this is all over, I'm sure not staying here."

"When what is all over?" Karis asks.

A fleeting grimace crosses Finn's face. "This round of sailing," they say, shoving off the railing. "I should be getting some shore leave soon."

Karis frowns, but Finn just stares her down and there's a dare on their face, as if challenging her to call them out. I expect her to. Only she doesn't.

Finn smirks. "Well, let's get you to work. You don't want to be known as Scriptorium and slackers."

They take us to the stern of the ship, where there's a pile of red fabric strewn over some crates. "First task for you lot," they say. "Mending sails."

Karis groans, but I step forward, eager. Mending sails. That means those new runes.

Eratian runes are only used to destroy, to lock, to attack, but that's not how Zara used hers last night. I look them over. There's a pattern to the weaving, slanting lines in the runes before matching lines in the runes that come behind. I press my hands against the cloth and the rhythm of pounding drums crashes into my head. It's fast. Thrilling. I've never heard anything like it.

"Supplies are in that crate there," Finn says. "Good luck."

12

———

KARIS

I run my fingers over the runes woven in dark red thread against the sails, their tint so close to the fabric they meld into the cloth.

Back on Tallis, there was nothing like this. I'm only a few days away from that place, and already I'm seeing how much bigger the world is than I ever thought before. Now it's right here at my fingertips.

And I'm doing a lousy job at fixing it.

I jab my needle back into the sail, narrowly avoiding piercing my thumb as I struggle to work it through the thick fabric. Sewing is not one of my skills. If one of my chitons ripped, it stayed ripped more often than not until I grew enough to be given a new one. Judging from the fact that Alix has already broken one of the bone needles on his hard fingers, I'm guessing it's not something his father insisted he learn either. Luckily, we have Dane. He actually cared about how he looked back on Tallis, and that meant sewing.

He catches me watching him and leans over. "That looks worse than the rip did," he says, right as Alix breaks a second needle. Alix looks dolefully at the snapped pieces as Dane gives an overdramatic sigh. "Am I the only one here with actual life skills?"

I can't help but grin. "Yes."

Dane rolls his eyes, but his lips quirk up. "Here." He takes the cloth from my hand and starts mending it. "I'm only doing this so we'll be done before midnight."

I fight back my smile, trying to look serious. "Of course."

Dane's needle dips into the sail, quiet for a few moments. "So what do you two make of all this?"

I bite my lip, sobering. They might be taking us where we want to go, but the *Streak* still has a captain I'm not sure I trust any more than she trusts us. Even the other pirates—Finn and Ava, Kocha and Wreska. There's something here that isn't quite adding up for me. "I don't know. Zara and her crew are playing friendly at the moment, but that could easily change." I hesitate, then look at Alix. "She hasn't tried to use your tome again, has she?"

Alix's hands still. "No, she hasn't. But there's something...strange about Zara. Almost familiar."

"Familiar?" I ask. "Like you've met before?"

"We couldn't have met. The last time I was awake was two hundred years ago. I don't know what it is. I...feel something when I'm around her, as if she has this energy to her."

An energy. I don't feel anything around Zara, except a

vague intimidation I wouldn't admit out loud to another soul. We have so many unknowns in our lives right now, I don't really want to add another one to the list, especially not one like her. How did someone as young as her become captain anyway?

"I don't think we should trust them too far," Dane says. He runs his fingers along his hurt cheek. "There are things here that don't make sense. Like how a pirate knows the Eratian Script. How she managed to get a gun."

"Are they that rare?" Alix asks.

Dane nods. "Notoriously so. On the whole island of Tallis there were only two. The runes are so complicated, most of the time they explode before completion." He drums his fingers on his hip, where his sword used to hang. "I'd feel better if we were at least armed. But our illustrious captain confiscated my blade with everything else."

"You have a problem with one of my decisions, soldier boy?"

Zara. I wince as she swaggers over to us, hands on her hips. How much of that did she hear? Not that it really matters, since all of it was incriminating.

Dane stands, facing her head-on. I resist the urge to kick him. If he gets us thrown in the brig, I'm spilling my gruel down his back.

"I should have my sword," Dane says.

"How do you figure that?"

"Because the Scriptorium may be tracking us right now. And if they find us, you'll need my help."

Chuckles sound from some of the nearby pirates, who've

drifted closer. I bite back a groan. Just what we need, an audience.

Zara rests her hand on the hilt of her own blade. "You think quite highly of yourself, don't you?"

"I know I'm a good swordsman. I won't pretend I'm not."

A slow grin spreads over Zara's face. I've never seen a shark before, but they must look like that right before they strike. "All right, soldier boy, you're so eager to prove yourself? Beat me and I'll give you your sword back."

That surprises Dane. "You want me to fight you?"

"What, too scared to take on a captain?"

Dane scowls. "No."

Zara steps back, pulling her sword from her scabbard and twirling it in an elaborate flourish that sends the pirates around us clapping and hooting.

One of her men throws his blade at Dane. He catches it easily. As soon as he has a sword in his hand, I can tell he's more comfortable. This blade is a curved one and it's long, too, with a weighty guard on its hilt. I know better than most it's not what Dane is used to, but if that makes him uneasy, he doesn't show it.

I'm uneasy enough for the both of us. Dane may not be humble, but he is right. He's a good swordsman—excellent, in fact. But he's never fought someone like a pirate captain before. I don't know much about fighting, but I can tell how adeptly Zara handles her own blade. Dane's pride might have wagered more than he can win.

The pirates form a loose circle around the two fighters. Kocha and Wreska push through to the front, glancing between their captain and my friend.

Dane is barely in his stance when Zara lunges forward. Their blades clash. Dane is already moving, slipping to the side and lashing out. Zara blocks his blade easily and twists away. Her eyes are feverishly bright. She rushes in and they engage once again, their swords blinding streaks beneath the midday sun.

They move as if in a dance, connecting, separating, connecting again. There's something beautiful about it and I feel a twinge of jealousy in my gut. If I could fight, Matthias and I might never have been separated. I might not have been forced to stay on Tallis all those years.

Dane and Zara separate again and slowly circle one another. Their chests heave as sweat slides down their temples. Around them the pirates lean in, eager. Expectant. They've stopped cheering and there's such a hushed silence I can hear the groan of the wood as the *Streak* rocks.

"I'll give you this, soldier boy," Zara says. "You are good."

Now it's Dane's turn to grin. It's the first time he's truly looked alive since we left Tallis. And she gave that to him, not me. "So, I get my sword back?"

"Oh no, I said you had to beat me for that."

Zara lunges forward, hard enough to drive Dane back toward the railing, the pirates scattering out of the way. She moves again, but in her eagerness she leaves an opening. Even I can see it. Dane's eyes glint in triumph and he jabs at her.

Quick as a trap clamping shut, she twists out of the way, grabbing his arm as it goes past. Dane's eyes barely have time to widen in surprise before Zara sweeps his feet out from under him. He falls onto his back, hard, his sword clattering away across the boards. He scrambles to get up but Zara presses the tip of her blade to the base of his throat.

She grins, still breathing heavily. "I guess that esteemed Scriptorium of yours never taught you how to fight dirty."

The pirates around us erupt with hoots and cheers as Dane gapes at Zara, flabbergasted. I can't think of the last time I saw that particular expression on his face. Really, I can't think if I've ever seen it.

Zara turns away.

"Will you teach me?"

The crowd quiets as Zara turns to me.

I straighten. "Teach me to fight, I mean."

Zara cocks her head. I need to phrase this the right way if I'm going to convince her.

"When we ran from the Scriptorium, when you caught us in that cave, I was useless, Captain. As an acolyte, the Scriptorium never gave me the chance to learn to fight."

Zara props a hand on her hip. "I must say, that's not a very convincing argument. It sounds like you want to know sword-fighting so you can use it against me and my crew. Why would I help you with that?"

I look at Zara. Part of me admires her after that fight. She is frenetic energy, sea grit, and sly smiles. It's been a long time since I saw Dane bested. I want to be able to fight like she does.

If I'm going to convince her, I need to be like her. I throw back my shoulders, folding my arms over my chest to copy her confident stance and stare her down. "Because you don't seem like the type who's all right with a girl not being able to defend herself."

Everyone is silent around us. I wonder if I've stuck out my neck too far and now my head's about to be lobbed off.

Zara laughs. "True enough." She jams her sword back through her belt and pulls out her smaller knife. "Someone get this girl a dagger."

13

ALIX

I watch the fight from the sidelines, perched on a barrel that groans beneath my weight every time I shift. Karis looks wobbly with her dagger but no matter how many times Zara knocks it from her hand, Karis picks it back up.

I don't know how she does it. Karis is all fire and spark. She's ready to take on anything.

The few times I've had to fight, I've hated it. There's nothing brave or fair about my way of fighting, of using my strength against others who could never match it. Yet here is Karis, wanting to fight, learning to fight, and as bad as she is, I can see the pirates' respect as she keeps going.

I look down at my hand, clenched into a fist on my knee. If I wasn't me, wasn't an automaton, would others respect me for my strength as well instead of fearing me for it? Would I stop fearing my own strength?

By the time Zara finally stops their training, it looks as

if only sheer stubbornness is keeping Karis upright. We head down into the hold. I walk slowly, trying to match Karis's hobble, as we round crates and hammocks and barrels, dimly lit by the shifting light coming through the portholes. Every once in a while, the light hits a piece of iron embedded in the wood, making it shine like a star. It's only been a short day, but I'm already getting used to the creaking wood and shifting shadows.

"Why didn't you ever ask me to teach you to fight?" Dane asks.

"How could I?" Karis groans. "The Scriptorium would never have allowed that. And now that I'm here, well…" She gives him a sly grin. "Of course I want to be taught by the winner."

Scowling, Dane rolls his eyes, then reaches out and lightly bops her on the head. "Brat." I thought he'd be upset by his defeat, but he's smiling. Perhaps he was simply happy to have a sword in his hand again.

The hammocks we've been assigned hang in the back corner of the lowest deck, swaying slightly between the posts. Dane collapses into his, then grimaces and pulls out a stinking boot from beneath his back. "And to think when I was a child I dreamed of being a pirate," he mutters, throwing it to the side.

Karis rolls into her own, wincing. She reaches over and pokes him in the ribs. "The glamorous life isn't quite as glamorous as you thought?"

"Hardly."

I stay standing. One of the hammocks is mine, but even if the mesh of ropes could bear my weight, I feel jittery. I want to move, even though there's nowhere to go on this ship, there's not even room to pace in the cramped quarters down here. It's so different from the gleaming spaces of my father's villa that it's hard to believe I've stood in both. More and more, that old life feels like some sort of dream.

"Alix?" Karis asks. "Are you all right?"

I'm embarrassed that she noticed. I try to shuffle my emotions into order, to pin down exactly what it is that's bothering me.

"What if the captain learns something about my runes, and it gives her more ways to control me?"

It's the first time I've said the words aloud. It's the first time I've really let myself think them. I drift my fingers over the lines beneath my sleeve. Once these must have been common knowledge, but they're obviously not anymore. If no one figures them out, then no one can ever turn them against me.

The only problem is, I don't remember what these runes mean either, so if I don't let anyone else try, *I* might never know.

Karis frowns as she levers herself up in her hammock. "Have you been worrying about that this whole time? Why didn't you tell us?"

She makes it sound so easy. It isn't easy to explain that I always worry about my runes. That's simply what it's like to be who—what—I am. I shrug as I settle on the floor, not caring about the sea grit packed between the boards. "The captain said she thought my runes could help her learn something. What if she does, and the temptation to use what she finds becomes too much?"

Dane and Karis glance at each other and in their expressions, I read the words they won't say. If Zara uses my tome, there won't be anything the two of them can do. Here on this ship we're outnumbered, and the only escape route would be through leagues of ocean. I could make that. Though the memory is shifty, I remember moving through the murky depths of water, my weight enough to hold me to the ocean floor. There wouldn't be any way for me to take Dane and Karis, though, and I'm not going to leave them to be thrown in the brig again, or worse.

"Do you want us to try to get your tome back?" Dane asks.

I startle, looking at him. Even Karis seems surprised.

"We're in this together now, right?" Dane says. "All three of us." He glances awkwardly away, rubbing the back of his neck. "And I'm not sure what it's worth, but I'm sorry for those things I said before. On Tallis and the wild island. I was wrong."

It is worth a lot. More than he could know. Perhaps I judged him too harshly as a Scriptorium soldier. However we started, he's not looking at me as if I'm some mindless automaton now.

"If you want us to try to get it back," Dane says, "we can."

They could try, and even by trying they could risk everything. I press my hand to my temple. "I don't know. Even if we got my tome back, it's not as if we could run. I'm not even sure what Zara might do. I'm just… I'm scared."

The word rasps in my ears. Before all this happened, my entire world consisted of my father and our villa. It might not have been large, but it was home, and it was safe. Now the fear inside of me is a cold leech, and I don't know how to stop it.

Karis gets up, wincing as she does and hobbles over to me. She sits down on the ground and takes my hand. The contact grounds me, pulling me back up out of the anxiety. Even though it's only a touch.

"It's all right to be scared, Alix," she says. "And Dane and I will be there tomorrow, no matter what."

I look at Karis. When I first met her, I didn't expect this softness from her. I felt as soon as I woke up for the first time that I knew my father. He was always open with me. Karis, though… I keep discovering sides to her that I don't quite expect. Both of us have lost and are lost. We both have to find our way forward again.

"Everything seemed simpler before," I whisper, and yet even as the words leave my mouth, I wonder if that was a good thing. Could I be content again living with the walls of a villa dictating my whole world? The thought bothers me. I'm not sure I'm ready to grow into someone bigger than my father's home.

"What was it all like back then?" Karis asks.

"I never had the chance to see most of what was out there. I was always in our villa."

"Will you tell me about that, then?"

I shrug. "It doesn't matter anymore."

"I'd like to know," she says. "More about your old life. More about you."

Warmth filters into my chest. It's strange, how emotions can tear me down and build me up. People, too. I think back, and even though the memories are painful, this time I don't shy away. I'm the only one who remembers who my father truly was: not a villain, but a gentle, fervent scholar. His memory deserves to be kept alive.

"My father was always kind to me. He never treated me like a thing. He never once used my tome. When I wasn't hiding, he'd take me out into the garden. I loved gardening."

Karis smiles. "You did?"

I nod. Unlike all the blurry memories that still beat like bird's wings against my mind, these come back whole and bright and good. "I liked watching things grow and bloom. There was something special in knowing the plants were only alive because of us and our care. The gardens were beautiful." Pale stone walls scrubbed clean by the sun, fig trees casting shade onto the paths, orchids and hyacinths growing like living splashes of color. I remember walking through them as if it were yesterday. Now that yesterday was centuries ago. "I suppose that's all gone now."

I miss him. I keep thinking this ache will go away, but it stays lodged in the center of my chest.

"Gardens grow back." Karis shifts closer, leaning her head against my shoulder. I'm caught between the urge to stiffen or to ease into that touch. "What else did you like to do?"

"Well..." I fiddle with the hem of my chiton. "I liked singing. Still like singing."

Her head pops up. "Really?"

I nod, pleased and embarrassed.

"Will you sing something?"

I should have expected that. I shake my head. "I don't think that's a good idea. My repertoire is dated and——"

"I'd like to hear."

Karis looks at me, expectant, and any refusal I might have made falls away. She woke me up, gave me back my tome, and didn't reject me. I never thought that anyone besides my father would look at me and see anything but a monster.

I never thought I might have a friend.

I think back, looking for a song she might like, and then begin to sing.

"'The moon was bright, the night was fair,
I wandered far not knowing where.
And at a spring where paths did meet,
I heard a song so low and sweet,
And saw a minstrel standing there.
And saw a minstrel standing there.'"

I start out hesitant, but the more I sing the more I remember, and my voice grows stronger. Pirates from some of the other beds poke their heads out to listen. Dane's hammock rocks slowly along to the melody, one leg hanging out. Karis leans against my side, a comforting warmth. Someone, it must be Kocha, begins to play his flute, the haunting melody winding with my own. I hear the gruff tones of a low voice joining in, too. I guess not all of these songs were lost to the ages.

My father was never a musician. Yet here, in this pirate ship, other voices join my own.

And together we sing in the night.

Finn and Ava lead us back to Zara's cabin. I tap my fingers on my father's pendant, now gleaming as it hangs around my neck. I can see its sigil again, a swan with olive branches twining around its open wings. It took me the entire night to clean two centuries of sea grime off of it, but it's not as if I could have slept anyway. Besides, it makes me feel stronger, having this piece of my father with me. The world is harder to navigate without him. Perhaps I'm ready, though, to be a bit braver and bolder.

Zara stands by one of the shelves, flipping through a dusty, leather-bound ledger. It's not my tome, but I can sense it's near, perhaps even in this cabin. I can't quite tell where, though. Being so close to Zara again, I feel that familiar tug once more, muddying even my connection with my book.

Zara sees us and slips the ledger back, swiping her hands on her pants. "Good, you're all here."

"Captain," Karis says with a slight nod.

Zara flashes a grin. "And you're learning. Even better. Well, Alix, front and center if you're ready."

I'm not ready, but I won't learn anything standing by the door. I step forward and unbutton my shirt before slipping it off. It's only my chest, but I still feel bare.

Zara's fingers float over my runes, not quite touching them. "Look here. This one is *see*."

Finn nods. "Over here is *touch*."

I twist so I can see, and Zara tuts at me to stay still. She steps over to my arm and frowns. "These I'm not so sure about. This one up here almost looks familiar, but I can't place it."

I glance at the rune she's examining, which has minimal damage. It's one of the few I do remember. "It's *decide*."

She looks up and her eyes meet mine. "*Decide?* Did your father teach you what your runes mean?"

I don't particularly want to talk about my father with her. She probably thinks of him exactly as everyone else does in this time. It's not something I relish being reminded of. "We said you could look at my runes, not that I'd tell you about them or about me."

"So, you do have a bit of a backbone."

I frown. "No, I don't. My back is metal."

Zara barks out a laugh. "It's an expression."

If I was able to blush, I'm sure I would be. "Not a very accurate one," I mutter.

Zara folds her arms, still grinning. "You know, we'll get further on this if we work together."

I sigh. I don't think I'm going to win this argument. "Yes, my father taught me all of my runes." I'm sure he did. "The problem is, I don't remember all of them."

"That's a pity." She leans in again to the *decide* rune. "It's fascinating, though. The marks on this side almost resemble a pattern from the Agafya scrolls."

She knows about the scrolls by Master Agafya? The woman's work was ancient even in my father's time. They are among the oldest preserved rune studies. How does a pirate captain know about them?

"Er, yes. That's what my father said he modified them from."

A flare lights in Zara's eyes, reminding me so much of my father I pause. He always got that look when he discovered something new. "So the stories are true," she says.

"He did manage to modify runes. What about these other lines? Do you know where they come from?"

"I don't, but I think that maybe…" I hesitate, trailing off. My father taught me runes, but that was only for the few short years when I was with him, and there are so many gaps in my memory. Only then I see Zara looking at me, expectant. Waiting for whatever I'm going to say. "I think they might be from Master Hieronymus's work."

She sucks in a breath. "Of course. Now I see the pattern." She steps back and gives me an appraising look. "Impressive."

A bit of a glow lights in my chest. I've never been called impressive before.

"So just how many of your runes do you remember?" she asks.

"Perhaps half of them." I gesture to the ones on my arm. "Most of these are gone, though."

"Well, what about special talents, then? Skills? It might help us to figure some of these runes out if we have an idea of what they should say."

"I can undo *lock* runes."

Zara taps my side. "That must be because of this one, *unlock*."

"I can feel runes, too. I used to be able to feel automatons."

"You could?" Karis asks.

"They let off this—" I search for the right word, but nothing can quite capture the way they used to feel, as if they called to me, as if they were a part of me "—this buzzing sensation. They don't do that anymore."

Come to think of it, the energy I remember from the automatons, the familiarity of it, isn't all that different from what I'm feeling from Zara. I glance at her. Why does she feel like that?

"Tell me about your tome, then," Zara says. "What limitations does it have? Do you have to keep it nearby?"

I'm sure I could claim that I've forgotten. The truth is, though, the day I tried to get rid of it is burned in my memory. I had finally worked up the courage to ask my father about why I had to be so careful with my tome, and so he told me.

The centuries that have passed have done nothing to numb the loss and confusion I felt at what he said. The anger, too. At it, at him. I was so new to my emotions back then. Each one burst too brightly inside of me. A few days later, when one of the woodworkers in the city came to deliver a new desk to the villa, I sneaked out and hid my tome deep in the scraps in his cart. It was naive, but tomes were so common those days I convinced myself that no one would be able to trace it back to me. The tome would be gone and I would be free.

Barely a half watch later pain had lanced through my head. My limbs had started jerking. My thoughts began to scatter. Panicked, I gasped out the truth to my father and he'd run from the villa, chasing after the cart.

When he came back, the tome in his hands, I was curled up in the corner of his study, phantom pain still lingering down my limbs. The cart hadn't even made it halfway across the city.

I shake my head, dissolving the memory. "It doesn't have to be right on me, but I can't stray far."

"And if your tome were destroyed?" Zara asked.

I startle, looking at her, and she holds up her hands. "I'm just asking."

If straying from my tome managed to hurt me like that, I don't want to know what destroying it would do. "I don't know. I don't…" I shake my head, forcing down the panic welling in my chest. It's better to live with the thing than to find that without it I'm nothing. "If that happened, I don't think I'd survive it."

Zara nods and perhaps she heard the strain in my voice, because she doesn't press any further. Her fingers tap meditatively on the hilt of her dagger. "All right, here's where we're at. I was hoping Finn and I would be able to figure these out on our own, but I don't think that's going to work. Most of these runes aren't even close to any I'm familiar with."

"How do you even know the runes that you do?" Dane asks. "*Unlock* and *see* and *touch*?"

Zara smiles and there's something dangerous in that expression. "What can I say? I have many talents."

Dane folds his arms. "Karis and I worked at the Scriptorium for years and even we weren't allowed to study runes like that."

"The world is bigger than your little island, soldier boy," Zara says.

Dane's eyes narrow. "I know that," he snaps.

Ava flips out her dagger and steps toward Dane, and as

she does her sleeve shifts up, showing lines tattooed on her skin.

"You have a rune on your wrist," I say.

Ava stiffens. Something like pain cracks across her face, bright and sharp.

Zara steps forward, her hands slamming into me as she shoves me away. Even though she's not strong enough to do it, I'm so surprised I let her, stumbling back. I'm fumbling for words to apologize, not even sure what I'm apologizing for, when Ava reaches down and pulls up her sleeve.

It is a rune. One I recognize because every single automaton has it on their body, even me, right in the small of my back.

Obey.

The silence in the cabin is so thick it presses into me like a palpable thing, stifling fingers smudging out all lightness.

"I don't understand," I finally manage.

Finn's staring at the ground, hands clenched at their sides, white-knuckled. Zara's angled herself toward Ava, as if sheltering the other girl. I can't quite make out the expression on Zara's face but her voice is cool and clipped when she says, "No. Though of everyone here, maybe you would." She looks over her shoulder at us. Dane stares at the lines, openmouthed. Karis just looks sick. "I wouldn't pry too deeply into the secrets of this crew. You might not like what you find."

I already don't like what I've found. Of all the lines in my skin, the *obey* rune is the one I hate the most. It's what forces an automaton to carry out any command they're given, even me, who has a mind and will of my own. There it is, inked on Ava's skin. Only, surely runes wouldn't work on people.

Would they?

The silence is growing thicker and I have to break it, so I say the only thing I can. "Why did you want to see my runes?"

Zara leans against the table, her eyes boring into me. There's a challenge there, and for the life of me I can't look away, as if her gaze is a snare that's rooted me to the floor.

I gather every bit of courage I possess. "I won't ask about the inked rune." I wouldn't. I know better than most how deeply some secrets are carved. "However, I deserve to know about mine. I want the truth."

I don't really expect that to sway her. She has all the power here.

Then, to my surprise, Zara tips her head toward Karis. "Your friend said that before all this happened, before you ever fell asleep in that cave, you remember this glowing light, this heat."

I knew I saw her interest when Karis told her about that. "Do you know what it is?"

"Perhaps. And perhaps your runes might have something to do with it." She looks so serious. So different from the unflappable, grinning captain we first met in that cave. Then she pushes off the table and the moment breaks. I'm left blinking as she goes to the map on the wall. "Unfortunately, as I said, I don't think we're going to be able to figure this out on our own. Luckily—" she taps an island on the map "—I know of someone who can help. He's a bit out of our way, but not too far, and he knows more about runes than any of us. What do you all think about a detour?"

A detour. I look over my shoulder at Karis. She shifts, biting her lip. I know how much she wants to go to Valitia to find her brother. I want to help make that happen.

Only, Zara is offering me a chance to figure out my runes, my memories.

I give her a pleading look, hoping she'll understand. She hesitates, and then gives a small, almost imperceptible nod.

14

KARIS

The *Streak* cuts through the waters, sails unfurled to catch the wind. I pull myself up the riggings, hand over hand, a salty evening breeze snaking through my hair. I try to focus on the feel of the wind and not on our detour. Zara said we'll reach where we're going by tonight, that we won't stay long. But we're still heading in the wrong direction, away from my brother.

The thought is unbelievably selfish. I know that as soon as I have it. This is important for Alix. Especially after what I saw in Zara's cabin.

Obey. Maybe some part of me knew that Alix probably had that rune. Every automaton I've ever climbed on or heard about has had that rune. But seeing Alix's expression when he looked at those lines still jabbed into me like a knife. I glance down at my wrist. Even when I had that bracelet on, even when it trapped me, at least it wasn't a part of me.

I want to help Alix find some answers. Because maybe that'll take away the pain that seems to cling to him. I'm not sure when I started feeling that way. It's like Alix is making me softer. And I haven't truly been soft with anyone since my brother. I could never afford to be.

Can I afford it now?

"You're turning into quite the pirate."

I'm so surprised to hear the voice, this high above the deck, that my fingers slip from the riggings. A small shriek escapes my lips right as a hand grips my wrist, steadying me. I look up, heart thudding in my chest, and see Dane crouched above me in the ropes, perfectly balanced.

He helps me climb the last few feet. The first time I did this I was so shaky it was embarrassing. The ropes, swaying with the ship and shifting with every gust of wind, were nothing like the solid automatons I was used to, and I could hear the crew chuckling from the deck below. But now I enjoy it, the *Streak* like a living thing rolling beneath me, the iron implants—Wreska's work—blazing in the evening light. Up here I feel as if I can scrape the blue off of the sky. It's a world of freedom.

"Thanks," I pant. "You as well."

I mean it as a compliment, but as Dane straightens again, leaning back against the mast, something flashes across his face so quickly I can't quite decipher it. Pain, maybe. Weariness. Then it's gone.

"Dane?" I ask softly. "What's the matter?"

He sighs, folding his arms and staring out at the water.

"I don't know. I guess I'm feeling a bit...untethered lately. I'm glad you're getting the chance to find your brother, Karis. I'm glad Alix is getting the chance to figure out his runes. But for me..." He shrugs, and there's an apathy to that gesture I don't like. "I don't know what I'm supposed to be doing anymore."

I thought I knew Dane better than anyone. That I would always be able to tell when he was putting on a show and when he was being real. When did that stop being true? "Dane, I know words aren't enough to change what I did but—"

"It's not even that. I chose to do what I did. But at the same time, in that moment, everything I ever wanted and worked for disappeared, and I made the exact choice I would have done back when I had nothing. What if a street brat is all I am?"

"I like the street brat," I whisper.

As soon as the words are out, I know I've said the wrong thing. Dane's face contorts.

"Dane, I..."

"Scribe! Soldier boy!"

Dane stiffens as Zara's shout echoes up to us. *Soldier boy.* I didn't realize until now how much that term must grate on him. A constant reminder of all he's lost.

I look down through the tangle of ropes. Zara stands by the base of the mast with Alix and Finn. Zara steps forward, shielding her eyes as she looks up at us. "We're drawing close. Get down here!"

Dane sighs, grabbing hold of a rope. "Duty calls," he

mutters and before I can say anything, he's swinging down through the riggings. With a frown, I follow.

"Well, you two are just natural-born pirates, aren't you?" Zara says.

Dane jumps easily to the deck, landing on his toes. He rolls his shoulders, looking at her coolly. "Is that an actual compliment?"

"Don't get too used to it, soldier boy."

"I have a name."

Zara grins, her eyes dancing. She spins her three-pointed hat before sliding it on. "I know." She flicks her hand. "Come on."

She strides across the deck as Dane scowls after her. He turns to Finn. "Why does everyone here follow her? Most of the crew's twice her age."

Finn shrugs. "Because she found us. And she gave us a purpose, every one of us." They follow after Zara.

As cryptic answers go, that one's right up there. I want to ask, but I don't. Zara told us not to pry into the secrets of this crew and I'm beginning to think she's right. We have enough problems without getting involved in theirs.

The island we're drawing near shows the first signs of life I've seen since coming on board, and it isn't much. A stretch of rickety docks barely clings to the shore, a few sad boats bobbing on waves that gleam faintly beneath the setting sun. Reaching up onto land is a hodgepodge of small houses made of mud bricks with thatched roofs, packed so closely together there's barely room for the streets.

I've never been here. Never been anywhere near this place. And yet I'm instantly reminded of Heretis. I recognize this world, of poverty and scarcity, of a life built off of stealing scraps. I glance over at Dane and see the troubled look on his own face before he shifts away.

Aiken navigates the ship to a cove off the side of the island. Zara and Kocha, then Dane and Alix climb down the ladder into the boat.

I look at Finn, surprised. "Not coming?"

They glance at their sister, working on the other side of the deck, and then they smile, slipping their thumbs into their belt. But there's something strained about their expression. "Not really for me, honestly. I should be helping Ava anyways."

"Karis!" Zara calls. "Hurry it up."

I shrug and climb into the boat.

Kocha rows us to shore and we follow a lumpy path up through the cliff side and across the island, back toward the village. There's not much out here, just a bit of scrubland with the odd goat who bleats at us in consternation before running off. Shadows stretch across the dry ground as the sun arcs toward the horizon.

Everything's so low, we can see the village long before we get to it. It doesn't improve on closer inspection. The clay walls are riddled with cracks, and so many chunks are missing in the thatched roofs I doubt they'd keep out a drizzle.

Kocha takes us down one of the twisting streets. I trail at the back. On Heretis, I knew every alley, every turn; which ones could give us a quick getaway and which were dead ends. Here, as soon as we enter the labyrinth I'm lost. The buildings aren't large, but they're so close they crowd over us. Crates and barrels crush out the little remaining space in the narrow streets. There aren't that many people, and those that are here mostly ignore us, scuttling on their way. The stink of fish and sweat hangs like a musk in the air.

A child dashes in front of us, thin, with tangles in her hair and suddenly I see myself as I was back then. The gaunt face that always looked at me from every puddle, the dirt that never seemed to rub off. I squeeze my eyes shut and take a deep breath. Coming here is bringing it all back: the dull ache of hunger in my stomach, the fearful restlessness that always kept us running, the exhaustion clinging to my limbs that I couldn't ever seem to shake. The memories slosh up over my head, trying to drown me.

"You all right there?"

Zara drops back next to me and when I glance at her, there's no sympathy in her eyes, only a keenness that I don't want to deal with right now. There are things about that life I haven't even been able to share with Dane, things no one knows beside Matthias. And I can't say I'm real interested in sharing them with her.

"I used to live in a place like this, that's all." I keep my voice flat. Flat is safer with her. "It's not a time I want to remember."

Zara looks around at the dilapidated houses, the cracked streets, and I wonder what she sees. She's a pirate captain now, so she might have grown up in a place like this. It's not like many aristoi end up in her position. And yet somehow, that sort of beginning doesn't fit her at all. Honestly, I'm not sure what sort of beginning would fit Zara. There's something about her I can't quite grasp.

"Almost makes you angry, doesn't it?" she asks. "When you see people having to live like this, when only a few islands away there are great, gleaming Scriptoriums."

I snort. I was right. She definitely wasn't a street kid.

She quirks a brow. "Something to share?"

"Not really."

"Come, Karis," she chides. "Don't start being shy now."

I roll my eyes, but I guess I take the bait because I gesture at the houses. "Look around you. Anger does nothing in a place like this. It changes nothing and it gets you nowhere." I should know. Back then I had so much anger I thought it'd burn me alive. When the fever claimed both my parents. When our landlord chased us from our shop. When I had to watch my brother being beaten as I was pinned to some dirty wall. I was so sure if I pushed back hard enough I could force the world to be fair to us. I might as well have been wishing on a star. "The world is what it is."

Zara lets out a bark of laughter, so brash the others ahead of us glance back.

I narrow my eyes. "What?"

"I didn't expect that from you."

"Meaning?"

"Meaning you've been nothing but fire since you got on board my ship. Wanting to learn to fight. Snapping at anyone on my crew who looked at you the wrong way. Even managing to escape from your Scriptorium, to come all this way...and then all I get is a shrug?"

I'm starting to get irritated. "What else am I supposed to do, *Captain*?"

She studies me for a long moment, and then a smile curls up at the edge of her mouth that I don't trust at all. "Fight."

Now it's my turn to laugh. But Zara's being serious.

"Fight who?" I finally say. "The Scriptorium? You can't fight people like them."

"Sure, you can."

"Says the pirate captain."

I mean the words as an insult but she simply laughs and spreads her arms wide. "I'm a thorn in the side of the Scriptorium and its master, and I'm proud."

She just doesn't get it. There are some fights that you can win. Like my brother. No matter what else happens, I'm getting him back. But other things you just can't change. All you can do is get out before you get killed. "Well, good luck with that. Try to drop us off before the Scriptorium shoots your little ship to the bottom of the sea."

I pick up my pace, irritated and flushed. Not even sure why I feel so irritated and flushed. If her goal was to make me angry, she certainly succeeded.

"Someone has to do it."

I glare over my shoulder. Zara has stopped walking, the others pulling farther ahead. Part of me wants to follow them, but there's a dare on her face and I'm not one to back down. I turn around.

Zara folds her arms over her chest, head tilted just enough that her eyes gleam in the shadows starting to swim through the alley. "And you know, I really expected you to rail about what the Scriptorium is doing. To want to change things for others who might be suffering just like you did."

"Others?" I spit. If she really wants to have this conversation, I'll have it. Because she has no idea what she's talking about. "Do you know what others did when my brother and I were all alone? We begged for food and they smacked our hands away. We tried to take shelter in their doorways from the chill and the rain and they kicked us out. I'm not risking my life fighting for others who wouldn't lift a finger to help me when I needed it, and I really don't see that I deserve this lecture from a pirate."

I throw the words in her face, and maybe that's risky, but I want a rise from her. Because I'd know how to handle a fight.

But Zara just smiles. "There's that anger. Funny how we use it to cloak what we're most scared of."

I gape at her. "Oh, yes? And what would I be scared of?"

She steps closer to me, so close I want to back away from the intense look in her eyes. I hold my ground.

"Caring."

"Captain?" Kocha's voice echoes back to us. "Everything all right?"

Zara flashes a grin over my shoulder. "It's fine." She strides down the street, without so much as a backward glance at me. I'm left staring after her, choking on the words I can't put together and say.

I am not scared of caring. I just know better.

"Come on, Karis!" Zara shouts back. "Or we'll leave you behind."

I growl and stalk after the others. Alix shoots me a worried look but I don't want his understanding right now. I brush past him.

As soon as I do it, I can almost imagine the hurt look on

his face. For one moment, I think of turning back around, but I push that thought away. He doesn't need to know what Zara said.

No one does.

Then I feel a hand on my shoulder.

Alix steps up to me. His face is hesitant. "I know I'm not good at this," he says. "I'm here, though, if you ever need to talk."

He follows after the others, and for the second time I'm left wordless. There's a crack opening my chest. It's been so long since I've let myself get close to someone. Even Dane. There's been distance between us for years. But I don't know what will happen if that crack gets any bigger.

I shove it down and pretend it isn't really there.

The sky has gone full-on dark when we reach a squat building that sits at the center of three different streets. Its shutters are latched shut, but light and raucous laughter spill out between the boards. Somehow even that seems dirty.

Zara looks over her shoulder. "Alix, make sure to keep your hood up and head low in here."

Alix looks vaguely queasy. I doubt he's ever been any-where near a seedy place like this. But he pulls his hood farther over his eyes.

Zara shoves open the door and struts in as if she owns the place. I trail in after her, and as much as my better in-stincts scream to keep my eyes on my feet, I can't help but look around.

It's a bar. Or at least I think it's supposed to be a bar. Running along the back wall is a counter, though it's little more than a long, notched plank of wood, bottles of a dozen different shapes and colors scattered along its length. The rest of the space is filled with tables and chairs, crudely fashioned from discarded barrels. Flickering candles jammed into the necks of bottles on the tables provide the light I saw from outside. Soot stains mar the ceiling and walls and I'm amazed this place hasn't gone up in flames yet. It reeks of sweat and smoke and alcohol, the stench so strong my eyes water, and when I take a step forward the floor sticks beneath my feet. Somehow, I manage not to look down.

It was mostly quiet out on the streets, but there are at least a good twenty people in here, most of them Eratians, no doubt spending what little coin they have on dice and wine.

We wind through the tables, in and out of snippets of conversation.

"The catch has been bad for weeks…"

"I don't know what's going on in that man's head sometimes…"

"Heard the Bandit broke right into the Acropolis and stole from the magistrate himself."

I stop. The Acropolis, that's in the City of Scholars. It's the central Scriptorium, the one all the others report back to. The ruling seat of the magistrate.

I look at the two people at the table beside me, a man and a woman, hunched over their drinks.

The man scoffs. "The Bandit is nothing but a story."

"He isn't a story." The woman thunks her mug down. "He's the greatest thief alive."

"Karis." Zara grabs my arm and yanks me along. "Stop gawking."

I scowl at her and pull my arm out of her grip. "Who were they talking about? Who's this Bandit?"

"A thief in the City of Scholars, just like they said."

"That's it? That's all you know?"

"What more do you expect?"

"Well, he's a criminal. You're a pirate."

I say it to annoy her, but she just grins. "I did see him in action. Once. He was pretty incredible."

"What did he do?"

She smirks. "Sorry. That's confidential. You know, for us criminals and pirates."

With that parting shot, she leaves me behind. I glare after her. I keep thinking I've just about grasped Zara, and I keep discovering that I don't understand her at all.

We go to a table in the corner. It's already occupied, by two boys with dirt packed in the creases of their skin and beneath their nails. They open their mouths as we come up, but Kocha pulls out his dagger and in the same movement slams the blade into the tabletop so hard it quivers. The boys' mouths click shut and they scurry off. Effective.

"You're going to wreck your knives doing that," Zara says.

Kocha frees his blade. "Yes, Captain."

We take our seats, me next to Alix. Kocha and Zara on the other side. It's only once I'm down that I realize there's only one place left for Dane: right next to Zara.

She grins as she pats the chair next to her. "Normally I wouldn't give a soldier boy the seat of honor, but I suppose for you I can make an exception."

Dane tenses, and I'm opening my mouth to interject,

when his shoulders settle back and he arches a brow. "Well," he says, his tone smooth, "I'll try to rise to the occasion."

Zara laughs, throaty and full. I smile, relieved Dane's gotten a bit of his fighting spirit back.

Someone, I assume the barkeep from her thick apron, winds toward us, squeezing her considerable girth through the crowd with practiced ease. Her hair is streaked with gray and piled atop her head in a messy bun. She looks as if she could snap my wrist with a flick of her little finger. "Ah, if it isn't the captain of the *Crimson Streak*. Wasn't expecting you so soon after your last visit."

Zara smiles. "Well, business comes as it comes."

"What can I get for you and your crew?"

Dane opens his mouth, but Zara speaks first. "A round for us, and something extra for you."

So quickly I barely see it, a slip of parchment passes between them. The barkeep gives Zara a cracked-tooth grin and sidles back to the counter.

Zara looks over at Kocha. "Go check if we have any packages to pick up."

"Yes, Captain." He leaves, back out the door we first came through.

I lean across the table and in as civil a voice as I can manage, say, "What package is this?"

Zara waves her hand. "You don't have to worry about that. It's my business, and Kocha can deal with it. Right now, we're waiting to see where exactly my particular friend is."

I narrow my eyes. I would not have agreed to come if I knew Zara would be running shady deals. I avoided things like that on the streets and I don't want to get swept up in that sort of trouble now.

The barkeep comes back with our drinks, as well as a note for Zara, which she quickly hides in her palm. Whatever it says, she looks pleased. At least that makes one of us.

"Well, well, now. If it isn't the pirate queen and her little crew of misfits."

The tables around us go quiet. I look up and see a man standing there, his face twisted into a drunken sneer. His chiton is stained and dirty and still smells of fish. A dockworker, if I had to guess. Zara's back is to him and despite the man's declaration, she simply lifts her drink and takes another swallow.

Pirate queen. I haven't heard any of her crew call her that. But looking at her now, sitting there so easily, with a wild glint in her eyes, I can see it.

Dane moves to get up, but Zara puts her hand on his arm. "Calm down, soldier boy." She turns, one arm slung over the back of her chair. "You got a problem with me, Lycus?"

"Yeah, I do actually. Last time you was here, you ran off with my boat hands."

Some of the men at a nearby table leer at us, but Zara grins. "Let's just say Ava and Finn were looking for alternate employment, and I offered it."

I frown. Ava and Finn used to live here? In a place like this?

"You didn't have no right," Lycus spits. "I demand you return—"

Zara stands. The movement is slow, but it reminds me somehow of the snakes I used to see on Tallis, sunning themselves on the rocks. Only slow until they struck. "Ava and Finn are part of my crew. No one touches my crew."

Lycus goes for the crude knife hanging from his belt. Zara's foot whips out, cracking him across the knee. The man hisses as his leg crumples. Before he can catch himself, Zara bashes him in the side of the head with her mug, hard. He falls to the floor, unconscious. The entire fight didn't last more than a few breaths.

Zara sighs, wiping flecks of ale off her sleeve. "Waste of a good drink," she mutters.

Dane, who'd leaped to his own feet, stares at her. And for the first time since we joined this crew, his contempt slips off his face. In its place is interest I know all too well. I saw it again and again on Tallis, for what seemed like his weekly dalliances.

I snort into my mug.

She's going to eat him alive.

A man walks up to the counter as the noise in the room returns to normal. He whispers something in the barkeep's ear and she looks over at Zara, giving a subtle nod.

"Well, that's us," Zara says, her voice low. "Follow me."

She leads us, not back to the front door but to one off of the side. It lets out into a small storage cupboard. Shelves line both walls, stocked with dusty old bottles, some filled, some empty, and crates of food that, judging from their smell, are long past their prime. The only other door is at the far end and, from what I can make out through the bent shutter on the window next to it, leads outside. It smells so thickly of dust and decay I can feel it clogging up my throat.

The shelves only allow a small aisle down the center

of the storeroom but it's currently blocked by a crate. On that crate is the oldest man I've ever laid eyes on. He looks Eratian, his white hair so thin it's barely more than wisps, his hands covered in liver spots. His head is down and I think he must be sleeping but then he looks up at us and the brightness in his eyes defies the rest of his frail, worn body. He wears a chiton and himation, both thick considering the season.

There's something I almost recognize about him, a sharp intelligence and quiet pride that I saw in so many on Tallis.

Zara steps forward and gestures to the man. "Everyone, meet Scriptmaster Leuwin."

15

ALIX

Scripmaster Leuwin. He's one of them. I stare at Zara. My whole life I've been warned to stay away from Scriptmasters. Now she's led us right to one. "You've taken us to a Scriptmaster?" I rasp.

The man raises a shaking hand. "Please, don't be afraid. That was in another life, one I do not wish to remember."

He looks me up and down and I'm tensing at being studied like that when he murmurs, "Astonishing. Never in my life would I have believed that someone like you would be possible."

Someone. Not something, but someone. Surprised, I look deeper into his eyes. There's a kindness there so like my father a pain lances through my chest.

The man pulls his himation tighter around his frail body. "Zara's note said you had something to show me. Some questions you want answering."

I nervously finger the edge of my himation. I don't know if I can trust this man, if it's naive of me to want to simply because he reminds me of my father. However, the only other option would be to give up, and that I'm not ready for. I step toward him, pushing my sleeve up and revealing the damaged line.

Master Leuwin reaches into his pocket and pulls out a thin pair of gold spectacles. He settles them on his nose before leaning in. The posture is strangely reminiscent of a bird cocking its head.

"Fascinating," he murmurs. "Absolutely fascinating."

"Do you know what they are?" I ask.

He touches a tangle of undamaged runes close to my elbow. "I believe these might be *think*... Up here, this looks like the sequence for *choose*." His fingers trace near my shoulder, where the damage is the worst. "It's hard to tell with the amount of damage but these... I think they might be *remember*."

Think...choose...remember... Perhaps that means we were right before. "Could those runes... I mean would it be possible for them to form something like a memory?"

Master Leuwin looks at me, his eyes enlarged by his spectacles. "Where is that question coming from?"

"My mind must come from somewhere. Much like these runes, my memory's been damaged."

Master Leuwin brushes the lines with his fingers. "These runes are so far beyond anything that's been studied for centuries I'm not sure anyone alive could find out the answer to that question. It is possible, though. The Script is very powerful, and it's only made more powerful with Script ink."

Script ink.

Those words bring a faint strand of memory pulsing against my thoughts, the same as when I read about the Automaton Heart. They're important, only I don't remember why.

Karis looks between me and Master Leuwin, confused. "What's Script ink?"

"They really don't teach you much in the Scriptorium, do they?" Zara says.

A blush touches Karis's neck.

"Zara, why don't you show them?" Master Leuwin says gently. "It may be easier for them to understand that way."

Zara fishes a chain out from beneath her tunic. Dangling from its end is a small golden ball, imprinted with runes no larger than a thumbnail. It glows in the dim storeroom like a miniature sun. "This is Script ink."

As soon as I see it, I feel that tug in my chest. That's it. That's what's been so familiar to me about Zara. The energy I've been feeling didn't come from her at all. "That necklace. All this time I felt drawn to you and that was why."

"That doesn't surprise me," Master Leuwin says. "Script ink is what allowed automatons to be made in the first place. You have some inside of you right now, in your seal."

I stare at him. Shards of memory piece back together in my head, jagged fragments of words and lessons from my father. Script ink… I was made with Script ink?

"Wait," Dane says. "I thought the runes were what made the automatons."

"The runes of the Script do have some power in and of themselves," Master Leuwin says. "Automatons, though, have always needed something more. Have you never wondered why Eratia was the only country to make automatons?" He looks at Dane and at Karis.

She shifts uncomfortably. "I guess I just assumed our runes were different here." She bites her lip. "Stronger here."

I think back to what Wreska had said earlier on the *Streak*, that Eratian runes were only ever used for one thing. For strength. To build automatons. It's true. I remember the way my books and scrolls had talked of automatons. They were the pride and joy of Eratia: proof of just how powerful our nation was.

"Runes are different no matter where you go. I've seen places where runes are carved into clay and stone, into wood and metal. I have even heard of a country that uses ice. No matter what a nation's runes look like, though, or what medium they are carved into, all Scripts all over the world are the same strength. Automatons are the one exception. They are the most powerful weapons to ever come out of Scriptwork, and they have only ever been able to be created here. It's because of this." He taps Zara's pendant. "Script ink connects the runes in the deepest way to the Script. It makes them stronger. It's why the ink is sometimes called automaton's blood."

I brush aside the wrapped edges of my tunic and touch my seal, ridged and warm and shimmering gold. Looking at it makes me feel as if I can sense the ink humming through my metal body. Is that all my mind is in the end? A by-product of this golden blood? I don't want to believe that.

"But at the Scriptorium, they never said…" Karis begins, then stops. "Why haven't we heard any of this?"

Zara snorts. "Probably because the Scriptorium doesn't want anyone to know they don't have it anymore. As long as people believe that at any moment they could unlock the secrets of the automatons again, they retain at least an echo of their power."

"If they don't have it, who does?" Dane asks.

"Script ink is everywhere and in everything," Master Leuwin says. "In the air, the ground, the water. Even in us. All Scriptwork from all cultures rely on it to work their runes. However, it was our ancestors who uncovered the alchemical secrets of refining Script ink, so that it could be used directly, seen and stored." He cups Zara's pendant, the glow spreading out over his wrinkled skin. "Refined Script ink is almost like caught sunlight. It disperses if it doesn't have anything to contain it. Vessels like this pendant were created to hold it. From there, the ink could then be transferred into the seals of tomes and automatons. However, most of the ink has been lost, as have the secrets to refining it. No one has managed to refine more, or to re-create the vessels."

"But what happened to all the old Script ink they used to have?" Karis asks. "Surely it didn't just disappear."

"It was destroyed," Master Leuwin says, "over two hundred years ago. If the stories whispered in the dark are to be believed…" He looks back at me, and somehow I know what he's about to say even before he says it. "Master Theodis destroyed it."

My father. I try to get my thoughts into some coherent

shape. "My father. You're saying that my father…" Another realization hits me like a physical blow: why Zara's necklace looks so familiar. I reach out to touch it but stop. "That glowing light I remember from before… You don't think…?"

"That it was a vessel?" Zara asks. "Yes. That's why I brought you here, Alix. That's the mystery I'm trying to solve. This necklace doesn't have much Script ink inside of it. But if what you described is really a vessel like this one, it's the largest I have ever heard of. Large enough to contain all the Script ink that would be needed to power every single automaton that still stands. The magistrate would have access to them all. We cannot allow that to happen."

Every single automaton. I don't even want to think about that, of them all becoming animated again and wreaking their destruction once more. My father might have believed that automatons were once built for good, but he was also very clear on what the Scriptorium used them for. I still remember the stories he told of how much the other nations feared and hated us. Of how much they would fear and hate me if they ever saw me. I don't want to go back to that.

"You were there, Alix," Zara says. "You said your father asked you to do something. So maybe one of those runes on your skin will have the answer."

I look down at my runes again, curling my hand over their ridges as if I can blot them out. Maybe they do have answers, but I can't read them anymore. Maybe I never could. Did I used to know this? Did my father ever tell me?

It's the first time I've ever truly doubted him, and the

thought sends waves of guilt crashing through me. If it was important, he would have told me. I know he would have.

"Alix," Master Leuwin says quietly. "Do you remember anything else about the light? Anything at all?"

Already, everything they're telling me feels too much, as if it's a weight pressing me down. Only they're all looking at me, waiting, and this might be my only chance. "I remember running to it with my father and it pulsing in the darkness. I remember it had a surface. I placed my hands on it and its music crashed into my head." I squeeze my eyes shut. "I remember... I remember it going dark." My eyes fly open again. "It went dark. That means..."

I can't say the words. So, Karis says them for me. "You were the one who destroyed it."

My head throbs. Is that what my father wanted me to do, destroy the automaton's blood so the Scriptorium could never use it again? I think of what we found in the Hall of Records back on Tallis. That record spoke of something called the Automaton Heart, which my father destroyed. Which perhaps I destroyed. Was that the golden light I'm remembering?

I step toward the man, desperate. "Master Leuwin, please. You need to fix my runes. If you do, maybe I'll remember everything."

He shakes his head, his hands trembling in his lap. "I'm sorry, but I dare not. Even if I had the strength, my mind is not what it used to be, because of the Scriptorium." A deep pain enters his eyes.

Zara glances away and I wonder what they did to him. I

don't ask, though. The last thing I'd want is to inflict any more harm on the man.

"If those runes truly are your memory," he continues, "there is no telling what the slightest mistake might do to you. I could not risk it. Perhaps you may someday find another Scriptmaster to fix them."

I don't want to wait until someday. I feel so lost without my memories, as if they're a hole torn out of the center of my life and now all I can do is hover around its edges. I need my memories to tell me who I am.

Dane straightens, his back tense.

"Dane?" Karis asks. "What is it?"

He holds up his hand. Listens. His face darkens. "Soldiers."

16

ALIX

Someone cries out in the distance, a keen of panicked noise. Zara crosses over to the window. "It's the Scriptorium. They're searching the houses."

Karis pales. "Searching for what?"

Zara looks around at us, and for the first time since meeting her, worry comes into her eyes. She doesn't need to say the words; they're searching for us.

No, not for us. For me.

"I'm sorry," Zara says, clasping Master Leuwin's hand. "For bringing them here."

He shakes his head. "I'll tell the others. For now, you and your friends must go."

"Wait, others?" Karis asks.

Zara waves her hand. "Later."

Karis clamps her lips shut, but she doesn't look happy about it.

Zara pulls her dagger from her belt. "Everybody, get ready. The soldiers are creating chaos out there and that'll give us some cover. Stay quiet and stay together."

"Captain," Dane says. "I should be armed for this."

She doesn't say anything, and he takes a step closer. When he speaks, his voice is softer. "Please, Captain."

Zara studies Dane, their eyes speaking a language I don't understand, then she pulls out a dagger from beneath her shirt. She hands it to him. "Don't make me regret this." She draws another one and holds it out to Karis.

Karis takes the knife, testing its weight uneasily in her palm.

Zara looks at me but I shake my head. "I don't need a knife." I don't particularly want something that will let me do more damage.

"Good luck," Master Leuwin says.

Zara nods at him and opens the door. From far off someone screams. I flinch, trying not to let it drag me back to a night two hundred years ago, when the only one running was me.

Zara hovers in the doorway, watching. "It's clear."

We dart away from the tavern, down one of the side streets. As soon as I'm out I smell the acrid smoke, sharp enough to even cut off the stink from the docks. Ash spirals in the air and everything has taken on a smoky, hazy quality. Fire. I can't see the flames, but something is burning.

There are more people out now, frantic and fleeing. Two women dash past us and I don't see what they're running from until a door bangs open down the street and four soldiers step out.

They don't look like the soldiers I saw on Tallis. Those had red sashes imprinted with the Scriptorium's sigil of an open book with the *knowledge* rune floating above it. These soldiers have black sashes, and their sigil has flames licking from the pages of the book, wreathing the rune. One of the soldiers has a torch and he lifts it up to the eaves. Fire catches instantly on the straw, a blast of heat against my metal skin.

"Back," Zara hisses.

We slip down another street, away from the smoke and the screams, even though it feels so wrong to run and to leave these people.

"Who are those soldiers?" Karis demands, voice low.

Zara's mouth is a thin, harsh line. "The magistrate's personal forces."

Karis's eyes go wide. "What?"

The magistrate. The most powerful man in the empire. He's sent his men here.

If they find us… If they trap me…

I cannot let that happen.

Zara leads us down the shadowy streets, each one looking like the last. Behind us the din and the stench slowly dim. We must be getting close to the edge of the village by now.

"Stop!"

I whip around. Three of the magistrate's soldiers stand behind us. One of them raises a gun, the runes on it glinting like fire.

"Run!" Zara shouts.

A crack splits the air. The shot goes into the building a foot to my left, clay and straw peppering my skin.

Karis dashes down a side street. I follow to provide cover. My skin can stop bullets. Hers can't.

A hand snakes out from the dark and grabs her arm. It's one of the magistrate's men. He knocks her to the ground, her knife clattering away.

"Karis!" I slam into the man, tackling him to the ground. He twists out of my grasp and rolls to his feet.

Our eyes meet. His widen.

"You…" He steps back, glaring. "You're not being controlled by a tome. How?"

In that moment of hesitation, I move. I throw a punch, aiming for the man's temple, just hard enough to knock him out, but he jerks his hand up. He's holding something and before I can stop myself, my hand touches it. Every rune on my arm flares bright and the limb falls limply to my side.

I stare at the small bronze seal the soldier holds, the *stop* rune cut into it. The man advances on me, an ugly sneer on his face. Panicked, I stumble back, trying to reach my arm. Behind him Karis, still on the ground, scrabbles for something I can't make out.

The soldier lunges, this time aiming for my seal.

There's a thunk and the soldier freezes, his arm still extended. I don't understand what's happened until he tilts, falling to the ground as I scramble out of the way.

Karis stands there, a rock clasped in her hand. She stares down at the man as if she isn't quite sure what she did.

"Is he…?" She trails away.

The soldier lets out a moan.

"Not dead," I say.

Karis stoops down and picks up the seal the soldier

dropped and then we're running again, away from the soldier's prone body, even though I know what this means. He'll tell. The magistrate will know.

We break out from the houses, back out into the scrubland, and a sharp whistle splits the air.

Dane and Zara stand there, not too far away.

"Hurry," Zara calls.

The path before us has been swallowed by the dark, making it treacherous. I'm half afraid that when we finally reach the water, the dinghy will have disappeared, but it's still there. Kocha is already inside. Kocha, and a young girl, clutching at his waist. I barely get a glance of a small, scared face, before she buries deeper into Kocha's tunic.

"Captain," Kocha says. "You made it."

"Did you doubt it?"

Dane unties our boat and pushes it off, clambering inside as it pulls away. Despite the child still clinging to him, Kocha grabs the oars and takes us out. I look back over my shoulder. I can't see the village past the cliffs but I can make out the thin trails of smoke, and a scream carries through the night.

We brought those soldiers here. I brought them here.

Guilt tears me apart. This happened because of me. I caused harm, like automatons always do.

Now all I can hope is that most of the people we left behind were able to run.

17

KARIS

We're barely over the railing when Zara shouts at her crew to cast off. She pulls her ledger from her pocket and writes a rune in it. The sails flare so suddenly that I grab a crate to stop myself from falling.

Ash coats the back of my blazing throat and burns scald my skin but I join the others, throwing myself into the work so I don't have to think about anything else. Not the screaming and the cries of children we just left. Not the homes so shoddy they didn't stand a chance against the flames. I never wanted to get involved in the lives of others.

Caring. Zara's voice in my head mocks me.

She's wrong.

We streak out over open water, racing against the dawn that fights to lighten up the sky. Dane and Alix work beside me, and as the hours go by, I see Alix beginning to be able to flex his fingers. I still have no idea what that soldier did, but at least it wasn't permanent. My own fingers brush the seal now in my belt pouch.

"You three." Zara comes toward us across the deck. "Time to take a break."

I straighten, my back protesting, and push my fingers through my hair, only to get a handful of ash.

"Is there any sign of a Scriptorium ship, Captain?" Dane asks.

Zara shakes her head. "Not yet."

My tired gaze wanders around the deck and lands on Kocha. He's still with that little girl, kneeling before her as she sits on a crate, head down. Her hair reminds me of straw, so thin and dry. The ends are ragged, cut short beneath her earlobes. She's so skinny it's hard to tell her age but she can't be older than ten. There's a detached glaze to her eyes.

"Who is she?" I ask.

Zara follows my gaze. "She's the package Kocha went to get."

Those words are as close as Zara's ever gotten to telling us her crew's secret. I need to know what's going on here. What all of them aren't saying. Why her crew has runes inked into their skin. How Zara got a pendant with Script ink. I'm sick and tired of the lies and half-truths. She kept us on board because she wanted answers. I want answers, too.

"Captain," I say, "you have to tell us what's going on. You owe us that."

Zara's eyes narrow. "No, Karis. This is my ship and I don't owe you anything."

A flash of temper lights in my chest. I didn't leave the

Scriptorium behind to put my life in the hands of yet someone else who won't tell me anything. I'm opening my mouth to snap back when Alix says quietly, "Please, Captain. We just want to understand."

We both stop. He looks tired, ash and dirt smudging his runes. But there's still this hopeful light flickering like the flames in his eyes, refusing to dim.

Zara sighs, something relenting in her expression. "The truth isn't pretty," she says. "And there's no unlearning it once it's out there."

Life hasn't given me the privilege of ignoring hard truths. "I don't care," I say.

She studies us for another long moment, and then with a shrug she turns toward her cabin. "Come with me."

Zara takes us back to the front room and gestures for us to sit at the table. Ava and Finn follow us, taking up spots by their captain's chair. Zara stares across the cabin, fiddling with her pendant, and that makes me even more uneasy than if she'd been glaring me down. Zara isn't the type to avoid someone's eye.

"I ought to tell you my story first," she finally says. "I grew up far from here, in Ariza. My parents were scholars there, experts of the Arizan Script."

"What was it like?" Alix asks eagerly. I forgot how little of the world Alix has seen. Not that I've exactly seen much of it. "Your home, I mean."

"Ariza? It's a country of hills and highlands, of sandstone and a night sky that goes on forever." Zara's voice takes on a faraway tone, almost wistful. It makes her sound so soft I almost don't recognize her.

She shakes her head, her tone going hard. "Then the Scriptorium in the City of Scholars invited both of them to go there. My parents were experts at Elder Imari's work, which influenced early Arizan and Eratian runes. The Scriptorium wanted to see what they could make of the automatons. At first my parents settled into their work well, but then I noticed how troubled they were becoming. In Ariza, the Script is used differently. It's a tool all have access to, that makes people's lives better. Our cloth and our weaving reflect us all. The Script is not a power to be manipulated by the few who have money and a position. I still remember the arguments I overheard, not just between my parents but also with other Scriptmasters who would visit our villa. They didn't agree with what the Scriptorium was using their Scriptwork for.

"Then one day my parents brought this home." She dangles the pendant from her fingers. The light of it casts harsh shadows against the planes of her face. "Most of the Script ink was destroyed all those centuries ago, but some vessels survived. I still don't know where the Scriptorium found this or what they'd been planning with it, but it was bad enough that my parents decided to steal it. We tried to run, but the soldiers caught up to us. I got away. My parents didn't. They were hauled to the Magistrate's Library, and they never came out."

She looks at Ava, standing nearby, who pulls her sleeve up, not just past her wrist but all the way to her elbow. Runes create a track down her skin. But unlike Alix, where each rune is unique, every one of Ava's says *obey*. They all look different, as if written by many hands, or maybe one that just couldn't get it right.

"That's what the Magistrate's Library is," Zara says, and for once her tone hides nothing. It's cold and dark. "They didn't have enough Script ink left to make more automatons or to wake the old ones up, so the magistrate decided to see if he could control people with runes. He takes criminals, rebels, anyone he views as lesser, and he inks these runes into their skin. All to see if he can make the perfect, obedient soldiers."

Horror creeps like ice water over my skin. Matthias. I think of him. Of that easy smile he had even after our parents were gone. Of the curiosity that always won over his common sense. And they sent him there, to ink those runes into his skin.

"But people can escape, right?" I lean forward in my chair, the wood digging into my palms.

Zara nods. "There are cracks in the system. Ava managed to steal a key and get out. Finn found her and the two of them hid out on that island until we came across them. Others are taken out with the magistrate's soldiers to test them in the wild. As far as I know, the runes have never worked, but some escape that way, too. We try to find those people, to get them to safety. That hideout you first stumbled into is one of our pickup places." She looks across the cabin, and past the hardness in her eyes there's something else: rage. Choking rage. "They don't always make it out in time, though. I've seen people come out of there who refuse to eat, to speak, to sleep. That's what happened to that little girl's father. He managed to get out. And he died anyway."

I'm having a hard time breathing. It's not rage I feel. It's despair. Matthias could be in that place right now, while all this time I was living on a safe little island. All those years I wasted, because I wasn't smart enough to find a way to him. He could already be gone.

As soon as I have the thought, I reject it. I'd know if my brother was dead. I don't know how, but the world would feel different if that happened. Matthias is a survivor.

"Why are people allowing this?" Dane's voice shakes. "There must be some who oppose the man."

"Not many people even know," Zara says. "It's his personal project. His secret project."

The way Zara is speaking... "Is he the one who actually does the work?" I whisper.

Ava looks away. And there's something about seeing her shy away like that that fractures my chest.

"Yes," Zara says. "He is."

This is it, the great secret behind Zara and her crew. What they're really doing. The silence in the cabin is so thick it's oppressive. I've always hated the Scriptorium and the magistrate. But I never thought that even he would be capable of something like this. Now he's hunting us. I've never felt fear like this before: a cold, slimy thing coiling around my lungs, suffocating me.

"You two should consider yourselves lucky," Zara says. "If they didn't think you'd be of use in the Tallis Scriptorium, you might have ended up there." She shakes her head. "People aren't meant to have commands written into their skin."

Alix glances down, running his fingers over the runes on his arm. Remembering the bronze seal in my belt pouch, I pull it out.

Zara frowns. "What's that?"

I slide it across the table to her, as far away from Alix as I can. Zara picks it up and rubs it with her fingers.

"That soldier had it," I say. "The one who—"

"The one who attacked us," Alix cuts in.

I look at him, startled. The fire in his eyes flares, and I'm reminded of those moments on Tallis when he just didn't seem to be able to control himself.

"The seal knocked my arm out. Because I'm not a person. I'm just a thing that has to obey commands."

Alix stands up so suddenly his chair falls, hitting the floor with a clatter. I open my mouth but Alix is already gone.

18

ALIX

I stalk over to the railing. Aiken and Het give me startled looks as I pass. Fear lights their eyes, fear that I thought they'd almost lost when it came to me. That should bother me. Only the anger and pain claw up my throat, shiver down my limbs, and I can't stop it.

Zara was right; people aren't meant to have commands written into their skin. Except I'd be nothing without my runes. Nothing but dead metal. These commands are all that I am. I reach the railing, wrapping my hands around it so hard the wood splinters beneath my palms. It's all so breakable. This ship. Everyone on this ship.

And me. I might be the most breakable one of all.

"Alix?"

Karis steps up to the railing. I hadn't heard her follow me across the deck. Her voice is soft. It makes me want to

crack, but then I don't know how I'd put myself back together. "Are you all right?"

"Am I all right?" I repeat, my voice tight. I touch the
rune near my shoulder. "If I'm not, it's only because of this."

"Your runes don't mean that your feelings are any less
real, Alix."

I spin on her. "Even when you had that bracelet on, you
didn't have to obey it. You could still choose what to do.
When someone writes in my tome, my body moves without
me telling it. My mind is trapped inside, screaming, and I
can't do anything about it." My voice rises, and I can't stop
it. I don't want to stop it. "I don't know what I am, Karis.
If I was made to be real or some puppet."

The last time I spoke to Karis like this, we were in that
cave, and I hadn't known her, only that she looked small
and scared. She's scared now, too.

Perhaps I want that. Then she'll leave. Being alone has
to be better than standing here, letting her see that in the
end, I'm only an automaton, with *obey* etched into my back.

She looks at me, and when she speaks her voice quavers,
but it's still determined. "Alix, you're not a puppet. Your
father didn't make you as a puppet."

"Then why did he give me a tome?" I yell.

Those words, which I've never let myself say, slip out
before I can catch them.

Karis stills. "What?"

My anger leaks away, leaving only black despair. I slump
over the railing. "If he didn't want me to be a puppet, why
did he make my tome?"

Silence stretches between us. I'm sure that where my

temper didn't scare her off, that admittance will. Who would want to be friends with someone like me? Something like me?

Karis's footsteps come closer. She presses a hand against my shoulder, warm despite the night air. It reminds me of when we first met. Her touch brought me back then, too.

"Did you ever ask him?" she asks quietly.

How are you supposed to ask a question when the answer might destroy you? "No." I was always too scared. Scared he'd admit it was a mistake and that I'd hate him for it. Even more scared that he'd admit it wasn't a mistake at all.

The words were always there, underlying every conversation we ever had, every moment we ever shared, but it was the one question I was never brave enough to ask.

Now I'll never know.

"Alix," Karis says. "No one who thinks and acts and feels like you do, who cares like you do, could possibly not be real. Different doesn't mean lesser. We're here for you. Me and Dane and even the captain and her crew. And maybe it's out there. A way to protect you from your tome. We could find it if we just look for it."

I raise my head and meet her eyes. They're steady. Stubborn. Passionate.

She didn't leave. She's still here, standing beside me. I'm not sure I want to give my heart that hope of freedom, when I don't know if it will ever come true, but I feel it anyway. Throbbing inside of me like the heartbeat I don't have.

I want it. I want it more than I can bear.

"Alix."

We both turn at Zara's voice. I shift, awkward. Having Karis see me like that was one thing. I'm embarrassed Zara saw it, too. I'm opening my mouth to apologize when she tosses me something. I fumble but catch it and stare down at the leather-bound volume in my hands, my seal flaring in my chest.

My tome.

Zara grins. "You don't have to look that surprised."

"But...why?" I ask.

"I shouldn't have taken it from you in the first place. I shouldn't have used it. I didn't realize who you were when we first met, and that's on me. I'm sorry." She nods at Karis. "She's right. You're more than those runes in your skin. All my crew are, and being made of metal doesn't change that. Don't ever let them define you on their terms. This is your life to live."

My life. I want to believe those words desperately, that no matter what I am or how I started, that what I have right now is mine. Standing here beside them, on this ship, I am so far from anything I imagined possible. For the first time I think it is.

Out of the corner of my eye I glimpse the figurehead, the woman with the crimson rune. "Captain? The rune on the figurehead, what does it mean?"

Zara grins. "It means freedom."

Freedom. How fitting.

The grin slips off Zara's face. She strides to the railing.

A ship cuts toward us, and as its black sails unfurl I see the sigil. The *knowledge* rune wreathed in flame.

They've found us.

Zara takes off across the deck. "Everyone to their stations!" she shouts. "Het, Ava, man the riggings. Kocha, grab the cannons!"

A bell rings out, and Karis and I race to our positions, dodging the crewmen bursting out of the hold, the deck turned into chaos in a moment. Dane appears beside us, hauling rope. I look back over my shoulder at the other ship. It's gaining.

"We can't outrun her, Captain," Finn says. "She's too fast."

I clench my fingers tighter around my tome, feeling even more vulnerable now that it's in my hands.

Zara points toward a chain of low islands clustered closely together coming up on our port side. "We'll lose them in there."

Finn's pale skin goes even whiter. "Captain, that'll be a tight squeeze for us."

"And even tighter for them. We're more maneuverable than they are." She raises her voice. "Hard to port!"

Aiken cranks the wheel and the deck shifts as we make a sharp turn. I stumble into a pile of crates. The rocks are coming up close. Too close. We aren't going to make it.

"Brace yourselves!" Zara writes in her ledger and the sails flare with light as they twist against their riggings. The wind catches them at their new angle, jerking the bow of the *Streak* to port.

There's a horrible grinding noise as we scrape the rocks to our left, cold spray sweeping over the deck.

"Wreska!" Zara shouts.

Wreska pulls out a scroll and dashes off some runes. The

iron implants on that side of the ship stretch, strengthening the weakened wood. Everything rattles as we scrape against the rock.

Then we're clear. Someone shouts from the magistrate's ship. I look back. Zara was right. They won't make that turn. They're not even trying to make that turn.

The magistrate's ship runs a parallel course to ours, still out on open water. Something's wrong. All we need is another channel off our port side and we'll be able to slip out of the other ship's reach. They shouldn't be risking that.

Then I see the cannons.

"Get down!" I shout.

I grab Karis and Dane and fling us all to the ground as a boom rips through the air. A cannonball screams above our heads and crashes through the deck.

"Incoming!" Aiken shouts. There's another boom and a cannonball slams through the foremast.

With a massive crack, it snaps. Kocha drops to his knees and writes in charcoal on the deck itself. Gold flares beneath our feet, racing across the deck, as the pole shudders. For a moment I think it worked, but then the mast falls, ripping a hole in the mainsail on its way. I fling myself over Karis as spears of wood drive down all over the deck.

Dane is already back on his feet, scanning the waters. I stagger up. Wood and cloth and iron litter the deck. Zara stands at the wheel now, struggling to keep us under control.

The cannons from the other ship have stopped firing as the magistrate's vessel slips down a larger channel among the islands, coming after us now that we're wounded.

"Captain!" Dane shouts. "Over there!"

He points to two larger islands with a narrow channel between them. It's not quite bridged by the dual half arches of stone reaching out to one another over the water. It must have been one island once, until the waves wore away at the stone arch, a little more every year.

"We'd slow down too much," Wreska yells back. "They'd be right on top of us."

"So, we bring the arches down behind us," Dane says. "Block them from following us."

Zara's eyes gleam. "To port!"

The ship turns but this time I'm ready, balancing as the deck rocks beneath my feet.

"We need a cannon back here!" Zara calls.

Two of the men slowly start hauling one across the deck. I run to them and grab it, pulling it over to the railing. The runes on its barrel hum beneath my hands and vicious music spills into my head. I grit my teeth against the sound as I position the cannon, dragging another to the opposite end of the deck.

The arch is getting closer. So is the magistrate's ship. Close enough that I can hear the crewman on it shouting and see their mouths as they form the words.

A shadow falls over the deck as we pass beneath the arches.

"Fire!" Zara shouts.

Both cannons explode in unison. They hit true and the arches crumble into the ocean, the world dissolving into a spray of wet and cold that obscures everything.

We shoot through, leaving the magistrate's ship trapped in our wake.

19

ALIX

The *Crimson Streak* limps through the water. Two of her three masts are gone. She has four holes punched through her deck and sides, each a gaping wound.

Her crew almost looks as bad, exhaustion heavy beneath their eyes, more than one with some slipshod healing job. In the two days since we were attacked, no one has slept much. I don't need sleep, but going this long with only scant breaks has given even me a sluggishness to my thoughts I'm not used to.

I grasp the mast in my hands, and as everyone stands clear, I heave it up. It's brutally heavy, the sheer weight making my feet carve into the wood of the deck. I grit my teeth and push harder, levering it up from the deck, step by labored step.

"Almost there," Kocha says, his hands coming to rest next to mine, guiding them.

I shake from the effort as the mast finally sways upright,

precariously balanced on its broken, bottom half. Kocha dashes off a rune like a whorl of wood and the jagged splinters twine around each other like snakes. A whisper of the music of his runes, a thin strain of a flute, pulses softly beneath my hands. I've never seen Scriptwork mend something.

"Wreska!" Kocha calls, his voice strained.

She steps up to his side, a thick piece of iron in her hands. Karis holds it flat against the wood as Wreska writes a rune in her scroll. The metal warps, wrapping around the mast until it encircles it like a cuff.

The others step back. I timidly let go, my hands at the ready to catch it if it falls. It creaks ominously but then settles.

I sag in relief. When I saw the damage to the *Streak*, I was so sure there wasn't any chance of us making repairs quickly enough to get away. With the right Scriptwork, though, with all of us working together, perhaps there is.

"How goes it?" Zara asks, coming up behind us. A scratch crosses her temple. I wonder if in the chaos she's even noticed. Everyone else seems worn thin, but there's an energy to Zara that makes her look even more alert. It feels as if she's the only thing holding this crew together right now.

"It's not the strongest patch job," Kocha says. He sits on his haunches, his hands hanging limply between his knees and his face drawn. Wreska comes up beside him, resting a palm on the nape of his neck, and he leans into her. "But it's as good as I can manage. With any luck, it'll get us into port on Valitia."

Zara nods. "Good work. You two have earned yourself a break. Alix." She turns to me. "I take it you're still fresh?"

Physically, yes. Mentally, I'm waning. I can't stop, though. We only went to that island because of me. The Scriptorium only caught up to us because of me. I'm the one they want in the end. I nod.

"Then come with me. I have something I want you to help with."

I follow Zara, Karis trailing behind us. We go to the mainmast, which Kocha fixed first. The sail, now also repaired, is roughly laid out in front of it.

"All right," Zara says, "so here's the problem. See the line of runes there?" She points to a string of them that runs along the edge of the sail, the ends of the crimson threads twining into the ropes. "Normally these runes let me raise the sail. But thanks to our spat—"

"That was just a spat?" Karis mutters.

One of Zara's eyebrows twitches up. "Thanks to our spat, the pattern has been broken." She points to the edge of the sail, where a rip cuts through the line. "It's fixable, but that would take a long time, time we don't have. However, if there's a second person working the Script, we can each handle one end of the line and it won't matter."

I'm so tired, it takes me a long moment to catch her meaning. "Wait," I say. "This is what you want me to help you with?"

She nods. "I've taught some of my crew Arizan runes, but nothing at this level."

"Captain, I can't. My runes are Eratian." The Script on

me is bound to this country. To Eratian runes. I thought she realized that. "I can't use the Arizan—"

"You know about Script ink now," Zara says and I hear the firmness in her tone and, behind it, the first hint of weariness. She looks at me and there's the tiredness that she can't quite push back or hide any longer. She's as exhausted as the rest of us. She's simply better at hiding it. Captain or not, she shouldn't have to. "You have some inside of you. That's what all runes operate on, and it might mean you can use any of those runes. I need you to try this. If we can't get the sail up from the deck, we're going to need to fix all the riggings as well. And if we have to do that, we won't beat the magistrate's men into Valitia."

I hear the words she doesn't say. Some of her crew were once in the Magistrate's Library. If we don't get moving, they'll all end up back in that terrible place.

"Right." I shake out my hands and step closer to the sail. They're simply runes like I've worked dozens of times. That's all.

As I touch the fabric, the pounding of the drums echoes into my head. I try humming, but before I get the first note out, I know it won't work. I'm used to hearing melodies from runes, but this is pure rhythm, vibrant and energetic.

I pause and then cluck my tongue. It's difficult. The rhythm is so quick, and my tongue feels sluggish. I keep going. I find myself connecting with the thudding in my head, with what feels like vibrations beneath my finger-tips, as if I'm not simply hearing the rhythm but feeling it.

The cloth twitches. I'm so surprised I falter.

Karis's eyes widen. "Alix, you're doing it."

I am. The cloth is moving. In stops and starts, but it's moving.

Zara pulls out her ledger, a gleam in her eyes that makes her look more like her old self. She writes something and her end of the sail moves. I can hear her runes resounding in my head, a counter-rhythm mixing with my own. It's the first time I've done Scriptwork with someone else before. It thrills me.

The music leaps faster and I join it as the sail rises, sliding on its own along the ropes, making me shift my hands. Rhythm and excitement buzz beneath my skin. Faster. Faster. I don't want it to stop.

The sail reaches its top and the runes flare before quieting. The music fades away.

The sail. It's fixed. I was a part of that.

Wearied applause scatters over the deck. I turn. Other crew members have drifted closer—Aiken, Manaka, Camila—and for once there's no wariness in their faces. They look at me, relieved. As if I belong here, standing among them.

Zara nudges my shoulder with her own. "Looks like you are more than your runes."

I stare at her. My whole life I thought I was constrained to the runes carved into my skin. Yet the runes that I worked on those sails were not ones my father gave me.

They let me do something good.

Zara grins and strides away. "Now come on, let's do the other one."

20

——

KARIS

A dot appears on the horizon midway through the second week and we slip through the waves toward it. Valitia. I knew from the maps the Scriptmasters made us study how much larger it is than any other island in Eratia, but I hadn't understood until now what that really meant.

The island rising out of the ocean must be at least ten times the size of Tallis, and it touches the horizon on both sides as if it wants to swallow the waves. A sheltered bay nestles at its base, dotted with the colorful sails of fishing ships. Even from here I can see the fisherfolk rushing about on the decks, pulling in nets full of flopping, shining fish. There are larger vessels, too, military from the cannons on their decks, flying sails emblazoned with the Scriptorium seal. Alongside them are other ships, with Eural seals, Anderran seals. Maybe they're here for diplomatic purposes, but soldiers stand on their decks even now, their spears glinting in the sun.

Near the docks are houses not so different from that fishing village. And then rising above the refuse of the tiny buildings is the famed City of Scholars.

It's built in tiers, reaching toward the summit, each one blocked off by a wall. The lowest tier holds smaller but orderly homes, with white walls and red pottery tiles covering their roofs. Then come the villas. As the city continues upward the homes grow larger, nestled among the hills and surrounded by vast swathes of green. Up above there's a tier of what looks like government buildings, schools and libraries, all with soaring architecture, surrounding the bustling central agora.

There are automatons, too, dozens of them. Standing among the buildings, in the hills and fields. An army, no less terrifying for being frozen. Here, time was never allowed to bury them in dirt and rocks, and the sight of so many, all of them caught in the moment they stilled, chills me.

At the summit of it all stands the Acropolis. It's massive, a half dozen stories high and large enough to encompass the entire complex on Tallis. The marble is so polished and white it shines like a beacon beneath the sun.

The seat of the magistrate and the heart of the Scriptorium. It's mighty, imposing, and yet it's nothing compared to what towers before it.

The Colossus.

It's an automaton out of legend. According to the stories, the Scriptmasters of a magistrate long dead toiled for a hundred years and a day to make it: the largest automaton to ever walk. It's always stood sentinel before the Acropolis, guarding the line of the magistrates. Except for once, during a great sea battle between Eural and Eratia. Our navy was losing badly. Their ships had almost reached our shores. The magistrate at the time took the Colossus's tome and sent the beast out into the waters. The legend says that even in the deeps it stood high over the Eural ships. By the time it was through, all that was left was driftwood.

I know we're running away from the magistrate's men by running toward the magistrate himself. We're being cautious—Zara even had Alix help her switch out the sails and we won't get too close to the capital until nightfall. But I can't help but be worried about how poorly planned this might turn out to be. Not that we have a choice. My brother is here. Alix's answers are here. And with any luck, those chasing us won't have had a chance to communicate what they know back to the magistrate yet.

Besides, some risks you have to take.

Alix drifts to the railing. "It's so different," he murmurs. "So similar, yet so different."

The raw loss in his voice catches me off guard. I shift closer to him, bumping his arm with my own. "Where's your father's house?"

"Up in the second tier, around the curve of the hill."

"I'm looking forward to seeing it," I say. "I'm sure there's something left." I hope there's something left.

Alix shakes his head, staring out across the water. "I forgot how...imposing this city was. I lived in it my whole life, and I barely saw any of it."

It's hard seeing Alix down like this. I search for something that might make him feel better.

"You know, Matthias and I were originally from Heretis," I say. "It's not exactly Valitia, but it was still a large city. I think we knew every street in that place and there was this...wildness to it, I guess you could say. Simmering just beneath the civilized surface. A sort of heartbeat."

Alix is looking at me now, interest clear in his eyes. It's strange to think of my time on the street positively. But maybe, like anything else, there was some good mixed in with the bad. I search for one of those moments, to share with him. He doesn't have many memories of his own, but he can have one of mine.

"I remember a time, we were having some problems with a group of older boys. Eventually, we started hiding down by the docks, which Matthias hated because it smelled so bad. And soon we smelled like it, too." I grin. "One night we were hiding on this flat roof with all these baskets of slimy fish guts. We heard those boys in the street below us, and without even hesitating, Matthias grabbed a basket and dumped it on them."

Alix lets loose a bark of laughter, so loud he looks surprised that it came from his mouth. Which immediately sets me off laughing. A grin splits Alix's face. And I'm proud. That I could give that to him.

Finn comes up behind us, looking between the two of us, their eyebrows quirked. "You two. The captain wants to see you and the soldier in her quarters."

I stifle the laughter still bubbling in my throat as we follow Finn. We pick up Dane on the way, from where he was learning a dice game I'm sure his old masters wouldn't approve of.

Zara stands in the corner of her quarters, examining the knife on her belt, but as we step inside she turns and nods at us. "Good, you're here. Front and center."

We line up in the middle of the room.

"We'll be docking soon," Zara says. "So, it's time for all of you to get ready."

"What will happen when we get there, Captain?" I ask.

I wonder if this is when we say goodbye. Dane sneaks a glance at Zara. I've seen plenty of people infatuated with Dane. I'm not sure I've ever seen him truly infatuated with someone else. I never realized it would make him so adorably obvious.

"Well," Zara says, "that depends on you three."

I wait to see if she'll explain, but she doesn't. She certainly enjoys being cryptic. "Meaning?" I ask.

Zara leans back against the bookshelf. "The truth is, I haven't been entirely honest with you all."

I tense. Alix takes a small step back.

Zara holds up her hands. "I mean you no harm. Surely you know me well enough for that by now. I just thought it would be best if I waited to tell you this." She looks at me. "You want more answers about the Magistrate's Library, right?"

I give a wary nod.

"Well, there's someone in the city who knows more about that place than anyone. You could say she's a friend of mine. And I think she'd want to see you all."

"But...?" I say.

"You asked me whether or not there were those in the Scriptorium who didn't approve of what the magistrate is doing. And there are. She's one of them."

Alix shifts. "You're saying she's Scriptorium."

"I'm saying she's a Scriptmaster, a high-ranking one."

"You know we're currently trying to run away from Scriptmasters, right?" I say.

Zara grins. "Master Leuwin wasn't so bad, was he? And at least I didn't keep it a surprise until you met her."

I roll my eyes. "Yes, thank you for that."

"Look." She pushes off the bookcase. "I know what you're all thinking, but you have no idea what she's done for this city and for Eratia. Caused riots. Turned Scriptmasters away from the magistrate's cause. Stolen from the man himself. I trust her, with my life, and the life of my crew."

The idea of willingly going to see a Scriptmaster—one of the people who trapped me on Tallis for seven years—is not comforting.

But Zara has even more reasons to hate the Scriptorium than I do, and she trusts this person. And in a strange way, I've come to trust Zara. She's kept her word. She brought us here. She told us about the library.

"You want to see her, don't you?" Dane asks me.

I nibble on my lip. Dane still knows me, because as soon as he says it, I realize it's true. We've reached the City of Scholars, but this place is massive, and the Magistrate's Library could be anywhere. And I have no idea how we're going to get in to get Matthias out. If this woman can help, I want to see her.

But I won't force that decision on Alix or Dane. I made

that mistake on Tallis. I'm not making it again. Even though the thought of leaving them, of going this alone, makes my chest feel tight.

"You two don't have to come with me," I say. "It'll be dangerous and—"

Dane shakes his head, cutting me off before I can even get the full sentence out. "Come on, Karis. You know we're not letting you do this alone."

Alix nods, smiling that soft, too-trusting smile. "Like Dane said, we're in this together."

Together. I duck my head, embarrassed at whatever might be on my face. I always expected to be taking this journey alone. I never thought there might be others beside me. I never thought that maybe I needed that.

That it was all right to need that.

"Thank you."

"Good," Zara says. "Then we leave at nightfall."

21

ALIX

Kocha rows us toward the shore, his oars whisper silent as they dip into the inky water. During the day the docks were bustling, but night has driven everyone inside, and down near the water, where people are too poor to afford oil for their lamps, everything has gone dark and still.

My fingers bounce anxiously on my leg. We're finally here, at this place I fled and where my father died. Where I left my father to die. All of my memories, the good and the bad, jumble up in a tight knot in my chest. Once, a long time ago, this city was my home, and even though I never saw much of it, as we approach the docks, I can tell how different it is. It's grown so much, the shacks pushing right up against the docks and the boathouses. The automatons, towering above the streets, are all stilled. I had a complicated history with them. Yet there's still something unnerving about seeing them all rooted to the spot, no more than statues. That could very well be my fate.

We aim for a deserted section of the docks, half of its wooden planks rotted away, their ends dragging into the water. I check to make sure that my tome is still secure in its satchel before pulling my hood down farther over my eyes.

Zara, barely a shadow in her dark cloak, wordlessly beckons us forward. We leave the docks and the thick scent of fish and enter the winding streets of the Lower City and its equally suffocating stench of sweat. Refuse clings to my sandals. The streets beneath us slope up, the houses on both sides built erratically on different levels, which gives the entire Lower City a hodgepodge look.

That ends abruptly at the first wall, cutting across the city like a wound, the buildings butting up against it. I don't remember seeing it like this before, from the villa. Was it always this desperate down here? Would I have noticed?

Zara raps on a thick door set in the pale stone. A slot opens at eye level and they exchange words too low for me to hear. Zara passes a cloth bag inside and the door opens.

We file through. The soldier on the other side is already rifling through the bag, silver drachmas slipping through his fingers.

Dane frowns.

The next tier is part of the city proper. The homes are not clay and straw but stone. I know this place: the Scribe's Quarters, home to the acolytes that serve the Scriptmasters and scholars of the higher tiers. Already the homes are larger, with prim shutters and neatly latched doors. Some even have small courtyards, bits of green climbing over the walls.

Synchronized footsteps sound on the path before us. Zara raises her hand and we duck behind a building as a squadron passes mere feet from us.

I don't remember soldiers roaming the city before either.

The soldiers pass and Zara waves us forward. Her purse gets us through the next wall, and we leave the streets and move out onto open lanes. Here the buildings are villas, grand with white walls gleaming in the dark and red clay tiles on their roofs.

We pass an elegant marble courtyard, fountains at its corners spilling water into a marble basin. A statue of a man stands in the center of the pool. I stop. The carving shows him dressed in simple leathers, the armor of a soldier, but the expression on his face, elegantly crafted but still lofty, isn't that of a common soldier at all.

Zara drops back to stand next to me. She nods at the statue. "Magistrate Agathon."

A spear of cold goes through me. Agathon. I look back over the statue. The magistrate in my own time, Reitas, wasn't a kind man. Sometimes my father would let me hide and listen in on his meetings with other Scriptmasters, but never when Reitas visited. I always imagined the man as some monstrous figure.

Agathon doesn't look monstrous. But I know he is. Outside the villa, I've come to realize how little the look on a face truly says about what's inside.

Zara's staring at the statue, too, her expression dark.

"Are you all right?" I ask.

I see the smallest flash of vulnerability cross her expression. Then it's gone. She grins, drawling, "Oh, you know me."

I'm beginning to think that I do know her. She's like Karis. Neither of them are particularly good at showing what they're feeling.

"You don't have to pretend if you don't want to," I say. "I won't tell anyone."

Zara stills, and now her face is carefully blank. I can't read her at all. She turns back to the statue.

"The Scriptorium took my parents from me, Alix. They weren't fighters. They were scholars. For them, the world was this beautiful thing to be shared, with everyone. With me. Nothing made me happier when I was a child than hearing them talk about their discoveries."

The smallest bit of doubt enters her eyes. It makes her look younger. As if she's just a simple girl, not a pirate captain aiding a rebellion.

"Sometimes I wonder if I've picked the right path," she says quietly. "If this is what they would have wanted for me. Sometimes I feel as if I'm nothing like them anymore."

I think of my own father. He, too, was a scholar. I was never able to see him out in the world, but I can't imagine him on an adventure like the one I've been swept up in. Am I doing what he wanted me to do? I don't even remember what that was.

"Your parents would be proud of you," I say. "How could they not? You said that they wanted to discover a world to be shared by everyone. Well, you're trying to make a world that can be shared, and fighting those who would reserve it only for a few. In the end, isn't that the same thing?"

Zara looks at me, and a smile comes on to her face, as

soft as I've ever seen. "You know, you're a good person, Alix. Don't ever let yourself lose that."

She turns, walking after the others who have already pulled a fair distance ahead. I follow, mulling over her words.

We head to a villa tucked away, off the main path. It's fronted by a beautiful garden, with arches of marble above our heads, and crocuses and poppies winding along the paths. Farther in, there's an automaton, crouched low to the ground, mostly blocked by the cypress shrubs that surround it. The shutters on the villa's windows are open, letting in the cool night air, but there's no light.

Zara takes us in. Red-and-green tiles embellish the walls and form mosaic patterns beneath our feet. The windows are carved with latticework, showing glimpses of the garden outside. Large pots stand on pedestals, depicting images of scholars and automatons, and rich silk tapestries soften the walls.

This place is the closest thing to my home I've been in since I woke up. It brings an ache to my chest. I can imagine my father walking these halls.

We reach a study, a carved desk in the center of the floor and bookcases filled with leather-bound volumes ringing the room. The shutters are closed, shrouding the room in shadows, but Zara lights the bronze lamp sitting on the desk, letting out a plume of smoke and light.

She turns to us. "I'm going to speak with my friend." She nods at the chairs. "Do me a favor and don't go wandering. All things considered, some of the people here won't take kindly to unidentified strangers."

She and Kocha leave.

Karis sits down on one of the chairs, rubbing her temples. Dane stays standing, looking out the window, through a crack in the shutters.

Karis's eyes are fluttering closed when the door opens again. Zara comes in, and this time she's followed by another woman. She wears the traditional white robe of her rank, the golden seal hanging around her neck polished to a bright shine. Her storm-gray hair is cut as short as a man's. Her flinty eyes are inscrutable.

Karis rises to her feet and Dane straightens. It makes him look like a soldier again. That thought bothers me.

"Everybody," Zara says, "meet Master Calantha. Calantha, this is Karis, Dane, and Alix."

The woman nods to Karis, then Dane. I thought Zara was good at hiding her emotions, but this woman gives away nothing. Only then she gets to me, and finally her expression changes. I see surprise.

Surprise and want.

I shift, very uncomfortable. This woman is a Scriptmaster, like my father. She is a rebel, like my father. Yet the way she looks at me... That isn't like my father at all.

"Welcome to my home," Calantha says, nodding her head. "I'm glad to see you all safely arrived."

Karis frowns. Exhaustion clings like a shadow to her edges. "I don't mean to be rude, but it's been a long night. Captain Zara thought you might want to speak to us?"

A smile twitches on Dane's lips at those words.

If they bother the woman, it doesn't show. She merely inclines her head. "I want your help taking down the magistrate."

22

—

KARIS

Taking down the magistrate.

Those words echo too loudly in a room that has gone silent.

Magistrate Agathon is the most powerful man in all Eratia. For as long as I've been alive he's always been here, as unmovable as the islands themselves.

"Ma'am." Dane straightens, his voice that of a soldier addressing his superior officer. Maybe he's relieved about this. It's probably more normal to him than anything on the *Streak* had been. "With all due respect, have you lost your wits?"

Zara snorts, a grin on her face.

Or maybe not.

Calantha's expression doesn't even twitch. "You don't believe me, soldier?"

I can see Dane carefully choosing his words. It's more

than I would have done. We've barely arrived and already I don't trust this woman. She's talking about the impossible. "The magistrate holds the Acropolis. He has armies at his beck and call, the entire navy. His own fighting force is elite."

"Don't think that makes him unstoppable. No one is."

She steps closer to us. Her eyes catch the torchlight, and they flicker. It almost reminds me of Alix, except I'd never see such calculation in his eyes.

"Zara tells me you know what the magistrate is attempting to do, that he wants to create a perfect army by inking runes into their skin, an army that has no choice but to obey him. I am not alone in finding his methods revolting. His power has been tainted for too long, and it's time for it to end. You could be a part of that."

I can hear the conviction in Calantha's voice. The idea of a world without the magistrate, where a man like that doesn't have the power to destroy a single other life.

But I can't forget who's telling us this: a Scriptmaster, standing in her beautiful home in her beautiful city, with a wall between her and people who are just like I was. We could join her, we could fight, and in the end we could just be left with the same Scriptorium, only with a different face.

I don't see why I should risk my life to get her a promotion.

I fold my arms. "And you think we could help you with that?"

"We can always use new recruits to the cause," Calantha says. "But you, Alix... You could be exactly what we need to finish this."

He looks startled. "Me?"

"Zara has told me about you. About your strength, how you can undo *lock* runes. You could be the perfect weapon to use against that man."

Alix's entire body goes rigid. "I'm not a weapon."

"We all must be what the world requires of us."

Alix flinches.

That's it. I step in front of him, anger boiling in the pit of my stomach. I was right. She sounds like every other Scriptmaster I've ever met. Maybe I'm naturally suspicious and maybe that's a failure of mine, but I'm not going to stand by and say nothing.

"Alix is not a weapon," I growl. I glare at Zara, silently demanding she step in.

Zara sighs as she boosts herself up to sit on the edge of the desk. "Weapon isn't the right word." She gives Calantha a look. "But, Alix, you could be a warrior for this cause."

"I don't want to be that either," Alix says miserably.

"I know." Zara's voice is uncharacteristically gentle. "You have a peaceful heart, and that isn't bad. But you can do things no one else can. You are something no one else alive can be. The Scriptorium is never going to stop looking for you. Isn't it better to fight now, when you could change everything, than to spend your entire life fighting to keep running?"

Alix looks down at his satchel with his tome, his face torn. I bite my lip. Zara still doesn't know Alix like I do.

There's just something about him, this hopeful light, that I don't want to see go out.

"Alix, you don't have to do this," I say. "Not if you don't want to. It will be risky. They could catch you."

I can feel Zara's eyes on me. I think back to our conversation on that island. What she said to me. That someone has to fight the Scriptorium. That's what Zara's doing with these people. I know that now.

But why does that have to be what we do? Why do we have to risk everything? We didn't ask for this.

"So you don't think I should do this?" Alix asks, his face still and serious.

I want to say no, to protect him from this. But he's grown so much since I found him, a sad, lost automaton alone in a cave. I won't make this choice for him. If I tried to force him into a decision that suited me, that would be just like me using his tome.

"You need to do what you think is right. Whether that's fighting or not."

He looks around the room, his fingers twined around the strap of his satchel. Even I don't know what he'll decide.

"If I agreed," he finally says, "what exactly is your plan?"

I let out a slow breath, trying not to think what those words could end up costing us.

Calantha glides behind the desk and seats herself on the chair there. "The magistrate knows about you, Alix, and he is desperate to get his hands on you. War is brewing. More and more Eural and Anderran ships are arriving, and still the magistrate sends out his own forces after you. We need to find out what he wants you for."

"But you don't know exactly what that is?" Dane asks.

She shakes her head. "No. But if he wants you, Alix, it must be for something only you are capable of doing."

Alix and I exchange a glance. His father also asked him to do something, something that might have involved a Script ink vessel.

I can see the question in his eyes of whether or not we should tell her. I shake my head. If Zara hasn't told her, I'm not about to. There's nothing wrong with keeping something back, in case we need leverage later.

"In order to uncover what the magistrate is planning, I do think we need to figure out exactly who and what you are," Calantha says. "Tell me, do you remember absolutely anything else you haven't told us?"

Alix thinks for a moment. "No. But I might be able to find out. At my father's villa. It's here in the city."

Calantha shakes her head. "Believe me, Master Theodis's home has been searched thoroughly since the Great Lapse, many times."

"Is it still standing?"

"Yes. Most of it at least. More than one magistrate has become convinced that if they search it one more time, they will uncover all the man's secrets. As far as I know, nothing has ever been found."

Alix reaches up and wraps his fingers around his father's pendant. "If it's still standing, then my rooms and my father's workshop will be there. He hid them well. Even if someone found the door, it can only be opened by a *lock* rune that only I know. I want to try."

"That may be difficult. His villa is in the second tier."

"I can get them there," Zara pipes up.

Calantha frowns. "You have duties out at sea, Zara, you know that. Important duties."

"More important than possibly taking down the magistrate? Calantha, you know how things have been in the city lately. Increased patrols. More members of the council being swung to that man's side. We're running out of time. I want to help the people who are stranded out there. Who have escaped. I do. But none of that will mean anything if the magistrate gets those *obey* runes working. My crew and I are needed here now."

"We also need to be cautious, Zara. There are lives at stake here, you know that."

Zara sits back, folding her arms. "Well, I'm not leaving. Whatever he wants from Alix, we need to figure it out before the magistrate gets a hold of it." A determined glint comes into her eyes. "Besides, I've got a score to settle with that man on behalf of my crew."

The two of them stare down each other, and to my surprise Calantha's the one who backs down first. She sighs. "Very well. But if you're going to Master Theodis's manor, I want you to search it yourself before you let these three anywhere near it."

"Fine."

"Now, Alix," Calantha says. "About your tome…"

Alix's hand covers his satchel. "It stays with me."

"If they catch you with it, everything will be over."

I hear the insinuation behind her words. If Alix is caught, it won't just be Alix who'll be in danger.

Alix must understand that, too, because his face twists. "So, you want me to leave it with you?"

"I want you to leave it here. That's not exactly the same thing."

Calantha rises and crosses over to a tapestry hanging behind the desk. She brushes it aside to reveal a box hidden in a hole in the wall behind it. Fishing a key from her pocket she unlocks the lid. "No one knows about this spot except for the people in this room and a few others among my closest allies. This is the only key." She holds it out to Alix. "Zara tells me you can't stray too far from your tome, but my villa should be close enough to the higher tiers that it shouldn't be a problem."

Alix looks at the key, then at her. And then he takes it. He slips the tome into the safe and locks it. As he lets the tapestry fall back, I see the hesitation on his face. I hope he's making the right choice. I hope we all are.

Calantha nods. "It's already late. Rest and gather yourselves for the night. Tomorrow you can—"

"My brother," I say.

Everyone looks at me. It's hard to hear over the pounding of my heart. But the reason I traveled all this way, the reason I'm risking everything, even joining a rebellion I don't believe in, is to find Matthias. "He was sent to the Magistrate's Library. He has low vision and his name is Matthias and…"

Surprise comes onto Calantha's face. Surprise and regret she isn't quite fast enough to hide.

"What is it?" I ask.

"I thought there was something about you that looked familiar."

My heart thuds so hard I feel it will burst from my chest. "Familiar?"

Calantha pulls open one of the drawers in her desk and takes out a worn parchment. She pushes it toward me.

A face looks up at me, and even though it's seven years older, sketched in black lines, I instantly recognize it.

Matthias.

I reach down and touch the paper with trembling fingers. Some part of me never truly believed I'd see him again, yet here he is, even if it's just a portrait drawn on paper.

There are words beneath it.

The Bandit.
Wanted for crimes against the Scriptorium. If seen, report to the Acropolis.
Reward.

The Bandit. That thief I heard about on that island. That's Matthias?

Zara leans over so she can see. "Wait, your brother is the Bandit?"

I look up at Calantha, confused.

"Matthias is one of our best thieves."

"A thief?" Dane says. "But his vision, it's…" He trails off.

Calantha smiles. "Matthias is a resourceful young man. He manages well."

I can hear the words she's saying, but I don't understand

them. My brother wouldn't have stayed here. He would have been out there, trying to find me.

"Where is he? Is he in this villa now? Can I see him?"

Calantha pauses. "I'm sorry. Three days ago, he went out on a mission with another of our people, Rudy. Rudy managed to escape, but Matthias didn't get out. He was taken by the Scriptorium."

23

KARIS

Three days. After seven years of missing my brother, planning how to save him, journeying all this way, I missed him by three days. That knowledge seeps into my lungs, my heart, my bones, scooping them out and turning me hollow. If we hadn't stopped at that fishing village out on the wild islands, hadn't met the magistrate's men, hadn't been attacked, I would be with my brother right now.

I follow Zara through the elegant hallways of Calantha's villa, barely listening as she points out the rooms and halls and studies. Dane and Alix exchange worried glances over my head.

Finally, Zara looks back at me. "Calantha will do everything in her power to find your brother. She is very loyal to her people."

"We must have different definitions of that word," I mutter.

Zara frowns. "Karis..."

"I'm sure you meant well, Captain, bringing us to this place. But you told us this woman knew more about the Magistrate's Library than anyone, and I don't see how, since she lives in this safe, grand villa, far away from—"

Zara stops. "Calantha worked there, all right?"

Silence drops like a shroud. I was right. About Calantha. About this place. Now the anger I'd been expecting to feel all this time comes lashing in, flaring hot against my breastbone. I thought we were done with Zara lying to us.

"And you took us to her?" I say. "After everything you've told us—"

Zara steps toward me so quickly my words cut off. "That's right, Karis. *I* told you. It was *my* crew who lived it. *My* parents who were taken there. If any of us have a right to be angry at her for her past, it's me. Don't you think there might be a reason why I'm not?"

Alix shifts nervously, glancing between us, as if debating whether or not to pull us apart. I can already feel the words rising in my throat—barbed words. I don't want to hear her defending the woman who sent my brother to his fate.

But somewhere in the back of my head I know that if I take up this fight now, it won't stop. If I'm to have any hope of getting Matthias back, I need to learn to get along with the people in this house. And if I can't do that with Zara, I won't be able to do it with anyone. So I do something rare for me, and I swallow my words down.

Alix speaks into the quiet. "How did she end up working in a place like that?"

Zara sighs. "She doesn't talk about it much. Even I only

know bits and pieces. Calantha was a rising star in the Scriptorium, one of the youngest to ever be promoted so high. Her success brought her to the magistrate's attention and he assigned her to work in the library for a short time. Whatever happened there convinced her that she needed to do whatever it took to stop the magistrate. Ever since then she's worked to save whoever she can. Including me. When my parents were taken to the library, I decided I was going to go in there, that I was going to save them. The only reason I wasn't caught is because she pulled me away and brought me back here. So if you won't trust her, then at least trust me. We need to find this vessel Alix remembers before the magistrate does, so we can stop that man. That's all Calantha wants, too."

Zara sounds so sure. I envy her that sureness. The world hasn't taught me to trust easily. Not back then and certainly not now.

"Give it some time," Zara says, "now that you're here. Besides, you're going to need her protection in this city."

Those words echo hollowly inside of me. I have the uncomfortable notion it's because they're true. My brother is gone, and I don't know how to get him back, or what I'm doing here anymore.

We keep going in silence to a hall filled with long tables, the walls decorated with tapestries and potted plants tucked into nooks. There are only two other people in the room, a man and woman in quiet conversation, seated at the farthest table. A few scattered lamps are lit, giving flickering, erratic light to the room.

Zara gestures to some seats nearby. "Just this once your

captain will go get the drinks. Something hot will do you good." She looks at me. "Should I find Rudy for you? If I'm remembering right, he's a bit of a night owl."

Anger flames like a burn inside of me. If I never see this Rudy person, it will be too soon. I'm shaking my head no when Dane touches my hand.

"You should meet with him," Dane says. "He's the last person who saw Matthias. Maybe he'll know something that could help us find your brother."

I know that he's right. I hate that he's right. "Fine," I mutter, slouching in my seat. But I'm not going to be happy about it.

Zara nods. "I'll be back soon." She leaves.

"We don't have to be here for this, if you don't want," Alix says.

"No," I say. "Stay." That's the only way I'll stop myself from doing something that will get us all thrown out into the cold.

Someone—I'm assuming the cook from her dirty apron—appears with two steaming mugs of spiced tea. "Compliments of the cap'n," she mumbles before leaving. I don't feel much like drinking, but I manage sips when Dane nudges me, not even caring when I scald my tongue.

I finish as much of my drink as I can and still we wait. The coward's probably too scared to face me. I'm half debating going and finding him myself, or maybe just hiding before he can find me, when the door opens and someone steps through.

He's not from Eratia. He's large, standing a good two heads taller than I do, and big-boned, his mussed robes barely fitting his frame. A silver scholar seal rests against his chest even though he's at least a decade younger than any scholar I've ever seen. He has the light skin and blond hair of those from some of the nations who live beyond Eural, and bright blue eyes. The color contrasts sharply with the restless red that circles his irises, the dark crescents worn into his skin. He looks as if he hasn't slept in, well, three days.

My hands curl into fists on my knees and I sit up straighter, glaring him down. Here's someone I don't care if I unleash my rage at. Because if he's mourning what he watched happen to my brother, he has no right. I don't need the full story to know that if Matthias isn't here, neither should he be.

Rudy sees me and a wave of pain crests over his face. There's something so vulnerable about it that even though I'm getting ready to lash out, the words stick in my throat. That expression reminds me of Alix.

Rudy pulls in a shuddering breath as he lowers himself onto the bench across from me.

"You must be Karis." His voice cracks. He swallows and tries again. "I'm so sorry for what happened to Matthias."

Underneath the table Dane slips his hand onto my leg and gives it a squeeze.

I take a deep breath, trying not to choke on the anger. "How could you leave him behind like that?"

Rudy flinches, and I feel the smallest twinge of guilt. It's like I'm physically hurting him.

"I didn't want to," he says hoarsely. "But stealing the seal was so important to him. He thought it would give us a clue to what the magistrate was planning. But we were caught. Matthias yelled at me to go and before I knew what was happening, he was running down the hall toward them. And then he..." Rudy pulls in another shaking breath. "He was just gone."

"And you let him do it. Let my brother sacrifice himself."

Rudy hunches his large frame. "I did."

I thought if he admitted it, I would feel better. But I don't. My brother is still gone. Fury and confusion and pain throb red hot inside my skull. What's the point of a rebellion if it can't even protect people? What's the point of fighting for others if this is the result?

Rudy raises his head, his bloodshot eyes studying my face. "You look so much like him, you know. And he talked about you, all the time. About finding you when things calmed down here, going to Tallis to get you. Please know how much he missed you."

I stiffen. Those words sound as if they're meant to comfort me but they must be a lie. He's talking as if my brother had the choice to come after me. I'm trying to summon an answer, any answer, when I notice Rudy fiddling with something in his hands, red paper flashing between his fingers.

My anger turns to ice in my lungs. "What is that?"

Rudy swallows and holds it out. "Matthias said he thought he was getting better at it." He shakes his head. "I guess you're the only one who can judge that."

I stare at the paper poppy. It was something special that Matthias had made for me, and only me. Here it is, held by someone else.

I don't understand.

When I don't speak, because I can't, Alix asks, "Were you two close?"

Rudy straightens, and a shine of defiance comes out past the sadness. He juts out his chin. "We're lovers."

I stare at Rudy. Lovers. That means Matthias...likes men.

Rudy looks at me. "I love your brother very much. Please believe me."

The last time I saw Matthias, he was only eleven. Had he known then? I hadn't known at that age that I was different. I didn't know the feelings that everyone told me would come never would. We had just been children. We never talked about any of this.

It forces me to face how little I know of my brother, after all this time. There are parts of him that he grew into while I wasn't there.

"I believe you," I whisper.

Relief crosses Rudy's face. And with that, every bit of anger leaves me. I sag, staring down at the table.

A calloused hand settles into mine. I'm sure it's Dane, but when I look up, it's Rudy. He gently opens my fingers and settles the poppy in my palm.

I shake my head, torn between want and regret and pain. "No," I say, "he made this for you." For Rudy, not for me. For Rudy who's grieving and who I attacked anyway, because I guess that's the sort of person I am. "I shouldn't—"

"Take it," Rudy says softly. "He'd want you to have it."

There's so much kindness in Rudy's face. I don't deserve it. So instead I look down at the little flower. Matthias has gotten better at it. He got better and I wasn't there to see it.

It's been seven years, but a part of me still believed that my brother would be the same as the boy I once knew. Why was he able to change when I wasn't? I feel as if I'm the same as all those years ago. Ever since we were separated, I refused to put down any roots. I decided to slip transiently through the world, because all I wanted was to get back what I lost seven years ago. But he was living this whole time. He made a choice.

And he didn't choose me.

I curl my hand around the petals. "Thank you."

24

ALIX

I no longer know how late it is when Zara shows us the hallway where we'll be staying. The others filter off to their rooms, Karis staring at the floor as she goes. She looks smaller than she did a few hours ago.

The doors all close, and I'm left in the sitting area, alone with my thoughts.

We all must be what the world requires of us.

I flex my fingers, watching the candlelight beside me slip over my runes. Maybe Calantha is right. Maybe I truly am a weapon, my fate and identity etched into my skin. She'd said the words so coolly, as if the damage they seared into me didn't really matter.

Only then I think about when I used the Arizan runes on the *Streak*. I did something I wouldn't have thought possible. That has to mean something. I desperately want it to mean something.

I wish my father was here. He always helped me to see things more clearly. But I'll never hear his guidance again. All that's left is the villa.

Soon, I'll be able to go back there. I hope whatever echoes of my father I might find there will give me some sort of peace.

Morning sunlight has filled the sky when footsteps enter the sitting area behind me. It's Rudy. He looks no better than he did when we last saw him.

"Is there any news?" I ask quietly. "About Matthias?"

Rudy swallows, shaking his head. "No."

A door opens to my left and Karis steps out. I've seen anger and fire and sadness from her, but never defeat. It hurts to see her like that, as if a piece of what makes her herself has broken. She isn't as strong as she sometimes wants people to think. I want to be there for her, to prove I've grown. Only I don't know what to say.

Rudy bows his head. "I'm sorry," he murmurs.

"Right." Karis glances away, fiddling with the edge of her shirtsleeve. She must have found a shift in her room, because she isn't wearing her clothes from the *Streak* anymore. There are still splotches of dirt on her skin, haphazard, as if she didn't care enough to clean it all off. "Is that what you came to tell us?"

"No. Calantha wanted me to come." Rudy turns to me. "You can probably tell from my seal, but I'm a scholar. A good one, or so I've been told. Calantha thought that perhaps your runes might give us some clue as to why you were...born. She wondered if perhaps you would be all right with picking up your tome and letting me..." He trails off.

"Study me?" I ask.

Rudy grimaces. "Yes."

If someone else had asked, it would have bothered me. To be studied. I can't be angry at Rudy, though, not when he's so obviously grieving. Besides, if it can help us take down the magistrate, perhaps without me fighting, I'll do it.

I nod.

Only Karis shakes her head. "What does it matter? Why do you keep fighting for all this when Matthias is gone? Don't you regret what happened?"

Rudy looks at her, such bright pain in his eyes that she drops her head.

"Do I regret it?" Rudy's voice is soft but not timid. "I knew how Matthias already suffered in that place. I knew better than anyone because he told me, gritted it out as I held him when he couldn't sleep. He would shake like he was falling apart and I couldn't stop it."

"Don't..." Karis whispers, but Rudy keeps going.

"I knew that, and I still watched him as he ran toward those soldiers, knowing what they would do to him. Knowing just as surely that I had to leave him, because it was what he wanted and what he asked of me. I regret what I did every moment of every day."

Karis's shoulders tremble and I stand there, ill, not knowing what to say, for either of them.

She looks up and I can't distinguish the plea from the pain in face. "Then why? Why do you still fight for that woman's cause when she took him from you?"

Rudy watches her, tired and solemn, but hopeful. "Because Matthias believed in that cause. Because when I fight for this rebellion, I'm still fighting for him, for the world he wanted. I'll always believe that."

Karis is silent, searching Rudy's face. Then she whispers the last words I ever expected to hear from her. "All right."

Rudy gives us clothes to change into: Scriptorium chitons. Karis looks as uncomfortable back in her acolyte chiton as I feel, though at least the himation they gave me is long enough to cover most of my runes.

He leads us to a small study that borders the courtyard. It looks as if a miniature storm has passed through. Books and papers are strewn about everywhere: on the desk, spilling from the shelves, littering the floor.

Rudy flushes. "Sorry, this is my study. I haven't had time to clean up lately..." He bustles about, grabbing piles of papers and stuffing them back into the bookshelves, only for them to cascade out again.

I help him, piling a stack of scrolls onto the nearby desk. There's a small pottery shard there, carefully kept free of the mess by the wooden stand it sits on. Bold figures painted in black stand out against the red clay of the pottery. It's an automaton and a girl.

In my father's villa I saw books and jars and tapestries depicting automatons. In all of them, the automatons were massive and set in violent poses, commanded by whoever was depicted with them. This one is different. The automaton isn't that large, perhaps only a few heads taller than I am. The girl sits on its shoulder, and its hand cradles her. There is nothing threatening about that pose.

Beside me, Rudy hauls up another sheaf of papers. He pauses. "That was found in an archeological dig north of the city." He carefully runs his finger over its edge. "Fascinating, isn't it? I've never seen an automaton depicted like that before."

"I haven't either," I whisper. My father had once thought that perhaps automatons weren't always used as weapons, that perhaps Eratian runes were once used more like the runes from Zara's or Kocha's home countries. I've never seen the smallest scrap of evidence to prove that.

At least not up until now.

Rudy picks up the shard and holds it out to me. "Here."

I shake my head, even though I do want to take it. I want to hold something like that in my hands. "You don't need—"

"Take it," he says, putting it in my hand. "You have more right to it than I do."

I look down and feel a tug in my chest. "Thank you," I murmur.

Rudy turns away and manages to clear a space. I gently tuck the shard into my belt pouch and then step forward. I unpin my chiton enough to bare my chest, trying to relax.

"May I?" Rudy asks.

I nod.

Rudy circles around me, studying my runes much like Zara and Finn had. I wonder if this feeling, as if I'm an object on display, is going to be a permanent fixture in my life.

"Fascinating," he murmurs. "The depths of these runes

are actually deeper than on a normal automaton and they…" He stops, looking horrified. "I—I'm sorry, I didn't mean…"

"It's all right. I know I'm not normal." The world disabused me of that notion a long time ago.

Rudy glances at the tome in my hands. "I don't suppose… Could I see a rune in action, just once?"

I look down at my tome myself. I know there will be more runes there, from when Zara controlled me. I've been hoping no more would ever be added. Each is a reminder of a feeling that pains me. Only Rudy is asking for my permission. It would be my choice. Surely there's something different about that.

I hold the tome out to Karis.

She startles, panic flashing through her eyes, and I wonder what she's remembering. Perhaps our first meeting. When she used my tome. When I lashed out at her. Does that moment haunt her as it haunts me?

"Alix," she says. "I would never—"

"I trust you, Karis."

They're words that I have never said, not even to my father. They're true, though. Karis wouldn't hurt me. I know her.

She nods and hesitantly takes the tome, and for the very first time, as it leaves my hands, I'm not scared.

Karis opens my tome to a new page. She takes a reed pen from the desk, dipping it into its ink pot. "Um, what should I write?"

"How about *reach*?" That seems safe.

She nods and bows her head, a strand of her hair falling onto the page. The rune on my right arm flares and I find it stretching forward. It's as disconcerting as always. I shake out my arm and Karis quickly gives my tome back to me.

Rudy scribbles madly on a piece of parchment. "So, it's an instant reaction," he mutters. "I thought there might be some delay…"

"Rudy," Karis says after a few moments, when it's clear he's lost in his work. "You said something yesterday about a seal. That it was what you and Matthias stole."

Rudy stills, bent over the parchment, and guilt takes over his face, as if for a moment he forgot what happened. "Yes." He crosses to a bookcase, where a small, ornamental chest sits. He opens it and pulls out a bronze seal.

"This is what we stole that night."

It's a larger seal, about the size of my two palms cupped together, and *unlock* is scrawled into its surface.

"We found something like that," Karis says, pulling the *stop* seal from her belt pocket. "It froze Alix's arm when he touched it."

Rudy nods. "The magistrate has been developing them. We've recovered over a dozen. Without Script ink, he can't have more tomes made, so he's been experimenting with seeing if he can use these seals in their place."

I rub my arm. "The *stop* seal certainly worked."

"It might have worked on you," Rudy says, "but none of the others have so far. The *wake* runes don't seem to be strong enough to reanimate an automaton, and without that, the other seals have nothing to work with."

"But what was so special about this seal?" Karis asks. "Why did my brother risk his life for it?"

"The *unlock* rune," Rudy says.

I don't understand. Judging from the confusion on Karis's face, neither does she.

"So?" I finally ask.

"Well, why would they need a rune like that? *Stop* I can understand, because all automatons have *stop* runes. It would be useful. But, Alix, you're the only automaton I know of who has the ability to undo *lock* runes. Scriptmasters use *lock* runes in the first place because only they can unlock them. It wouldn't make sense for them to create a seal so that anyone could undo their locks. Which means we have to assume there's something out there that not even the Scriptmasters can get open. That they need, I don't know, some sort of key to open, like this seal. And there's something else odd about this rune." He runs his fingers over it. "All *unlock* runes are structured off of the same base rune, with different strokes added on top. But look here."

I lean forward, studying the rune, but I don't understand what Rudy is hinting at. Reaching out, I brush my fingers across it and a melody floats through my head, new and yet familiar.

"The base rune," I breathe. "It has an extra stroke."

"Exactly," Rudy says. "I work here in the City of Scholars and even I don't know a single Scriptmaster who has the knowledge to modify a base rune. It just isn't done. But this extra stroke clearly..." He stops, his gaze snapping back to me.

"What?" I ask.

"This rune. Your rune..." He rushes over to me. "They're the same. You don't have just any *unlock* rune, you have this one."

I twist so that I can see. He's right. The rune on the seal and on me are identical.

"That means that whatever they want to unlock, whatever the magistrate wants to unlock, you already can, Alix," Karis says slowly. "That could be why he wants you."

I struggle to sort back through my memories. Is that what I've been missing this whole time? Is that what my father wanted me to do? Perhaps that means if I unlock whatever this is, I'll feel a little more complete. I'll have done whatever it is that I'm supposed to do.

Only, isn't that what the magistrate wants? Surely my father wouldn't have wanted the same as that man. I'm missing something here.

"There have been rumors, too," Rudy says quietly, glancing at the door, as if afraid of being overheard. "About something called the Automaton Heart."

That name again. Karis and I look at each other.

Rudy frowns. "What is it?"

Last night, Karis didn't seem to want to be completely open with Calantha. But I'm sure Rudy's safe. "Back on the Scriptorium on Tallis," I say, "we sneaked into their Hall of Records and I found some information on my father. It spoke of something called the Automaton Heart. My father was the one who caused it to stop." I hesitate, then add, "I was the one who caused it to stop."

Rudy's eyes widen.

Karis steps forward. "Do you have any idea what it is?"

"We aren't quite sure." Rudy glances at the door again. "But we think it might be a Script ink vessel, somewhere here in the city."

A Script ink vessel. That means it could be the golden light that I remember.

"And you think the magistrate is looking for it?" Karis asks.

Rudy shakes his head. "No. We think he's already found it. That he's trying to get it to work."

All that's left after his words is silence. Zara had said that a vessel that size would contain enough Script ink to re-animate every automaton still out there. If the magistrate gets that sort of power, we'd never be able to overtake him.

It would all be over, and we'd be left standing in the ashes.

25

—

KARIS

I slip out a side door, not sure where I'm going, only knowing I need some space to separate this clog of thoughts swirling through my head. Of Matthias taken, days before I arrived. Of this rebellion and of Calantha. Of the magistrate and his library and the Automaton Heart.

I think of all that power come back into the world. It makes me want to run, to find my brother and to get out of here before something happens to one of us that I can't undo.

It makes me want to stay and do something.

The thought surprises me, but it's already digging its way into my head. I know now what Zara had really been asking me when we'd walked through the streets of that fishing village. At the time I was so sure I knew my answer. That all I wanted was my brother safe. That I didn't owe anything to this world that has only ever kicked me down. Why do I have to start doubting now? Matti tried to help and now he's been taken. For all I know, the same thing could happen to me, to Alix, to all the rest of us, too.

My steps slow and then stop as a sour prick of wrong touches the back of my head. When I first came outside, I could hear the villa. Talk drifting out the windows. The clanking of clay bowls in the kitchen courtyard. Now there's nothing but a silence that hangs like a weight over the grounds.

Something's happened.

I shove my way back through the gardens, trying to remember where the villa sits without the noise to direct me.

Ahead of me there's a row of cypress shrubs. I remember those, surrounding the automaton we passed our first night here. I step through the bushes and stutter to a halt.

A man stands in front of the automaton, his back to me, hands clasped loosely behind him. He turns as I scrape through the bushes and somehow I know who he is before he even faces me.

The magistrate.

There's a marble bust of him on Tallis, pale and cold. It's not painted. I knew the man himself couldn't possibly look the same, but I'm still thrown at the shock of his red hair, neatly oiled and streaked with gray, like fire with ash. He wears a simple leather breastplate over a linen robe, with a knife at his hip. His eyes, as they latch on to me, are as deep a blue as the bottom of the ocean.

The world goes still, silence pressing against my ears. I'm waiting for him to arrest me, when, of everything, he smiles.

"Ah." His voice is surprisingly soft. "I was expecting Master Calantha."

I make myself move, ducking my head in the hopes that it will distract him from the movement of my arm as I slide it behind my back, to hide that I wear no bracelet—if the acolytes here even wear bracelets. "I'm sorry." The words drop like stones from my tongue. I stare down at my feet. "I didn't mean to intrude. I'll just..." I take a step back.

"It's all right. Why not keep me company until she arrives?"

My stomach tilts down. Please no.

"What's your name?" he asks.

"Demetria." The word comes out without me even thinking, and as soon as it does, I inwardly wince. Why did I give him my mother's name? After all these years?

"Demetria. That's pretty."

I nod. I know I should be saying something but I'm scrabbling, trying to think of what he's doing here. What he's doing smiling like that? A monster shouldn't be able to put on a human mask.

"You know," he says, "most acolytes are at the Scriptorium in their classes this time of day."

I freeze. This is a man who could throw me into a dark, dank cell and forget about it before the door clanged shut. He and the other magistrates before him have held sway over our nation for as far as Eratia's history stretches. How did I ever think I could come here and face him? A man as powerful as him?

I'm sure this is it. But when I risk a glance up through

my lashes, he's still just smiling. There's no venom, no malice in that smile. It's like we're sharing a joke.

"Don't worry, I won't tell. I skipped plenty of my own classes when I was your age."

"You?" The word is out before I can catch it.

But he laughs. Honestly laughs.

"Yes, even me. School is important, of course, but I think we both know there are things that no records room or lecture hall will teach you."

We *both* know. A slow shiver crawls up my spine, even though his voice didn't change. His face didn't change. Maybe he truly thinks I'm a truant student who shares some sliver of familiarity with his own past. Then again, maybe he didn't. I haven't gotten this far by ignoring my gut.

I raise my head and look at him. It is unbelievably reckless. But whatever game this man is playing—this man who inked runes into the skin of Zara's crew, who has my brother—I will face him head-on. If I'm going down, I'm going down in flames. "And what would those things be?" I say, putting as much brazenness as I can muster into my voice.

Something in the magistrate's eyes changes, so quick I almost miss it. It isn't surprise. It isn't annoyance. It's knowing. Then it's gone, and he's back to amusement. "I'm glad to see a fire in our youth. You remind me of myself when I was younger."

"I am not like—" I clamp my jaw shut, dizzy with what I almost admitted. Saying those words would have been treason.

"Ah, I see you don't approve of some of my policies. Then

again, that opinion is hardly irregular nowadays. But you know, Demetria, everyone always appreciates what I give them. Peace. Security. Thirty years of it." He waves his hand, rings glittering in the garden's light. If my words faze him, if he cares that someone as young as me is speaking back to him, it doesn't show. "Such a long time that some have started to think that such things—peace and security—are given. They aren't. Nothing is ever given to you. You either take what you need no matter the cost, or you watch it be taken from you. Then again—" he looks down at me "—I suppose you already know that, don't you?"

Ice water floods my veins. There it is, that knowing again in his eyes. But he can't know. To him I'm just some acolyte standing in this garden. A bit outspoken, but no rebel.

Right?

My throat feels so dry. There's something calculating to this man. I'm grasping at words, already falling behind. "I—"

Footsteps sound behind me and I don't turn, I can't turn, because I'm not as bold or as brave as I thought. A hand settles on my shoulder. I suck in a sharp breath, sure it's a soldier. Then I look up and see Calantha.

"There you are, Calantha," the magistrate says. "Young Demetria and I were having a fascinating discussion while we waited."

"My apologies, Magistrate. I had something I needed to deal with in the villa." Calantha's voice is calm. But her fingers dig crescents into my shoulder, she's gripping me so hard.

The magistrate steps toward us. He's no longer a young

man, but the movement is lithe. I see the warrior he must have once been, who murdered his predecessors and took his power by force. He was a fighter long before he was a ruler. "I fear you've been avoiding me, Calantha."

"I have been busy, Magistrate."

"Yes, so many side projects. It's a wonder you can make time for them all."

Beside me Calantha is like stone. If she's stone, I'm all cracks. I want to run, but even if Calantha's hand wasn't pinning me in place, I couldn't have moved.

"I think you'll be pleased by my efforts, Magistrate," Calantha says. "If I could just have some more time. I'm working on a new way of structuring the *wake* rune and I—"

The magistrate reaches up and catches her chin.

Calantha's hand clenches so suddenly tighter around my shoulder I jerk. The two of them are roughly the same height, but there's a presence to the magistrate that makes Calantha seem breakable.

"You know, I've always admired how well you lie," he says, so quietly I can hear the leaves rustling above us through his words. "Perhaps the best of all my pupils. The problem with lies, though, is that you have to be careful or else you might drown in them." He leans in closer and something flickers in his eyes. Something dark. Something wrong. "I would be careful if I were you, Calantha. And know that I'm watching. Always."

He lets go and he's gone, striding back through the gardens. Guards in black, with his sigil on their sashes, melt out of the nearby bushes to trail him like shadows. I hadn't realized they were watching.

Still we stand there. I look up at Calantha, who stares after them, a distant glaze to her eyes.

"Calantha?" I finally ask.

Her eyes come back into focus and she lets go of my shoulder, leaving only an ache behind. I rub it.

She turns away. "Come with me."

I follow her through the gardens, only then realizing how hard I'm shaking. I stare down at my trembling hands as if they're betraying me, but I can't make them stop.

We go to her study. I close the door behind us as she pours herself a drink.

I sag against the door frame, struggling to gather my thoughts as a dozen questions clamor for attention. I want to ask if he knows. What he knows. What he was doing.

Instead all I can manage to say is, "How long?"

She turns, confused.

I try again. "How long was my brother with that man? The first time."

Grief settles over her expression. "Almost a year."

I squeeze my eyes shut. A year in a place like that. With a man like that.

"How did he escape?" I ask through gritted teeth.

"They brought out a few of the prisoners to test them. I heard about it beforehand and sent some of my people in. They managed to cause a distraction. Matthias was the only one smart enough to run. The only one we recovered that day."

I open my eyes again and look around at the sunlight

shining through the windows, the smell of nectarine blossoms wafting in from the gardens. I don't understand why I'm here and he's not.

"Was he...?" I trail off. No one who went through something like that could ever be all right.

Calantha lowers herself into a chair, her goblet dangling from her hand. "I've rescued many who have come out of the library. Some give in to anger. Others to darkness. Some rage. Some go silent. Your brother did a bit of all of that. He'd slip from the villa in the middle of the night and go walking, not caring about the danger. He'd return with things he stole. Tools. Weapons, occasionally. Once even a Scriptmaster's golden seal that I don't want to think how he managed to get. There was no purpose to it. I think he just wanted to hurt the Scriptorium any way he could. He never got caught. I asked him if he would like some training. There's an old Scriptmaster here who lost his eyesight as a young man. He trained Matthias, and when Matthias was ready, I paired him with Rudy. Rudy's a good scholar, but he doesn't have the instincts for covert missions. They did well together."

"Until that night."

Calantha nods. "Yes, until that night."

I'm sure Matthias went out on this woman's orders. Does she regret it? I look her in the eye, wanting to see her expression as I say this. "Zara said you worked there, with him."

A dark flash passes over Calantha's face. Maybe saying that was cruel. But I won't be part of this with only half the answers.

"Yes," she says. "I've always had a talent for the Script. It led me to rise quickly in the Scriptorium and I relished it. When the magistrate said he had a special opportunity for me, I was eager. Eager and foolish.

"I went with him to the Magistrate's Library. He wanted to see if I could improve the design of his *obey* runes, to make them work." She gets up suddenly, her expression hard. "I was there for three weeks, working for him. He wouldn't allow anyone else to lay hands on his prisoners. But I would give them the drinks to make them sleep. And I would stand at the magistrate's side as he did his work. In those three weeks, every bit of glory I ever wanted from the magistrate soured. I knew I could never be like him. It was my mistake, Karis, and I will spend the rest of my life atoning for it."

It's hard to stand there, her gaze boring through me. Even though I knew she'd worked there, I didn't expect that story. I didn't expect to hear such potent regret. For the first time, I glimpse why my brother might have chosen to follow this woman.

"How did you get out?" I whisper.

"I made it seem as if I couldn't give the magistrate what he wanted. He said I was a disappointment and told me to return to my former position. I don't think he's trusted me since. Luckily, I have an influential enough family, and he isn't as powerful as he was when he first took control— there have been too many rumors darkening his work, and the talk of war with Eural is only splintering things further. He hasn't dared to lay hands on me yet. Not without proof. I'm very careful. I'm sure he'd love to see me in chains."

Would he take her there, to his library?

"Making the *obey* rune work on people, it's all he's ever wanted. It's never been done before, but he is determined to see it through. With every delay he grows more frustrated. Every failed experiment makes him more desperate. More dangerous.

"That is why we fight, Karis. The Script could be a force for good in our nation. It could benefit all. It does, in other places. But here, the magistrate believes its power should only belong to a few. He's distorted it into something it was never meant to be. Now, finally, others are rising. He knows his power is weakening. Whatever he is trying to do now is his last attempt to regain power." Passion blazes in her eyes, and I see someone so dedicated to her cause that she would do anything. It terrifies me.

It thrills me.

She's asking me the same thing Zara did. Challenging me. And all I can think are the words that the magistrate said to me:

You either take what you need no matter the cost, or you watch it be taken from you.

He said it so knowingly. And maybe I found truth in those words, too. Because when it came to survival, when it came to my brother, I would have done anything.

But I did that for family. I'm not like him.

There's a knock at the door and we both stiffen.

"Calantha? I'm back."

I let out a breath. Zara.

She opens the door, stepping inside, and I stare. Her usual jaunty captain's outfit is gone. She wears the prim chiton of a scribe now, each fold perfectly arranged. She looks the image of a studious scholar and if not for that light in her eyes I'd be sure she had a twin she never told us about.

"How did the scouting go?" Calantha asks.

"Good. I found a route that should serve our purposes." She turns to me and grins. "I hope you're ready because it looks like Alix is going home."

26

KARIS

Zara waits for us outside of our rooms the next morning, dressed again as a scribe. Dane stops when he sees her, his eyes widening. Zara grins back. Her gaze trails slowly down his body. "You clean up good, soldier boy."

Unlike me and Alix, Dane was given a soldier's uniform to wear. He tugs on his sash, not that it hadn't been perfect before. "Thank you, Captain."

"Not Captain today. Today, and today only, you can call me Zara."

Dane's eyes spark as a deep light comes into them. "Of course. Zara."

I'm seriously debating stepping between them before something happens that I'll regret watching when Zara turns on her heel to appraise Alix. He's so wrapped up in his himation I can only make out the slight flicker of his eyes, from deep within the cloth. It's a bit eerie.

"You're going to have to be the most careful out there," Zara says. "If anyone sees your eyes, we'll be in a world of trouble. As far as anyone is concerned, you're an incredibly shy student who keeps your eyes on your books."

"My books?"

Zara pulls out a stack from her pack and thunks them into his arms. "Here you go."

Alix picks up the first one and twists it to see the gold print stamped into its spine. "A study of automaton runes dating from the first century."

"I remember stealing that book," I say.

"Now," Zara says, "there's one last thing you all need to wear."

She reaches into her pack and pulls out three Scriptorium bracelets.

I take a rapid step back. "No."

Zara sighs. "Believe me, I know how horrible these things are. But they aren't official bracelets. Rudy made them to hoodwink the gates around here. I promise no Scriptmaster will be able to track you with these and you can even take them off yourselves. There's a hidden release here." She demonstrates on her own.

I swore to myself I would never wear a bracelet like this again, even if I could take it off myself. But the only other option would be forcing Alix to do all this on his own. I might have made some questionable choices in my life, but I'm not about to do that.

I take the bracelet and snap it around my wrist. A seed of panic sprouts at its cool touch. I take a deep breath. We'll be fine. I'm sure Rudy and Zara know what they're doing.

Rudy and Zara had better know what they're doing.

Dane reaches out and touches my shoulder. "Are you all right?"

"Getting there." I glance at the other two, who've drifted off to ready the supplies, then back at Dane. "What about you?" No matter what I might be feeling, this is going to be rougher on him than on me. Sneaking through this city, dressed like a soldier but not one.

Dane runs his finger along the sash. "I used to dream about becoming a captain and going to a place like the City of Scholars." He shakes his head, and something new enters his eyes. Not the carefree expression that had been there on Tallis. Not the uncertainty that's been there ever since. Something more determined. "I'm glad, to find something to fight for. Something real this time."

Dane is so different from me. He needs something to fight for, to believe in. It drives him. It's always driven him. It's how he settled so much more easily on Tallis than I did. And now it's how he can give himself to this cause and make it sound so simple, while I still can't seem to manage the same.

What do I believe in?

Awkward, I let my gaze drift around the room. Zara is in the corner securing a dagger to her belt.

"Something to fight for, or someone?" I ask, aiming for a light tone.

He rolls his eyes and knocks his elbow against mine.

"I'll have none of that from you, thank you very much," he says. But his eyes stay on her. I get a confused pang that he's found something in her that I'll probably never feel myself. Even though I don't truly want it, in that moment a part of me envies him. Would normal be better? What is normal?

"I'm happy for you, Dane."

He looks at me, a smile playing at his lips. "You know, you've changed. You're softer now. In a good way." He glances over at Alix. "I think he's changed you."

Those words catch me off guard. Dane doesn't look like he's joking.

Zara swings her pack onto her shoulders. "Come on. Let's get going."

Dane pats me on the shoulder and follows Zara as she heads out. Frowning, I trail after him. It's true, I've never met someone like Alix. As sincere as he is. As trusting as he is. It makes me want to protect him, and I've never had someone to protect before. I'm not sure I want to change, though.

Zara leads us out of the villa toward the crest of the hill. From up ahead comes a swell of noise and we step past a row of prickly bushes onto a wide lane made of stone. A crush of bodies walks up the road and every single one of them is Scriptorium, dressed in chitons or longer robes, seals and sashes denoting their ranks. There must be more people walking up this one road than there were on all of Tallis.

Zara taps my chin, and I snap my gaping mouth closed.

"It's called the Grand Thoroughfare." Her voice is pitched low, but that can't quite hide the laugh tucked into it. "And it leads all the way from the harbor to the Acropolis."

The gate in the wall ahead of us is open, but traffic slows as it funnels to pass through. Two soldiers stand on either side. The man and woman lazily scan the passing crowd, spears idly clasped in their hands.

I finger my bracelet nervously. Zara wasn't exaggerating before. This is perhaps the most dangerous place in the world for us to be, for Alix to be especially, and we're just willingly walking into it.

Zara loops her arm through my own. "Talk to me," she murmurs.

"About what?" I ask.

"The lovely day. The nice weather. The fine company we find ourselves in."

I raise an eyebrow. "Fine isn't the word I'd use."

"Better than those dangerous pirates you've been hanging out with."

"Have to say I prefer them to this lot."

She flashes a grin at me. "It sounds like someone has been a bad influence on you."

"Don't let yourself take all the credit. I was the scourge of my masters back on Tallis. They were all… *Karis*." I strike my best imitation of Master Vasilis. *"Your thoughts are wandering. Go fall off that automaton over there."*

Zara bursts out laughing. "You fell off an automaton?"

"It was the Scriptmaster's fault…mostly."

She snorts.

I realize it feels strangely…right to be walking with her, arm in arm. I've never really had a female friend.

Are we friends?

We're at the gates. I step forward and my bracelet flares with familiar heat against my skin. I suck in a breath. But no alarm sounds. No one shouts. When I glance back at the soldiers, they're still looking down the road at the approaching crowd.

On the other side of the wall, the city opens up into the agora. I remember the marketplace from Heretis. With so many bustling vendors and shoppers, it was one of the easiest spots in the city to slip a roll or piece of fruit into a belt pouch. Back then, I thought the large, spread-out agora must be the busiest place in the world.

It's nothing like this.

The central area is lined with stalls, cloth canopies overhead to shelter from the already blazing sun. The stalls sell fruit and grains and salted fish, fabric and weapons and jewelry, clay bowls and pots and jugs. The smell of bread and smoke from a nearby kiln hangs in the air. There are stalls with Scriptorium wares: parchment and reed pens and leather-bound books. A tangled weave of hundreds of people fills the space, browsing the stalls or hurrying off to wherever they're going. At the back there's an amphitheater, wide steps cluttered with students.

"Where's the Magistrate's Library?" I ask Zara under my breath.

"Farther up. It's in the Acropolis itself."

Of course it is. The incline of the hill above us doesn't let me see the Acropolis, but I can make out the Colossus. It towers over us, a malevolent guardian, its shadow splitting the agora into halves. Its bronze skin is wreathed in morning light, as if it's trying to swallow the sun. It's only now, when I'm so close to that behemoth, that I understand how our tiny island nation sent so many other countries to their knees.

Beside me, Alix drops his gaze, squeezing his books so tightly there's a crack in one of the spines.

I walk closer to him, laying a hand on his arm. "We're right here for you, Alix. We're going to do this together."

"I know. It's just…the Colossus is—"

"Nothing like you," I say firmly. "And if you need a distraction, well, just think of slimy fish guts."

Alix chokes on a laugh. I mime fish guts spilling down onto my hair, and he hunches over his books, shoulders shaking.

It's nice to know that my inappropriate sense of humor, as Master Vasilis called it, is good for something.

"This way," Zara says brightly, as if she's a student giving us a tour of the place. The pirate queen with brine in her veins has completely been transformed into an eager, young scholar. It's terrifying, really.

She slips between two of the buildings at the edge of the agora and we come out into what must be the back lanes of the Scriptorium. Here there aren't official Scriptorium buildings but more villas. They're all secured behind high walls, some with small windows that let us see beautiful gardens with fountains and busts and fruit trees, others just impenetrable stretches of white. I'm sure these walls have gates somewhere, but we're at the back of these homes, not the front, our little shale path squeezed between the walls on both sides.

Every time we pass one, I wonder if this is Master Theodis's home. But every time I glance at Alix, he still stares forward.

The farther we go, the older our surroundings become.

The houses don't gleam quite so brightly. Plants cling to cracks in the walls. The path turns derelict beneath our feet. It feels as if we're walking back in time.

We come around the corner and Alix goes so suddenly still, I don't need to ask to know we've arrived. We silently follow the wall around to the front road. The wooden gate has rotted off its hinges, leaving a large gap through which I can make out the villa. Its worn and sad, with stained walls and broken tiles, its garden long overgrown into a snarled mass.

Alix pulls his himation from his face. The loss in his eyes stabs like a knife. I recognize that look because I felt it, when my brother was taken away. This place has sat abandoned for centuries. But not for Alix.

"Are you all right?" I ask softly.

He shakes his head. "But I need to do this."

Slowly he squares his shoulders. And he steps into his old home.

27

—

ALIX

I slip through the gap in the gate and onto the front pathway, plants poking up around my sandals. I still remember every stretch of my father's meticulously tended garden. His favorite nectarine tree over there that used to give the sweetest fruit. The bed of crocuses surrounding the bench where he used to read to me in the evening. The herb garden he and I tended together. It's all gone, replaced by a snarled mass of yellow leaves and thin, decaying branches. Everything he and I worked on together has been erased, as if it never existed.

As painful as that is, it's worse seeing the villa. I used to love looking at it, lying on my back in a hidden part of the garden. I thought it had a nice face. A welcoming face. Now it sags, its once gleaming shutters broken and dirty, its once white walls smeared brown and riddled with

cracks, pottery tiles from its roof lying on the ground broken and chipped.

The villa once had a set of great wooden doors to greet
guests, carved with the sigil of my father's house, the swan
with the olive branches. Now nothing but the hinges remain. I climb the steps, my fingers nervously drumming
against my books.

I brace myself but stepping inside is still a blow. The
dust kicked up by our entrance glints in the light stream-
ing in at our backs. At my feet, I can barely make out the
mosaic pattern of marble and gold, which would look like
the sun if all the dirt in here was swept away. The nooks
in the walls, which once overflowed with each day's offer-
ings from the garden, are empty. The tapestries and statues
have been stolen away. All of the grandness of the villa is
gone. It looks dead, like my father is dead.

All I want is to find my father's study and his library and
all the other rooms I spent so many happy days in back
then. Only we don't have time, and perhaps it's better if
they live on in my memory as they used to be. I know
now that whenever I think of the spaces I've seen so far,
my good memories will always have to compete with how
it looks now.

Leaving my books on the ground by the door, I head
down the side hallway, the others following me silently.
Our sandals leave footprints in the dust with every step. If
anyone comes here, it will be very clear where we've gone.
Why would they, though, after all this time? This is a corner of the world that's been long forgotten. The house of

the great traitor. Even if it was once a home—a good home, a happy home—what would the rest of the world care?

I stop at what seems to be a normal stretch of wall, with golden sun decorations running along at chest height. The chip near the one I'm looking for is still there, where I dug it out of the wall too forcefully once. Now I'm more careful, grasping its raised edge and easing it out. It reveals the bronze seal behind it, the rune still emblazoned on its surface.

I should unlock it. Instead I stand there.

"What if I don't like what I find in here?" I ask. My words sound far too loud for the silent hallway. "What if I find out what I am and it's something that I don't want?"

Karis steps up to me, lacing her fingers through mine. "You're you, Alix. And nothing you learn in there will change that."

I want to believe her. I'm just not sure I can. At least I'm not alone. I squeeze her hand and reach out with the other to press my fingers against the seal. The rune in it is so familiar, the humming tune I made up for it springs to my lips before I think about it. The rune on the back of my hand flares brightly and a rumbling shudder quakes down the hallway as the entire wall in front of me shifts toward us.

Karis frowns. "What rune is that? It's an *unlock* rune and yet…"

She trails off. I understand why. The rune she's looking at isn't one but two, built on top of each other. I look down at the familiar lines on the back of my hand. "My father told me it meant home."

Home. Even though he isn't here anymore.

The wall swings out. There's a small tunnel on the other side and I have to let go of Karis's hand to navigate my way through. The world goes dark as I close the wall behind us, the dim light from my eyes not strong enough to let us see anything. I don't need to see. For me, it's only been a few short weeks since I last stood here, not enough time to hold centuries.

I take three steps. Turn to the right. The lamp is somehow still there. I strike my flint and a golden glow springs to life. I move forward, not focusing on anything but the lamps scattered throughout the room, leaving brightening light in my wake. It's only once they're all lit that I turn.

A fresh blow of pain hits me in the chest. As bad as it was seeing how much the rest of the house had changed, it's worse seeing what's happened here. The walls are still painted with pictures of gardens and the ocean and the islands, but they're flaked and crumbling. The furniture is still here, too, the only pieces I've seen so far in the house, but dust clings to them in a thick layer, smudging out everything.

The rest of the villa always looked elegant. Father said it was important that his home look the way the other Scriptmasters expected it to. These secret rooms alone were decorated for comfort, with soft couches to recline on, roomy bookcases, and a round table off to the side, where even now some dice lie, in the middle of a game I wish I remembered. Everything is still and quiet. Not that it was loud back then, but it wasn't like this.

Two doors lead off the main room, one open, one closed. I go to the open one first, taking a lamp and holding it high.

"My room," I say, not sure who I'm talking to.

Karis looks in, Dane and Zara hanging back to give us privacy. I wonder what Karis sees. There are definitely some things missing, such as a bed. Windows. Besides that, though, I think it looks like a normal room, with a desk and more bookcases and a chair in the corner. This room I made mine more than the other, so there are also vases, which once held flowers but now only hold dust. None of them match. I never had enough of an aesthetic sense to make things look good together.

A map of the islands decays on one wall and a map of the world decays on the other. Little figurines and boxes and trinkets sit perched on every remaining available space, objects from the outside world that Father would bring me whenever his duties called him away. It was as close as I got back then to being able to touch the outside world.

I pick up a little swallow carved from stone, its mouth open as if singing. It was the last piece my father brought home, because he said he missed the way I sang while he was away. I rub the dust from its head and slip it into my belt pouch.

"I like it," Karis says.

"I liked it, too."

Liked. Past tense. As soon as it's out, I wonder if it's true. When it became true. Suddenly, I'm so glad that Karis is standing here beside me and that I'm not facing this alone. Karis is fierceness and stubbornness, and she makes me feel braver.

I turn away, knowing we don't have much time, and go to the other door where Zara and Dane are waiting. There's no *lock* rune on it. No locking mechanism at all, and yet it still feels wrong to lay my palm on the wood. "This is my father's workshop. He asked me not to come in here, and I never broke that rule."

"Surely he wouldn't begrudge you that now," Zara says.

No, he wouldn't. Maybe, after all these years, he'd want me to see what's inside. I'm the only one left who really knew him, the only one who can carry on his memory, his work.

I lift the latch on the door and push it open.

28

ALIX

After so long I expect the door to creak, but it soundlessly gives way.

My father's workshop is dark, and I don't know where any candles in here might be, so I hold my lamp in front of me and take a hesitant step inside. My light slips over a workbench, wooden and sturdy even after all these years. The light finds a face.

No, not a face. *My* face.

I jerk back. Beside me, Karis holds up a candle, and as she moves the light over the length of the automaton, I see it's missing an arm and a leg. It doesn't even have a seal. Its face, though… Its face is still mine. I reach out with shaking fingers and touch it. Shivers crawl all over me at the feel of its cold metal.

Zara steps forward, too, raising a lamp she must have grabbed. Her circle of light shows more workbenches and more automatons lying on them or leaning against them. Most are missing limbs, some are less than half-built. All of them are still. All of them bear my face.

A vice clamps around my chest, squeezing tighter and tighter. No matter where I turn, I see myself. Lying on the benches, covered in dust, staring blankly with eyes that look exactly like mine except without the fire. They're exact copies. Dead copies.

"Alix?" Karis's voice is so soft, I almost don't hear it.

"I thought I was unique," I whisper. "I thought he made me to be unique." All this time, these things were right on the other side of the door.

"You are unique." Karis steps closer, and the ferocity in her voice pulls me back. "They might look like you, but they aren't you. Whatever spark of life makes you yourself, they clearly don't have."

Couldn't they have had it, though? I don't understand how my father made me, but couldn't any one of these automatons have easily become me? And couldn't I have easily become one of them, half-finished and lying in the dust? Maybe all I am is the copy that worked.

Griefs splinters in my chest. How could my father have not told me about this? He didn't tell me, and now he's gone, and I'll never have the chance to ask him.

Zara clears her throat. "I'm sorry, Alix, but we can't linger here long. Everyone spread out. See what you can find."

"Why don't you wait in the front room?" Karis says.

A part of me wants to do that, to run from here and never come back, but I shake my head. This room might be the only place in the entire world that can tell me about myself.

That can tell me about my father. The only thing worse than losing him would be realizing I never really knew him at all.

Karis opens her mouth, but I move forward before she has a chance to say anything, toward the nearest workbench. There's an automaton lying on it—or half an automaton. It has no legs. I look away. I never quite knew what people meant when they said that they felt sick to their stomach. Now I do.

Bronze tools carved with runes lie scattered over the benches alongside hammered sheets of metal. There are papers, too, and even though they're decaying, I can see my father's meticulous printing. I think of him, working in the front room or in his study in the house proper, bent over his papers and his letters. Teaching me to do the same. All that time, he never told me what he was working on. Was I on the other side of the door as he studied these other automatons? Waiting eagerly like I always did to spend more time with him?

Did he ever think of telling me the truth?

I can't stand those thoughts slithering through my head. I force myself to keep moving.

I see a fully finished automaton, identical to me down to the last rune. Somehow, that's even more disturbing. I'm already turning away when I notice the book tucked beneath its arm.

I don't want to touch this dead twin, but I don't see a way around it, so I shift its arm and pull the book free, the leather cover flaking away beneath my fingers. I turn it over in my hands. It isn't a tome, or if it is it's unfinished. The unmarked cover doesn't have a seal on its spine. I open it. There are more notes here. I flip through them, and then stop at the image of a great, glowing orb, covered with runes. It's labeled near the top: *The Scrivolia "The Automaton Heart."*

We were right.

I press my fingers over the words. The Automaton Heart. This time it brings forth a thin strain of memory, of my father calling it that, a Heart to hold the automaton's blood, the Script ink.

I shift the book and parchment flutters from it down onto the workbench. A broken seal stares up at me, bearing the crest of the Scriptorium. I pick it up with shaking fingers.

Master Theodis,

We've completed our deep study of the runes inscribing the surface of the Scrivolia. They have revealed that it should be possible to unlock the Heart to even greater levels of power. All of our attempts to regain the secrets of refining Script ink or to build more vessels have failed. With the rumors of war only growing, we must find a way to gain more of the Scrivolia's power so that we can increase our automaton forces.

Knowing of your expertise in the area, the inner council has appointed you as head of the project. We need you to find a key to unlock the greater treasures that the Scrivolia can provide. We need it now. You will be provided with whatever funds and supplies you require.

The magistrate thanks you for your service.

Councilor Reill

The world doesn't feel quite solid beneath my feet, as if broken, empty sky spools out from beneath me. I look back at the notebook and see a single scrawled note in my father's hand:

The fools. Don't they know that any key can lock as easily as it can unlock?

"Alix?" Karis steps up to my elbow. "What did you find?"

I numbly hold it out to her. Her eyes, burning like my own in the candlelight, look over the letter. Her mouth opens in surprise.

"Me," I say hoarsely. "This is why my father made me. I'm this key the Scriptorium wanted." I know it with a certainty I can't even try to deny. This is what I was made for. This is what I am. The magistrate wanted a key to unlock the Scrivolia to greater power. My father wanted a key to take the Script ink away from them. So he made me. All along, a part of me knew that I had been made for a reason but facing the truth of it is still wrenching. I'm a tool.

My father built me to be a tool.

I look back down at the picture of the Heart. The memories press in, blurs sharpening into images. Of my father coming into my rooms dripping wet, a frantic look in his eyes that I didn't recall ever being there before.

"I remember," I whisper. "My father rushed into my rooms one night. He said we'd been discovered and that we had to do it now."

"Do what?" Dane asks.

"Do this." I press my hands against my temples, not wanting to lose the memory of that night. Of sneaking with my father into the highest tier, through the pouring rain that darkened the shadows and stung cold against my skin. Moving through the Scriptorium like ghosts while we heard the shouts of those looking for us. Stumbling down a stairway that curled deep into the ground until we reached the Automaton Heart, burning in the crypts beneath the Acropolis like the sun.

"We went to the Scrivolia. I locked it." I remember placing my palms against the metal surface, burning hot as fire. I remember the melodies that had crashed into my head when I touched it.

The memories are already breaking apart, splintering even as I try to dig deeper into them. "The Automaton Heart went dark but then men found us." Scriptorium soldiers found us. My father shouted at me to run. So I did. I ran, and he fell. The memory hits me like a thunder strike, searing me to my core. A soldier advancing on my father, his sword gleaming in the light from his torch. My father's eyes going wide as the metal bit through his body. The way he'd been shucked off the blade like a discarded rag, the light already leaving his eyes. "They killed him," I whisper. "I left him to die."

"No, Alix." Karis steps up to me. "That isn't your fault."

"Yes, it is, it's all my fault!" I cry and see the surprise in her eyes, the flash of fear she isn't quick enough to hide. "He built me to be a key, raised me like his child, but when it mattered, I wasn't able to do what he wanted, and he died."

"You did do it," Zara says. "You locked the Script ink down. You took its power from the Scriptorium. Thanks to you it's been gone for two centuries."

"That wasn't all my father wanted me to do." Something else is coming back to me, something I've forgotten all this time. He taught me how to lock the Scrivolia, yes, but he also taught me something more. "He wanted me to destroy it." That's the secret that's been hovering around my edges. "He said that as long as the Script ink in the Heart was un-locked, the Scrivolia was indestructible. If the Script ink was locked, though, the actual vessel could be destroyed. I managed to lock the Script ink, but the magistrate's men found us too soon. The Automaton Heart still exists. While my father..." My father doesn't. When it really mattered, I failed him. I failed what I was meant to be.

There is quiet for a long moment until Karis asks softly. "Do you still remember how to destroy the Heart?"

No, I don't. That part of my memory is still locked deep inside of me. I shake my head. "It must have something to do with the runes, though, and with the Script inscribed on the Heart." Not that it matters now. It's too late.

I look around at the workshop, at the automatons whose master...whose father...is long dead because I left him.

In the end, child or tool, I was no more use to him than any of them.

29

ALIX

I don't speak the entire way back through the city, ignoring the concerned looks the others are giving me. I stare down at the books in my arms, my father's notebook hidden among them. My father, who built all of those other automatons. Who lied to me. A seed of coldness has been planted in my chest and I can already feel it growing.

We reach the villa and I retreat to my room, even though I know that's running away. I catch a glimpse of Karis's face, her mouth opening, as I shut the door. I throw the books on my bed, then sag back against the door. Whatever Karis was about to say, I don't want to hear. Because, in the end, she doesn't—can't—understand.

My uncovered runes emit pale light in the dark. Script ink. Runes. The Heart. Is that truly all I am? When I decided to go back to the villa, I was so sure I'd find something that would prove I'm more than an automaton. Only I didn't.

I wearily lift my head and see my father's notebook, fallen open on the bed.

The fools. Don't they know that any key can lock as easily as it can unlock?

I can't stand this, being here alone in the dark. All of these emotions are creeping over me, biting away at my edges. There are no voices outside the door anymore. I leave, slipping through the sitting room and pacing down the hallway. I head out the first side door I find, away from this villa holding so many people who are nothing like me. Anger and confusion pulse inside me and I walk faster, as if I can outpace everything I'm feeling. I shove between two bushes, branches splintering beneath my hands, and then I stop.

The automaton. The one I saw on the way in. It crouches in the garden, frozen in mid-movement. Plants twine up its arms and legs, leaves scattered over its skin, as the garden slowly claims it. It has no eyes, but it still seems to stare into me.

Seeing it saps every bit of anger from my body, even though what's left behind is far more frightening. This feeling of breaking. Of drowning. My knees give, sending me into the grass.

What am I supposed to do now?

"Alix?" Karis's voice sounds behind me. Her footsteps come closer. "Are you all right?"

I choke out a laugh. No. I am not all right.

I look up at the automaton. At this thing that, in the end, is exactly like me. "You know, my father used to tell me that he thought automatons might not have always been used as weapons." My voice sounds strange in the garden.

Too distant. That should bother me. Why doesn't it? "He looked at the designs of the oldest ones, and thought that many centuries ago, they might have served different purposes. That someone later decided automatons could only be one thing. There was always a part of me that desperately hoped it was true." I shake my head. "Only now I realize it doesn't matter. In the end, is being built as a key any better than being built as a weapon? I'm still a thing."

"Alix." She kneels down beside me in the grass. "You are not a thing. None of us think that."

"I was built for a purpose, Karis. I am bound to a tome and I have no idea if one day something will take away everything I am. All this time I thought maybe I could come back here and find something that will make me feel normal. Only I won't ever be normal. I won't ever be like you or Dane or anyone else because my will is bound up in paper and what I was meant to do is etched in my skin. I exist to do one thing, and I couldn't even do that."

The words burn off my tongue. I hang my head. I journeyed all this way for nothing.

Karis takes my hand, but for once I find no comfort in it. "Alix, you are not just some key, some thing. Look at everything you've done. You got us off of Tallis. You fixed the *Streak*. You have come so far since I found you in that cave."

I can feel those words trying to reach me. Only they don't. I'm tired of pretending I'm something I'm not.

I get up, my hand slipping from hers. I pad forward, until I'm standing right before the automaton. "All those things that I've done, I only did because of my runes. They allowed it. What if this is just what I am?"

I reach out, brushing some of the plant matter away, my fingers skimming the giant seal on the automaton's chest.

There's a tug in the center of my chest, and every rune on my body flares with heat as a wave of light races across the automaton's skin. The ground heaves beneath me, throwing me onto my back as the automaton twitches, one of its massive arms shifting up out of the ground.

It's awake.

"Alix," Karis cries, "shut it off!"

I scramble to my feet, pressing my hands against the automaton's seal. Nothing happens. Its runes still flare gold, glowing like a beacon in the evening light.

"I don't know how."

A door bangs open like a gunshot in the night. I flinch. Calantha hurries into the clearing, Zara on her heels.

Calantha pales at the sight of the automaton. "What have you done?" she demands.

"I just touched it." I hold my hands out in front of me as if they're poison.

That's when we hear shouts echo across the garden. Loud. Authoritarian.

Soldiers. They must be able to see the light. They'll find me. They'll find all of us.

Calantha straightens. "Zara. Make sure everyone gets out of the villa and to the tunnel. You three go with her and—"

"My tome," I say. It's back in the house. Already I can hear the soldiers getting closer. "I can't leave it," I plead.

"I'll hold them away for as long as I can," Calantha says. "When you get your tome, take the path that goes be-

tween the marble arches at the back of the villa. There's a
tunnel at its end."

"Wait," Zara says. "Calantha, you can't go back in there."

"Zara..."

Her eyes flash. "You know what the magistrate will do
if he catches you. With this automaton woken up, it will
give him enough of a reason to bring you in for question-
ing, and your position won't be enough to protect you."

They stare at each other, pirate captain and rebel leader,
and I see just how similar they are. So I already know how
Calantha will answer.

"Get the others out." Calantha leaves, striding back down
the path.

Zara stares after her. "Get your tome," she says tightly.
"And get it now."

I take off.

Through the trees I catch a glimpse of others, all hurrying the other way, and then I'm at the villa, pushing
through the side entrance. Outside I could hear the soldiers
but inside it's quiet until a heavy pounding on the front
door echoes down the hall. I falter.

Karis comes through the door behind me. She looks
down the hallway. "We can make it," she says.

We slide down the deserted hallways, slipping into the
study even as we hear footsteps clattering inside. Karis pulls
the door shut as I push aside the tapestry and unlock the
box. My tome is still there, and I sag with relief as soon as
my fingers close around it.

"Come on," Karis says. "Let's—"

Voices sound right outside the door.

We both freeze. Calantha's voice comes, muted but still sure and steady. She's distracting them.

"The window," Karis mouths.

We dash over to it. Karis easily vaults through, back out into the garden. I follow, but my shoulders catch on the window frame. I'm too big.

Behind me, I hear the door creak open.

Bracing my hands on the walls, I shove myself through, feeling the crunch as I take some of the window frame with me.

We don't stop to see if anyone noticed but run. I see the marble arches at the back of the villa. We follow the path through the garden. It's wilder here, more snarled, the trees creating a dense canopy over our heads.

I glimpse a figure and hold out an arm, so suddenly Karis runs into it. She bites back a grunt of pain. A soldier stands ahead of us. It's one of the magistrate's men, his sash dark against his chiton. He isn't facing us, but he is in our way.

I slowly step back, into the shadows of a nearby tree.

A hand touches my shoulder. I spin.

It's Rudy. His face is pale and he clutches a satchel to his chest, papers spilling from its sides. Gesturing silently, he steps away from the path and the soldier.

We plunge into the thick of the garden, branches tearing at my clothes. Then we're back on the path. We reach its end and I see a trapdoor covered in grass, propped up. Finn and Ava stand beside it.

"Are you the last?" Finn asks.

"I think so," Rudy pants. He disappears down the steps.

I look over my shoulder, back at the villa and the garden, where the animated automaton must still stand.

I did this.

I turn and follow Rudy down into the dark.

30

KARIS

We seem to walk forever in the dark tunnel, the only light the lamp clenched in Ava's fist, the only sounds our footfalls against the stone. The steps, when we reach them, come up into a small shed in the Lower City.

Finn leads us out, toward the bay. I wonder if we're going to the *Streak*, to set sail right now and leave the city.

But we don't. We go to a deserted area of the docks, the planks slick with seawater, the air thick with brine and rotting fish. Dark water swirls through the cracks beneath our feet. Large decaying buildings that look like they might once have housed ships crouch over us in the hastening night.

Finn takes us to one near the back. The windows are dark and there's no noise but the ocean. They remove a fragment of rotted wood wall and we slip in, and it isn't empty at all.

The people inside are shadowy blurs in the cavernous

space. It's sparsely furnished, mostly with pallets, worn and unmatched. I don't recognize many of the people but then I see Zara. She stands in the center of the room, in a small patch of moonlight created by a hole in the roof. She points to some crates, directing others.

"Captain," I say, wincing when my voice echoes too loudly.

She turns, and I see how different she looks. Her usual jauntiness is gone. There's a new weight settled onto her grim expression, into the tense set of her shoulders. The others in the boathouse all orient themselves toward her. I never thought to ask who would inherit the responsibility of this rebellion if something happened to Calantha.

Now she's standing in front of me.

"You made it," Zara says, relieved.

I look around for Dane. I haven't seen him since we got back.

Zara must read the question on my face because she says, "Dane asked to go back out to help the others, so I let him."

He went back out. I know better than anyone what that request must have meant to him. He'll be fighting other soldiers, who represent what he once wanted. And he still did it.

"What can we do to help?" Alix asks, a catch in his voice.

"There are blankets in those crates," Zara says. "Hand them out and show people to the pallets. There'll be more coming from the other villas as soon as word spreads about what happened."

Alix nods. He goes to leave and I take his arm. "Alix, this isn't your fault."

Guilt clearly eats into him. "Yes, it is." He pulls his arm away.

I open my mouth, but whatever I might have said comes too late. Alix strides between the pallets. Exhaustion weighs me down as I stare after him. Ever since we saw his father's workshop, it's like a part of him shut down. And I hate that. I don't want to see him lose his softness, his hope.

I don't want to have to watch him become like me.

More and more people filter in through the hole in the wall, dressed in Scriptorium wear and peasant wear and noble wear—and those terrible runes on so many of them.

It must be near dawn when a piece of wall moves and two lone people stumble in. One I don't recognize. The other is Dane.

"Dane." I run to him as he sags to his knees. He's dirty and bloodied, one of his eyes swelling shut, a long cut tracing down his left arm.

I uncap the water skin in my hand and pour some on a rag, pressing it against his hurt eye. He winces, his free hand coming up to cover mine.

"Archius, soldier boy." Zara trots over. "What's happened?"

Dane shakes his head. "I'm sorry," he says hoarsely. "We tried to get the last group out, but they were caught at the corner of the market."

Zara's face falls, and I see her incredible exhaustion. But only for a moment. She gathers herself up. Slips back into the role of commander. "You did everything you could. That's all I ask."

"There's more," the other man—Archius—says. He swallows. "The Scriptmasters, we overheard them talking. Master Calantha has been taken into custody."

★ ★ ★

The boathouse has turned into a gathering of ghosts. From the moment the news spread that Calantha was taken, whatever flame we'd managed to salvage went out. I skirt through the pallets, offering the last of the blankets, some food I found, and only get listless stares back. That same emotion sinks through my own skin and wraps around my heart. There was such passion in Calantha's voice when she talked about the new Scriptorium she wanted to make. Now she may very well be in the Magistrate's Library, alongside my brother and everyone else who was just taken.

I look around the boathouse at all these people who have suffered so much. Who will suffer again if the magistrate unlocks the Heart and reanimates the automatons. At their grieving and scared faces.

This isn't right. None of it.

I abandon the pile of blankets I'm carrying and go to find the others. They're all together—Zara, Dane, Alix, and Rudy—in a small room that must have been an office once, sitting on some crates that have been dragged together. There's a window, half-boarded up, but I can still catch glimpses of the black ocean, of the night sky through it. It's a world that goes on like it always has, even though so much has changed for us in here.

It's dark, but I can just make out the exhausted faces around me, the creases in their skin and the bags beneath their eyes. Even Zara. There's a defeat in her expression I've never seen there before.

Dane sits next to her. Their hands rest on the crate between them, their fingers brushing one another, and they both lean into that touch. For the briefest moment I wish I could have something like that, a relationship that's as close as that, where I don't need words to explain what I'm feeling. Because I feel tired and alone and I could use it right about now.

Alix looks up. Offers me a shaking smile. It's a shadow of his usual one, but it's still there. I manage a smile back. I might not have what Dane and Zara do, but that doesn't mean what I have is weaker. Standing here, it feels as strong as stone.

I go over to Alix and perch on the crate beside him. The heat wicking off his skin helps to banish the numbness sunk into my bones.

"I'm sorry about Calantha," I say to Zara.

She rubs a hand across her eyes. "We all knew the risks. The most we can do right now is keep everyone safe for her. There are other villas on other islands. We'll ferry everyone to them."

Rudy, who'd been staring at his satchel, lifts his head. "But what about what's happening here? The rumors are only growing. The magistrate could be days away from whatever he's planning. And what about the people we're leaving behind?"

I hear in his voice the heartbreak of the name he doesn't say. If we leave, we abandon Matthias to whatever is being done to him here. We abandon Calantha and all the others. However she phrases it, Zara's plan amounts to running away. That wasn't something I ever expected to hear from her. She's always been so quick to rush in, to fight for what she believed in.

"We don't have a choice," Zara says, and at least now there's a flash in her eyes. "So many of our people have been taken. Calantha won't talk, but the others…" She cuts off, shaking her head. "After all they've suffered at the hands of the magistrate, they might break, and I can't blame them for that. Most of them have seen Alix. Once the Scriptorium knows he's here, they won't stop until they find him. Calantha is gone now. All these people are my responsibility, mine alone, and I won't risk their lives for nothing."

A thick silence settles over us, broken only by the quiet noises filtering in from the rest of the boathouse and the slosh of water beneath our feet.

This can't really be it. After everything that's happened, how can this just end with us running away?

Across from me, Rudy is hunched over, rubbing the seal he holds in his hands. It's the one he and my brother stole, with the *unlock* rune.

Unlock.

Wait.

I snatch the seal out of his hands.

Rudy blinks at me. "Karis?"

This *unlock* rune matches the one on Alix's side. Alix, who was built to be a key for the Scrivolia.

"The magistrate… He's going to use a seal to unlock the Heart," I say.

The others all stare at me. Zara's brow furrows. "What?"

I hold out the bronze seal. It's all coming together, disparate pieces connecting in my head. "This rune matches Alix's. At his father's villa, we learned Alix was built to unlock the

Scrivolia. That's what the magistrate's trying to do. He's trying to make a seal, so he can get into the Heart without Alix."

The color leeches from Rudy's face. "But if he manages to unlock the Script ink, he'll gain control over all of the automatons. If that happens…"

He trails off, but he doesn't need to finish. If the magistrate gains access to the Heart, the Scriptorium will be returned to its former power.

Alix shakes his head. "No. The Heart can't be unlocked. My father…" His voice cracks. "My father died so the Scriptorium wouldn't ever have access to it again."

"Then we have to stop him," Dane says.

Zara shakes her head. "We can't. There are people counting on us, people we need to get to safety."

Safety? What safety could exist after this? I think of the magistrate, of everything he's done. If he manages to re-animate the automatons, he'll be unstoppable. And I know the ragtag group around me will be first on his list.

I can't let that happen.

That resolution shudders through my bones. This whole time, all I wanted was to get my brother and me as far away from all of this as I could. I'm sick of it. I'm sick of standing to the side as others choose to fight. I'm sick of fearing and hating the magistrate's cruelty and doing nothing to stop it.

"We should strike now."

Everyone turns and looks at me.

I straighten my spine. Maybe I never wanted this to be my fight, but it is now. Alix is right. We can't allow the magistrate to gain access to that Script ink. I can't allow it. And if I'm doing this, I'm going all in. If we flame out, we'll burn like stars.

"Alix just woke up an automaton," I say, "which means the Scriptorium will be in chaos right now. Scouring Calantha's villa for news. Checking on the other automatons. Searching the city for us. Right now, they don't know what Alix is capable of doing, but we know. If we can get Alix to the Heart, he can destroy it. And then the magistrate won't ever get the Script ink he needs."

"She's right," Rudy says. His words start out slow, but then come faster. "They won't be expecting us right now. And if there are *lock* runes in the way, Alix can get us through them. All the security in the Scriptorium is built to yield to Scriptmasters, which means it should yield to Alix, too."

"And what about when we get to the Heart?" Zara says. "Alix doesn't remember how to destroy it. We'll be risking everything to get there, and he might not even be able to do anything."

"I'll figure it out, Captain," Alix says. "Please. I'm good with runes. You know I am."

"Do we even know where the Heart is?" Dane asks.

"It's in the Acropolis," Alix says. "There was this stairway that spiraled deep into the ground. At the top was a statue, one of the old masters. Master Killia, I believe."

Zara closes her eyes.

"What is it?" Dane asks.

Zara's mouth is a grim line. "I'm not sure what was there in your time, Alix, but now that's the entrance to the Magistrate's Library."

The Magistrate's Library. Where our people were just

taken. Where Matthias might be. That information should terrify me. It does terrify me. It's the last place I want to go.

But it means that maybe I'll have the chance to stop the magistrate and save my brother, too.

Alix straightens, his hand finding the medallion at his neck. "I have to try." There's an undercurrent in his voice, of determination, of desperation, like there was in Master Theodis's villa. It makes me worried about what Alix is feeling. About what he might do. The look in his eyes is so brittle. "I have to finish what my father started and destroy the Heart, before it falls into that man's hands."

Zara drums her fingers on her knee as we all wait in silence for her decision. I can't imagine what she's going through, the whole weight of the rebellion suddenly on her shoulders. All of these people looking to her. But we need our captain right now.

She straightens, a familiar fierceness crossing her face. It makes her look more like herself. "Then I guess we're all in." One by one she looks at the others. One by one they nod. Finally, she looks at me. It's a heavy look. I'm sure she remembers what I said to her as we walked through that village. But things were different then. I was different then. And I'll prove it.

I nod.

"All right," Zara says. "So, we go now. We save our people. We destroy the Heart. And we deal a blow to the Scriptorium they'll never recover from."

She's right. We can do this. We must do this. There's too much at stake now if we lose.

We'll just have to make sure we win.

31

ALIX

The Acropolis.

The last time I was there, I locked the Heart, my father was murdered, and I ran, beneath waves and across islands, until at last I staggered to a stop and somehow centuries passed without me waking. I feel as if ever since that time I've been running. From the Scriptorium. From the magistrate. From the fragmented pieces of my own past that chased me like shadows.

Until now. I rub my father's medallion. Calantha was right. We all need to be what the world asks of us. No matter what that is or what it costs us. Perhaps once I do this, I'll finally be free of the thoughts that won't let me go. If I'm made for a purpose, then I have to complete it. It's what my father would have wanted.

First, though, I have a favor to ask.

I skirt through the pallets, looking for Karis. She stands

near a stack of crates, uneasily fiddling with the knife on her belt.

She straightens as I step forward. "Are you ready?" she asks. There's a slight waver in her voice that she can't quite hide. I'm afraid, too. Of what we'll find in the Magistrate's Library. Of what stepping back into that chamber with the Scrivolia, that place of memory, will do to me.

Which is exactly why I have to ask her what I'm about to.

I hold my tome out to her. "Karis, I want you to take this."

She stares. "What?"

"I can't leave it here. The distance from the docks to the Acropolis is too far. I don't dare hide it either, not with so many soldiers scouring the city. Which means it has to come with me."

"But, Alix, it will be safest with you. You're the strongest of all of us. Or with Dane or Zara. They're both better fighters than I am."

"You don't understand. I'm not asking you to protect it." I pause and then force the words out. "Karis, if it looks like there's any chance it will fall into the hands of the Scriptorium, I need you to destroy it. Stabbing it through the seal should be enough."

The dawning horror on her face nearly breaks my resolve, but I can't let it.

"I'd do it myself," I say, "but I'm not sure what will happen, so I don't know if I'd be able to see it through."

"Alix, no." Karis backs away from me, shaking her head. "Destroying your tome could kill you."

"I would rather be dead than be helpless as they force me to do terrible things. You know they will."

"But at least if you're alive we could save—"

"If you had the choice between dying or going back to Tallis, where they would clamp a bracelet on your wrist again, only this time you knew you would have to do everything they told you for the rest of your life, what would you choose?"

Karis opens her mouth as if to deny it, but I see the truth in her eyes. I saw it in that cave, when she first woke me up. Her desire for freedom, exactly like my own.

I step closer. "Please, don't let them take away everything that I am. I'm asking you, as my friend, to do this for me."

I never thought I would have a friend. But Karis stayed with me through everything. She was never afraid to look at me and truly see me.

Her eyes search my face. She reaches up and touches my cheek. "Alix?" she says. "Are you sure you're all right? Ever since we went to your father's house...you've been different. It isn't like you."

Those words weren't what I expected, and something sleeping in me twitches, nudged awake. I do feel different. Colder. Perhaps I appreciated that, since it kept some of the grief at bay. Now, though, her words make me doubt. They make me face all those feelings that crashed into me at the villa.

Only, I don't want to feel those things anymore.

I take her hand and lower it. "This is what I am, Karis. It's time we both faced that."

A long silence stretches between us. She stands there,

as if waiting for more, but I don't have any more to give. Then she reaches out and takes my tome.

I nod, trying not to let my uncertainty show, to not focus on my hands, which feel suddenly empty. This is better for everybody. At least now I know that when I go in there, I'll leave that place of my own free will.

One way or another.

"Thank you," I whisper.

She mutely nods.

"Karis? Alix?" Zara weaves through the beds toward us. Her eyes go to my tome, now in Karis's hands, but she doesn't say anything. I can only hope it's because she understands. "The rest of us are ready to go."

I look at Karis and then take her hand and squeeze it. She squeezes back.

We started all of this, her and me, in that cave. Even after everything that's happened, we're still standing here together. It's only fitting that we end this together, too.

Myself, Karis, Dane, Zara, Rudy, Kocha, and Wreska. It doesn't seem like enough to take on the Acropolis, but it's us or no one.

Zara keeps us to the side roads as we head up through the Lower City. As careful as we are, I still catch glimpses of soldiers in Scriptorium uniforms and hear the clatter of the wheels of chariots ferrying Scriptmasters about, the barked commands of the Scriptorium authority. The city pulses with fear and a terrifyingly bright energy, a web trying to ensnare us.

We approach the first gate and Rudy takes the lead. I

nervously rub the bracelet on my wrist, the exact color and texture as my metal skin. There are eight soldiers standing there, each holding a naked blade in their hand. One even has a gun holstered at her hip, inscribed with runes of fire and death. The torches anchored to the wall cast a harsh light on their sharp swords and sharper expressions. There's a crowd waiting to get through, mostly acolytes, a few scribes.

Rudy strides toward them, his demeanor changing from a shy young man in mourning into a proud, successful scholar. The others in the crowd glance at his gleaming seal before scuttling out of his way. Rudy walks up to one of the guards and thrusts the seal at him. "Master Aquitaine sent me to catalog runes on one of the automatons in the Lower City. My assistants and I are back to report." His voice is steady and brazen. For the first time I realize how well he fits in with this rebellion.

The guard looks at the seal and then over at us. I stare down at the ground, sure they'll see the glow of my eyes, or a patch of oddly textured skin I forgot to cover. The moment stretches out, too long and tense.

"Go on ahead."

We slip through the gate. Beside me, Karis lets out a breath of relief.

"One down," Rudy mutters. "Three to go."

We head up through the Scribe's Quarters, every street packed with bodies and nervous whispers. Then the tier we fled only a short day ago, where the crowds thin and the villas stare down at us, seemingly every window lit. Two hundred years ago, I ran this path. At that time, I was going the other way, fleeing from my failure. Now, finally, I have the chance to make it right. To do what I'm meant to do.

We reach the Acropolis tier. The Colossus stands in front of us, so tall that up close I can't crane my neck far enough back to see its full height. Our heads barely pass the top of its ankles. All its runes are out of reach, but I'm sure each one is at least as tall as I am. The lines flare, and I'm struck with the sudden dread that we're too late and that the magistrate has already unlocked the Heart, but it's merely a trick of the torchlight.

Behind the Colossus, the Acropolis shines pale in the moonlight. I'd forgotten how magnificent it looks. Seven stories of pure marble reach to the Colossus's waist. A set of broad steps, edged with gold, lead to imposing wooden doors that stretch far above our heads. The pillars surrounding all four sides of the building are carved to look like automatons holding the roof up, accurate down to the runes in their skin.

Looking at it now, it's more than a building. It represents all the hurt Agathon has caused within its walls. We somehow have to conquer that.

Rudy leads us to the side of the building, where there's a smaller door. It has a *lock* rune, but I place my hand on it and immediately catch its song. One mental twist and it yields.

We slip inside.

As soon as Wreska closes the door behind us, the noises from outside disappear. My father's home had been grand and elegant. So is Calantha's villa. They're nothing like this. We stand in a sheltered alcove at the edge of a large room, a great arched roof soaring over our heads held up by pillars crowned in gold. Reclining couches and low tables are scattered about, the wood ornately carved and the cushions crafted from silk. It's deserted.

Rudy beckons us forward down a side hallway. I can make out the tread of feet, but it's quiet, far off.

We wind through the halls, slowly, carefully. The only sounds are our footsteps padding across the ground, the slightly erratic draw of the others' breaths. As we move farther, I begin to see things I remember: that mosaic of a Scriptmaster holding a tome; that window looking out at the Colossus; that carved nook with the vaulted ceiling. I was on this path before. I don't remember if it was when I came in with my father or when I ran out of here alone, but I've walked these steps once already.

We turn a corner. The statue stands in a great atrium, slits in the roof sending moonlight shafting down. Master Killia's stone robes flare out around her legs, caught in a moment of movement, and she stares down at an open ledger.

We gather around the statue and I take in the determined expressions of Zara and the other pirates. Some of them have been in this place, and they aren't turning back.

"Anyone who's down there who we aren't here to save, kill," Zara says, her voice deathly dark. "Because the people in this place don't deserve to live."

Kocha and Dane pull out their daggers. Wreska slips her ledger from her pocket, and with a dash of charcoal across the page, one of her bracelets unfurls into a thin knife. There's a prickling at the back of my head that tells me to shy away from this violence because, like Karis said, it isn't me, but it's too late for that. If this is what I was made to do, then I will do it.

And then... I don't know what I'm supposed to do then.

Zara gestures to me. I remember where the *lock* rune is even as I step forward, my fingers finding it hidden in the fold of Killia's cloak. The melody that spills into my head is discordant. Chilling. As if even the rune, even the song, knows what kind of place it's guarding.

I hum a few notes, gritting my teeth against its severity. Golden light shoots out from the rune, framing a large marble tile on the floor. The lines of light connect together and there's a soft chink as a marble square rises slightly. Kocha grabs its edge and swings it up, showing a rough staircase descending into the dark.

Zara nods at us all, and one by one we slip down, down, down, until we're swallowed by the shadows.

32

KARIS

Wreska, Dane, and Kocha hold the lamps, the sway-ing light throwing erratic shadows against the rough stone floor and walls. But the dark is so thick even the lamplight isn't strong enough to keep back the shadows that bite at its edges. A slow shiver crawls over my skin, prick-ling out goose bumps. I can't shake the feeling that there's something in the black, watching us. Waiting.

And then, between one step and the next, something changes. Like we've stepped into an invisible fog, even though there's nothing there but the dark. Its nails raking through my head, a sudden burst of pain that makes me gasp. In front of me Alix stumbles and falls to his knees, his face contorted.

"Alix." I stagger over to him, pressing my hand to his shoulder. He shakes beneath my touch.

"What is that?" he forces out.

Zara looks back, her pained face ghoulish in the weak lantern's light. Her hand, braced against the wall, trembles. "That's what happens when you try to turn Script ink into something it's not. When you twist it."

"But there's nothing here," Dane grits out.

"This Script ink isn't refined. You won't be able to see it." Zara shoves off the wall. "But it can still be affected by the things people do through the Script. The magistrate is messing with things he shouldn't."

The thought that this force is surrounding us, hanging in the air, makes my skin grow clammy.

"Are you going to be all right?" I ask Alix.

His face is twisted, but he braces his arm against the wall and hauls himself to his feet. "I'm fine."

"Alix—"

"I have to do this, Karis."

He keeps going. I follow, fighting to push down the unease that grows with every step. I can't explain it, but it feels like something has already gone wrong. Alix's tome weighs down the satchel resting against my hip, far too heavy for such a small book. I don't know how I'll ever be able to do what he asked. I don't know how I'll be able to refuse.

The distorted Script ink in the air only thickens the farther we go, sloughing at my limbs and making every step forward a challenge. Alix starts humming, the notes sharp and pained. I don't know if he's trying to dispel whatever is in the air or only to comfort himself, but it does comfort me.

We reach the bottom of the stairs. There are two torches

there, and their weak, guttering light barely illuminates the hall in front of us.

As soon as I see, I wish there was no light at all. Because then I wouldn't be able to make out the hallway in front of us, bare except for a row of cells on both sides, with gritty iron bars that look like teeth. A scent hangs in the air, so rank I clap my hand over my mouth. I always thought that people saying you could smell fear was just an expression. It isn't.

I'm taking a step back when Dane says, voice tight, "Is this...?"

At his words, a murmuring comes from the cells. Dark shapes shift inside, the torchlight reflecting eerily off their eyes. It's the only indication that they're people. A crushing weight suffocates me. I don't need to hear the answer to Dane's question. This is it: the Magistrate's Library.

I lived out on the streets for years. Slept in some of the dankest, dirtiest places in all of Heretis, where you could hear the scratching of rats all night long. I thought I was ready to face anything. But I wasn't ready to face this. The terrible, stark reality of it punches a hole through my chest.

"Captain?"

The wavering voice is familiar, but it takes me a too long moment to realize who it belongs to: Aiken, from the *Streak*. It hasn't even been a day since he was taken, but he's already stinking and dirty, and there's a wild look to his eyes as he slumps behind the bars. How could he not, with the Script ink like this, worming its way into our heads? "Captain, you came for us."

Zara goes to him, clasping his hands between the bars.

"Of course. I always come for my crew." She raises her voice. It's strung tight as a whip. "Find the keys."

Wreska and Kocha separate down the hall as Zara turns to us. "You know the plan?"

I nod. Zara, Wreska, and Kocha will stay here and unlock the cells. Me, Dane, Alix, and Rudy will keep going. Alix will destroy the Heart once and for all. In the ensuing chaos we'll get everyone out or die trying.

I know that's the plan, that it's my plan, that we need to go now. But Matthias could be right here, in any one of these cells, separated only by a few bars and shadows. That knowledge stifles everything else out.

"My brother," I whisper.

Zara doesn't look surprised, even though we hadn't discussed it. But there's a clear warning in her eyes as she says, "Whatever you do, do it quickly. His isn't the only life we've come to save."

I hurry away, down the row of cells. My heart hammers against my ribs as I look into each one for the person I crossed an ocean to find.

Faces peer at me through the bars, so gaunt and smudged it's hard to tell that some are young and others old, some are Eratian and others not. Rudy haunts my steps, and now I'm glad he's here because I don't think I could face this on my own. At every cell my heart lifts and crashes down again. We reach the last one.

He isn't here.

No. I look desperately back up the hallway, as if somehow we missed something—another row of cells, a door. Anything.

"I don't... I don't understand," Rudy says. He presses his hands to his eyes. "This is all my fault. If I'd just reached out and stopped him. If I'd just done something..."

I stare into the last cell, disbelief ringing through my head. He's not here. After all this, he isn't here.

How can he not be here?

Horrible, stifling silence stretches out until Dane speaks softly into the quiet. "Karis, Rudy. I'm sorry, but we have to go."

I numbly look at Dane, whose expression is steady even now. My heart aches as if there's a hook in it, slowly tearing it in two. But I promised to do this. I told myself I would do this. If I can't save Matthias, I'm going to save everyone else.

It's what he would have done.

There's only one way to go, farther into the library, so that's where we head. There are no more cells here, but bare hallway. Another intersects ours, and when I glance down it, I see a door at the end. I don't want to think about what lies behind it. There are no lights, yet the shadows around that door seem thicker than they should be, as if they have weight.

One of the shadows twitches.

I jerk, my heartbeat rocketing up. I'm sure I must have imagined it, until Alix speaks.

"Did that..." His voice is weak. "Did that shadow just move?"

Dane grips his blade, even though there's nothing to attack. He swallows and I pretend not to notice the fear in his eyes. "Let's keep moving."

We hurry down the hall and now there's no mistaking the way the shadows move, twitching and spasming against the walls. Zara had said the magistrate was working with things he shouldn't. I see the proof all around us of what she meant.

The hallway abruptly ends, at a stairway that spirals down a rocky shaft.

We stop at the landing, none of us quite ready.

"Is this it?" I whisper.

Alix nods, and for once I have no idea what's going on behind his expression. It's locked down into a place I can't understand.

"This is it," he says.

He steps forward down the stairs. Dane has the only lamp and it shines at our backs, throwing our wavering, elongated shadows in front of us. At least the distorted Script ink in the air has slackened down here, giving me more room to think. I peer over the edge of the stairway, and a flash of gold catches in the torchlight. The Scrivolia.

We reach the last step and I get my first true look at the Heart. It sits in the center of a large, circular crypt, the edges of the space bordered by rough archways that lead to more darkness. I wasn't sure how big the Scrivolia would be, but it stands twice as tall as I do. Its entire surface is covered with gold polished so brightly it shines even now when I know the Script ink inside of it has been locked.

Then I notice its runes, gliding and swirling into one another, as if they're caught in a dance. I've seen so much Eratian Scriptwork in my life, carved into automaton metal or inscribed in ledgers. It's always been clunky. Brash. But on the Scrivolia it's beautiful, with an elegance to the lines that reminds me of Alix. They're all connected, dozens upon dozens of smaller runes flowing into one another. I thought the Scriptwork I saw on Alix's arm was the most intricate I would ever lay eyes on, but it is nothing like this. The entire surface of the Heart is one massive rune.

"This is the Scrivolia?" Rudy asks.

"Yes," Alix whispers.

This Heart once held the Script ink. It once gave our nation the power to create and control automatons. Even though that has only ever caused me pain, there is still something awe-inspiring about standing before it. This vessel was created so long ago, no one even remembers when or how it was made. It's a piece of history that few know about and even fewer understand.

A piece of history we've come all this way to destroy. I turn to Alix. "Finish what your father started. For all of us."

His eyes meet my own and they hold loss, too. And I see that he understands. He nods, squaring his shoulders, and moves toward the Heart.

"So, you made it after all."

The voice is cool, crisp, and I know it with gut-wrenching certainty.

The magistrate steps out from the shadows at the end of the room. He's dressed just like the last time I saw him, but down here the white of his robe and the gold of his seal seem smudged, as if the shadows cling to him. He claps his hands, and the sound is so sharp in the quiet crypts, it makes me flinch. "I wasn't sure if you would show."

"Magistrate Agathon," I whisper.

He turns to me, and my breath lodges in my throat. His eyes. Up in the gardens I thought I'd seen a flicker of shadows in them. Down here it's as if they're dead light, all the life sucked out, and I can make out shadows twining in their depths. He is as wrong as the place he stands in.

That's when I know exactly how deeply in trouble we are. Because he doesn't look surprised to see me, not at all.

"Ah, little Demetria. Or should I call you Karis now? My little runaway, come back to me."

The possession in his voice steals away my breath. How much did he know back in that garden? How could I ever have thought he didn't know?

He turns to look over my friends. "Then there's Dane, the soldier who all his masters had such high hopes for, now nothing more than a common rebel." Dane twitches. "Rudy, one of the greatest scholarly minds to come through our halls in a generation, wasted." Rudy juts out his chin, but it trembles.

"And you." The magistrate looks at Alix and something finally comes into his eyes: hunger. Hunger that could swallow a hundred nations. "The automaton with the mind. Master Theodis's little monster. What a remarkable creature you are."

Alix flinches, and in that moment he's the scared, lonely automaton I first woke up.

I stumble forward, placing myself in between them. "Alix isn't the monster," I spit. "You are."

The magistrate just smiles like he did in the garden. "A monster? No. I already told you, Karis, I'm simply a man who is willing to do whatever it takes to protect what I care about. I would have thought we had that in common."

I jerk back and he laughs. "I've read your records, Karis. Do you think your masters didn't notice your single-minded obsession with finding your brother? No, that was something I admired about you."

I am nothing like this cruel man. But the cold of his words creeps in, making me doubt every choice I've ever made. All the decisions that were only meant to get my brother back, even if it left the rest of the world to burn.

Decisions that led me right here.

"In the end, though, you were as predictable as anyone. As predictable as your new friends. As predictable as Calantha. I knew you would come to Valitia searching for your brother, that Calantha would find you and want to use you. Then it was simply a matter of slipping you the right clues."

He looks pointedly at Rudy, who goes ashen.

Rudy shakes his head. "No, the seal, you—"

"I started a rumor, knowing Calantha wouldn't be able to resist. But you, Rudy, I truly thought perhaps you might be smart enough to see through it. That you would realize no single seal could possibly unlock the Scrivolia. Maybe your masters thought too highly of you." The magistrate clasps his hands behind his back and looks up at the Heart. "No, there is only one thing in the entire world that can unlock the Heart." He turns back around. "And now it's standing in front of me."

Alix takes one faltering step back, right as soldiers pour out from between the other archways. Six, ten, fifteen, twenty, spilling around the magistrate's form, surrounding us. It only takes a moment and we're hopelessly, desperately outnumbered. My head spins.

"Karis." Alix's voice is a whisper, but I hear. He looks at me, and I know what he wants.

My numb fingers slip inside the satchel and brush the cover of his tome. I pull it out, my other hand finding the dagger at my belt even as a dozen thoughts spill into my head, screaming for attention.

I have to do this, for Alix. I promised. Promised him I wouldn't ever let anyone control him again. If I don't do this now, the magistrate will get his tome and he'll be trapped forever. But I can't do this to my friend. I can't make the fire leave his eyes, turning him back into dead metal. My breathing rasps in my ears and I can't make it stop. I can't make any of this stop.

"I wouldn't do that if I were you," the magistrate says.

I look at him, wary.

He snaps his fingers, and two soldiers step out from behind the others. They throw who they're holding to the ground.

Time rocks to a standstill. My brother. Matthias. That same high forehead that looks back at me from the mirror. That same tousled hair he's had since he was a boy. His lip is puffed up and there's a gash in his forehead, still seeping red. His arms are bound behind his back, and as he struggles to his knees, I see his shirt is in tatters, showing the bruises and cuts and inked lines that cover his skin.

"Matti."

The breath of a word barely escapes my lips, but he still looks in my direction, eyes searching and confused. I know he can see basically nothing at this distance, yet somehow, he finds me.

I take a staggering step forward and instantly one of the soldiers holds a knife against Matthias's throat. He winces, and I stop.

"It's me," I say. "It's Karis."

"Karis?" There's a note of wonder in his voice. It's the voice that comforted me a dozen times when we were cold and exhausted and hungry. It's the voice that threatens to push me over the edge. My brother is right in front of me, his life in the hands of a man who breathes cruelty like air.

"I'm here, too," Rudy says. "I'm right here."

"Rud?" Matthias's voice tears. "Why did you come back?"

"I had to."

The magistrate sighs. "This is all very touching, but it isn't why I brought him."

I force out the words. "What do you want?"

"We both know you're quite intelligent, Karis, so don't pretend. You already know what I want. I want the Scrivolia unlocked again and you want your brother back. A simple trade."

Bile rises in my throat. A simple trade that isn't simple at all, with everyone I love on one side and everything I promised to do on the other.

"Karis," Matthias says. "Don't do—"

The soldier on his left hits him hard with the pommel of his dagger. I let out a cry as Matthias slumps, dazed and blinking, to the ground.

"No," Rudy runs forward, voice strangled, but Dane grabs his arm, struggling to hold the larger man back.

"Or I could kill him," the magistrate says with a shrug. "And you can watch."

Kill him.

I turn to Alix. "Alix."

His expression twists with pain. And beneath the pain, a plea. "Karis, I can't. You know what he'll do if he gets the Script ink."

"This is my brother's life!"

"Karis," Matthias says. "It's all right." He's barely able to get the words out before a punch in the gut doubles him over.

Icy panic is taking me over, swallowing me whole. It's not all right. I meant what I said to the others. The magistrate needs to be stopped. We need to stop him before he gains power that can't be undone. Maybe somewhere in the back of my head, I even thought there might be a cost to it. But not this. Not the cost of watching my brother be murdered in front of me. Not the cost of stabbing the seal that keeps Alix alive and having to watch the light leave his eyes. Zara had said I was scared of caring, and in this moment, I know that's true. Because everyone I've ever cared about has been taken from me. My parents. My brother. Now Alix. I'm always being left behind.

I can't do this again.

"Well, what's your choice?" The magistrate looks at his soldier who presses a knife into Matthias's cheek. A trail of blood traces down his jawline. Matthias grimaces. But he doesn't look afraid. Doesn't look regretful. He's willing to die, to die and leave me like everyone else.

I look down at the tome, still clenched tight in my hand.

The tome that could change everything.

I don't know where that thought comes from, but as soon as I have it, it sinks its fingers into my skull. Even if it's a betrayal. Even if it makes Alix hate me. The idea burns like a flame in my mind and I can't turn away from its haunting light. If I can just make Alix unlock the Heart, the magistrate will let my brother go, and then all of us can get out of here. Whatever happens with the Script ink and the magistrate, we can fix. I'll find a way to get Alix back to the Heart so he can lock it. But I can't fix both of them dying. I can't fix them being taken to a place I'm unable to follow.

With shaking fingers, I pull a piece of charcoal from my belt pouch. I flip open Alix's tome and before the doubts can consume me, I write a rune on the page.

33

———

ALIX

My legs pull me forward. I whip my head around, sure a soldier grabbed Karis while we were all distracted. Only she's alone, my tome open before her, her hand holding charcoal over it.

"Karis," I whisper, my whole body numb. Sure I must be missing something.

Then she looks at me, the guilt torturing her before she turns back to the page.

Betrayal washes over me, so sharp and sudden I don't have a moment to brace myself before I'm drowning in it. Karis. My first friend. The person who has been with me through all of this. She's doing this to me.

"Karis?" Dane looks between us, confused. "What are you doing?" His hand grips the hilt of his sword, but he isn't moving. Even Rudy is standing there, frozen.

I fight my legs, throwing every bit of me that makes

me who I am against the movement of my body. It isn't enough. My steps don't even falter. The Heart looms over me, monstrously beautiful, its gold flashing in the torches. I'm thrown back to that night, to the glow draining out of it, rendering it useless. The pride and joy on my father's face. The shouts as soldiers flooded down the stairs. My father falling even as he yelled at me to run. Falling and dying so that no magistrate could ever use its power again.

Now that will all be undone, by my own hands.

"Karis." My voice breaks as I look over my shoulder. "Please."

She raises her head, her face pinched and pale, a battle waging in her eyes. The smallest hope flares into my heart. She wouldn't really do this, not to me.

"I'm sorry," she whispers. "But I can't watch you die."

"Karis!" The word rips from my throat but it's too late. She writes another rune and my arms reach out, my hands planting themselves on the surface of the Heart, burning so hot that even my metal skin stings.

The music of the runes cascades into my head, intertwining melodies that come together like some siren's song. It's beautiful, ethereal, so radiant that even through my panic and despair I want to weep from the sound. I remember this, the most wondrous melody I'd ever heard. Hearing it back then nearly made me hesitate when locking it away, as if it was wrong to touch anything so beautiful.

I feel no hesitation now, only the anguish of needing to end this, but it doesn't matter because I'm not the one unlocking the Heart. It's the lines carved into my body, that my father put there. They blaze over my skin, hot and terrible, even as I try to make them all stop. I can't. The melodies keep reverberating through my head, and I can't tell them apart. I can't catch on to any of the individual melodies long enough to find their beginnings. It's all too powerful, too complicated, too much.

A prick of numb touches my toes. Panicked, I look down. The numbness crawls up my legs and a rune peeking out from beneath my chiton goes dark.

A cry wrenches out of my throat. Light pulses around my fingers like a heartbeat even as the Scrivolia fills with a blazing shine, and the numb keeps stealing over me.

Suddenly I know. Who I am. What I am.

All this time, I thought the Script ink was locked down inside of the Scrivolia. It wasn't. The Script ink is inside of me. I took it all those centuries ago. My father didn't build me to be a weapon. He didn't build me to be a puppet.

He built me to be a Script ink vessel.

Another rune beneath my chiton goes dark. The Heart is stealing all the Script ink back, draining it from my body. I need it. I know that with everything inside of me. I need the Script ink to stay who I am.

I try to wrench my fingers away, to break contact, but Karis's rune keeps me frozen in place. Someone shouts behind me, but I can't turn because everything is going fuzzy, my surroundings and the Scrivolia shifting in and out of focus. The numb creeps down my arms, up my neck, piece by piece my body falling out of reach. Despite all that, one blazing thought manages to pierce through.

I don't want to die.

Whatever I am—vessel or tool or weapon—I want to live. Whatever my life is, I don't want it to end like this.

Only it's too late because the world is still going fuzzy.

Fuzzy.

Fuzzy.

Dark.

34

KARIS

*U*nlock.

As I write the word, a rune flares hot on Alix's side beneath his chiton, and a glimmer shoots through the lines on the Scrivolia like a heartbeat.

The Script ink.

The magistrate stares at the Scrivolia and there's no mistaking the triumph in his smile. The triumph that I gave him. Dane looks at me, and the helpless disbelief on his face is worse than anything else I could have seen there. But I don't stop. I don't write the rune that could undo all this. It's too late.

Golden light leaks into the Scrivolia. It's beautiful and terrible, burning so bright it's hard to look at. Alix stands at its center, wreathed by the blaze. I clench my hands around his tome, shaking, wanting this to be over.

Alix lets out a cry, terrified, guttural. His runes, blazing in the reflected light of the Scrivolia, wink out, one by one.

"Alix?" I whisper.

He doesn't turn. I don't think he can even hear me.

Something's wrong.

I scribble the rune *move*, but he doesn't obey. Alix still stands there, nearly all his runes dark. He sways on his feet.

"Alix!" I cry.

I write *turn, step, lock* but nothing happens. My breath rasps harshly in my ears. Why isn't it working?

The light filling the Scrivolia reaches its top and it lets out a flash, so bright that gold is all I can see burning against my eyelids. As my sight clears, I see Alix falling. Doing nothing to catch himself. He hits the ground with a thud that reverberates in my bones, staring up at the ceiling with sightless eyes.

No.

I frantically scrabble *wake* in his tome, but he doesn't move. I write *wake* again and again, my writing growing increasingly distorted, but nothing happens. The tome falls from my fingers, hitting the floor with a thump. I clap my hand over my mouth.

What have I done?

"Yes," the magistrate says. His soldiers have all backed away and he steps forward alone, into the fiery light that burns like it wants to consume him. He pulls a tome from his robe and touches the book to the Heart. A tendril of gold seeps into the seal on its spine. "At last. After all this time. The Scriptorium will regain its power."

Rudy darts to where Matthias was left by his guards, cutting the ropes binding his arms and hauling my brother to his feet. The magistrate doesn't notice. The soldiers still don't move, staring at their leader as he writes something in the tome with a reed pen. A massive shudder tears through the building, sending tremors through the ground beneath our feet. Hunks of stone fall from the archways, clattering to the ground. And even though I can't see it, I know what the magistrate has done, what automaton he would choose to reanimate first.

The Colossus.

Feet pound down the steps behind us. I go numb, sure it'll be more soldiers. But Dane's eyes widen in surprise and relief.

I turn. It's Zara. Following her are some of her crew, the people she rescued from the cells. She looks from the magistrate to Alix to the Scrivolia.

A slow smile spreads over the magistrate's face. "Ah, the infamous pirate queen. The girl who got away. I've been hoping to meet you."

Zara grabs her dagger and throws it. The magistrate sidesteps it and the blade clashes against the Heart. A bolt of Script ink sparks off it like lightning. The magistrate stumbles back, his eyes widening.

"Kocha," Zara shouts, scooping up the tome at my feet. "Get Alix!"

Four of her crew move, rushing to Alix and hauling his stiffened body up onto their shoulders, straining beneath the weight. But the soldiers are already closing in on them, on us. My hand gropes for my dagger, because I have to help somehow, but as it brushes my belt pouch, something inside it shifts. I pull it out and stare down at the bronze disc in my hand.

The *stop* seal.

I have no idea what it will do to the Heart. And I don't care.

I throw it. It connects and bolts of Script ink explode from the Heart, scouring the walls, the roof, the ground. One hits a soldier and he's flung into an archway, his body making a sickening crack before he tumbles to the ground. Chaos erupts as everyone tries to avoid the lashing light. It strikes one of the arches and the entire thing collapses in a cascade of stone.

"Karis," Rudy cries, struggling to maneuver Matthias. "Help me."

I run to him, grabbing Matti's other arm and throwing it over my shoulder. Air hisses between my brother's teeth.

"I'm sorry. I'm so sorry," I whisper, the words cracking at their edges. After all these years my brother is finally at my side and I can't summon a scrap of triumph.

We reach the stairs, Dane and Zara in the back, as we leave the scathing light behind and head into the darkness above.

"After them!" the magistrate shouts.

The Heart is still in turmoil but some of the closest soldiers obey. Dane pulls his sword, metal clashing against metal as he engages one of them. They lock swords and Dane twists, sending his opponent tumbling off the edge of the stair.

There's another massive shudder and we fall to our knees.

My stomach lurches as I look over the edge at the Heart and the pandemonium still below.

"Keep moving!" Zara shouts.

I heave Matthias up. His face has gone white, and his head lolls against his chest.

"Hang on," Rudy whispers. "Just hang on."

We come out into the cells, empty now, the others gone. We've barely staggered forward when there's an earth-shattering crash right behind us.

A massive hand, carved with runes, plunges down through the layers of floor. The entire building shakes, threatening to crush us all. I stare, gasping for breath, as the hand comes back up, clutching the Heart like a ball, pulling it out through the new hole in the roof. I catch a glimpse of a massive body before it shifts away, the thud of its feet rattling through my bones.

We haul each other up, stagger out of the library and through the elegant hallways. The quiet from earlier is replaced by screams, pressing against the outer walls. We burst out of the first door we find.

The yard has devolved into mayhem. Scriptmasters, soldiers, and scholars alike scream and run for cover, backlit by the light from the torches. In the middle of it all stands the Colossus, wide-awake, its runes flaring in the dark against the harsh glint of bronze. Terror pulses through every piece of me. This is the mightiest automaton ever created, a monster from legends come alive.

It takes a step, its foot moving over us like a cold shadow, landing so close we all hit the ground again as it bucks beneath us. Rocks sting into my palms and lash against my cheek.

We pull each other up and then we run, for all we're worth. Through the gates, no longer manned in the mass panic. Down the main road, shoving our way through the flood of people. Behind us we still hear screams but I focus on the pounding of my feet, the draw of my breath, as we race away from the Acropolis and all my mistakes.

35

—

KARIS

The *Crimson Streak* cuts through the inky water. We're running scared. Trying to take as many as we can as far away as we can. We left so many behind. Too many.

I sit in the sick bay, in a chair that digs into my spine. Off to my left, Matthias rests on a bed anchored to the wall. Rudy sits next to him, stroking his hand and murmuring softly. Off to my right, Alix is in another bed. His tome sits beside him on a table. I tried writing *wake* again when we got here, but it didn't work.

Despair as thick as ink twists through my veins. Alix had been so scared of losing what made him himself. In the end, I was the one who took it away. I still remember how he looked in that cave when we met—lost and lonely in this world that wasn't his own. And yet he trusted me. He let me in. Willingly gave me his tome.

And I used his tome against him and broke everything. I

don't know if whatever made Alix himself is gone for good. I don't know if automatons can die. All I know is that for the first time he's cold to the touch, and his tome doesn't have the power to do anything. The panic and fear that I put on his face haunt me like a sickness.

A groan escapes my brother's lips. I look over, my neck already stiff. He's stirring and not even the knowledge of what I did is enough to choke out my sudden burst of hope.

Matthias tries to sit up, only to groan again. Rudy gently eases him back down.

"It's all right," Rudy murmurs. "Just rest for now."

Matthias smiles at him. It's a smile I've never seen on his face before: so tender and soft, it makes my heart ache that I wasn't around to notice it growing. "Missed you, Rud." Matthias says, a bit drowsily.

Rudy presses his lips to my brother's. I glance away, wanting to give them some privacy.

"Karis?"

My brother's head tilts in my direction. At this distance he can probably vaguely make out my form, maybe the light of the lamp behind me. I doubt it's enough for him to know it's me sitting here. But at the same time, he must know that it could only be me, because his smile shifts.

And it's that boyish smile—the same one I remember from our days together, the one I know I don't deserve anymore—that breaks down every wall I've built in the last seven years. I throw myself into Matti's arms, remembering a moment too late that with his depth perception he won't be expecting it. He sucks in a sharp breath, but before I can apologize, he's squeezing me back.

My brother, my only family, is finally here. I cling to him

as if he's the last rock left in my swaying world. So much of my life has led up to this moment, and now it's here, and it's nothing like what I thought it would be. I feel so lost. My world should have been put right when Matthias and I were finally reunited but it wasn't.

I'm not sure how long I hold on to him, sobbing, before he starts rubbing my back. I remember all the times he did that when we were young, after our parents died, when we were cold and hungry. Bit by bit I pull my shattered pieces back together, until I feel as if I'm some sort of whole again, riddled with cracks but still there.

I pull away, sniffling and rubbing at my eyes, the tears sticky against my cheeks. Rudy has retreated to the far side of the room. Clearly, he's more considerate than I am. After what I did, everyone is more considerate than I am.

Matthias's tunic, already ripped and dirty, now has splotches of wet on it as well.

"Sorry," I say.

"Don't be." Matthias's eyes crinkle with his smile. He reaches out to me and the movement is so familiar that without thinking I guide his hand to my cheek. His thumb gently wipes at my eyes. I can already feel myself—feel us—settling back into the patterns we lived before. And yet this isn't before. It isn't the same.

"I'm so glad you're here," he says.

"Are you?"

As soon as the words are out, I want to take them back. His brow furrows. "Of course I am."

I hunch my shoulders. I shouldn't say it. I need to say it. Because after everything I've done, I have to make us right, or what was the point of any of it? "You didn't come for me," I whisper. I need to know why. Why he stayed. Why he was so willing to die down in those crypts when the brother I knew was determined to survive.

Why he chose to leave me behind.

His hand falls and finds my own. It's so much bigger than mine now. But the sincere look on his face is the same. "I'm sorry, Karis. I wanted to. I was just…" He shakes his head. "When I got out of the Magistrate's Library, I was in a bad place. I was so angry. I wasn't eating, wasn't sleeping. Every night I'd have these nightmares, and so many of them were of the Scriptmasters catching you and taking you to that terrible place. I wanted you to be safe, to be far away from this life."

I touch his arm, near where an *obey* rune is inked. I wasn't there for that either.

Matthias shakes his head. "I should have known better. You were always built from tougher stuff than that."

Once I might have agreed. Once I thought if I was determined and reckless enough, I could do anything. But I don't see a way ahead. And I don't feel strong anymore. "I don't think I am."

Seven years have passed, but my brother still knows what I mean without having to ask. "How's your friend?"

I shake my head, clamping down the tears because if I cry, I don't see how I'll be able to stop. "I don't know. I don't know why the Heart shut him down."

"From what I heard, he seems like a pretty unique automaton."

He is. And I still took his will away. That look in his eyes… It makes the panic come back, burning in my heart and turning everything to white-hot ash. I press my hands against my face. "How could I have done that to him?" What if that wrenching betrayal is the last thing that's ever on his face? A memory to be replayed over and over in the lifetime he should have had.

"Karis..." Matti begins, but I don't want to hear the understanding in his voice. I don't deserve it.

"It was my fault." I drop my hands. "All of this was my fault. And you should be mad at me, too." Just like everyone else. Pile on the hate until I can't breathe, can't think. "You told me not to do it, and I did it anyway."

Everything I did, everything I risked... It was all to get Matthias back. The only reason I used Alix's tome was to make sure he got out of there alive. But everything went wrong. "I just wanted to save you," I whisper. "To save him."

Matthias doesn't say anything, even though I desperately want him to, to break up the creaking of the *Streak*, the lapping of the waves. The sounds are too normal after everything that's happened. I want them all to stop. It isn't right that the world should keep going when Alix lies still and cold on the bed across the room.

"Maybe he didn't need to be saved by you," Matthias finally says. "Maybe he just needed you to be there for him."

I look up, Matthias's face blurry through the tears. But I catch his expression. Soft. Serious.

"I know you, Karis. I saw the way you reacted after our parents died. How hard it was for you to open up to people after that. It was like you shut a piece of yourself off. And honestly, maybe I did, too." He shakes his head. "It's why I didn't go to find you. I was scared of what would happen, that I would bring all my troubles to you. Even after I got out of the Magistrate's Library…it was like the despair was trying to pull me under. I had no idea what I was supposed to do. Where I was supposed to go. Even when I started training, that wasn't enough to fill the hole I felt inside of me. But then Calantha assigned Rudy and me together."

Matthias smiles and the look on his face is so gentle. "We went on missions together. We fought for the rebellion. And all that was important. But you know what really helped me? Just being with him. Talking to him. Laughing with him. He was this ray of sunshine that split the black apart. He made me hope again. And I didn't have to do anything to get that, except to let him in."

His hand squeezes mine. "It's all right to let yourself care about people, Karis. Even if it hurts, and it will hurt. Even if you can't always be together. It's worth it to try."

Caring. Just like what Zara had said. Somehow, it always comes back to that.

But can I risk that again?

Matthias wraps his arm around me and I curl into his side, pressing my head against his shoulder. I catch a glimpse of Rudy, fidgeting by the far wall, glancing at Matthias every few moments while obviously trying to hide what he's doing. "You know," I say, my voice muffled by his chiton, "Rudy is much too sweet for you."

Matthias pokes me in the side. "I'll have you know I'm as gentle as a lamb."

I choke on a laugh. It hurts. It's good.

My brother is different now. Maybe it's just from getting older, but there's a calmness to him that I don't remember being there before. Rudy was the one who helped give him that, who helped him to change.

Just like Alix changed me.

I'm tired of holding people at arm's length. Of not letting them in. I tried that and it never worked. I think about all those who I've gotten to know on this strange journey. Dane. Zara and her crew. Calantha and her rebels.

Alix.

I want to be a person who can fight for a better world alongside them. I failed them all once.

I won't fail them again.

I come up onto the deck. A salty wind blows off the endless leagues of ocean surrounding us. Up above the stars flare in the tapestry of the sky, burning against the dark. I feel so very small on this ship beneath a sky like that. A sky that will keep blazing, no matter what happens to any of us down here.

The music of Kocha's flute, low and melancholy, drifts over the deck, only to cut off when he sees me. He whispers to Aiken who's sitting beside him, the younger pirate still shaking after his ordeal. They both look at me, and I want to wilt beneath the pain in Aiken's face, the cold blankness of Kocha's, to run back down to the safety of the hold. But I can't let myself. I step forward, even though that makes more of the people up on deck notice me, turn on me with suspicion and resentment. I clench my hands into fists and take a deep breath. If this is my punishment, so be it.

Zara stands on the other side of the *Streak*, leaning on the railing and staring out over the water. I take a step toward her. Only then I see Dane coming from the opposite direction. I hang back, feeling awkward.

Zara doesn't glance at Dane as he comes up, but she must hear him because she says, "Whatever you're going to say, soldier boy, I'm not in the mood."

Dane pauses but joins her at the railing. "I just wanted to make sure you were all right."

Zara stares out over the water. I can't see her expression, but I can see the tense set of her shoulders, hear the wear in her voice. "I could have gotten everyone from Valitia to safety if I'd been more cautious. Instead we had to run and leave so many people behind. I shouldn't have risked it. Calantha wouldn't have risked it."

Dane picks at the railing, silent for a long moment. "You don't know what would have happened if we'd left instead of going to the library. But now, thanks to us, those trapped in the library are free. And those in Valitia—yes, they're in hiding, but that doesn't mean they aren't safe." He turns to Zara. "You're not Calantha. You're you. It's all right for your choices to be different than hers. Sometimes you have to stand and fight."

"Even if you lose horribly?" Something catches in Zara's voice. She looks away from him.

Dane shakes his head, even though she can't see him. I wish she could the way he's looking at her. I've never seen him look at anyone like that. "We haven't lost yet. And failing the first time doesn't change the fact that we had to try. No matter how it turned out, when we went down to the library, I was nothing but proud that you were my captain."

Zara looks at Dane, something changing in her expression. "Just your captain?"

Dane blushes. He actually blushes. Zara reaches up, brushing his cheek with her fingers. She looks so soft. In that moment, they could be two people anywhere. Not a pirate captain and an ex-Scriptorium soldier. Just themselves. I edge away, regretting listening in when Zara raises her voice. "Do you need something, Karis?"

It's as if I'm a bucket of cold water. Zara turns to me, expression tight. Beside her, Dane grimaces and looks away, running his hand through his hair. He doesn't say anything, doesn't step in to save me from whatever wrath might be coming. I don't blame him. He once told me he was scared he'd always just be a street brat, always make the same choices he would have back then. But I was the one who did that. I was the one who chose my friends over the world and ended up risking everything and everyone. And I'm done.

I step forward. "I wanted to say I'm sorry."

Zara folds her arms over her chest. She doesn't speak and I shrink a little more on the inside before forcing myself on. "You told me what the magistrate has done, how much suffering he caused, and I still let him get the Script ink. I made a selfish choice that put everyone's lives at risks, and because of me that cruel man now has the power to hurt so many others. It was my fault. All of it. And I'm sorry."

Zara's expression doesn't flicker. My words don't bring a single speck of warmth back to her eyes. Even as they leave my mouth, I know they aren't enough.

The silence stretches out so tense I'm debating changing my mind and running back to the hold anyway when Zara says, "Alix trusted you, you know. We all trusted you. Now Alix might be dead and we're running for our lives.

We had to leave people behind on Valitia. Good people. Who might not have another chance to get out."

Each one of her barbed words finds their mark. Dane glances between us, hesitating now, but I don't want him to intervene. This is mine to face. I made the decision alone and I'll bear it alone.

"I know," I say.

"So then," Zara says, and something flashes in her eyes. "What are you going to do to make it better?"

A thin ray of hope pierces me at those words, that she's actually asking me them. That she's giving me the chance to answer. Losing Zara's respect was an awful blow.

There's only one problem: I don't know how to fix this. I don't know how to stop the magistrate when he'll soon have an army of automatons answering to him. I don't know how to bring Alix back—if he even can be brought back. I remember the way the Heart filled even as the light from the runes drained from Alix. I'm sure the Scrivolia stole the automaton's blood out of Alix. Which means maybe if we had some Script ink, it would be enough to bring him back, but…

Zara's pendant.

"Your necklace," I breathe.

It only takes Zara a moment. She pulls it out, the light spilling over her palm.

"Will it be enough?" Dane asks.

I don't know. When Master Theodis animated Alix, Script ink wasn't as rare as it is now. I'm sure a Scriptmaster like him would have had more than this tiny pendant. But for the first time since Alix fell, I actually believe I'll see him again, that my mistakes won't take him away forever. It's a flicker of a flame coming back to life in my heart.

Only then I remember what Zara told me about that pendant. About her family. "I don't want you to have to give up the last piece of your parents..."

Zara slips the necklace over her head. "I don't need a pendant to remember my parents or what they did. And I'm not about to let Alix stay the way he is." She holds the necklace out to me.

I shake my head, backing away. "No, it shouldn't be me. Not now."

Zara doesn't budge. "This is your mess, Karis. And I expect my crew to clean up their own messes."

Her words aren't a command, but her tone is. I take the pendant, the gold warm against my skin.

The others follow me silently down to the hold. Alix is still lying in bed, his hand open on the sheets. I place the pendant into his palm, my heart straining against my ribs. He looks just like when I first found him in that cave, only now I know how much more he is. He isn't a mindless automaton to be used and controlled. He's my friend. He's kind and brave and strong. And I have to believe he's still in there somewhere.

"Come on, Alix," I whisper. "You can do it. Come back to us."

Nothing happens, and black despair threads its way into my heart. Then the light coming from the pendant dims and his runes give a weak flash. I barely dare to breathe as the moments pass. One. Two. Three.

And Alix's eyes flicker open.

36

ALIX

I drift up out of the darkness, fuzzy shapes shifting from the black. My memories blur together and I can't quite remember why, but this all feels familiar. This cold and this dark, and this struggling to surface. I fight against the cloud that's taken root in my head and slowly the fuzzy shapes sharpen. A figure leans over me and as my vision clears, I see it's a girl.

No, it's not simply a girl. I know her. I know her because this has all happened before.

Karis.

Her face trembles with relief. Relief, and guilt. With that, all of my memory comes crashing back over me. The Heart and the magistrate. Karis using my tome, and the Scrivolia being unlocked against my will. The Script ink being pulled out of me, and my body going numb. Betrayal engulfs me once more, as fresh and as sharp as when I first felt it.

The Scrivolia took away what I was. I could feel it stealing all the pieces of me, and I don't understand how I'm back until I notice the prick of heat against my palm. I look down and see Zara's pendant clasped in my hand. It's dark now, all the Script ink in it gone. Over it are Karis's fingers, curled around my own.

I move my hand away, and Karis's face crumples. Some part of me wavers, wanting to reach out and comfort her. As quickly as that emotion comes, it's gone, replaced by a hollow ache in my chest. Everything I thought I knew about how she felt for me was a lie. When it really mattered, to her I was simply a thing to be used.

She turns and flees from the sick bay, out into the hold.

I don't call her back.

There's a thick silence before Zara steps up to me.

She clasps my shoulder. "Welcome back to the land of the living."

The cloud around my thoughts is dissipating, leaving a splitting headache behind. I didn't realize I could get headaches.

"Thank you," I say, my voice coming out foggy.

The others crowd closer around me. Dane shakes my hand. Finn gives me a slap on the back. Rudy wraps me in a bear hug, looking elated, and it's only then that I remember Matthias and glimpse him in the bed across the room from mine.

All of these people were worried about me. They were waiting for me to wake up. Back before, I was so alone.

It was only ever the two of us, and when my father was gone, all I could do was sit and wait for him. Now here's a room full of people who wanted to make sure I was all right. That should be enough.

Only it isn't. A chunk has been torn out of me, leaving a yawning pit in my center. And I don't know how to fix it.

One by one the others leave. Each of them asks if I want them to stay, but my head still pounds and for the first time in my life I'm tired, exhaustion weighing me down into my bed. So I force a smile I don't feel and I tell them it's all right to go.

It's quiet once they're gone. Matthias is still there in the bed across the room, but he's asleep, and so is Rudy, his head resting against Matthias's side and their hands entwined on top of the blankets. The only light in the room comes from the two lamps, one beside my bed, one beside Matthias's, like watchmen signaling that we're both still alive.

My tome lies beside my bed on a table. I feel its closeness even before I look at it, this thing that allowed all this to happen. Some part of me doesn't want to see the evidence of what Karis did. Only these are my runes, this is my tome, and for once in my life I'm going to own them.

I pick it up and flip to the last page with runes on it. There's *walk, halt, reach, unlock*. I expect the runes to end there. They don't. There's *move, turn, step, lock*, and then *wake*, over and over and over again, the writing growing increasingly frantic. It's Karis's writing, I know that much. Which means she tried to stop it, after she started. She tried to wake me up. I see her panic and fear in the erratic lines and the smudged strokes. She changed her mind.

Only it was too late.

The door creaks. I look up and see Karis, in the shadow of the doorway. She's pale and exhausted and wearing the same chiton as before, stained and streaked with dirt. As soon as I meet her eyes, she drops her gaze.

She doesn't say anything, and neither do I, because I can't. Seeing her has brought it all back: my limbs moving against my will, my body taking me to a place I didn't want to go, and then the coldness and the darkness swallowing me whole.

She steps closer. Her hands clench in front of her and the words start spilling out, faster and faster, as if she's scared I'll stop her. "I'm so sorry, Alix, for what I did. I have no excuse. I knew exactly what I was doing. I knew how much it would hurt you. And I still did it. I know I can never make it up to you. I know you have every right to hate me." She shakes her head, her breath catching in her throat. "But I am so, so sorry."

Her words peter off. She means what she says. Despite what happened, I'm sure I still know Karis well enough to judge that. Yet it does nothing to take away this pulsing knot in the center of my chest.

"Is it supposed to hurt this much?" I ask.

Karis's face twists. "I don't know. I don't have Script ink so—"

"I don't mean that." I clutch my hand to my chest. I thought when I learned about what had happened to my father that was the worst I could possibly ever feel. Only even that had been a shock turned to numb disbelief turned to a heavy ache. This is a wound that's still being carved. "I didn't think emotions could feel like this." Father never warned me what others could do to you, even the people you cared about. Even the people who you thought cared about you.

Karis pulls in a sharp breath. "I don't know. No one's ever treated me the way I treated you."

I sag, even though I wasn't sure what I expected from her. To make this all better? Perhaps the lesson to be learned is that some things can't be fixed. Karis used my runes against me. My father gave me those runes in the first place. The two people I thought really cared about me... The two people I thought saw me as something more... They each had a hand in what happened.

"You treated me like a thing, Karis." My voice comes out strangely flat. The coldness should bother me more than it does. It's taking me over and pulling me down until I can no longer glimpse the sky. "You took away my choice and broke the promise you made to me. I'm not ready to forgive you for that. I'm not sure I can."

Karis's face falls. "Right," she whispers.

Silence swallows us once again, silence I'm not used to, not when it comes to her. She looks smaller than usual, that stubbornness and energy normally blazing in her expression gone.

I stare numbly down at my hands. How did everything change so quickly? I set out to complete my father's work, and instead I undid it. I failed what I was meant to do. Even if the magistrate hadn't shown up, even if Karis hadn't done what she did, I wouldn't have been able to destroy the Heart. I wouldn't have known where to start with those melodies.

I desperately want my father. He would never have gone to the Acropolis that night without a solid plan. Which means somewhere in my head I already know how to do this, somewhere locked down along with every other one of my memories. If only Calantha or Master Leuwin had fixed my runes. If I remembered everything, none of this would have happened.

Then I realize there's someone who can fix runes, right here on this ship.

I look at Karis, still standing there, shoulders hunched as if melting into herself. As if she's waiting for me to say the words to send her away.

"I'm not ready to forgive you," I say. "But I do need your help."

She looks up at me, eyes bright, and nods.

I'm finished with not remembering. One way or another, I'm getting my memories back. Tonight.

37

ALIX

"Absolutely not!" Rudy cries. His hair is flattened against one side of his head from his rest. Matthias blinks sleepily on the bed behind him. Zara and Dane are here, too. It only seemed right that we all be together for this.

Karis steps forward. There's a space between her and me, negative energy pressing us apart. I see it there between her and the others, too, as she stands in the middle of our group and yet alone. What happened while I was sleeping?

"Rudy," she says, and her voice is quieter than what I'm used to. "Do you know how to fix Alix's runes?"

"Theoretically, yes. But if I made the smallest mistake—"

"I'm willing to risk that," I say firmly. I've already decided and I'm not changing my mind. "It's my choice to make."

Rudy throws his hands up. "I'm the one who might kill you, so I'd say some of it is my choice, too."

"Look what happened because I didn't know."

Rudy tugs the silver scholar seal hanging around his neck, gaze darting around the room, looking as if he'd rather be anywhere but here.

Karis steps closer to her brother. She squeezes his shoulder and he grins at her before piping up, "I think you should do it."

Rudy stares at him. "Matt…"

"Rud," Matthias says. "We owe him my life. And he's right. This has to be his choice. I know you can do it."

Rudy swallows, once, twice. Then he turns to me. "If you're sure…"

Something quivers inside of me. I silence it. "I'm sure."

"Right. I'll just, um, fetch my tools, then."

He leaves. I watch him go, trying to ignore the fears that are already creeping in. That he won't be able to do it. That something will go wrong. This is my mind we're talking about.

Rudy comes back, in what seems far too short a time, but when he gestures to my bed, I sit on the edge of it without comment. I don't want my nerves to convince him that he doesn't want to be doing this.

He unrolls his leather carrying case on the table beside my bed, revealing a line of bronze tools. I recognize most of them from the tools my father worked with. There's a carving knife and a scraper, a broad scriber for the strokes and a finer one for the smaller details. I run my fingers over the destroyed runes on my arm one last time. After this I'll remember everything about my father, and maybe that will finally be enough to dispel these doubts that won't let me go.

Rudy selects a carving knife with runes etched into its

metal blade. "I'll need to engrave the runes deeper to correct them," he says. "I have no idea if this will hurt."

I look at Karis. I don't know why. Perhaps it's instinctive after all this time, that she'd be the person I'd look to for comfort.

Karis opens her mouth, and then closes it, looking miserable. She stares down at her feet.

I glance away. "I understand," I say quietly.

Rudy leans in. His fingers explore the edge of the topmost rune. I clench my hands around my knees as Rudy delicately presses the knife to the rune. He takes in a measured breath and digs its tip in.

I go rigid. It's the most terrible sensation I've ever felt, as if the knife is scraping against my seal's flame, freezing me from the inside out.

Rudy stops.

"No," I say through gritted teeth. "Keep going." I can handle this.

I have to be able to handle this.

Rudy has gone pale but he does what I ask. Line by line, rune by rune. So cold it scalds. The world fuzzes around the edges as my thoughts blur into one another, like when I stood in front of the Scrivolia. Only this time maybe I won't be lucky enough to wake up again. Maybe this time it will take something from me that I won't be able to get back. I try to push the panic away, but it claws deeper into me. It's too much. It's not working. I open my mouth to tell Rudy to stop when a memory bursts across the surface of my mind.

I stand on a dark island, black waves crashing against pale rock. Tallis. The destroyed runes on my arm are numb, the chilled water I came out of sliding down my skin.

I look far off in the distance and see the lights of the magistrate's ships, bright against the dark ocean. I stagger along the coast when I see an automaton in front of me, still and frozen. Exactly like all the automatons will now be frozen, because of what I did. I jerk back away from it, but my foot catches and I fall, hands scrabbling to regain purchase on the steep cliff side. My fingers catch on a crack and I see a cave in the cliff, just beneath me. The ships are drawing close. I swing inside.

In the dark I slide down the wall, clutching my hurt arm. The numb from it is already spreading, taking me over, sending me to sleep, and before I know it, I'm gone.

Another memory comes, from earlier, during my escape through the islands toward Tallis. Trudging across the ocean floor, the world murky and dark as it undulates around me. Climbing up each time a land mass shifts out of the water, hoping it will be a safe place to hide. The Script ink that I just took from the Heart blazes inside of me like fire. It's bright and beautiful and terrifying.

Then back to that night in the Acropolis. I lock the Heart down and take the Script ink, as if I'm pulling a wondrous melody into my veins. I hear shouts and my father yells at me to run even as he falls, blood blooming through his robes like a crimson flower. I push through the soldiers when blinding pain runs down my arm. I look and see a line of destroyed runes that makes the world spin around me, but it doesn't matter because I'm already climbing the stairs.

The memories slide back then to good ones. My father in his study, showing me a book on automaton structure and pointing out the way the movement runes work together.

Us in the garden, tending a sickly tree. Us in my rooms, and in the dining hall, and in the study.

One final memory comes.

My father and I sit on the marble bench in the back of the garden, where we always let the plants grow a bit wild because we both liked it that way. The birds are out and I throw pieces of bread to them, marveling at the way their little bodies move, so quick and light as if they're made of air. I need the distraction. Father's words hang between us: the truth of how and why I was born. I don't know what to think about any of it.

"Please talk to me," my father finally says, in his soft, dusty voice. "You know you can say anything to me."

I try to sort out my feelings, even though feeling anything is so new to me. "You made me for a reason, because Magistrate Reitas wanted you to."

"Yes, I did. The Scriptwork on the Scrivolia is the most elaborate ever created. Even the greatest masters in our nation have failed to fully understand it. An automaton, though, someone who was part of the Script but who had a consciousness and who could think for themselves... That was the one being I believed would be able to work the runes on its surface and unlock it. Or lock it."

Those words twist something inside of me. I wanted him to say it isn't true, that he made me for me. I look down at the little birds who have strayed closer to my sandals, searching for bread, confusion and grief pounding inside of me like the heartbeat I don't have. Before I can stop myself, I stomp my foot. The birds all take flight, scattering up into the sky in a flurry of wings. I watch them go, aching.

A hand settles onto my shoulder and I look into my father's deep eyes.

"That's why I made you, Alix, it's true. Then you woke up and there was a fierce intelligence in your gaze that I wasn't expecting. As I taught you, I discovered that you had likes and dislikes. That you love to sing and the runes sound like music to you. That you hate arithmetic. These are things that I didn't give you, that your runes didn't give you. They are things that you simply are. I'm ashamed now at my reasons for creating you, but at the same time I'm glad, because if I had never gotten that missive ordering me to create a key, I wouldn't have you now."

He places something in my hands. It's a golden medallion, his sigil inscribed onto its surface. "You are my child, Alix. This is your life to live. I'm telling you all this now, because it is your choice. If you want to leave this place, you can. I'd go with you if I was able. If you want to stay for this, I will do everything in my power to prepare you for it. Whatever you choose to do with your life, know that I couldn't be prouder to call you my son."

He gets up and leaves. I rub my fingers over the medallion. My life to live. My choice. As I stare after my father's retreating form, I know, somewhere deep inside of me, that I've already decided. I will destroy the Heart. For my father and for myself.

Hands clamp down on my shoulders and the memory dissolves. I blink and see Karis, her face tight with worry.

"Karis?" My voice comes out groggy.

She lets go and steps away, curling her hands into the folds of her chiton. "Your face went suddenly vacant. It scared us."

The others are all huddled closer than they were before. "Are you all right?" Rudy asks, looking sick.

Am I all right? I don't know how to answer that question. My father made me to be a Script ink vessel, that's true. He also loved me. He gave me runes, but he also wanted me to have my freedom.

"I remember it," I whisper. "The time I spent with my father. When I locked the Heart and took the Script ink. When I ran and found that cave." Until I opened my eyes. I saw Karis and everything changed.

I sink back into my pillow. I feel as if I've relived a life's worth of sadness and happiness, joy and fear. Each memory is its own shard of light. "Well, I remember how to destroy the Heart." My father had gone over the sequence of runes again and again, until I could recite it backward. I'd even already crafted the melody I would use. "Not that it matters now."

Zara sighs, fiddling with the pendant back around her neck, its gold dark. "That's true. I don't see any way of scaling the Colossus. Not while it's moving. Which it will be."

I press my hand against my eyes. Everything—what I was made for, what I chose to do, what my father wanted for me—is all jumbled up in my head. I'd hoped that once my memories were back, I'd see some way through this. Only I don't. My father had said that I could be anything that I wanted. Calantha had said that I needed to be what the world asked of me. I did what each of them had asked and it led all of us here.

I shake my head and look at Rudy. "Thank you for this."

He nods. "Sorry I couldn't fix the cracks." He pauses. "Is that a broken rune on your shoulder, too?"

I glance down and see that my chiton has slipped. I rub the dent Zara gave me the first day I met her. It's admittedly one of the strangest mementos of this journey. "Err, no."

Zara grins. The expression is tired around the edges, but it's there. "I might have shot him. But I still stand that it was justified."

Rudy's eyebrows go all the way up into his hairline.

Karis glances at my runes and her eyes light up. I recognize that look, which always seems to come before some foolhardy plan. Despite everything, a faint hope flickers inside of me. I could use some foolhardiness right now.

Dane must see it, too, because he says, "Karis, what is it?"

"Umm…" She looks around at the others, hesitating.

"Come on, Karis," Zara says. "You made a mistake, but you're still part of this crew, so out with whatever you wanted to say."

"Well, what if we didn't have to scale the Colossus?" she says. "What if we could just make it drop the Heart?"

"How would we do that?" Dane asks. "The thing's a behemoth."

Karis steps toward me, then seems to think better of it and stops. "They didn't have things like guns when the automatons were built, so automatons were never built to withstand them. Look at what a bullet did to Alix." She glances up toward the deck. "What do you think a cannonball would do to the Colossus?"

38

KARIS

We gather around the table in Zara's quarters. A weathered map of the City of Scholars has been spread out on top of it, weighed down by stones on each of its corners. The different tiers are marked out, as well as the positions of all the automatons. Or at least where the automatons used to be. I'm sure the magistrate has woken up every single one he has a tome for, just like I'm sure he's already started making tomes for the others. This isn't going to be easy.

Good thing we're not used to easy.

"All right," Zara says. "Chances are the Colossus is still going to be stationed near the Acropolis." She taps the map. "The magistrate isn't as strong as he once was, so right now, he'll no doubt be trying to shore up his powers again. Few things will do that as effectively as him towering the Colossus over all those who thought to oppose him. Unfortunately for us, there's no way the *Streak's* cannons will reach as far as the Acropolis. The only way we're going to hit this thing is if we lure it to the docks." She looks around at us. "Any ideas?"

We're all silent. I hadn't thought that far. Really, I hadn't thought far at all. I'd just grabbed at the idea of the cannons because it seemed like there was a chance it would work. Then again, I thought my last plan would work, too, and look how that ended.

"I'm sure the magistrate still wants me," Alix finally says. "So why don't I be bait?"

Bait. I don't like that idea. At all. But I force any of the words I might have said down. Even if he would listen to me, I don't have the right anymore.

"We would still have to somehow get the magistrate's attention," Dane says.

"I'll shut down one of the automatons," Alix says. "Or as many automatons as I need to until the magistrate notices me."

"Do you remember how to do that now?" Zara asks.

Alix nods. "My father taught me. I need to reverse the rune in the seal. I don't think there's any chance I'll be able to reach the Colossus's seal to shut it down, but I should be able to on the smaller ones. I can draw the ink out of them just like the Heart drew it out of me. If I am going to go through with this, I could use more Script ink than I have now." He rubs his temple. He looks tired in a way I've never seen before. It's one more guilt to pile up with the rest.

"So, Alix knows what he'll be doing," Zara says. "Karis and Dane, I'm guessing you want to go with him?"

I nod, bracing myself for Alix to reject my offer of help. But he doesn't. Then again, he also doesn't so much as look at me.

"I'll keep as close to a skeleton crew on the *Streak* as I can," Zara says. "The rest of my people, and any of Calantha's rebels who are up to it, I'll send into other parts of the city to cause as much trouble as they can. We'll try to strip the magistrate of as many of his forces as possible."

Alix nods. "Once we shut down the Heart, that should drain the Script ink from the tomes and the automatons. They'll all shut down with it."

"I'm going after the magistrate," Matthias says.

I look over my shoulder at my brother. Unlike the rest of us, he leans against the wall, rubbing the end of the staff Rudy dug up for him. There's a dangerous edge to his expression that's all the Bandit.

"The magistrate won't trust the Colossus's tome to anyone else," Matthias says. "That means he'll have to stay close. If I get a chance, I'm taking it."

"If you're going, I'm going with you," Rudy says.

Matthias flashes a grin.

"Well then, it sounds like everyone knows the plan," Zara says. "We'll drop everyone off who needs to be off at the closest safe house, the little ones and those too weak to join us. And then we'll go back to Valitia, and finish what we started."

By the time we reach Valitia again we've only been gone four days. And yet as the City of Scholars comes into view, my breath lodges like a stone in my throat.

A dozen automatons move about in the tiers, lumbering through the streets and in the lanes between the villas. For two hundred years, the automatons were stilled, and all we had left of them were frozen statues and stories. Terrible stories that I would have been happy to forget. Now, after all this time, their power has returned. And we have to face it.

There are soldiers out, too, marching in rigidly straight lines. Even from here I can see they bear the black sash of the magistrate's forces, each one a shadow against the white stone walls of the city.

And that's it. There are no civilians. No scribes or acolytes or scholars. Besides the magistrate's forces, the tiers are empty.

I tilt my head up to see the Colossus. It stands by the Acropolis, and even from this distance I can make out the glint of its lit runes. The Heart shines fiercely in its hands, as if it's snatched the sun from the sky.

When I suggested robbing the Colossus of its prize before, it had seemed like a good idea. Why had it seemed like a good idea?

Aiken navigates the *Streak* away from the city, to a sheltered beach, before saluting Zara.

She steps toward the crowd that's gathered on the deck, clasping her hands behind her back. She's abandoned the chiton she wore in the city and is back to the same clothes I first saw her in, boldly patterned fabrics, her hat perched on her head. She looks wild and strong, every bit a pirate queen, born of brine and waves and sea. The sight of her raises goose bumps on my skin.

"Everyone, today is finally the day." Zara's voice is bold.

"When we face the magistrate. When we face the Scriptorium. We all know what they've done to us and to ours. We all know how strong they are. How powerful." A low ripple of voices crosses the deck as she looks over us all. "But know that we're strong, too. That the power we have has nothing to do with misguided notions of control and force. It's in who we are and what we've gone through. And that's a strength the magistrate will never understand.

"Together we are fierceness. Together we are change. And no matter what happens today, know that I'm proud to be your captain and to call you my crew. This piece of history belongs to us, and it is ours to rewrite. So let's not waste it."

Zara's gaze sweeps over the deck and as it lands on me, I shove every scrap of my fear away and I choose to believe. That we can do this. That we will do this. This might be the magistrate's city, but today we take it from him.

We separate to our boats. Matthias and Rudy will be heading ashore in a different one than us since they'll stay with the *Streak* crewmen until they get closer to the Colossus. I throw my arms around my brother's neck. He squeezes me back.

I don't ever want to let go. We just patched up what was left of our family. But he has to go. Just like I have to go. So, I step away. Trying to project lightness into my voice, I say, "I'll never forgive you if you get yourself caught again."

He laughs. I want to memorize the sound. "Believe me, I'm not planning on it."

His hand finds mine and he presses something into my

palm. I look down. It's a little butterfly, folded out of yellow paper, its wings bright like buttery sunshine.

"A butterfly?" I ask.

"Rudy described them to me. I thought I'd try making one. For luck." He steps closer, and when he speaks again, his voice is more serious. "If anything does happen, this time I'll find you. I promise."

I look up into his eyes, so sure. Full of the belief that what we're doing today is right. I wrap that belief around my own heart. "I know you will."

I squeeze Matthias's hand and then guide it to the rail. He swings himself onto the ladder. I tuck the butterfly into my belt pouch. I'm not going to regret leaving my brother. And this won't be the last time I see him. I won't let it.

Kocha is with Alix and Dane farther down the railing. The big pirate ties off a rope ladder and climbs down into the waiting boat. Dane is about to do the same when Zara saunters over to us.

"Surely you weren't thinking of leaving without saying goodbye, soldier boy."

She's caught Dane with one leg over the railing, off balance, and he sways precariously for a moment. "Goodbye," he manages.

I snort. He's so articulate. He scorches me with a glare.

"Don't get yourself killed out there," she says.

"I won't. And you, too. Good luck with those cannons."

She pats the railing. "A captain doesn't need luck, not when it comes to her ship. I can count on the *Streak*." She steps forward, placing her hand on his chest. With the wicked glint in her eye, I'm not sure if she's planning on pulling him closer or pushing him overboard.

She draws him in for a kiss on the cheek and swaggers off.

Dane stares after her, a dazed look on his face, then turns and sees me watching. He scowls. "Not a word." I grin, but he's already over the railing.

Alix steps up to the ladder but for a moment he just stands there, looking at it. He's quiet, and his expression is distant. It's painful seeing that. All I want is to make things right between us, but maybe I realized my mistake too late.

"Are you ready for this?" I ask quietly.

His fingers thread around his father's pendant. "The Heart will be destroyed today. At least then this will all be over."

Those words throw me back, to before we went to the Acropolis, when it was like he was trying to force himself to be what the world wanted him to be. Or even farther, in the gardens by the automaton, when he was in such pain. I'm not good at this—at comforting people—but I have to try. He so clearly doesn't see what I see. There is a bravery to being kind and gentle, to being hopeful. One I didn't recognize before I met him.

"You know," I say, "back on Tallis, all I cared about was finding my brother. And when I first saw you in that cave, all I saw was a tool that would help me reach my goal."

Alix stiffens, and I stare down at the railing, too much of a coward to face him. I can't blame him for being distant with me, not after what I did. But I couldn't bear to spill out my heart, and still see him look at me with that detached gaze. He deserves for me to let him in, for once. Even if he leaves me in the end.

"But I was wrong. Alix, you're right, you have runes and a tome. And you're right that I can't possibly know what that's like. But I do know you." Now I do look up, because I owe it to him to face him as I say this.

"What you said in the boathouse, that this is what you are... It isn't true. You're our friend. And the person who you are, the decisions that led you here, that made you our friend, none of that is because of your tome or the Script. Destroying the Heart doesn't make you a key, it doesn't make you a vessel. It just makes you yourself, someone who would do anything to save those who need your help. Someone who refuses to stop trying, no matter what happens. You have a spark that refuses to dim. And that doesn't come from here." I lightly press my fingers over his seal, glowing faintly beneath his chiton. "It's all you. Your light is stunning. It's brave and beautiful. So just be you, because that's enough. It's always been enough."

Vulnerability creeps over his face, and he looks like the Alix I crossed an ocean with again. The Alix who makes me want to be a better person. I'd give anything for him to smile again like he used to, soft and hesitant and warm.

He opens his mouth.

"Alix! Karis!" Kocha calls up. "Get down here."

Alix looks at me for a moment, emotion flashing across his expression, and at least it's there now. He swings himself down onto the ladder. I have no choice but to follow, not sure if I made things better or worse.

As I seat myself on the bench, Kocha takes the oars.

He guides us through the bay, toward the beach. There's no wind and the sea is surprisingly still. We're hidden by a peninsula of rocks that sticks out into the water, so we can't see the city or the Colossus or the other automatons. It's so strangely calm that if not for the nervous energy sizzling beneath my skin I could almost forget what we're rowing toward.

Almost.

Our boat scrapes into the sand on the beach and we climb out. Kocha nods at us and then he's gone, rowing back to the *Streak*.

For a moment we stand there, me and Dane and Alix. It's the first time in a long while that the three of us have been alone together and it takes me back. To escaping from Tallis and hiding on that island. Before we ever met Zara or her crew or went to Valitia.

Dane leads us inland, past farms and vineyards, ramshackle homes of clay and sticks surrounded by whatever crops and vines manage to grow on the rocky, hilly terrain. Stones poke through the soles of my sandals and the sun beats down on my head and shoulders. There are no farmers tending to the vines or the fields. Not even any goats or sheep bleating from the fields. The dirt path we're on is as deserted as the farms and maybe that should make me relieved, but instead a prickle runs up my spine. Farmers don't take days off lightly.

Unlike the higher tiers, there's no wall surrounding the Lower City, so as the outermost hovels come into view, it's a simple matter to slip down a side street. I've only been here briefly, but as we track through the winding lanes with the small houses brushing close on each of our sides, I see how the few days we've been away have changed this place. A tense, stifling silence has descended upon the city, as if it's scared even to breathe.

Then we hear it. The thud of a massive footstep that shakes the ground beneath our feet. An automaton.

We find a squat house with a stack of crates next to it and climb onto its roof to get a better vantage point. We hunker down side by side in the straw, the stiff stalks poking through my clothes. I end up next to Alix. It's the first time we've been this close in days, and that thought clamps around my chest like a vice.

There are three automatons nearby. They're all large. Not as large as the Colossus, but I'm still not used to seeing the things activated. Each is at least half again as tall as the biggest of the houses. Two of the automatons are moving. One is stationary. I'd have said that would be our best chance, but it's also the largest of the three.

If I'm being honest, none of them look like a good chance.

"Do you see any of their masters?" I ask quietly.

Dane scans the area, alert and serious. In that expression I see the captain he might have been. The even better rebel he's becoming.

"There, in that window." He points to a nearby building. After a beat, I see it: a flash of gold that must be a seal, draped around the neck of a shadowy figure.

"Let's do that one," Alix says. "We can stay in the master's blind spot and I can reach the automaton's seal from one of the rooftops around it."

Dane nods. "Now we just wait for the signal."

We stay silent and still, my heart thudding in my chest. Every moment that passes strings the tension tighter. They must be getting close to position soon.

A plume of smoke erupts on the west side of the city, sending a tremor through the streets, followed quickly by another one on the opposite side. There are shouts from soldiers a few streets away and the tramp of feet as they run off.

There. All we can hope is that Zara's people have drawn off enough of the magistrate's forces for us to do this.

The three of us slip off the roof and steal toward the automaton. There's no chance of us losing it, even down here at street level. The thud of its feet shakes the entire block.

Dane slows us as we approach. "Karis, you climb that building there. I'll stay on street level. You and I will be lookouts. Shout if you see anything or if the Scriptmaster moves. Alix, good luck."

"Good luck," I whisper to Alix, but he's already slipping into an alleyway between two buildings. He doesn't look back.

I obediently clamber up the side of my building. I keep the position of the Scriptmaster in the window in my head and use the slope of the roof to shield myself as I scramble over the edge. The automaton is only one street away, lumbering along slowly. Maybe that's as fast as it can go.

Hopefully that's as fast as it can go.

Alix creeps over the side of another roof, careful just like I was to stay hidden from the Scriptmaster. He's almost to the automaton. Just a few more feet.

Gold flashes in the opposite window. It's a second Scriptmaster, and I can clearly make out the open tome in her hands. She's the one controlling the automaton. And she has a perfect vantage point for seeing Alix.

"Alix!" I shout.

The automaton moves, and instantly I know I was wrong in thinking it could only move slowly. It lunges toward Alix, hands outstretched.

Alix jumps back, barely escaping the cage of grasping fingers, but not quick enough to evade the blunt force of the automaton's arm. He's slammed back across two rooftops before hitting an upper wall so hard it caves around him in a cascade of clay and stone.

The automaton is already moving again. I get up and sprint across the roof, struggling to keep my balance in the unwieldy straw. I scream as I leap the gap between two of the houses, heading for the second Scriptmaster, sure that if it's a choice between attacking Alix or saving themselves, I know what they'll choose. And I'm right. The woman frantically scribbles in the tome and the house I'm on trembles with the thud of the automaton's footsteps.

"Karis!" Dane's cry echoes down the street. "Look out!"

I throw myself to the side as a massive hand pounds where I just was, taking half the building with it.

Alix launches himself onto the thing's back. The automaton's arms come up, spraying bits of straw and clay into my face. I scrabble away, trying to avoid the crushing weight of its limbs. It raises its hands above me, ready to crash down, and this time I have nowhere to go, trapped by the caved-in roof at my back. I throw my hands up as if I can somehow fend off the incoming blow.

The automaton freezes.

Alix's one arm is wrapped around the thing's neck and his body hangs down over its chest, his fingertips just low enough to touch the seal. He squeezes his eyes shut as his seal flares with light beneath his chiton, and when he opens them again, there's a brightness that wasn't there before.

I let out the trapped breath in my chest, the world spinning around me in a dizzying way.

Still not dead.

I wonder how many more opportunities I'll have to think that today.

Alix slides off and rushes over to me. "Karis. Are you all right?"

He reaches down to me, and even though I was just about crushed, I'm so relieved he still cares enough to be worried.

"Yes." I take his hand and let him pull me to my feet. My shaky knees barely hold me. "I'm all right."

I look for the Scriptmaster. She's still trying to write in her tome, her partner long gone. And then Dane slips through the window. He snatches the tome from the woman and stabs his dagger through the seal. The woman runs.

Dane tosses the tome to the floor, then steps up onto the windowsill, making the short drop to the roof we're on. "That wasn't too bad."

He can speak for himself. He wasn't nearly turned into a splatter.

"This isn't over yet," Alix says.

He uses the automaton's still outstretched arm to boost himself up, climbing onto its shoulder. Alix looks up at the

Scriptorium, clear-cut against the sky, eyes blazing with twin fires. He looks so sure. So strong.

"You want me," he says in a low voice. "Come and get me."

A rumble like distant thunder vibrates down to my bones. The magistrate. He's seen Alix.

I look up to the Colossus, towering so high above us that its head seems to split the clouds.

And then it turns toward us.

39

ALIX

The Colossus steps forward, easily clearing the wall between the Acropolis tier and the one below. The entire city quivers with the impact of its weight. It takes another step, and another, and with that it's already halfway through the agora, rapidly eating up the distance between us.

I throw myself off the automaton, landing on the roof next to Karis and Dane who both stare at the thing with wide eyes.

"We need to go!" I shout.

We swing down onto street level and race toward the harbor, our feet pounding the ground. I don't know where we are but it doesn't matter, because the way to the harbor is obvious from the slope of the ground beneath our sandals and the tang in the air wafting off the ocean.

The thud, thud, thud of the Colossus's footsteps grows louder. It's so close now the ground shakes every time one of its feet lands, threatening my balance. I careen into a wall as the ground rocks once more, but I push off and keep going.

We break out of the labyrinth of narrow streets and skid to a stop on the docks. There's more open space out here, giving me enough of an angle to see the Colossus, already midway through the lower city. Beside me Dane scans the water, chest heaving.

The *Streak* isn't there.

The Colossus takes another step and Karis stumbles, grabbing a barrel that reeks of fish to keep her balance. I step in front of the two of them, not knowing what I'm doing. I only know I have a better chance of stopping that thing than they do. The Colossus looms into view over us, so large it blots out half the sky.

A crack splits the air and a cannonball hits the Colossus smack in the middle of its chest. It staggers, its hand moving a sluggish moment later to catch itself on one of the boathouses. The building creaks in protest, wood cracking at the impact.

I whirl and see the *Streak* cutting through the bay. Finn, Ava, and the others scramble about the deck, loading more cannons. Zara stands at the wheel, hair flying free. Even from here, I can hear her cackling. Dane lets out a whoop.

The Colossus rights itself, in time to get two more cannonballs, one to its chest and one to its shoulder. It careens again, but the Heart stays balanced in its hand.

It's not dropping it. We won't have much time before either some of the other automatons or the soldiers get involved.

I see a thick chain on a spool, used for reeling in ships. Not too far from where the Colossus stands.

"Dane, Karis!" I point to it.

As soon as I say the words they must understand because they both race for it. We grab its end. It's brutally heavy, but together we drag it toward the Colossus's feet. It steps forward, and for a sickening moment the shadow of its foot looms over us before it's pushed back by another cannonball. The noise cracks through my head.

"We can wrap it around that," Dane shouts. He points to a boat anchor, a large column of rough gray stone where the docks meet the land.

We wrap the chain around the stone. With any luck, whatever vantage point the magistrate has chosen won't let him see what we're doing.

But Zara sees. She shouts, the noise carrying across the water. There's another crack and a cannonball whizzes to the right of the Colossus, then another. The Colossus steps left to avoid it. Closer. Closer.

"Now!" I yell.

We heave the chain tight against the automaton's ankles. It trips, and the Heart falls from its hand, smashing through a boathouse roof.

I'm about to crow when the Colossus lurches, its one foot moving forward a moment too slow to try to balance itself, so close the impact throws us all to the ground. The Colossus sways above us, still off balance, and then it falls, not forward like I'd been expecting, but sideways into the bay. Right where the *Streak* is.

The Colossus's arm snaps the mainmast before plowing

through the center of the ship. Wood splinters and explodes, spraying out into the bay. Someone screams. Then there's nothing but churning, frothy water around the Colossus's massive form, bits of wood surfacing like refuse.

The *Streak*... She's gone.

"Zara!" Dane scrambles to his feet and runs toward the edge of the dock.

Karis grabs his arm, struggling to hold him back. "Dane, you can't go in there!"

He tries to throw her off, a vein sticking out in his neck, but she clings on. "Zara!"

The water roils violently as the Colossus tries to heave itself out. I stare at the broken pieces of the ship. The figurehead with the *freedom* rune bobs to the surface of the water, one of its arms snapped off.

No.

A figure breaks the surface of the water, out where it's a bit calmer. It's Finn, Ava right behind them. Others surface. Het. Aiken. Manaka.

Zara surges up. She grabs the figurehead as relief bursts through my chest.

She looks across the water to us. "Move it!"

The Colossus is still pulling itself from the bay. Dane, Karis, and I take off toward the boathouse. Its doors are secured with a lock, but I punch it and it smashes into pieces. Dane and I haul the doors open and we rush inside. The place is a mess of jumbled beams and wood, cracked and broken and forming a thicket in front of us. Still, it's impossible to miss the light of the Heart, rays of gold shining through the wreckage like streaks of the sun.

"Look out!" Dane shouts.

I catch a glimpse of the Colossus's hand right before it slams into us. I go flying, hitting the ground hard, my head smacking against stone. I struggle to my elbows, blinking sluggishly. My hand gropes for the satchel at my side.

It's gone.

I lurch up to my knees. My satchel lies right in the path of the Colossus's steps as it forces its way into the boathouse, the roof splintering before its legs.

Karis is across from me, a long scratch on her cheek, but she's on her feet. She looks at the Colossus, and then at the tome. She runs for it.

"Karis!" I cry.

She throws herself at the satchel, grabbing it and rolling out of the way right as the Colossus's foot comes down. The boathouse shakes and she falls.

I stagger over to her. The Colossus takes another blind swipe and I grab Karis, pulling her to the side. We stumble into the small shelter a broken corner of the boathouse offers.

Karis looks up at the Colossus as it takes another swipe, demolishing an entire wall. She shakes her head. "Alix, it's too close. We should regroup, try this a different time."

There's fear in her eyes, and I know it's fear for me. But I shake my head. "I need to do this now. While there's a chance."

She looks down, and we both realize at the same time that my satchel—my tome—is still in her hands. I freeze. Suddenly I'm thrown back to the last time we stood this close to the Heart. When she wrote words that I couldn't refuse but to obey. When she betrayed me. The memory crawls all over me, paralyzing me. What if she takes my will away from me again?

Karis swallows, then she presses the satchel into my hands. "I know you do," she whispers.

My fingers instinctively curl around the leather, my seal flaring with warmth. She gave it back.

She looks out at the Colossus. "Dane and I will get the magistrate's attention and try to distract him long enough to give you a chance."

Her and Dane, alone against that thing? "Karis, the Colossus is enormous, and—"

"Alix." Karis's quiet word stops me. The fear is gone from her eyes now. She looks at me, her gaze stubborn and strong. "You can do this."

Then she's gone, running toward the bronze giant. "Dane!" she shouts. "Try to lure it away!"

I look at the two of them, so small compared to the behemoth before them. Yet still doing this, to give me a chance. I'm torn between the two of them and the Heart, so close. I have to decide. What I want to do. What I need to do.

I run, scrambling over broken pieces of building, shoving anything aside I can't get past. I can hear the Heart calling out to me with that brilliant melody. Its buzzing energy makes the very air vibrate. I don't know what will happen when I touch it again, but this time I know I'm doing this not because of what my father wanted, or what Calantha might want, but because I want it. For all of us. Then I'm there, potent golden light stinging my eyes.

I stand before this ancient Heart. There have been other

vessels, like Zara's pendant, that have controlled automatons over the ages. But none have been as large or contained as much Script ink as the Heart. This is the one that truly gave the Scriptorium their strength. This is the one my father knew we had to destroy if there was ever to be peace.

I throw my hands against its blazing surface, falling into its song. This time I don't hesitate. I open my mouth and sing, loud and strong.

The runes respond, and the Script ink plunges down my arms. It fills me up, all light and life and wonder until I'm blazing with it, as the Heart dims and goes dark. The melody fills my world, until the light is all I see and the song is all I hear. It dims the sounds behind me, of the building creaking and cracking as the Colossus tries to force its way through, of the waves beneath my feet.

Even drained of Script ink, the Heart feels as if it's pulsing in front of me, as if it really is alive. I change my song to one my father and I worked on together, and I sing it out.

As I sing, I finally know that Karis was right. I'm not a weapon. Not a tool. I'm me. Choosing to destroy the Heart doesn't change that. Using the runes my father gave me doesn't change that. I am not bound to these lines on my skin. I can do more than I ever imagined. I know that now, and I won't doubt it again.

I spent my time in the villa dreaming of a world just out of reach, a world of islands and waves and starlight. Now, I'm a part of that world, and no matter how I started, I get to decide what to do with this beautiful, brilliant life of mine. I'm done making myself into anything less than I am.

My notes touch the runes my father told me I needed

to, and each one is a flare of light piercing my vision. I feel rather than see sheets of gold peel from the Heart. It's heart-wrenching, but I keep singing, my voice strengthening even as the melody of the Heart grows fainter and then silent.

The notes fade from my lips. My vision clears. I'm back in the boathouse. There is no Automaton Heart in front of me anymore, only twisted, golden sheets lying on the ground. I drop my hands to my side, my palms still burning from the Scrivolia's touch.

The Heart is gone. The magistrate will never be able to use it again. The Scriptorium will never be able to use it again. After all these centuries, all this pain, I finally did it. I can scarcely bear the emotions welling inside of me, the joy and triumph and relief. It's done. It's finally over.

"Karis? Karis!" Dane's voice filters back to me. It comes again, even more desperate. "Alix, I need you!"

I race back, stumbling around the wreckage, even as the room blurs around me. The Colossus is frozen once again now that the Heart is gone. Its hand has reached down to the ground, fingers curled. Trapped in those fingers is Karis. She isn't moving.

Dane's struggling to pry the Colossus's hand open. He looks at me, panic in his eyes. "Alix, help me," he begs.

I run to him, grabbing the automaton's fingers and lifting. My metal skin groans beneath the weight, but I can't stop. I can't look down at Karis who is so still and pale.

Crying out, I give one last heave, and the fingers part. Dane grabs Karis beneath the arms and pulls her out.

He brushes the hair from her face. "Karis?"

She doesn't respond.

I stagger back, panic engulfing me. If I'd only stopped...
If I'd only helped... Then Karis... I can't say it. I can't think
around the pain that's splitting all over me.

Karis's body convulses, and she heaves in a breath, her
eyes flying open. She coughs, hacking in air.

I sink to my knees as Dane wraps her in his arms, elic-
iting a strangled yelp from her.

She's alive.

He slackens his grip. "Sorry."

Karis struggles to sit up, wrapping her arm around her
ribs. She looks at the Colossus, frozen now. "D-did we
win?" she manages weakly.

Dane buries his face in her hair.

"Yes," I say. "It's done. The Heart is gone."

Relief spills over her face as we look at each other, both
of us on the ground in this broken boathouse. Both of us
still here. I open my mouth, not sure what I want to say,
needing to say something because I almost lost her, when
footsteps sound behind us.

Dane and I whip to our feet, but it's only Zara, and Finn
and Ava behind her. They climb over the Colossus's frozen
arm, all of them dripping wet.

Zara raises a brow as she slides down to the floor. "I take
it the mission was a success?"

A grin splits Dane's face. He runs to her and lifts her off
her feet, spinning her around. Then he seems to realize
what he did, and his eyes widen. Before he can apologize,
Zara clasps his face in her hands and presses her lips to his.

I stare. I've never seen anyone kiss before.

Zara laughs as Dane sets her back on her feet. "You did good, soldier boy. I'll give you that."

"After all this time, I'm still just a soldier boy?"

She grins. "Always."

Behind me, Karis struggles to get to her feet. I take her arm and help ease her up. "What about the others?" she asks.

Zara nods. "Let's go find out."

40

KARIS

The Colossus is frozen, but this isn't over. I have to make sure my brother and everyone else is safe. And we have to find the magistrate. As long as that man is out there, none of us will ever be safe.

We climb up through the tiers, my ribs burning like pokers in my chest. As we go, I see the destruction from what we did. Streets are cracked. Whole buildings are reduced to rubble. These were the magistrate's people. And this is what he did to them: sent the Colossus down here without a care about the damage it might cause. Suddenly the burning in my chest has nothing to do with the pain.

I rage.

Fire seethes inside of me. For everyone he's hurt. For everyone he's killed. For everyone he's crushed for the sake of his own power.

And today is the day we make him pay.

A crash rends the air and someone shouts.

We pick up our pace, bursting out into a small central square. The magistrate stands there, the side of his face bloodied and his robes torn. The chariot he must have been trying to escape in—to flee like a coward in—is on its side, a spear sticking out between the spokes of its wheel. A dozen soldiers are with him, all wearing black sashes. Facing him, already in the square, are some of Zara's pirates and Calantha's rebels, as well as Rudy and my brother. Rudy leans against a building, nursing a nasty cut on his arm. Matthias stands protectively in front of him, livid, clutching his staff as if he wants to beat someone with it.

The magistrate's gaze swings toward us as we come barreling in. His lips peel back in a snarl.

Zara swaggers forward and plants her hands on her hips. A slow smile curls over her lips. "You seem to be surrounded, Magistrate," she drawls.

Calculation ticks in the magistrate's eyes. We've shut down his automatons, drawn most of his forces away, but what he has left is still roughly equal to our own numbers. Even I can see that.

"Attack!" he orders.

The square erupts into the chaos of clashing blades. One of the magistrate's men comes toward me and I grab for my dagger, but the pain in my ribs blinds me, and my hand fumbles. I gasp, staggering sideways, and then Dane's there.

"Karis, stay back!" He knocks the man's blade to the side, driving him away.

The pain in my chest makes my head swim. The screams in the square are deafening. One of the magistrate's men

falls. And then another. We're winning, and I'm still standing frozen and useless.

That's when I see the magistrate. He isn't trying to fight.
He's edging away.

He's running. Leaving his men to die on his behalf and
running. Fury strangles out my air. No. He doesn't get to
cause all this and just run.

I force myself to move, even though each step makes the
world blur around me in pain. I stagger around the others,
my hand pressed to my side. If he gets into the network of
streets, we'll lose him. I push myself harder and get there
before him, barely. This time I do manage to draw my
dagger. I hold it out in front of me, only to find that my
hand shakes.

He sees and smiles. Not the smile from the garden, calm
and serene. This one is cruel. He pulls out his own knife,
gleaming and sharp enough to cut air. Traces of the Script
ink shadows cling to his skin and clothes. His eyes have
been taken over by a frenzied sort of energy, as if the shadows are consuming him. Whatever they are, he can't control them.

The magistrate's lips twist. "Here she is, the stubborn
little rebel, so willing to die for her cause. I truly expected
more from you, Karis."

His words are meant to cut, and they would have found
their mark before, when I was still that selfish girl from
Tallis. The orphan, alone and lonely, wanting only a future where I found my brother and left all the problems of
the world behind. But I'm not her anymore. I am willing

to die for this. That knowledge, that resolution, resounds inside of me.

"I would happily die," I grit out, "if it would mean stopping you."

It's not the answer he expects. I can tell that by the way his eyes narrow. "And what do you think happens when you stop me? Do you truly believe the world those rebels want to build will ever be strong enough to survive? A world without automatons, where other nations constantly prey on our shores? Where we're weak and defenseless against our enemies? Your little rebellion has built your beliefs on naive ideals that have no place in the real world. The Scriptorium is power because that is what it needs to protect itself. You can't stop it." He edges toward the road and once more I step in front of him, trying not to sway as the pain ricochets inside of me.

His words once spoke to some of my deepest fears. That even if we remove their leader, the Scriptorium will remain just as it's always been, with only the face changed. And that all the people like me, like my brother, will stay crushed beneath their feet.

But I think of Calantha, who sacrificed herself for us. Rudy, a great young mind, willing to risk everything to build a new world. Dane, who was a Scriptorium soldier and turned away from that life.

"You were only right about one thing," I say. "Peace doesn't just happen, not as long as there's people like you ruling over us." And I realize, standing here now, he's just a man. I was the one who made him into something more.

Someone to my left shouts. I look. It's just a glance, but

in that moment the magistrate lunges at me. I jerk back, my bruised body protesting, and narrowly avoid the swipe of his dagger. His blade flashes silver in the sun. I frantically try to meet it with my own, hoping I can stall long enough to give the others time to notice.

Over the magistrate's shoulder I catch a glimpse of a figure, his wooden staff sweeping soundlessly over the ground. Matthias. The Bandit. Danger glints in his expression.

I don't want my brother anywhere near this man. I want to yell at him to run. But I decided that this time I would fight, no matter what. So did he. And seeing my brother has given me a plan. It might be my most reckless yet, but it's all I have. Matthias needs an opening and I can give him one. I just need to let him know where the magistrate is going to be.

"Look lively!" I shout. The words from the code my brother made, to guide him to the left.

It's been years, but Matthias still remembers and still trusts me like before because he strides in that direction.

The magistrate's brows furrow at my shout, but I'm already moving toward my brother, feinting to the side. My ribs scream in protest. But the magistrate is faster than I thought he'd be. He moves with me, his knife swiping out, so close.

Matthias's arms snap around the magistrate. The man snarls, writhing in Matthias's grip, and Matthias grunts as the magistrate's elbow connects with his gut. I'm staggering forward to help when Matthias presses his knife into the man's side, hard enough to draw blood. Instantly the magistrate goes still.

Matthias leans in closer. "Miss me?"

The magistrate's face pales, scraggly hair trailing down his temple, and for the first time, fear enters his eyes, pushing back the darkness.

Fear of us.

My body burns, but the pain dims behind sheer disbelief as I take in the square around us. The magistrate's men, noticing what's happened to their leader, are surrendering, raising their hands in the air, laying down their arms.

Is it...over?

Alix stands at the far side of the square and I meet his eyes, filled with blatant relief. The relief and something else, an uncertainty, a thawing, as we stand on either side of this square, so much between us. Hope flares painfully into life in my heart.

I step toward him, but Finn is already there, slapping Alix on the back, Wreska and Het close behind. Dane comes up to me, laughing as he wraps me in a hug.

Aiken, standing nearby with a bloody cut on his cheek, lets out a cheer, and then all around us pirates and rebels and my friends join in. The sound fills the square, seeping into my body and bones and heart.

I squeeze Dane back even though it makes me dizzy with pain.

It's over. The Heart is destroyed. The magistrate is captured.

And the city is ours.

41

KARIS

We're in the Acropolis, the actual Acropolis. Sitting on its carved chairs. Looking out its latticed windows. When I was back on Tallis, dreaming about rescuing my brother, I never would have believed something like this would be possible. Then again, I'm here and I still don't quite believe it.

I'm dressed in clean clothes—not Scriptorium clothes but an ocean-blue chiton, and I'm relishing my newfound freedom to make that choice. My entire torso still feels like one gigantic bruise. I have to either move gingerly or not at all, so I've settled myself in a chair. For the first time in a long time, I have nothing to do except bask in the sunlight from a nearby window.

And it's wonderful.

The others are here, too. Dane and Zara polish their daggers—not something I'd bond over but whatever works for them. Matthias is perched on Rudy's lap on one of the reclining couches and they're laughing about something. Alix is reading a book on automaton anatomy on a window bench. He's been quiet since it all ended a week ago. It's a prick of wrong in all this right.

Zara admires her dagger before sliding it back into its sheath. "Well, this has been fun. But I'm ready to be back out at sea. Being on land this long makes me itchy."

She's already told us she's been granted a new ship by the rebel Scriptmasters working with Calantha; they have formed a provisional government while they try to figure out what to do next. They were going to give Zara a ship from the Scriptorium fleet, but instead Zara chose a junk bucket the Scriptorium had captured from another pirate. She says she's going to rehabilitate it. I'm happy for her. She seems more relaxed now, as if a weight has been lifted. Maybe this is closer to who she really is.

"Will you be leaving soon?" Matthias asks.

"Yes. There are plenty of people out there who were hurt by the Magistrate's Library that we have to track down. If we can help them in any way, we want to."

I glance at Dane with raised eyebrows. He grins back, and I know he's made the decision to go with her. I can't blame him, but it will be strange not having him around. It was only a few weeks ago when I was back on Tallis thinking I'd have to leave him. Now he's the one leaving me. But at least it's not forever. We made it so it wouldn't have to be.

"Well, I'm certainly staying here," Rudy pipes up. "Without the Script ink no one will be able to make automatons anymore, so there's a real chance we can use the Script for good. I want to be part of that."

Matthias gives a stretch, lounging across Rudy's lap like a contended cat. "Good, I'll help."

"You don't know the first thing about the Script," Rudy says with a laugh.

"I can learn. Besides, with any luck, there won't be a need for the Bandit for a while. I think I'm overdue for a vacation anyway."

I look at Alix.

"What about you?" I ask quietly.

He glances at me and I see the indecision flash over his face. It's the same emotion curling around my own heart. Whether it was surviving or finding my brother or taking down the magistrate, I've always had something to fight for. And I'm glad I've done all those things, but it's also left a void. I don't know what I'm supposed to do next.

Alix reaches up and fiddles with his father's medallion. "I'm not sure."

"Why don't you join the council?"

We all jump to our feet, except for Zara, who sits there, grinning.

Calantha stands in the doorway. I knew she was liberated the day the magistrate fell and that Zara's seen her since, but this is the first time I have. She looks thinner now, but she's dressed once again in her Scriptmaster robes and that determined, passionate look is back in her eyes.

And I'm glad. Even though I was at times suspicious of her, even though we didn't always get along. She wouldn't be Calantha without that passion.

She smiles at Alix. "What do you think?"

Alix stares at her. "The council? You mean for the Scriptorium?"

"Yes, we have to rebuild it from its foundations. There is no longer going to be a magistrate, but we'll keep the governing inner council. I want you to be on it."

He shifts awkwardly. "I don't know anything about politics."

"We can teach you the politics. You're the only automaton still awake. The only one that will probably ever be awake now. For better or for worse, the Scriptorium has spent its whole history studying automatons. I think it only right that you be part of guiding us on to our next goal." She turns to me. "And I would like you to be on it as well."

Now it's my turn to stare at her. Alix, I understand. It's perfect for Alix, a path forward when he seems so lost. But me? "What?"

"For too long the council has been solely comprised of old men and women with old ideas. You're an intelligent young woman, Karis, and you have so much potential. In some ways, this all started with you two. It seems only fitting then that you both be part of this new era."

I'm not used to people thinking I have potential. I was always just one orphaned brat among many. Could I really be something more here?

I glance over at Alix. He meets my eyes for a long moment before looking away. My heart twists.

"You don't have to decide now," Calantha says. "But promise me you'll think about it."

I bite my lip and nod. I am already thinking about it, and I'm already confused about it.

"What about the magistrate?" Zara asks. "And his council?"

"Their trial will be next month."

Zara snorts. "A man like that doesn't deserve a trial. Get me my ship and I'll find a nice shark pod to drop him off in."

Calantha shakes her head. "No. That is what he would have done. According to the law, everyone has the right to trial, so he'll get one." She smiles. It's an evil expression. "Then we'll throw him into the dankest cell we have."

Zara grins.

"And his other supporters that are out there?" Rudy asks.

"They'll be trickier," Calantha says. "Many of those who are still loyal to him have already fled, but they'll still be out there, planning. We're trying to track them down, but we can't risk sending too many of our forces away, not with Eural clamoring for war."

Zara says something else, but I'm not paying attention. Alix sits quietly on the window seat, staring out at the Acropolis yard where the Colossus once stood. I wonder what he's thinking about. A world without the magistrate and the council, maybe, where we're the ones who are trying to shape this new future. This journey started so long ago, but we got through it together. I'm sure we can get through whatever comes next as well.

The only problem is, I don't know if he wants that anymore.

Calantha and the others are still talking when Alix slips out the door. I wait for him to come back but he doesn't. So instead I go after him.

I check his rooms, the dining hall, the studies, and don't find Alix anywhere. Finally, I stop for a rest at the end of a hallway, leaning against a windowsill to catch my breath. My ribs have been feeling better since the healers saw them, but they still burn, the most apparent wound that came from all this.

A light scraping sound echoes up the hallway and when I turn, I see Matthias coming toward me, his cane sliding across the floor in front of him.

I straighten. "Matthias."

He grins. "I thought that might be you, guzzling in breath. I could hear you from two hallways away."

I roll my eyes but can't stop the smile from tugging at my lips. "You know, a kind brother would ask me how I was doing."

He laughs as he stops in front of me. "My apologies. How are the ribs?"

"Terrible."

That just makes him laugh again. He rubs his fingers on his cane. It's different from the one he had on the *Streak*. That was a spare piece of timber. This one is dark wood, polished so brightly it gleams, with a silver head. Standing beside my brother in this magnificent building, him holding such a beautiful cane, truly makes me realize how far we've come.

"Nice cane," I say.

"Rudy got it for me. As a gift for not dying. Though now that the Scriptorium is open to trying runes from different nations, he thinks he might be able to make a better one with Scriptwork."

That tenderness is back in Matthias's voice and I'm glad

that he's found someone to be happy with. I'm ashamed I ever thought that meant he was replacing me.

"What are you doing out here anyway?" he asks.

"I'm trying to find Alix."

"Ah, thinking about Calantha's offer?"

I poke him in the arm. "Jealous I'm about to be promoted past you?"

"Not at all. I hate meetings. It's a lot of paper rustling and paper studying and everyone forgetting I don't read. Besides, I prefer being out there." He gestures vaguely to outside. "Less stuffy."

"Did you just call the Acropolis stuffy?" I ask. "This building has centuries of history to it, most of it before the magistrates started twisting everything. Think of what we might be able to find here."

"It's still just a building."

I grin. "You're so uncultured."

"Says the girl I used to have to beg to stop pitching rotten fruit at the Heretis Scriptorium."

"I'll have you know I just did that because I wanted to make you proud."

Matthias's face goes soft. "You've always made me proud."

A wad of emotion sticks in my throat. I never realized until now how much I needed to hear those words. How much I needed to know I still had his approval. I step closer to him, wrapping him in a hug. Laughing, he ruffles my hair.

"Listen, you know Alix better than anyone," Matthias says. "I'm sure you'll be able to find him. And maybe after you can spend some time with me and Rudy. I'd like you to get to know him better."

I step back. "I'd like that, too." I want to get to know Matthias again as well. We can't return to what we were before, but we can build something new that's just as good.

He readjusts his grip on his cane and goes to stroll away. "Matthias?"

He turns back.

"Promise me you'll show me the Bandit at least once." There have been hints, but I want to experience the Bandit full force, sneaking through the city.

His teeth flash in his grin. The expression is all mischief, and it's nothing and everything like the brother I remember. "It's a promise."

He leaves. I think back to what my brother said: *you know Alix better than anyone.* He's right. I do.

And I know where he'll be now.

42

ALIX

I sit on the steps of my father's villa, staring out at the wilted garden. When I first came here, I planned on going back to his workshop, but I wasn't brave enough to head in there alone. So instead I sit, thinking about Calantha's offer. My father served on the council. If I served, too, I'd be following in his footsteps.

Only my father was so many things I'm not. He was always so sure of himself, so driven. While I've seen so little compared to everyone else. I don't know if I'm ready to do what Calantha thinks I can. I do want to find my own purpose for my life. I simply didn't expect that idea to be so intimidating.

There's a rustle and I snap my head up. Karis is squeezing through the gap in the gate, wincing as she does. Then she sees me. She stops, nervously tucking a strand of hair behind her ear that's escaped from her braid. "I was looking for you. I thought you might like some company."

The hope in her voice is vulnerable. I'm still not quite sure where we stand with one another but the truth is I don't want to be alone. I nod.

Karis's face gives way to relief and she gingerly comes and sits next to me.

We sit silently for a few moments. I gaze up into the sky, where a swallow darts across the blue. It's the first one I've seen here. I wonder what it would take to bring the birds back to this place.

"I bet these gardens were beautiful back then," Karis finally says.

"They were." Zara told me this villa is mine, whether or not I want to live here. I haven't decided yet. "I suppose I could replant them if I wanted. It isn't ever going to be the same, though."

"You can still make it beautiful," she murmurs.

I sigh, pressing my hand to my forehead. There's still this ache deep in my chest whenever I think of what she did to me. At the same time, though, suddenly I want to talk to her, because she's here, and I need somebody. I need her. My friend. "I don't know what to do now, Karis. Destroying the Heart was everything my father and I worked for. I'm glad it's gone, but I don't know what I'm supposed to do next."

She pulls out a little paper butterfly from her pocket and runs her fingers along its wings. "You know what, Alix? That just makes you alive. Deciding what you want to do.

Finding something that gives you purpose. We all have to do that. I have to do that."

A hitch enters her voice and I glance over at her, but she shakes her head. "A life is no more than that. And you have that life, same as anyone else." She meets my eye and that hesitation that's grown between us slips away for a few moments. She's back to the same stubborn girl who crossed oceans with me. "So, what is it you want to do?"

What do I want to do, with this life that is mine? For the first time I truly ask myself that, not wondering what my father would want or what Calantha would want or what the world would want. I've carried my past for a long time, and I'll carry it for the rest of my life, but it's time to let go of the anger and the sadness. I'm ready to let it go. My father is gone. I'm still here. It's up to me to build my life now.

"I do want to join the council," I say. "If I can make a difference, I want to." For myself and for the future I want to see. "Will you join me?"

She shifts nervously. "Would you want me to?"

Perhaps we can't change what happened. The decisions she made. The decisions I made. That doesn't mean we have to let them ruin us. Even if what happened stays between us forever, there will be other things there, too. Better things. I reach out and squeeze her hand. "I would."

A smile comes onto her face only to tremble as tears prick at her eyes. I stare, flummoxed. In all the time we've been together, I've never actually seen her cry.

"Sorry. I'm just really happy." She hurriedly starts to swipe at her eyes, but I stop her, gently wiping her tears away. It seems odd now, how afraid I used to be of hurting others. Those feelings, of anger and grief and sadness, that once seemed so overwhelming, I'm learning to handle.

"Thank you," she whispers. "I'll do it right this time, I promise."

"And the council?" I ask. "Will you do that, too?"

She squeezes my hand. "If you want me there, of course."

I do. I want to build a new Scriptorium. I want to build it with my friends. Even if we hurt each other in the process. Maybe, in the end, it's impossible to grow without hurting others. Without being hurt in turn. Maybe that's all right, as long as we try to do better. All these moments make us up. They're all precious in their own way.

There's still this gnawing ache inside of me, though.

Somehow, she knows.

"What is it?" she asks.

Perhaps it's time to say it, what I've barely been able to admit even to myself. Only sitting here, in front of my old home and yet a lifetime away from it, I know there's something else I need to do. "I want to learn more about my father's work. Most of it has probably been lost by now, but I want to understand how he made me. If what he said about automatons was true." That once they were good. I rub the pottery fragment Rudy gave me, nestled in my belt pouch. I'm more than those other automatons could ever be, but it's still a history I want to know. I want to figure out the ways I'm different and why.

"And your tome?" she asks quietly.

I pull my tome out of the satchel, touching its worn cover. I still fantasize about being rid of the thing, so that nothing has the ability to control me like it can. But I don't feel that so urgently anymore. This tome doesn't define me, no matter what other people might think or say.

"I'm not going to destroy it." Maybe one day I will, if I find out it's safe. For now, though, I can live with it.

Karis stands up and holds her hand out to me. "Well then, let's change the world. One more time."

I take her hand, and in that moment our entire history is spread out before us. Her waking me up. Our trek across oceans until we came here. Her betraying me. My destroying the Heart. The good and the bad are both a part of us now. And they make us who we are.

I smile at her, and with her hand in mine, I get to my feet.

★ ★ ★ ★ ★

ACKNOWLEDGMENTS

This book would not have been possible without the support of a wonderful group of people. I cannot thank everyone enough for the time, care, and attention that they put into this novel.

To Rebecca Strauss, the best agent I could ask for. You were the first one to believe in Karis's and Alix's story, and I would never have thought to write this book without your encouragement.

To the superb team at Inkyard Press who guided the story's development and were there for me every step of the way. I'm so glad my book found a home with you. A special thanks to Lauren Smulski, Bess Braswell, Connolly Bottum, Allison Draper, and Chris Wolfgang.

To Anna Prendella. Your notes pushed me to make this book so much stronger and it was such a pleasure working with you.

To Dill Werner and Rawles Lumumba. Thank you for all the incredible insight and the ways you changed my book and my characters for the better.

To Gigi Lau, Mary Luna, and Maciej Frolow for creating such a beautiful cover. It was such a special moment seeing an element of my book brought to life, and I couldn't be happier with it.

To the wonderful critique partners who helped me in the early stages of writing, especially Rachel and Ellie. Thank you for taking the time to read some pretty rough drafts.

To all the debut classes I've been a part of. The great part about my book's release date being changed was that I got double the debut love. It was wonderful being part of The Roaring Twenties, the 21ders, and the Class of 2K20. I'm looking forward to reading all of your books.

To my amazing writer friends. Thank you, Kirstie, Brittany, Amber, Bianca, and Kaleen for always being there with good laughs, good tea, and good times. I'm so excited for when all of our books will be out in the world. Thank you, Rebecca Ann, for the many, many chats we've had. Also, a thank-you to Michelle and Kit.

To my wonderful colleagues at work, who have supported me throughout this process.

And, of course, to my family.

To my parents. You have encouraged my dreams ever since I was little and made me believe that I could do anything. You gave me such a deep love of reading and the written word that I decided I would make it my career two times over. I wouldn't be where I am now without you. To Sara, for sharing my love of YA and all things libraries. To

Rebecca, for being so excited when you heard about my book deal (the first call!). Also, to my friends who are like family, Ella and Nicole and Peyton.

To God, for guiding me onto this path.

And finally, to all of the readers who have picked up this novel. Thank you for sharing in this story with me.